PRAISE FOR MELANIE SUMMERS

"A fun, often humorous, escapist tale that will have readers blushing, laughing and rooting for its characters." ~ *Kirkus Reviews*

A gorgeously funny, romantic and seductive modern fairy tale...
I have never laughed out loud so much in my life. I don't think that I've ever said that about a book before, and yet that doesn't even seem accurate as to just how incredibly funny, witty, romantic, swoony...and other wonderfully charming and deliriously dreamy *The Royal Treatment* was. I was so gutted when this book finished, I still haven't even processed my sadness at having to temporarily say goodbye to my latest favourite Royal couple.
~ *MammieBabbie Book Club*

I have to HIGHLY HIGHLY HIGHLY RECOMMEND *The Royal Treatment* to EVERYONE!
~ *Jennifer, The Power of Three Readers*

I was totally gripped to this story. For the first time ever the Kindle came into the bath with me. This book is unputdownable. I absolutely loved it.
~ *Philomena (Two Friends, Read Along with Us)*

Very rarely does a book make me literally hold my breath or has me feeling that actual ache in my heart for a character, but I did both." ~ *Three Chicks Review for Netgalley*

ALSO AVAILABLE
ROMANTIC COMEDIES by Melanie Summers
The Crown Jewels Series
The Royal Treatment
The Royal Wedding
The Royal Delivery

Paradise Bay Series
The Honeymooner
Whisked Away
The Suite Life

Crazy Royal Love Series (Coming in 2020)
Royally Crushed
Royally Wild

WOMEN'S FICTION by Melanie Summers
The After Wife – coming January 2020

STEAMY OFFERINGS by MJ Summers
The Full Hearts Series
Break in Two
Don't Let Go – Prequel to Breaking Love - E-book only
Breaking Love
Letting Go - Prequel to Breaking Clear & The Break-up
Breaking Clear
Breaking Hearts
The Break-up

Copyright © 2019 Gretz Corp.
All rights reserved.
Published by Gretz Corp.
First edition

EBOOK ISBN: 978-1-988891-20-0
Print ISBN: 978-1-988891-21-7

Whisked Away

~ a paradise bay romantic comedy ~

By Melanie Summers

DEDICATION

For my dad, John Edward Close,
I hope you're somewhere riding horses, reading books, and
fixing machines of some sort. I'll be down here working hard
and dreaming big, just like you taught me.
Love you forever,
Mel

AUTHOR'S NOTE

Dear Reader,

I'm not going to lie. This past year has been the shits for me. We thought my dad's battle with cancer was over (and that he won), but it turns out, it was launching a horrific comeback. Losing him slowly, ounce by ounce, day by day, knowing we were coming to the end, was a pain so excruciating, I'm certain it'll take me a lifetime to get over.

He passed away on New Year's Eve at two minutes to midnight, and I'll be forever grateful I could be there with him as his journey here ended. It was a moment I never would expect to describe as beautiful, but there really is no other word. We got a chance to say *all the things* in the weeks leading up to the end, and we made the most of it, which is an incredible gift.

Since he's been gone, I realized something that may be obvious to you, but just in case it isn't, I'm going to mention it now. We *always* have the chance to say all the things that are in our hearts. Most of us just aren't in the habit of doing it. We're lazy or scared or don't want to sound cheesy. But those are just excuses that keep us from truly connecting with our own very important people on the deepest of levels. But imagine if we got in the habit, if we loved fiercely and fearlessly...what kind of world would that be? I suspect it would be kind of sort of wonderful. This world just might be kinder, more meaningful, more honest, and I venture to guess, we'd all feel more loved.

So, if you, like me, aren't in the habit of letting those you love know how you feel, take every effing chance you can to tell them. (Unless the person you love is the guy at work you fancy but he doesn't know you exist. In that case, maybe hold off until you've been dating a while so you don't scare him off.)

But I digress...and you probably want to start reading this book, so I'll leave it there. I hope you will enjoy getting to know Harrison's little sister Emma better, and that she and Pierce make you laugh and feel all those wonderful squishy romantic feelings you get when you're falling for someone. They've seen me through some sad days myself, and if they can do the same for you, I would be most pleased.

Wishing you love, peace, and laughter,
Melanie

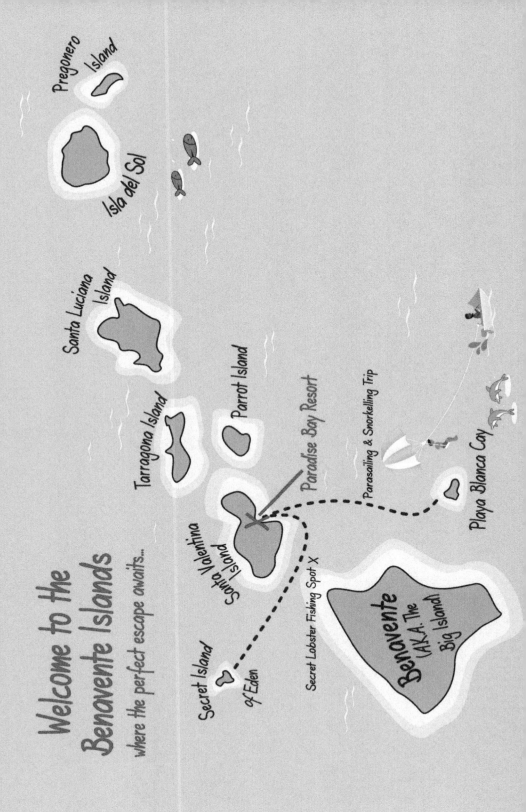

Welcome to the Benavente Islands
where the perfect escape awaits...

Pregonero Island

Isla del Sol

Santa Luciana Island

Tarragona Island

Parrot Island

Santa Valentina Island

Paradise Bay Resort

Parasailing & Snorkelling Trip

Playa Blanca Cay

Secret Island of Eden

Secret Lobster Fishing Spot X

Benavente (A.K.A. The Big Island)

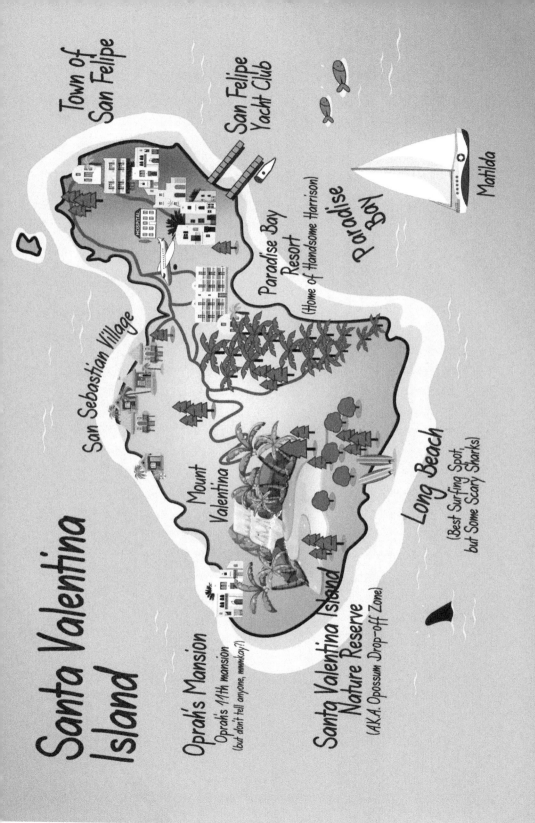

MUSINGS FROM A FANTASY MAN

THE WORLD'S BIGGEST AUTHORITY ON ALL THINGS FANTASY FICTION

THE CLASH OF CROWNS: A MUST READ

WRITTEN BY JOE 'FANTASY' WILCOX

Okay, peeps! I have just finished the first book in the epic fantasy series *The Clash of Crowns* by newcomer Pierce Davenport, like literally five minutes ago, after reading for 14 hours STRAIGHT! It is, without a doubt, the greatest piece of fantasy literature ever written.

Davenport - who is only 24 years old - has out-Gaimaned Neil Gaiman, he out-Tolkeined J.R.R. Tolkien, and outshone the rest by a mile. *The Clash of Crowns* series is set in the medieval world of Qadeathas, where three brothers are forced to battle it out for their father's crown.

Davenport doesn't bore you with a hundred pages of backstory and world-building before he gets to the action. He literally kills off one of the brothers on page one, then builds the world as he goes. This book is the perfect blend of action, drama, horror, and fantasy. It has it all - dragons, elves, manananggals, witches, epic sex scenes, and battles that will keep you on the edge of your seat.

According to publishers Sullivan and Stone, this is the first in a four-book series, but if you ask me, he could keep writing in this world forever and it would NEVER be enough. Word on the street is that NBO is already in talks with Davenport to create a series based on the books. We can only hope they'll do justice to this work of literary perfection.

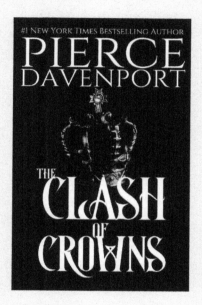

#1 NEW YORK TIMES BESTSELLING AUTHOR

PIERCE DAVENPORT

THE CLASH OF CROWNS

RATING: 5 SWORDS

So, do yourself a massive favour and pick up this book like RIGHT FRIGGIN' NOW!

Join me on Twitter at #clashofcrowns to discuss this epic tale!

MUSINGS FROM A FANTASY MAN

THE WORLD'S BIGGEST AUTHORITY ON ALL THINGS FANTASY FICTION

THE CLASH OF CROWNS BOOK 2 IS HERE!!

WRITTEN BY JOE 'FANTASY' WILCOX

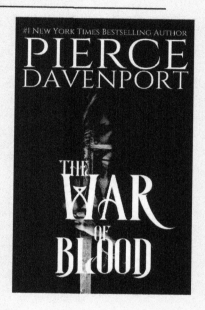

Davenport does it again. He had me up ALL night and most of the day (after waiting in line until midnight in front of Waterstones to get my hands on a first edition of *The War of Blood: Clash of Crowns, Book 2*).

And HOLY SNAP! You will not BELIEVE what Davenport does to King Draqen's sons, Lucaemor and Matalyx, this time around. These two brothers are not only in the battle for the throne, but he's added a whole new threat in the form of Zhordal mo Rhandar, the Lord of the Underworld (and the baddest badass of any fantasy book ever).

Book 2 is every bit as exciting and horrifying as the first one. Davenport keeps the pace lightning fast as he throws in the biggest plot twists I've ever come across. The heat between Lucaemor and Oona burns so hot, you could get singed just reading about it. I cannot wait until they are finally alone together to consummate their feelings.

Next April, NBO will release the first season of the series based on the books, and I promise I'll be binging on it the second it comes out....

RATING: 5 SWORDS

Join me on Twitter at #clashofcrowns to discuss *The War of Blood*!

ISSUE NO. 78

MUSINGS FROM A FANTASY MAN

THE WORLD'S BIGGEST AUTHORITY ON ALL THINGS FANTASY FICTION

THE CLASH OF CROWNS

APRIL 7

NBO

IS IT AS GOOD AS THE BOOK?

WRITTEN BY JOE 'FANTASY' WILCOX

You bet your ass it is. I don't know how, but the folks of NBO managed to capture the very essence of the Qadeathas world, bottle it, and put it on screen. My only wish is that I could have watched the first episode in the theatre with my fellow Crownies.

I'll write more later, but for now, I need to rewatch Episode One about ten more times until it soaks into my very life force.

Join me on Twitter at #clashofcrowns to discuss all things Clash of Crowns!

MUSINGS FROM A FANTASY MAN

THE WORLD'S BIGGEST AUTHORITY ON ALL THINGS FANTASY FICTION

THE CLASH OF CROWNS BOOK 3 HAS FINALLY DROPPED!

WRITTEN BY JOE 'FANTASY' WILCOX

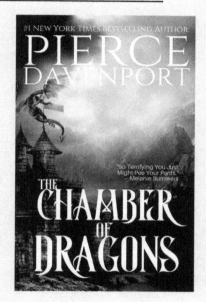

Was *The Chamber of Dragons* worth two days of waiting in line in the rain and cold?

Yes. Yes, it was.

The book picks up where *The War of Blood* leaves off, with Ogden about to be hanged and Surryn on her way to stop it. I won't tell you what happens because I'm not a total douche-canoe who spoils books for people, but let me say this - I almost crapped in my pants.

The Endless Night has started, which quite frankly speeds up the frantic pace of the series and turns up the heat even more for Luc and Oona's relationship. Two characters were never meant to be together more than this pair. I don't want to sound like a girl, but I think I might die if they don't end up together. Like, literally die.

I honestly cannot figure out how Davenport is going to get Luc and Mat out of the bind he has them in. Seriously, no idea. It looks like Davenport has written himself into a corner, but with his level of genius, he must know how to finally end the race for the crown.

RATING: 5 SWORDS

Join me on Twitter at #clashofcrowns to discuss all things *Clash of Crowns*!

MUSINGS FROM A FANTASY MAN

THE WORLD'S BIGGEST AUTHORITY ON ALL THINGS FANTASY FICTION

WHERE THE EFF IS BOOK 4???

WRITTEN BY JOE 'FANTASY' WILCOX

TWO YEARS. That is how late Pierce Davenport is on turning in his homework, ladies and gentlemen. And I, for one, have HAD IT! That's why you will find me, along with a few dozen other die-hard Crownies, camped out in front of Pierce's downtown luxury apartment building until we have the ending we deserve!

Honestly, I'm starting to fear that I was right when I suggested Davenport has written himself into a corner and there is no feasible way out. If he did, this will be THE GREATEST DISAPPOINTMENT OF MY LIFE.

Join us there at 152 Richmont Street, Valcourt, Avonia, for a 24/7 vigil for the people of Qadeathas who are currently waiting in peril while Davenport dicks around doing God-knows-what!

Bring your own sleeping bag, food, and water. We're welcome to use the bathroom at the Starbucks across the street but you must purchase something, so make sure you have some money...

Join me on Twitter at #piercesucks to discuss all things *Clash of Crowns!*

ONE

Bellinis are a Bad Idea...

Emma Banks - Culinary Institute of America, New York Campus

"**E**mma, you're not still asleep, are you?" The voice of my roommate, Priya Bhatt, interrupts what is most definitely the best dream I've had in months.

"No, of course not. I've been up for hours. That's how I made the greatest Baked Alaska Gordon Ramsay has ever tried," I say, rolling over onto my stomach and snuggling into my pillow. "Now, if you'll excuse me, he was just about to offer me a job."

"Well, you may want to save salary negotiations for later. Your flight leaves in just over two hours, and those packing fairies you were hoping would stop by overnight haven't shown up yet."

I flip over and bolt upright. "No, no, no, no, no! How did I sleep through my alarm?" Grabbing my mobile off my tiny wood veneer night table, I swipe the screen. "Oh, that's how. I set it for six *p.m.*," I say, tossing my phone on the single bed and rushing to my closet.

"In hindsight, we probably should have set our alarms *before* we made the first pitcher of Bellinis," Priya answers, tugging her towel off her head and shaking out her wet, black hair. "I tried to wake you before I went for my shower, but you were out cold."

Priya and I have been roommates here at the Culinary Institute of America for over three years. The big graduation ceremony was yesterday afternoon and things may or may not have gotten out of hand last night. Okay, they definitely may have. And by 'may have,' I mean I don't remember anything that happened after we got to the third pub.

"Damn Bellinis," I mutter as I toss my scuffed soft-sided suitcase on my bed. It takes two quick steps for me to be in front of my rickety dresser. Pulling out the top drawer, I dump its contents into my waiting suitcase.

"Here. Let me help," Priya offers, opening the second drawer and carefully lifting an armful of sweaters out of it. She's not in nearly as much of a rush to clear out as I am. Priya can *drive* home to Philadelphia at her leisure, while I need to be at JFK Airport *tout suite* for the nine-hour flight home to the Caribbean.

I pivot around Priya to replace the drawer. Glancing at the sweaters, I say, "Do you want those?"

"Seriously?" she asks. "Like, *all* of them?"

"Yup." I won't need them when I get home to Santa Valentina Island. "Oh, except my green cardigan. I'll take that with me."

Grinning, Priya hurries to her side of the room—the much neater side that has been thoughtfully decorated with a white and gold bedding set and matching area rug that say 'Sparkle' on them in flowy pink writing. While Priya is all about the sparkle, I'm more of a 'get in, get it done, move on' kind of girl. I've been using a sleeping bag since I came to school and I sleep just fine, thank you very much.

"You're so lucky," she says as she refolds her new sweaters. "You're *literally* going home to paradise to have your pick of restaurants to run."

"But there's no In-N-Out Burger on the Benavente Islands," I answer lightly, trying to deflect her comment. I know it shouldn't bother me, but the only reason I'm so 'lucky' is because some jackass ran a red light when I was seven and killed both my parents. My uncle, who owned a large, all-inclusive beachfront resort, took my brothers and me in. Then, when he died (a week before my grade twelve final exams), we inherited the resort, the staff, and all the responsibility that came with it.

Not that I'm complaining, because, as a student of the culinary arts, having guaranteed employment when you graduate is kind of like finding a talking unicorn that poops cash on demand. But, still, I'd much rather have had my mum and dad at the ceremony yesterday, snapping photos and cheering for me in embarrassingly loud voices.

I actually had no one in the audience because I purposely didn't tell my family until it was too late for them to book flights. My little brother, Will, is somewhere on the other side of the planet filming the adventure/nature docuseries in which he stars, so there's no way he could take a break with all those people depending on him. And my big brother, Harrison, is preparing to open the resort's premier private island villa this week, which has basically had him working around the clock for the better part of the last year.

Priya was the only other graduate without family in the audience. Her parents are both super busy surgeons who also happen to think this 'cooking thing' is just a phase, like trying weed or making out with a girl your first year of college (which they actually told her they would have preferred, since in either of those cases, they could have hidden it from the family). But don't worry, they're not all bad. They're planning to attend her *real* graduation when she finishes med school. So, that's nice of them, isn't it?

Poor Priya.

She's going home to live in their basement while she tries to find work and pay off her student loans. (They'll pay for her med school tuition, but cooking school? Not so much.) She could move in with her sister and brother-in-law, a cardiologist and an impossibly brilliant pediatric cardiologist, but according to Priya, they're even more judgy than her disapproving parents.

I finish with the dresser and rush over to the closet, grab at the thigh-high laundry pile, and start stuffing it all into a duffel bag I 'borrowed' from Will when I moved here. (Don't tell him; he thinks he lost it. He's about to become a big TV star so it shouldn't matter to him that I didn't exactly ask if I can use it, but he's also a jackass, so if he finds out, he won't shut up about it.)

Oh, God. I just realized my brain feels like a wool sweater that's been washed in hot and dried on high. I'm going to need to guzzle a couple of litres of water during the cab ride so it'll return to its normal size.

Mmm...my breath must be delightful right now. Not to mention the *eau de exam stress and booze* I'm wearing. "I don't even know if I'm going to have time to shower," I mutter, glancing at the clock and feeling my stomach tighten.

I eye Priya's bottle of Febreze for a second, considering it. How bad could that be for you, really? I mean, if you just Febreze yourself the one time...

She must know what I'm thinking because she's looking at the bottle too, and her tone is slightly urgent when she says, "I have some wipes you can use."

"Much better idea. Thanks!" The outfit I was going to wear on the plane is jammed into my dirty laundry, so I dig through my suitcase to find something appropriate for travelling. I'm out of clean knickers so I'll have to go commando, but I do find a pair of yoga pants, a tank, and a long-sleeved tee that I can take off when I land at the San Felipe airport. It'll have to do.

Priya hands me the wipes, I grab my change of clothes and my toiletries kit, and sprint down the hall to the communal washroom. As I brush my teeth, I feel a surge of excitement building. Or maybe it's terror. So hard to tell the difference sometimes.

For the first time in my twenty-eight years, I'm finally going to run my own kitchen. And not just a homey little café that seats twelve and serves soup and sandwiches. I'll be in charge of a large, world-class restaurant with a staff of somewhere between sixteen and thirty people, depending on which of the resort's seven restaurants my big bro, Harrison, hands over to me.

The thought makes my heart race along with the furiously quick strokes of the toothbrush across my tongue.

Oops! Too far. I just gagged. I hate it when that happens. *Slow down, Emma.*

That's going to be my mantra because I tend to work a little too quickly which can lead to mistakes (or the odd tiny grease fire). But not anymore. Head chef Emma Banks will slow down just enough to cook everything to perfection.

I wonder which restaurant Harrison is going to give me? I'm secretly hoping it's the Brazilian steakhouse. I absolutely *adore* serving meat on swords. There's an element of danger to it that I find quite alluring. But, now that I think of it, Junior Gonzalez has been the head chef there for over fifteen years and I don't think he's ready to retire yet. Damn.

Oh! Maybe Harrison is going to let me run the main buffet. It seats two hundred people and features over forty-eight different dishes with the menu changing each weeknight. It's easily considered the most difficult kitchen at the resort to manage, and Harrison *did* text that he had a 'special challenge' for me when I got back. He also said I'd be quite pleased with my new assignment and that he was sure I'd be up for it. Squeee! I cannot wait!

I grin at myself in the mirror while I brush out my chestnut brown hair and put it up in a high pony.

A toilet flushes and Tina Jones comes out of one of the stalls. She gives me a slight nod. "You're still here? I thought you'd be in the Caribbean by now, taking your brother's handouts."

I don't like Tina very much.

I pick up my things and spin toward the door, calling back. "Just leaving now. Good luck with...being you."

She's wrong about me taking handouts. Well, technically, Harrison did finish raising me, and he paid my way through culinary school so I could graduate without debt, so, yeah, I guess a totally jealous bee-otch might call it handouts, but I'm going to *devote my entire life* to paying him back, so I call it being part of a family.

Oh God, what if I'm not up for the challenge? What if I totally mess things up like I did last year when I had to drop out because I was going to fail Sauces 201 and needed to start my entire semester over? What if, instead of finally paying Harrison back, I end up making his life much, much worse because I actually suck at running a kitchen and he has to fire me or—and this thought is even more terrifying—he keeps me on but everybody knows I'm just there because my family owns the resort and the rest of the staff start to hate me because I'm the worst head chef of all time?

I break out in a cold sweat while my mind takes off without my permission. *Okay. It's okay, Emma. You got this.*

Everything is going to be just fine. I graduated third in the entire class. Plus, I practically grew up in a restaurant kitchen. I can totally do this. In fact—and here's a little secret between you and me–I'm going to put Paradise Bay Resort on the map as the world's greatest culinary destination. I haven't told anyone else yet, but for months now, I've been scribbling down what I think will be absolutely genius Caribbean fusion recipes that will melt on the tongue, thrill even the most delicate palette, and earn me more Michelin stars than Joël Robuchon (who holds the world record of 31).

Someday, in the not-so-distant future, there is going to be an entire movement of Caribbean fusion restaurants everywhere, and I'll be the mother of it all. My name will be among all the top dogs: Gordon Ramsay, Wolfgang Puck, Emma Banks. Of course, I'll have to publish a series of cookbooks so people around the globe won't be afraid to 'try this at home,' but for the most part, they won't be able to capture the flavours that will be found at the resort because their dishes won't be bursting with the freshness of fruits picked that morning at the height of ripeness. So, they'll come to Santa Valentina Island in hopes of catching a glimpse of the famed, young chef extraordinaire and having *the* authentic Caribbean fusion experience, right where it all began.

And please don't think me conceited because I haven't accomplished any of this yet. But I will. Because once I set my mind to something, I *never* give up. Just ask Harrison what it was like for our mum to get me to stop sucking my thumb when I was two.

Anyway, the point is, I'm not going to simply pay Harrison back for everything he's done for me over the years. I'm going to make him rich beyond his wildest dreams. I'm going to be the heroine my family and all the staff at the resort have been waiting for all these years. No more struggling to make ends meet, no more panicking about what will happen if another hurricane comes along and we have to shut down for a few months. Fear not, Paradise Bay staff! Emma is about to change everything!

But, not if I miss my flight.

I rush back into our dorm room, only to find my luggage zipped up and standing by the door, my bed stripped, and the concrete wall above my bed barren where it used to hold a collage of family photos. "Wow. It looks so...final."

Priya nods at me, her eyes filling with tears, even though we've promised each other not to get all sappy about parting ways. Clearing her throat, she says, "Everything's packed up, and your pics are in an envelope in your laptop bag. I couldn't fit your sleeping bag in, so it's either going to be making the trip in a garbage bag or you'll have to leave it."

"Leave it. Maybe someone will need it next semester."

"Do you have your passport?"

"In my purse," I say, shoving my toiletries kit into my laptop bag and zipping it shut.

"That's it, then."

A lump forms in my throat. "Thank you so much, Priya. For helping me this morning and for..." My voice cracks and I cut the sentiment short.

"You too," she says, her face crumpling.

We both burst into loud sobs, hugging each other while we cry and laugh at ourselves and say things like, "I don't know what I'm going to do without you," and "You're the best friend I've ever had," and "We'll Skype every day."

And before I'm really ready, I find myself alone in an Uber on the way to the airport, silent tears running down my cheeks. A sense of melancholy sets in at the thought of finishing such a wildly fun and, in many ways, carefree chapter of my life. But as I watch the buildings zip by, I start to feel a tiny flicker of excitement for the incredible life that lays ahead.

TWO

Revolving Nannies and Soft Launch Guinea Pigs

Pierce Davenport - Valcourt, Avonia (A Picturesque City in the Fairy Tale Kingdom Just to the East of England and Slightly North of Belgium)

They say no man is an island. They are wrong. The very idea that we must make ourselves reliant on other human beings for our basic needs, our own fulfilment, and our happiness is absolutely absurd. Because in case you haven't noticed, most human beings suck balls. Not literally. Well, some of them do, I'm sure, and that's fine if they like that sort of thing, but that's not the sucking to which I am referring. The average human being is completely unreliable, and therefore, if you can avoid them, you should—a lesson I learned as a young child.

A man can, in fact, be an island. It's just a matter of how large said man's bank account happens to be...

Take me, for example. I am disgustingly rich. I'm the guy Jesus was referring to when he said (and I'm paraphrasing here, because to be honest, I'm not a big bible guy): it's easier to squeeze a camel through the eye of a needle than for a rich man to sneak into Heaven. Or something like that. Anyway, the point is, I'm rich enough to *not* have to rely on a living soul other than Mrs. Bailey, my housekeeper, who I pay very well to be here as little as possible whilst managing to get through all the tasks I'd rather not do (which includes anything a 1950's housewife would have done). Other than Mrs. Bailey, I'm ecstatic to be alone most of the time.

Although lately, my fortress of solitude has become more of a prison of luxury. Now, before your hand shoots up and you shout that you'd happily trade places with me, allow me to fill you in on the fine print...

Instead of growing up with a close-knit family in a cozy three-bedroom home on a quiet street, you would have spent your formative years in a very cold mansion with marble floors (quite unforgiving for a toddler learning to walk). You'd also have formed attachments to a string of nannies, all of whom were unceremoniously dismissed by your mother for various inane reasons such as 'her hair was too brassy,' 'her laugh gives me a migraine,' or my personal favourite, 'she ate the biscuit I offered her.'

But the fun doesn't stop there, because as a grown man, life will then present some challenges most people don't have to suffer. Imagine that privacy is as foreign a concept as loving parents—something you only read about in books or see on the telly—and I have to say, it is the one thing for which I often long. (Privacy, that is. I can do without the sentimental mum who keeps a scrapbook of every inconsequential thing I've ever done, like a photo of the first time I made a poop on the potty.)

As the grandson of the great Lord Davenport—founder of Davenport Communications, the UK's largest telecommunications, digital cable and satellite service provider—and son of Lord Alistair and Lady Bunny of the House Davenport, you'd have grown up under a microscope, being examined by every well-to-do person in the entire kingdom. (And yes, Bunny is her real name—disgustingly rich people can get away with ridiculous baby names.)

Were you in my Testoni dress shoes, you'd find yourself subjected to relentless curiosity and intrusion by nearly everyone you meet, and after thirty-one years of having strangers believe themselves entitled to the inside scoop on your father's alleged affair with a certain Victoria's Secret model (not a chance in hell, by the way), you'd likely find yourself growing a little bitter. In fact, I'd venture to guess that you'd also find yourself overwhelmed with a desire to retreat to your own personal fortress of solitude.

That's where I am at the moment—in my 4000 square foot penthouse flat that overlooks the Langdon River. From my bedroom window—or, to be more accurate, my wall of windows—I can see all the way to the Langdon Bridge, which incidentally is not falling down, but only because it has undergone more facelifts than my mother.

Unfortunately, at the moment, even my fortress in the sky isn't enough of an escape, because for a man seeking privacy, I've fucked up entirely by writing a certain series you'll have either read or watched on the UK's biggest subscription-only channel NBO. Alternatively, you've refused to watch because it's too gory and sex-filled. Yes, I'm *that* Pierce Davenport, writer of *Clash of Crowns.* Had I known it would become a mega-hit, I might not have written it at all.

Other than the cash that pours into my account faster than that Rain Man fellow could count it, the entire experience has been a disaster. Well, I suppose that's not completely fair. The series has definitely been responsible for yours truly getting a whole lot of action in the boudoir, so that's a bit of perk.

But here's the thing about writing the world's most popular epic fantasy drama series: if you don't know how the hell it ends, and you've got millions of people waiting for the final installment, a good percentage of them are going to get impatient. Brutally impatient.

They will turn on you in a way that no other reading audience will because they have a bloodlust to begin with, and then you've gone and put some rather violent ideas into their heads. And when that happens, you really are trapped because every time you leave your home, you'll be bombarded by angry super fans who want to know just what the hell you think you're doing out in public when you should be holed up at home writing. These same people tweet, email, and send IG messages to me *demanding* I finish. They then grow unreasonably angry when I don't reply, which I find rather ironic because were I to spend my time writing back to thousands of people per week, that wouldn't exactly leave me with time to finish the novel, now would it?

But set the irate nerds aside for a moment because I'm even more fucked than you'd think. This is because the executive producers of the television series *Clash of Crowns* are also out of patience and are now threatening to bring in a team of screenwriters to complete the series for me, which would be an unmitigated disaster. First off, the writers on staff aren't capable of an original thought between them. NBO had me in for a 'planning sesh' with the writers once, and one of them actually suggested the old 'it was all a dream' ending and that all the characters I've mercilessly killed off are actually alive. I'm not shitting you. They even put that little gem up on the 'Board of Possibilities.'

They'll take what *Rolling Stone* magazine has called "the most unpredictable, horrifically beautiful, gut-wrenching masterpiece in the history of television" and tame it down so that nobody dies and the good guys win. In other words, they'll FUBAR it (fuck it up beyond all recognition).

Let's be honest, the brass at NBO are in it for the cash. They don't care how the series ends, because at this point, they've already hooked hundreds of millions of viewers so it's totally irrelevant to them if the last season satisfies the hungry fans or ends up being the next *Lost*. And the moment they realized that, I was totally fucked. Unfortunately, I didn't know it until last week when the head of NBO—a total bellend by the name of Kent Cromwell—gave an interview on ABN's (Avonian Broadcast Network) Entertainment Weekly Round-Up stating that they've given me two months to write the ending so they can start turning it into a script or they'll do it for me. Rumour has it, they're already amassing a team to be on call should I fail. Thanks for that, Kent Cromwell, you colossal douchenugget. This has caused every entertainment media cockroach from around the world to camp themselves outside my building, along with a couple dozen "Crownies" as they call themselves, who are holding a candlelight vigil until I emerge with the completed manuscript. A little dramatic, no?

I don't know how the hell they think this works. It's not like I'm up here madly typing each page on an ancient Typemaster Five and will grab the entire stack of papers when I'm done and run down the street to my publisher with my bathrobe flying behind me.

I haven't stepped foot in Sullivan and Stone Publishing House for years. Everything is sent via email. And I'm certainly not coming out of the building the moment I finish to hand out free copies. That is not going to happen, no matter how much they wish it did.

I know they believe themselves to be supportive, and I really am grateful for my Crownies (at least the ones who haven't threatened to castrate me), but seriously, people, it's a lot of fucking pressure to know you're out there while I wrack my brain for the perfect ending.

To be honest, I sort of wrote myself into a corner in the third installment of the series, and I've spent the last two years holed up thinking of ways to get out of it, but to no avail. I've tried everything to figure it out—rereading the books, watching the entire series in one go, reading all sorts of books about how to beat writer's block (useless, all of them). Meditation, hot yoga, self-hypnosis (total sham). I even spent six tedious months building the entire Qadeathas world out of Lego pieces on my massive walnut dining table in hopes that having a miniature version of my creation would lead me to the answer. I now have an intricate 3D model depicting every castle, ship, mountain, river, lake, road, and township in all five realms that has done absolutely nothing other than take up thirty minutes per week of Mrs. Bailey's time when she dusts it.

And now this very public, very shitty deadline has been set.

Fear not though, because in exactly two hours, I'll be sneaking out the back door of my building (out of sight of the paparazzi) and slipping into a limo that will take me to the airport where a Learjet will be waiting. Once aboard, I'll be disappearing to a private island in the South Caribbean where no one will be able to contact, harass, bother, badger, or beg me to finish the fourth book. And that's when the book will finally get written.

As a side note, if you've ever wondered why it rains so much in the UK, it's karma getting back at the horrid so-called 'reporters' who make their money selling stories to the gossip rags. And the paparazzi here in Avonia outdo them all—they're the worst of the worst. I like to think that today's pea soup fog and unseasonably cold drizzle is payback from the heavens for the crowd of vultures waiting for me downstairs. I don't need to call down to the doorman to know that they're down there waiting for me. I can *feel their presence* just as certainly as I feel my Zaffiro gold razor skimming along my jawline.

The sound of a chime tells me my editor/best friend, Zach Shulman, is calling through on my private line. He is one of only three people to have this number—and the other two are not my parents or my idiot brothers. I make sure my towel is secured around my waist, then say, "Answer call."

Zach's face appears on the screen embedded in my bathroom mirror. (I got a little bored last winter and had the guy who did Bill Gates' home electronics flown over to tech out my flat.)

"You're up early," Zach quips, referring to the fact that it's almost eleven and I am only now through the shower.

In my defence, I generally work until around two a.m., and I did get up to run on my treadmill already today.

"You could sleep in too if you hadn't saddled yourself with that lovely wife of yours." She's not lovely at all, actually. She loathes me because I won't allow her to use me to help her climb the corporate ladder over at ABN where she works as a producer for the news. She's been on me for years to allow her cameras into my fortress of solitude and bare my soul on television and, because I have politely declined on each attempt, she looks at me like Taylor Swift looks at Katy Perry—with an unmistakable bitterness.

"Don't remind me about the single life. If I don't think about it, I don't miss it nearly as much," Zach says, even though he definitely doesn't miss the single life at all. He yawns widely while he scratches at his overgrown, thick brown hair.

Zach is chronically tired because even though he starts his workday a full three hours after his wife, Kennedy, he insists on getting up at the arse crack of dawn every morning so they can eat breakfast together. Apparently, they miss each other so much while she's away bossing people around and he's crammed in his tiny office at the newly merged Sullivan and Stone Publishing House that he simply *must* get up to prepare her tea and toast each morning. Pathetic, no?

"I don't think you're going to be escaping today." He lifts his enormous coffee mug to his lips and takes a long gulp of what I know to be coffee so strong it could lift a car to save a trapped baby—a little habit he picked up when he was studying

English literature at Harvard. Why anyone would leave the birthplace of the English language to study the subject is beyond me, but somehow Zach came home with an incredibly keen eye and the ability to spot a plot hole from a mile away. That combination, and his dry sense of humour, make him the only person to whom I would trust one of my books. "That fog has grounded all of this morning's flights."

"It'll lift by noon and my plane isn't scheduled to leave until three."

His expression says 'damn, foiled again,' because Zach, along with my agent, Judith, do not want me to disappear into the jungle for the next two months. Apparently, they not only doubt my ability to be any more productive there than I am here, but they're also terrified that if word gets out that I've disappeared into the jungles of the West Indies, NBO may just relinquish the two-month deadline.

Seeming to decide to drop the topic (a wise choice), he asks, "How did the writing go last night?"

"I'd rather not talk about it."

"You know, if you just show me the pages you've got, I'm certain I could help you crack the story wide open. A lot of my clients—"

I hold up one hand. "I'm going to stop you right there. You know my process better than anyone. Let's not mess with the process." I rinse my razor under the tap, then start on my right cheek.

"Yes, I'm well aware of your process, Pierce. But it doesn't appear to be working for you this time. I'm not sure if you saw the interview Cromwell gave last night when he was leaving the Prince's Gala, but I'm afraid you've pushed him to his limit."

"I saw the interview but it's really nothing new. Kent said the same thing last week. Many thanks for calling to remind me my career is hanging on by one bending fingernail, though."

"Anytime. Now, about this trip... I've thought of a delightful alternative—somewhere much closer to home, with a more moderate climate, no mosquitoes carrying the Zika virus..."

36

"If you're referring to the cottage in Bath, my stupid brother is hiding out there at the moment, so you may as well give up." My younger brother, Leopold—yes, *that* Leo, the one who allegedly (read: definitely) flashed the Queen at the garden party celebrating her 90th birthday—has managed to stir up a hornet's nest here at the Valcourt Palace. His latest antics have finally resulted in our father washing his hands of him, which has upset our mother (who believes the sun rises and sets out of her youngest son's behind) to no end. My eldest brother, the tow-the-family-line, uber-responsible (read: total prick) Greyson, actually issued a statement on behalf of Davenport Communications that the corporation has severed ties with Leo and that he is no longer welcome at any of the properties owned by the corporation. So, that's going to make for a lovely family Christmas dinner, don't you think?

"How about a quaint castle on the north shore? Remember when you met Princess Arabella and she offered it up for you if you ever needed a quiet getaway?" He waggles his eyebrows at me. "A little getaway with a possible side order of royal action?"

"As tempting as that is, I probably should focus on my work at the moment." Flipping open the lid of my towel steamer, I pull out a face cloth and clean off the remaining shaving cream.

"God, those warm towels always look so inviting. I tried heating a wet cloth in the microwave the other day, but it didn't work out as well as I'd hoped."

"Is that how you got that angry blister on your forehead?"

Nodding, he says, "Apparently when you heat something like that in the microwave, it comes out with hot spots that will scald you."

"Do you really have to shave your forehead? You've never looked that hairy to me."

"Very funny. I was trying to give myself a bit of a man spa." A sheepish look crosses his face.

If it were anyone else admitting that to me, I'd go after them *hard*, but with Zach, I just can't. The poor bastard really doesn't have a lot going for him, so I'm not about to have a go at his expense. "Now, I believe you were about to try to talk me out of my badly-needed escape from the crushing pressure under which I've existed for over seven hundred days..."

"Right. Yes, back to this snake-infested island of insanity where you will certainly spend the next two months typing, 'All work and no play makes Pierce a very dull boy...'"

"I'll be just fine. I've been assured it's heaven on earth, which I doubt includes snakes or insect infestations."

"But Zika is a definite possibility. The entire Caribbean is crawling with it."

"You may want to fact check that one. But even in the event you're right, Zika doesn't frighten me because I'm not trying to get pregnant this year. Besides, I shall pretty much be inside the villa day and night until I can finally type 'THE END,' so unless there are dangerous wild reptiles *indoors*, I shall consider myself much safer than I am here in Valcourt with all the snakes camped outside my building."

"What about having to go through the torturous process of adjusting to a new set of servants? Remember how long it took for Mrs. Bailey to figure you out and how annoyed you were until she did?" Zach asks.

"Ha! Here's the funny thing—the housekeeper on the island is Mrs. Bailey's sister, so really it will feel very much like home. I'm sure she's filled her in on my little quirks."

"Seriously?"

"Yes, that's how Mrs. Bailey got me in on the soft launch of the island."

"Soft launch? Aren't you the one that always says a soft launch is just an excuse to turn a poor man into a guinea pig?"

"Trust me, for what I'm paying, I guarantee there will be no experimenting."

"I still think you should reconsider. What if—?"

"Zach, while I appreciate your concern, I assure you everything will be just fine. All I need to finish this book is complete privacy, my laptop, and my two hands, all of which I will have."

"What if you run into trouble with the book and you need me?"

"They've got Wi-Fi, so in the unlikely event that I require help, I'll email. Just a second." I push a button on the screen, transferring the call to my dressing room. A moment later, the lights turn on automatically as I walk in.

"I hate it when you do that," Zach says, referring to transferring him to another room. "It's always so dark before you get here."

"Well then don't call me when I'm about to get dressed," I say, opening my underwear drawer.

"Hey, is that a set of Hermes Orion luggage?" he asks, suddenly distracted by the suitcases my housekeeper packed for me last night.

"Could be. Mrs. Bailey ordered them for me."

"She did well. If you're in need of birthday gift ideas for me, look no further."

"I was thinking of getting you a towel steamer so you don't scald your face again."

"Either would be good," he says with a big smile. "Speaking of my birthday, it presents a very strong argument for you to remain in the country. Kennedy's hosting a dinner for me next Friday and all our friends are only coming because they think you'll be there."

"Then they're not real friends. I'm sorry I won't be there to see you blow out your candles, but honestly, Zach, this truly is my last chance and I refuse to fuck it up. In order to immerse myself fully in the realms of Qadeathas, I must separate myself from all things in this lesser world. Now, if you'll excuse me, I should get dressed."

"That's a sight I can do without."

"See you in two months."

"That is if you don't get eaten by a crocodile."

Sighing, I say, "Do you not think I can handle myself in the wilds of the Caribbean?"

"Asks the man whose housekeeper pressed and packed his clothes for him..."

"I'll have you know I've lived in a tent in the Canadian wilderness."

"And if memory serves, you came home after three days with a scorching case of poison ivy."

Okay, he's got me there. That did happen and it was awful. Rolling my eyes, I say, "Two distraction-free months in a tastefully-appointed villa on a remote private island and I'll give you the best damn ending to the greatest fantasy series this world has ever seen."

"If you survive, that is."

"Goodbye, Zach. Enjoy your birthday."

THREE

It's My Not-Party and I'll Cry If I Want To...

Emma - Santa Valentina Island

I dig around in my purse for a pack of gum while I wait for Harrison to pull up in front of the San Felipe airport. The flight landed ten minutes early (yay!). I've already collected everything I own and made my way outside so I can breathe in the fragrant scent of the Benavente Islands for a few minutes. Actually, I'm secretly hoping to dry out my pits and let the breeze blow the smell of booze off my body, but to be honest, I'm doubtful that it'll work. I really reek. I made three attempts at an 'in-flight sink bath,' but each one was thwarted by cranky passengers needing to get to the toilet. So far, I've managed to clean exactly one foot and my face. But that's okay. Nothing that can't be fixed with a long shower and an entire bar of soap, right?

Watching the people coming and going from the airport, I look for familiar faces. So far, it's just a bunch of tourists, but that's okay, too. Their relaxed smiles and floral pattern shirts mean I'm home—and this time, I'm home to stay.

A turquoise open-topped jeep belonging to the Paradise Bay Resort pulls into the arrivals lane and I wave way too enthusiastically for someone who smells like this. I can't see who's driving yet, but I bet it's my brother. He probably brought his girlfriend, Libby, with him. I really like Libby. She's a bit uptight and a little crazy, but she's madly in love with my brother, and since he's never been so happy in his life, I can't help but love her, too. I bet Rosy's in the jeep, too. There's no way the woman who pretty much took over as my mum when

41

we moved to the Caribbean would be able to wait to welcome me home.

Ooh! The jeep is getting closer! Yippee!

Hmph. Fidel LeCroix, my brother's right-hand man at the resort, is driving. And he's alone.

Ooh, I bet everyone else is at the resort getting ready for a big surprise party for me!

Fidel pulls up and stops with a screech of the tires. "If it isn't Emma Banks, Paradise Bay's new master chef!" he calls, hopping out to give me a hug.

"Hey, Fidel!" I hug him back, completely forgetting how I smell until he stiffens up, then quickly lets me go.

"Are you all right?" he asks, blinking.

Oh, God. I'm make-you-blink stinky, like a freshly opened can of Surströmming. "Sorry about the smell. I ran out of time to shower before my flight."

"What smell? You're fine," he lies, quickly moving away from me under the guise of being in a rush to load my luggage in the back of the jeep. "How were your exams?"

"Since you asked, I had the third highest average in my class. No biggie." I shrug, climbing in the jeep and buckling the seatbelt.

"No biggie," he says, giving me an 'as if' look while he slides into the driver's seat.

"Okay, it is pretty huge. I was only four points off the top chef's marks, which is a minuscule difference, really. The head instructor said I'm one of the most talented poissoniers he's ever seen." I grin widely at Fidel, who chuckles at me.

"God, I hope you don't poissonier anyone. That would be really bad for business."

"Haha. A poissonier is someone who works with seafood."

Fidel pulls out of the arrivals lane, and we head toward the main road to take us south to the resort.

I yawn loudly as we make our way across the freeway into the fast lane. "God, I'm really wiped. I could use about forty-eight hours of straight sleep."

"You may not get it," he says, glancing at me. "Things are pretty nuts with the opening of Eden. Harrison and Libby have been working full out for the last six months to get everything ready."

"Did I say I needed forty-eight hours of sleep? I meant a shower, a pot of coffee, and I'll be good to go."

The Island of Eden is sort of the last resort for our resort. We had a hurricane nearly wipe us out two years ago and the wolves have been at the door ever since. If the launch fails, the bank will own everything by the end of the year—the thought of it makes my stomach churn. But, never mind, I'm home to stay, and for the first time, I'll be able to make a *real* contribution to the family business. I can take a lot of the load off Harrison and Libby's shoulders at the main property so they can focus on making Eden a complete success.

I watch as the palm trees whiz by, and I let myself enjoy finally being warm all the way to my bones. "How are Winnie and baby Harrison?" Fidel and his wife, Winnie, named their firstborn after my brother. I'm secretly hoping they have a girl next, so there could be a baby Emma around too.

Fidel's entire face lights up. "Great! He's a little spitfire, though. Always on the move and ready to try anything. Winnie says she's never been in such great shape in her life on account of chasing him around all the time."

The next fifteen minutes, Fidel talks non-stop about his son, then switches to filling me in on the gossip from around the resort. One of the towel-folding girls and a very married pool cleaner started up a relationship and got caught in cabana number ten doing the mambo number five by his wife, who works in laundry services. She tried to strangle them both with a pillowcase, so that's got everyone talking.

Unfortunately, Fidel doesn't give me any sort of hint about which restaurant I'll be hanging my chef's hat in. I know Harrison wants to tell me himself, but I was hoping for some type of clue. Not that I won't be happy with any assignment I'm given. I'm really just grateful to be home where I can start phase B of my 'become the world's most respected chef and make my family rich' plan.

My heart pounds as we start down the long, palm tree-lined driveway to the lobby where I'm sure my entire family and a bunch of the staff will be waiting to greet me. I bet they put up a big sign and everything! Damn, I wish I'd showered.

Grabbing out some lip-gloss, I try to make myself slightly more presentable. I flip down the visor and glance in the mirror briefly before giving up. No way to salvage what I've got going on here.

When we pull up in front of the large open-air lobby, my heart sinks. Nobody is here. Well, a smattering of security staff and porters and several guests are milling about, but there are no signs of a welcome home party. Huh.

Fidel parks in front, then starts to get out.

"Hey, Fidel, you wouldn't mind driving me to Harrison's so I can dump my stuff and have a shower, would you?"

"Sorry. Harrison said to take you straight to his office."

Oh, so the party's *inside*.

"Okay," I say nonchalantly even though I'm super excited.

"You go ahead. I'll stow your stuff in the luggage storage room for now."

"Thanks!"

Taking the steps two at a time, I wave and say hi to the staff as I hurry inside and through the lobby to the back offices. As I pass Rosy's office, I see the lights are off. I can hear Harrison's voice coming from behind his closed door. He's pretending to be on a call when I'm pretty sure everyone's crammed in there waiting to surprise me. What a guy! My brother's the best, isn't he?

I knock lightly, then practice looking genuinely surprised before I open the door.

Huh. He really is on the phone in his otherwise empty office.

He waves me in and gives me the 'just a second' sign with one hand. "Well, it was supposed to be here three months ago, and I've got our first guest arriving in less than three hours. What am I supposed to take him out to the island on? A catamaran?" Pause. "I know Riva Aquaramas aren't exactly easy to come by. That's why we placed the order nearly six months ago." Pause. "I'm looking at the email exchange right now and your response that says it would take three weeks tops." Pause with Harrison scowling and shaking his head (a rare sight, to be honest, because nothing rattles my brother). "It had better be." Pause. "Yeah, you too." Hanging up, Harrison stands and says, "Sorry about that. Recreating Eden has been tougher than I thought."

"You probably should have left it to God," I tease as he walks around his desk to pull me in for a hug. "Oh, you might want to wait until—"

Too late. He's hugging me. Now he's wincing and pulling back fast. "Jesus. What happened to you?"

"Long story."

"If I had to guess, I'd say you stayed up all night partying then overslept and had to rush to the airport."

"Yeah, here's a little tip for you: when someone says 'long story,' it's usually an indication that they don't want to talk about it."

"Harrison, bad news." Libby's voice comes from down the hall as her heels click along the tile floor. She walks through the door carrying an armload of files, and her expression goes from worried to delighted as soon as she notices me. "Thank goodness you're here!" She gives me a quick side hug with one arm then asks Harrison excitedly, "Did you tell her yet?"

"I was waiting for you so we can tell her together."

"Tell me what?" I ask, looking back and forth between them, wondering if they're about to announce the location of my surprise party at which they will then announce my new position as executive chef of *all* the restaurants at the resort. Not that I need *that* kind of validation. I'm honestly thrilled just to be able to give back in any capacity.

Come on, be all *the restaurants!*

Libby takes two steps toward Harrison, and I wait while they give each other a kiss on the lips and she tells him how sweet he is to wait for her. Kind of yicky, to be honest, but in a weird way it warms my heart.

Harrison turns to me with his arm still wrapped around his girlfriend's shoulder. "First, an apology. Libby and I wanted to host a big welcome home-slash-graduation party for you, but things have been more than a little crazy around here with us trying to get ready to open Eden."

"Oh, geez," I scoff. "As if I need a party."

Harrison looks slightly skeptical but I'm going to ignore that. "I take it you're all done being mad that I didn't give you enough notice to make it to my grad ceremony?"

He gives a conciliatory shrug. "As much as I hate to admit it, you were right to keep it from me."

"I know," I say, feeling a teensy bit smug. "Because you would have come and from the looks of things, there's no way you would have had time for a trip to New York."

"It's been *insane!*" Libby nods. "But we promise to have a celebration for you as soon as we can."

He looks down at me and clears his throat. "Second, let me say well done, you. If mum and dad were alive, they'd be incredibly proud to see the young woman you've become and how hard you've worked to get here."

Libby cuts in with, "It's not just your parents who would've been proud. You should see this guy going on and on about you to anyone he meets. I'm pretty sure every guest at this resort knows that his little sister just graduated from culinary school." She grins up at him adoringly and rubs his abs.

Okay, this is starting to be a lot less cute. We're moving into 'toothbrush too far down my tongue' territory now.

Harrison grins down at me. "Now, I know you must be exhausted after finishing exams and making the trip home, but I'm afraid rest will have to wait because we'd like to offer you the most important position for any chef to ever have at Paradise Bay—and you need to start today."

Oh my God, I'm being offered the resort's executive chef position! My knees feel suddenly weak, and I have an urge to sit down. I nod solemnly, ready to take on the biggest challenge of my life. "I'm up for it, believe me."

"Good, because in two and a half hours, the biggest VIP in our resort's history is about to—"

"An hour and forty-eight minutes, actually." Libby gives Harrison a sideways look.

"What?" Harrison's head whips around. "His plane wasn't supposed to land until 6 p.m."

"That was the bad news I was bringing down the hall. Somehow his pilot managed to jump the queue on the runway and then make up twenty-three minutes in the air."

"Shit. But the Aquarama hasn't arrived. Plus, there's no way Emma can prepare that fast."

"Prepare for what?" I ask, trying to appear calm. Even though my brain is two steps ahead of me in knowing what my new assignment is, the rest of me hasn't figured it out. And when it does, all of me will be sssooooooo disappointed.

The two ignore my question. Libby says, "It'll be fine, really. Justin's cleaning the *Rogue Fun* right now. Besides, we haven't advertised that guests will be taken to Eden on a Riva, so he won't know the difference."

"Prepare for what?" I ask again, leaving a clueless grin on my face.

Harrison nods at Libby. "I guess you're right. I just wanted everything to be perfect."

"It's a soft launch, so I'm sure he'll expect a few hiccups," she answers, reaching up on her tiptoes to kiss him on the lips. "Hey, I'm supposed to be the one who worries, not you."

"Good point. I'll try to calm down," he says.

"Ahem," I say loudly. "What exactly am I meant to be preparing for?"

"Oh right, sorry," Harrison says, with a shake of his head as if he suddenly remembers I'm in the room. "*You* are about to become the personal chef at Eden Island!"

The pair beam at me while I try to muster a shocked, happy look. "Really?" I ask through a too-wide smile.

"Now, the kitchen leaves a lot to be desired," Libby says apologetically. "I'm afraid it's rather cramped, and, well, it's on a houseboat actually. But the good thing is you won't have any other staff, so it's not like you'll be bumping into anyone while you're working."

Umm. What now? No other staff? "I don't get it. I thought the island has a super incredible world-class villa."

"Oh, it does," Harrison says. "I can't wait until you see it. It's turned out better than we could have hoped. The villa's equipped with a state-of-the-art kitchen in case some guests prefer to prepare their own food—"

"—or have you prepare it in front of them, you know, for a fun chef's table experience," Libby adds excitedly.

"But in order for guests to have a real private island experience, we decided it's best if the meal prep is done offshore," Harrison says. "First, we were thinking that we would cook everything here at the resort, but it's a twenty-minute boat ride to Eden, even in the *Rogue Fun*, so there's no way the food would still be at its finest. That's when Libby thought of the houseboat idea." He gives her a proud stare that makes me want to vomit on his smug flip-flops.

"Are you okay with this?" Libby asks, a worried expression on her face.

"*Okay* with it?" I shake my head and wave my hand as though that's the craziest question I've ever heard. The truth is I'm *so* not okay with it, I could burst into tears. But I won't because that's not what my brother needs right now. He needs co-operative, will-do-anything-for-the-family Emma, not whiny, I-want-to-do-what-*I*-want-to-do Emma. "What's not to be okay with?"

"The whole houseboat thing. We were worried that you'd be looking forward to cooking in a world-class kitchen and bossing people around all day," Harrison teases.

"*He* was worried about you wanting to boss people around," Libby says, rolling her eyes.

I bark out a loud laugh. "Ha! Boss people around. No way. That's *so* not me," I scoff. "I don't need some fancy kitchen. Just give me a good set of carbon-steel pans and some eggs, and I can whip up a gourmet meal."

"Thank God, because if you had said no, we'd have been totally screwed," Libby says.

Shit. I could've said no? Why didn't I say no?! "No, this is *brilliant*, really. I'll be a private chef for two people at a time. Brilliant." For some unknown reason, I put on a French accent. "Quite a challenge to cater to their every whim."

"Well, the first two months, it'll just be the one guest," Libby says, then quickly adds, "But he's an incredibly well-connected, famous author, so if you—well, *we* as a team—can impress him, it'll really cause Eden to take off."

"No pressure, though," Harrison says.

"And don't worry. We're not sending you out into the wild alone," Libby adds. "We've hired a lovely couple from Avonia to take care of the housekeeping and butler services. Alfred and Phyllis Willis—you'll *love* them. They're right out of *Downton Abbey*. They worked at Valcourt Palace for a combined total of forty-eight years, so they really know their stuff. Lucky for us, when they retired from the palace, they decided to continue working in a tropical location."

"Libby snapped them up as soon as they became available," Harrison says, pulling her in for a shoulder squeeze. "Alfred will serve as butler and take care of any minor maintenance issues that crop up. He's also a master sommelier, which is a huge bonus."

"Huge!" Libby beams. "And Phyllis will take care of housekeeping."

"Oh, terrific. That's...who doesn't love *Downton Abbey*? This is...great," I answer. You know what else would be great? A nice cold, stiff drink right about now.

Harrison nods. "It's a pretty cool setup, actually. Their houseboat is moored next to yours so you can feel secure out there at night—"

"If you decide to stay on the boat, that is," Libby cuts in. "Alternatively, you could come back to the resort when you finish up with dinner service."

"But you can sort all that out later. For now, we better get you and some grub over to Eden stat," Harrison says, clapping his hands together.

He and Libby simultaneously usher me out the door, and I find myself being rushed down the hall toward the back entrance.

The walkie-talkie on Harrison's belt crackles, and Rosy's voice fills the space. "Big Momma to Honey Bear. Come in, Honey Bear. Over."

Harrison pulls his walkie-talkie out of the holster. "Hey, Rosy. What's up? Over."

"Who is this? Over."

"You know who it is. What's up? Over."

"Just say it," Libby suggests as the radio crackles. "She's not going to move on with the conversation otherwise, and you know it."

Harrison sighs. "Honey Bear here. What's up, Big Momma? Over."

"The crew from housekeeping and I are on our way back. We should be there in about fifteen minutes. Over."

"Great work, everybody. Hey, Big Momma, there's someone here who wants to speak to you. Say hello to Baby

Bear. Over." Harrison snickers as he hands me the walkie-talkie.

I glare at him and yank it out of his hand.

"Baby Bear? Is that you? Over."

"It sure is. I made it home!" There's a long pause until I say, "Over."

"And Baby Bear, did you finish your degree this time? Over."

"Yes, Big Momma," I say reluctantly. "Over."

Loud squealing sounds come from the walkie-talkie, and when Rosy's ready to speak, she's sobbing audibly and saying something about Big Momma being so proud of her Baby Bear. As cringeworthy as this is, it's good to be home again.

Now, if only I can magically be clean, put together, and prepared to impress some snooty old wanker in the next hour and...shit...twenty-minutes...

FOUR

The World's Nastiest Bunny...

Pierce - 1000 km Northeast of the Benavente Islands

Ahh...that's better. After nearly eight hours in the air, I finally have managed to loosen the grip that the permanent knot has had on my gut for months. Special thanks to the makers of Bombay Sapphire gin and Bob Ross for this blissful state. I sigh contentedly as Bob puts the finishing touches on another happy landscape. He really is the most soothing person to grace the telly, no? Even that perm is delightfully fun.

And before you say, 'But, Pierce, shouldn't you be writing?' you should know I do, in fact, have a plan. I'm going to use these nine hours to fully unwind and let go of the real world so that upon arrival at Eden, I can fully immerse myself in my work. Yes, this is it. I can almost feel the creative juices flowing like a spring brook.

Christ. 'Bunny Davenport' is flashing across my mobile screen. My mother's calling again. (And, yes, I have her down by her real name rather than World's Best Mum or some other cutesy way people list their parents in their contacts. In my case, reminding myself of the limits of our relationship is imperative.) I roll my eyes as my phone vibrates on the plush cream-coloured leather seat next to mine.

Damn. Since I intend to shut off my mobile for two months, I suppose I should answer, even just to tell her I'm disappearing for a while.

"Hello Mother, what seems to be the trouble?" I ask, then take a sip of my drink.

"Why, Pierce, I'm insulted that you think I only call when something is wrong." Her shrill voice blasts out of my mobile. "Is that what you think of your mother?"

"Name one time in the fourteen years since I left home that you have called just to say hi."

"So, I'm not one for idle chitchat. Is it really necessary to throw that in my face? You and your brothers act like I have no right to my own life, but honestly, after everything I sacrificed to bring you into the world and raise you properly, is it so much to ask that I have a little *me time*?"

Other than her time spent in labour, my mother's entire life could be classified as 'me time.'

Rolling my eyes, I say, "Of course not. As I've told you before, take all the 'me time' you need." After all, our relationship tends to be much smoother when she's completely self-absorbed. "Mother, I can't talk long. I'm working at the moment, so if you could quickly fill me in on the latest scandal your youngest son has caused, I will give you my customary sympathetic answer, offer no solutions, and get back to the task at hand."

"What's that noise in the background? Where are you?"

"Somewhere over the North Atlantic."

"Going where?" she asks, suddenly sounding panicked.

"A writing retreat."

"Not that silly *Battling Kings* thing still?"

So nice to know she cares. "*Clash of Crowns*, and yes. Now, what exactly did Leo do this time?"

She instantly shifts gears back to full drama mode. "You really don't know what's happened?"

"Haven't the faintest."

"It's Arthur. He's broken off his engagement with that awful girl."

She's referring to Prince Arthur, the heir apparent of Avonia and a former classmate of mine. "Really? With the wedding only weeks away?" I say. "Well, I can't say I'm surprised. They did rather rush things."

"Especially since he was about to rush into marriage with someone so very low class," she says, lowering her voice to a whisper, as if somehow the volume will reduce the nastiness of her words. "There was a photo spread of her family home in

The Weekly World News last week. They have *garden gnomes*."

I gasp, feigning shock as I stare out the window at the ocean below. "Not *garden gnomes*. So, it *was* doomed from the start."

"I can do without the sarcasm, Pierce. And here I thought for once we were on the same page."

"We are, just perhaps not for the same reasons." I dislike Arthur's choice in brides because she's a horrid blogger who makes her money writing about how much she hates royals of any kind. She's written especially awful things about Arthur himself, and as a loyal friend, it's not something I can easily overlook.

But the *real* reason I'm against this particular coupling is no different than why I'm opposed to every other marriage—because it's a monumental misstep. There's no such thing as lasting love—just temporary insanity followed either by divorce or fifty years of waiting for your spouse to kick off so you can get back to watching what you want on the telly.

"... ring him up and be there to support him during this difficult time."

I suddenly realize my mother has been talking without me hearing a word of it, but there's really no point because the only reason she called is because I have a connection that can help improve her own position in amongst the other Botox cobras at the country club.

"Arthur knows how to reach me if he wants. Now, if that's all, I should go."

"Fine. If this little vacation is more important to you than your best friend's welfare, I guess you should carry on as though nothing is happening," my mother sniffs.

Best friend is definitely stretching it. Arthur and I see each other a couple of times a year at most. As fond as we are of one another, it's not like we've had slumber parties and told each other our deepest darkest secrets. I could mention this to my mother, but there really is no point. She believes what she wants to, and at the moment, she wants to believe I can parlay Arthur's breakup into a closer relationship with him so *she* can be the one with the inside scoop on spa day.

She sniffs again, no doubt hoping I'll ask if she's crying. She's not and I won't. I can picture her right now laying on her gold velvet chaise in her private bedroom—the massive three thousand square-foot suite which she does not share with my father. She is likely fanning herself like a Victorian duchess whose overly cinched bodice is making her feel faint.

"It's not a vacation, mother. It's a work trip—"

"So *money* is more important than your dearest childhood friend. Now, Pierce, I don't think that's how I raised you."

Yes. Yes, it is. "Just exactly why does this matter so much to you?"

"Because it's a *tragedy*."

"That's exactly what you said when they *announced* their engagement."

"Oh, not about them breaking it off. About *the wedding* being cancelled. I've had the entire house redone because of all the parties we were to throw surrounding the big event. Not to mention the dress I've had Stella toiling away on for months."

Ahh...there it is. "That *is* tragic. Hopefully he'll find a new bride before your dress goes out of style."

"I should have known better than to call you for sympathy."

Truer words were never spoken. "You should have called Leopold. He has a lot more patience than I do."

"I tried him first, but he didn't pick up. Have you heard from him lately?"

"No, I haven't, but I'm sure the little birds you have everywhere are keeping you abreast of his every movement."

That's not entirely true. I did receive a rather incoherent text message from my little brother two nights ago—something about the 'meaning of life, perky tits, and happiness.' Needless to say, I haven't gotten back to him. The less I have to do with Leo, the easier my life tends to be. As fond as I am of him, he's a bit of a mess, and since I have my own shit to work out, it's not like I'm in any position to play his keeper.

"If there's nothing else, I really must get back to work." Okay, I know I'm technically lying, but mental preparation is key.

"Honestly, why are you insisting on living the life of a Tibetan monk, tapping away on a keyboard alone all day, when you could be out meeting a suitable woman?"

And here we are again. My mother is the Michael Schumacher of making sharp conversational turns. "Okay, first, I don't think Tibetan monks spend much time on laptops. Second, I don't *want* to meet a suitable woman. I *like* being alone. Not everyone has to get married and procreate. It's not like we're trying to populate the colony."

"*Nobody* likes being alone, Pierce. That's just a lie people tell themselves when they're too scared to put themselves out there. Happiness cannot be found in isolation."

"Trust me, it can. For example, before I answered your call, I was having a very pleasant day."

My mother sighs dramatically. "All I want is to see you in a fulfilling, happy relationship. Is that too much to ask?"

"You mean like the one you and father have?" The sarcasm drips from my tongue like molasses—thick and heavy.

"He and I have been doing better, thank you very much," she quips.

She's referring to the fact that he's been in Scotland for work for the last four months, which means they haven't had to see each other. Rather than challenging her on it, however, I'm just going to let that one go in the interest of ending this conversation. "I'm very glad to hear that. Now I really must run. If I don't talk to you in time, good luck with your next procedure."

With that, I hang up and power off my mobile so can I get back to forgetting everyone I know. I stare out the window at the early evening sky, feeling every bit as discontent as I did when I stepped aboard the jet. Bunny has a way of doing that to me, which is why I avoid eighty percent of her calls. Her voice invades my mind. *Battling Kings*. There is literally nothing I can do to impress that woman. My father, too. This is not a new revelation for me. I've known it since I was a boy, more content to read than hunt foxes with my father and my other brother, Greyson.

The truth is, no matter what I accomplish, it will never be enough. They will never know me for who I am, not that I need that of them. But should I fail over these next few weeks, whatever relationship I do have with my parents will be even more unbearable than it is now. My achievements may not impress them, but a spectacular public failure shall not escape their attention...

FIVE

How *Not* to Make a First Impression

Emma

Why do people say 'no pressure' when there is clearly a hell of a lot of pressure involved?

Seriously, I'd much rather be told the truth. *Hey Emma, there's a shit-ton of pressure on you to gather everything you'll need, transform into the world's most professional-looking chef, and get yourself out to an island in the middle of freaking nowhere in the next hour. Oh, and once you arrive, you'll have to prepare a delectable, Michelin-star-worthy dinner for a guest who, according to Libby, hails from one of the most influential families in the UK (the Davenhams or Binglyports or some other snooty rich family I've never heard of), so his recommendation could either make or break us among the elite. If there was ever a time to panic, it's now.*

But, instead of honesty, I was repeatedly and uselessly reassured by Harrison and Libby that there was nothing for me to worry about as they handed me the keys to one of the speedboats and told me to get my buns out to Eden—pun intended.

Ha ha ha. Aren't they hilarious together?

In the last forty minutes, I've raided the pantries and fridge at the main buffet restaurant, commandeered a clean chef's uniform, and endured a bumpy ride out to Eden driving full throttle whilst attempting to plan a perfectly impressive meal for Mr. Important. I still haven't thought of anything, by the way, since my brain is on empty. I also haven't showered, brushed my teeth, put on makeup, or sucked down an entire pot of high-test coffee. I'm angry, bitchy, tired, and disappointed right through to my bones. Every expectation of my homecoming has been put through the meat grinder because, let's face it, so far it has left a lot to be desired.

No party.

No fussing.

No quiet moment of reverence as I walk around the kitchen of my restaurant, running one hand along the cool stainless-steel counter-tops, knowing it's all under my control now.

No luxuriously long shower followed by a twelve-hour nap.

But since I'm now down to twenty-four minutes until the arrival of his nibs, I'll have to pout about everything later.

When I reach the island, I have to circle around almost the entire way to find the spot where the houseboats are docked. Just as I start to worry that I'm at the wrong place, I see them—both well-scrubbed but utterly unimpressive vessels that hardly look seaworthy as they rock in the waves created by the speedboat. Libby told me mine is the blue one and the Willis's will be living on the white one (which, by the way, is roughly double the size of mine). Apparently, Phyllis is up at the villa completing the final preparations, and Alfred is going down to the guest dock on the other side of the island to greet Mr. Important, so I'm going to have to transfer all the supplies from the speedboat to the houseboat alone in this heat.

By the time I've unloaded all the food and my box of cookware, I'm drenched with sweat. When I finally unlock the door and step inside the cabin, my last hope of being pleasantly surprised today is snuffed out. "No, no, no, no, no." *This cannot be my new life. My* dorm room *was better than this.*

The 'kitchen' is all of four-square-feet and holds the world's smallest three-burner stove. Why *three* when there is room for a fourth? The stovetop isn't a triangle, after all. In place of the sub-zero walk-in fridge I daydreamed about during my flight, I find myself staring down at a minibar fridge that I'm pretty sure would barely fit Charles Manson. There are exactly four cupboards—two upper cabinets and two holding up the minuscule laminate wood countertop that will serve as my preparation area. And there's a built-in three-skinny-person banquette in a lovely combination of pea green vinyl and silver duct tape that will serve as my break room/planning area.

I dump the box of food on the counter and make short work of unloading everything I brought. I crouch, staring into the fridge as I rack my brain for the perfect meal to please the pompous middle-aged foodie who is about to arrive. According to Harrison, he's an author who will be using the island for his own private writing retreat. I don't know much about book royalties, but if I had to guess, I'd say he's gonna have to sell a hell of a lot of copies in order to pay back the special soft launch price of $12,500 per night.

Not my problem, though. *Focus, Emma! What are you going to make?*

The radio crackles and I take the three steps required to reach it and pick up the mic, hoping it's anyone but Rosy. "Emma here."

"Emma, it's Harrison. Fidel is on his way with Mr. Davenport. They should be there in fifteen minutes. Any chance you could have yourself up at the villa with an appetizer and some cold beverages waiting?"

"Absolutely." As in, *Absolutely! There is a very slim chance I'll make it up there in time.* "Any hint as to his food and or drink preferences?"

"No, sorry. He didn't return the guest preferences sheet." *Of course, he didn't.* "Okay, 10-4, Harrison. I'll get to it."

As I rush back to the kitchenette, a wave of inspiration hits in the form of cherry bruschetta. Easy, fast, and (hopefully) impressive. The oven door groans when I open it to make sure there are no animals nesting inside. All clear. Okay. Maybe this won't be so bad after all...

Oh, yes it will. This damn oven doesn't have a broil setting which means slow-toasting the bread. Setting the dial to 350°F, I quickly slice a baguette, lightly brush six slices with olive oil, place them on a small cookie sheet and pop them in the oven while I get to work on the cherry compote.

While the liquid cooks out of the compote, I gather everything I'll need to take with me to the villa, including a bottle of Pinot Noir that pairs well with the appetizer. When everything is ready, I pack the small cooler that thankfully has been provided, grab the uniform I borrowed, and climb down off the boat and onto the small wooden dock. A golf cart waits for me, plugged into a solar-powered generator. Seconds later, I'm zooming up the steep, windy path.

When I reach the villa, I momentarily forget how much of a panic I'm in and am awed by what Harrison and Libby have managed to accomplish since I was last here during my 'hiatus' from school. There used to be a tiny one-room cabin with no electricity or running water, but the building before me screams luxury. Surrounded by jungle, the villa has floor-to-ceiling windows and an enormous wrap-around porch that sits under a dramatically sloped ironwood roof. The extra-wide double doors are made from polished mahogany. I sound like a travel brochure, no? If this whole cooking thing doesn't work out, maybe I could have a career in marketing.

The door swings open and a middle-aged woman with gray hair in a tight bun hurries out. She's dressed in a light gray, short-sleeved dress with a white apron tied at her waist and she looks as stressed as I feel. "You must be Emma," she says, rushing down the steps. "Why are you not in uniform? We've only got a few minutes to finish preparations."

She takes the cooler and rushes ahead of me back into the villa with me at her heels.

"I only just landed and haven't exactly had a chance—"

"No time for excuses. Go get yourself dressed in there. I'll lay the food out," she barks.

Well, that's a bit rude. Does she think I work for *her*? Deciding to let it go, I rush to the washroom, calling over my shoulder that she needs to plate the bruschetta with the cheese first, then the compote.

"This is not my first rodeo," she replies in her upper-crust accent as I shut the door to the washroom.

I snag a perfectly rolled facecloth off the tray on the counter, rip open a bar of soap and get to work washing out some of the stench. According to my watch, I have about two minutes until Mr. Important arrives. "Not my first rodeo," I mutter. "As if she's ever even been to a rodeo. She's probably never even seen a cow in real life. '*Oh, Emma, you'll love Phyllis and Alfred. They're so wonderful.*' Pfft."

After my thirty-second sponge bath, I squeeze myself into the borrowed uniform, only to realize it must be child-sized. Seriously? Who can fit in this thing? The sleeves come up to the middle of my forearm; the pants, which are tight enough to display my lack of knickers, come up just below my calves; and the buttons on my jacket strain to pop open as I squish my boobs in. *Come on girls, could you be smaller, just for a few minutes?*

I help myself to a swig of mouthwash and give myself a few seconds to freshen my breath. Just as I'm preparing to sneak out with my dirty clothes, the soap I'm liberating, and the cloth I used, the sound of male voices makes their way through the washroom door.

Shit. He's here.

I hurry out of the bathroom without watching where I'm going, only to crash into a very solid structure.

Mr. Important.

Of course, I make a loud 'oofing' sound while the contents of my arms drop to the floor between us. The soap slides across the room leaving a wet streak on the Brazilian hardwood, hitting Phyllis in the old lady nurse shoe. When I look up, I see her and her husband gaping in horror.

I risk a glance at Mr. Davenport, who incidentally is much younger and much hotter than I anticipated. He's easily over six-feet tall, lean with ramrod straight posture, and has rimless glasses that frame his gorgeous green eyes. His dark brown hair sits perfectly in place as though not one strand would dare stray from the pack. His sharp features, chiselled jaw, and full lips have an expression that is so severe, it makes me want to catch a flight back to the U.S. and find a Wendy's in need of a fry cook. He's dressed in rich guy casual—a pair of jeans that probably cost more than my first car, some brown loafers, and a crisp white button-up shirt with the sleeves rolled up to display a muscular set of forearms.

He tilts his head and narrows his eyes at me a little. "Who are you and why are you stealing my soap?"

His soap? He's just renting this place. "I'm Emma Banks. I'll be your personal chef during your stay and I'm not stealing your soap. I'm...commandeering it."

Raising one eyebrow, he says, "Is it required for some urgent government business in which you're involved?"

"Something like that," I answer, crouching quickly to pick up the dropped items. *Rrrriiippp!*

Annddd...my pants have split open at my bottom, which is just perfect since I'm not wearing any knickers.

"Did your pants just—"

I shoot up to standing and cut him off by loudly saying, "I've prepared a cherry bruschetta with goat cheese and paired it with a Pinot Noir to welcome you. I hope it will be to your liking."

He stares down at the tray of carefully crafted appetizers but instead of doing what I hoped he would, he stuffs both hands in the front pockets of his jeans and says, "I'm not really a fan of goat cheese."

Oh perfect. So, even though he's young and hot, he's every bit the rich-guy arse I knew he'd be.

Plastering a phony smile on my reddened face, I say, "No instructions were given as to your dining preferences so I had to guess." There's an ill-advised edge in my voice, but I'm exhausted, disappointed, and starving. Oh, plus there's a draft from the air conditioner blowing up my nether regions reminding me of how naked my behind is at the moment.

"I didn't bother to fill in the preferences form, but I was just telling your co-workers here that you'll find I'm not at all picky."

"Other than disliking goat cheese, that is?" I ask.

He stiffens slightly at the question. "Well, all soft cheeses, really. And come to think of it, I've always felt that sundried tomatoes ruin any dish."

"Since it's not 1993, I won't be using those anyway."

He smiles for the briefest instant and I'm temporarily blinded by his hotness. My brain gives a mental slap to my lady bits and tells them to calm the hell down. *We will* not *be attracted to this wanker.* "Anything else I should avoid?" Other than him, that is...

Mr. Snooty Pants looks up at the ceiling for a second, then says, "I dislike onions, pecans, anything caramelized, anything with gristle, and gazpacho of any kind."

"But you're not picky."

"Exactly."

"Or apparently, at all self-aware," I mutter.

"Pardon me?"

"Nothing." I crouch—gingerly this time—and gather my clothes, then stand, all the while careful not to turn my back to Mr. Low Maintenance or Mr. and Mrs. Perfect Servants.

Phyllis, who is now holding the soap with two fingers as though it's a dirty nappy, hands it to me while she addresses our VIP. "The bar is stocked with a selection of premium beers, fruit juices, sodas, and top-shelf liquors. Next to it, you'll find a cupboard filled with various snack foods such as nuts, crisps, and chocolates. There is a handheld radio on the bar which you can use to reach us should you need anything."

"Thank you," he says, his eyes never leaving me. He zeros in on my tiny uniform while I do my best not to fidget. Smirking, he says, "Have you recently had a growth spurt?"

Oh, he's a regular Kevin Hart with the jokes.

Lifting my chin, I say, "This is the new look for chef uniforms in Paris, actually. The shorter sleeves don't get caught as easily in an open flame."

Raising one eyebrow, he asks, "And the short pants?"

"That's for style." I give him an icy glare then remind myself that I need to dial back the snark for the good of the resort. Raising the corners of my lips in an attempt at a smile, I say, "For your dinner tonight, I'll be preparing a light grapefruit and avocado salad served on a bed of spinach and lamb's lettuce with a balsamic vinaigrette dressing followed by a fennel and lemon risotto with prawns caught this afternoon."

"Ah, risotto," he says, wrinkling his nose ever so slightly. "The signature dish of the rookie chef."

I stiffen at his words. "I assure you, I'm no rookie."

"Really? How long ago did you graduate from culinary school?"

"Yesterday," I murmur. "But believe me, I'm very experienced."

An amused smirk crosses his face and he stops himself just short of laughing. "I'm sure you think you are."

"Do you want the risotto or not?" I ask sharply, then taking a breath, I soften my tone a little. "I'd be happy to whip up something else if you prefer."

"No need. Risotto is fine," he answers. "As I was saying to Mr. and Mrs. Willis while you were using my washroom, I won't be requiring their services this month other than a weekly cleaning while I'm out for a run. I'll need complete privacy so I can finish the novel I'm working on. I don't care who brings me my food so long as they're quiet about it," he says. Looking at me, he adds, "I work until well after midnight and don't eat breakfast until close to noon, lunch at four p.m., and I take my dinner around nine. I expect that won't be a problem."

"No, of course not." Except it *totally is* a problem, because it means I have to sleep on the houseboat every night for the next two damn months. There's no way it's safe to make the ride back to the resort after dark.

Nodding, he says, "Thank you, that will be all."

"Very good, sir," Alfred says, picking up the plate of bruschetta. "I'll just remove this unwanted food for you."

In lieu of answering, Mr. Snooty Pants picks up his laptop bag and turns his back to us. I stare for a moment while he makes his way across the large room to the mahogany desk, my entire body seething with hatred. He is everything that's wrong with this world. I can see his epitaph now: Mr. Davenport. Writer. Entitled, rude arsehole. Missed by no one.

Covering my bottom with my clothing-filled hand, I follow the Willis's out the front door. Once it's closed, I watch helplessly as Alfred dumps the food into a rubbish bin on the back of his golf cart.

They stand for a moment watching me as I slide into my own golf cart. "So, that went well, don't you think?" I ask, then laugh a little at my joke.

Apparently, they're not into ironic humour because they both just stare, poker-faced.

"You are Mr. Banks' sister?" Alfred asks.

Nodding, I say, "Yes."

"I see," he says. "Perhaps I should bring Mr. Davenport his meals so as to maintain a professional atmosphere."

"Perfect." Since I don't want to ever see His Royal Arsiness again, that suits me just fine.

With that, Alfred starts up his cart and pulls out, leaving me to follow my new neighbours down the trail to the beach, repeating what will become my new mantra: "I love my brother, I owe him everything, and I will do whatever I have to do to save the resort—even if it means being nice to these awful people."

SIX

Insert Feet Here (Points to Mouth)

Pierce

"Way to go, Pierce, you gargantuan idiot," I mutter as I cross the room to the bar. "Have you recently had a growth spurt? I don't like goat cheese."

Cringing, I pour two fingers of vodka into a crystal tumbler. Filling the glass with ice from the mini-bar freezer, I then crack open a can of tonic water and add a healthy serving of it to my drink.

The first sip cools my overheated mind, swirling with self-loathing over my inability to hold it together around this woman. Honestly, what is wrong with me today? It's not like I haven't been around my share of attractive women. Normally, I have no trouble pulling out the charm, but around her, my attempts at humour came off as high-handed judgment.

So what if she's pretty? Well, beautiful is a more fitting description—those lips, those athletic curves squeezed into what is clearly no more her uniform than the soap she was using. Stunning really, even without makeup or her hair done. And there's a feisty edge to her that I'm drawn to like a Kardashian to a camera lens.

Snap out of it, idiot. You have no time for women right now!

I grab a bag of pretzels from the cupboard and head over to the desk to get to work. As soon as I sit down and open my laptop, I'll forget all about a certain stunning chef and dive straight into the realm of Qadeathas where my characters await.

Yes, by this time tomorrow, I'll be well on my way to another year on the New York Times Best Seller list.

***

So, apparently I have jetlag or something because it's now almost nine o'clock in the morning and I haven't written a single word in spite of staying up all night to work. My plan of spending the entire night locked in the frenzy of words has instead been usurped by Ms. Emma Banks, whose face pops into my head every few minutes as I stare at the blank screen of my laptop. And it's not a sex thing, I promise, so before you go accusing me of being some simpleton who is helplessly led by his umm...pen, allow me to explain.

It's the expression on her face when I exhibited my ill-mannered side that haunts me. She was all defiance and strength when most people crumble in my presence. And for every ounce of strength she showed, I was reduced even more into an awkward, forty-two-year-old gamer who lives in his parents' basement with his tarantula, Spock, and Sulu, his crested gecko. I found myself with absolutely no hope of stringing three coherent words together. My brain seized up and my tongue continued on with absolutely no direction from my frontal lobes. And now, I can't stop reliving the horror of it...

I spent the first few hours of the evening waiting for my dinner, secretly hoping she would be the one to bring it so I could attempt to redeem myself. Instead, the older chap appeared, silently setting the tray of piping hot risotto down on the dining table, then disappearing. It was delicious, by the way—creamy and cooked to perfection with prawns that absolutely burst with flavour.

So now, having not slept and not written, I find myself laying on the floor in the living room, tossing a squash ball up in the air in an attempt to have it loop around the rafters and land back in my waiting hand. FYI, I have yet to get it up high enough. Oh, not that way. Believe me, when the moment arrives, I can get it up high enough to suit any woman. I'm referring to the ball.

You may be wondering, why not just go to sleep, Pierce? Because sleep is for people who accomplish something. Since

I'm not in that group at the moment, I'm forcing myself to stay awake until I write something. Anything at all.

I'll let you in on a not-so-little secret (and please don't tell anyone because you're really the only one to know): I have no fucking clue how to end the series. Not even a hint. And each hour that passes without me writing something, *anything* really, is another nail in the coffin of my career. Because the first three novels took more than eighteen months each to write, and I don't have eighteen months. I have exactly eight weeks until a crew of hired guns will be sitting around a conference table at the NBO offices brainstorming ways to ruin my legacy.

Once they get started, they'll be able to work much quicker than me because *I'm* writing the novel on which they should base their script, and scriptwriting is a much faster process. It's just a matter of listing the setting, the characters in the scene, then bang—action and dialogue, and move on. No flowing descriptive paragraphs. No painstakingly-developed window into the very souls of the fully-fleshed out characters of Qadeathas. No way am I letting this happen to my world.

The truth is, the writers at NBO really won't give a pebble shit how to finish the series. They just need to have enough content for ten episodes. And if they should beat me to the finish line, *they* will win. Their sub-par climax of my epic fantasy will reign supreme because millions of people who *would have* read the book won't once they know how it ends. Even worse, it will spark huge controversy over what the 'real ending' should have been—mine or theirs. Mine, obviously.

But, there's even more pressure than that on yours truly because if they finish before me, my writing career is over. Done. Finito. My fans will never forgive me. I'll *never* get picked up by another publisher again after tanking so publicly and costing Sullivan and Stone tens of millions. I literally will go from being considered one of the most brilliant minds of my generation to being one of the biggest failures. So, it really is do or die for me, the thought of which doesn't exactly allow me to relax enough to get into a creative mindset.

An image of a group of bearded unkempt writers sitting around a conference table eating crisps springs to mind. One of them gets up and writes "Finish with Bollywood Dance Number" on the whiteboard.

Fuck.

SEVEN

I hate to complain, but...

Emma

It's a grey, rainy day, which suits me just fine because I'm every bit as miserable today as I was when I first arrived back home three days ago. Phyllis and Alfred are really cold, which means I'm basically living in solitary confinement out here. It's more like Ryker's Island than the Island of Eden. I'm a social girl. I *love* people so this is definitely not for me.

Plus, it's honestly a little scary out here at night. I find myself laying awake half the night wondering if Phyllis and Alfred are actually axe murderers waiting for their chance to off me.

During the day, it's not much better either. It's desperately boring and lonely so I've been going back to the resort as often as possible. I tell Alfred and Phyllis my frequent trips are supply runs, but I'm secretly doing a little recon to see if any of the other chefs at the resort might want to trade places with me. I considered telling Harrison how badly I hate it here, but since I'd rather bring him solutions than problems, I want to find someone willing to swap before I approach the subject.

Actually, that's not entirely true. The truth is—and this is between you and I because I could never admit it to anyone else—I don't want to ask Harrison for a better position because I'm the teeniest bit angry with him for sticking me out here. Well, more than a teeny bit, actually. Extremely pissed would be more accurate. I suppose I'm more hurt than angry.

Very, very hurt.

I know he and Libby said this is a super important position and all, but I can't help but wonder if maybe I wasn't given a proper kitchen to manage because they thought I couldn't handle it. I know I'm young, but I've been working in the restaurants in one capacity or another since I was in a training bra. And deep down, I know I can do it. I could run the hell out of a kitchen. (In a good way of course. That didn't sound quite how I meant.) I just need to get someone to give me my shot, and it hurts that Harrison doesn't have the confidence in me to let me try. He says he's proud of me, but then he sticks me out here like I'm the family screwup or something.

So, I figured I'd be like Tess McGill in *Working Girl* and decide that 'I make it happen.' Unfortunately, it turns out no one wants to be stuck on a tiny houseboat with no air conditioning, scrubbing their own pots, when they can be in a nice, cool, well-equipped kitchen planning meals and delegating all the crap jobs. I approached the subject with Frieda, who runs the Japanese restaurant. She basically laughed when I tried to Tom Sawyer her. Norman, the head chef at the buffet said he'd love to trade with me but couldn't on account of his seasickness. Apparently, he completely forgot he was standing in front of a framed photo of himself on a boat with a marlin on a fishing line at the time.

Word must be getting around that I want off Eden, because yesterday afternoon all I did was smile at Junior Gonzalez when I saw him on the way to the Brazilian steakhouse and he shook his head and said, "No way, Emma. I'm not trading."

Unfortunately, this means putting my dream of becoming a world-famous chef on hold indefinitely. I'm basically working as a personal cook for parties of one or two, which is going to get me exactly nowhere. And, let's face it, it's not like the next guests will be any better than this guy. They're *all* going to be uppity rich people who treat me like the help while they spend their stay posting photos of their ridiculously expensive vacay to make everyone back home jealous.

The truth is, the longer I stay here, the longer it's going to take for me to earn any R-E-S-P-E-C-T from the culinary world. I'll wither and die here on this shitty little houseboat, having never shared my talents with the world.

Oh dear, I am a whiny thing when I'm alone too long with my own thoughts. Think on the bright side, Emma.

It has given me the chance to relax after all that hard work at school. I've actually started reading again for pleasure, which is rather nice, really. And I've been taking mid-afternoon naps to make up for the rotten nights out here. Oh, plus I haven't had to see He Who Shall Possibly be Maimed in days since Alfred is bringing the meals up to the villa. I do have to take his calls on the radio which, quite frankly is bad enough, but at least I don't have to see him in person.

The radio crackles and I hear his snooty voice. "Mr. Davenport here. I require breakfast now."

"I require breakfast now? What an arse," I murmur as I pick up the mic. Pushing the button, I say, "Yes, Mr. Davenport. I'll prepare some French toast, eggs, bacon, and fruit, if that would be to your liking."

"That will definitely hit the spot, thank you," he says, his voice straining at his attempt at being human.

Raising my middle finger at the radio, I put on a syrupy voice, "I'll have it to you as quickly as possible, sir."

***

By the time I've finished preparing everything, I'm like a ball of rage. Between Big-Brother-Knows-Best and Mr. Thinks-His-Shit-Doesn't-Stink, I've had it with anyone with a Y chromosome. *I require breakfast now.* Grrr. I *cannot wait* for him to get back on his stupid jet so I never have to hear his snooty voice again.

A knock at the door snaps me out of my thoughts. "Come in!"

Oh *perfect*. Another irritating man has just walked in. Alfred stands at the door, dripping wet in his Paddington Bear outfit, complete with the red rain hat and blue coat. "I'm afraid we can't use the golf carts today."

"What? Oh no! Why not?" I'm only acting like I care. This really isn't my problem. It's his. I'm the chef, *he's* the guy in charge of butlering and maintenance.

"The carts can't make it up the hill when it's this wet. Mr. Banks said as soon as he can afford to, he'll replace them with all-terrain vehicles, but for now, in cases of heavy rain, we have to walk."

"Well, it shouldn't be too much of a problem. The cooler is insulated so it'll keep the food warm on your trek up to the villa." I snap the lid on and hold the cooler out to him.

Alfred looks down at it, but makes no move to take it from me. "I'm afraid I won't be able to make it up there in a timely fashion. I have a trick knee that acts up during storms."

Well, isn't that convenient?

We stare each other down, while I try to determine what exactly the trick is even though I'm pretty sure it's on me.

Alfred continues, "I'd ask Phyllis to go since you did all the work so far this morning, but I'm afraid she has terrible bunions and wouldn't be able to walk that far."

Narrowing my eyes, I say, "Why don't I go?"

"That would be most kind of you, Emma," Alfred answers with a smile and nod. Glancing down at my attire— peach striped pyjama pants and a tank top—he says, "I'll let you get changed into your uniform. Provided you have a clean one that fits."

"I do, thanks."

"Excellent. Good luck." With that, he disappears into the storm, leaving me to dress.

***

I mutter curse words the entire five minutes it takes for me to dress, put my hair up in a twist, and apply a light layer of makeup. Well, light might be the wrong word. I did go a little heavy on mascara. Apparently, there's a tiny but strong-willed part of me who badly wants to show Mr. Important what he can't have. She won the argument with feisty, independent Emma, who is now completely disgusted as she applies her shiniest lip gloss in the mirror above the toilet. Yes, the toilet. The sink has a small window above it so I have to straddle the toilet to use the mirror. Isn't this delightful?

Okay, Emma. Just get this over with so you can come back and have a long nap and dream about a land where men don't exist.

Grabbing the umbrella from the tiny closet, I pick up the cooler and start on my way.

EIGHT

The Mysterious Ms. Banks

Pierce

Okay, so things aren't exactly going as planned. I've burned eight days already—eight!—without accomplishing anything other than doodling some mildly inappropriate sketches. I finally gave up on sleep-as-a-reward after about thirty-two hours of torturing myself needlessly. Not that it's helped.

I also haven't had a chance to redeem myself with the lovely chef. I've been hoping she'll bring up one of my meals so I can compliment her culinary skills (which truly are well-refined) and apologize for my unforgivably rude behaviour, but so far, it's just been Alfred. And for some stupid reason, I can't even manage to order food properly. You'd think speaking to her through the safe distance of the radio would help, but no. I still come out sounding like a total arse.

I've been sitting at my computer tapping my fingers on the desk for the past thirty minutes while I obsess over our brief conversation. *Why on earth am I letting this woman get under my skin? Forget her. You have one job, Pierce. And you're failing miserably.*

Thunder rolls through the air as the door opens. In walks Ms. Banks, dressed in a suitably fitting uniform this morning that happens to be dripping wet and rather muddy around the ankles and knees. Her cheeks are rosy, her hair is dripping, and her mascara is running. She says nothing as she carries the cooler in one hand.

I jump to my feet, wanting to help her, but then stop when I see the haughty expression on her face. "Good morning, Ms. Banks."

"Good morning," she whispers. "Where would you like me to set this?"

"The dining table would be fine. Why are you whispering?"

"Because the other day you insisted on silence while being served," she whispers, her expression nothing if not facetious.

I wince at the memory, then say, "I was a little out of sorts when I arrived, I apologize."

"That's fine. No need to apologize to the help," she whispers, setting the cooler down on the table with a thump. She lifts the lid, taking out a carafe of coffee, a plate, a mug, a glass, cutlery, and napkins. I watch as she opens metal containers holding my breakfast and deftly arranges everything on the plate.

Scrambling to think of something intelligent to say, I come up blank and end up settling for something cliché. "I feel like we got off on the wrong foot."

"Not at all, sir," she says, her voice barely audible. "You were just making your expectations clear."

"There's really no need to whisper or call me sir. It's Pierce."

She finishes and turns to me, speaking in a normal voice. "Coffee, French toast, poached eggs, bacon, an array of locally grown organic fruit, and orange juice squeezed a few minutes ago. Not to worry, there are no onions, pecans, sun-dried tomato, goat cheese, anything caramelized or covered with gristle, and no gazpacho of any kind."

I wasn't expecting the side order of feisty with my meal, but I can't say I don't deserve it. "It looks delicious, thank you," I say, unable to pull my gaze from her mesmerizing hazel eyes. Realizing I'm likely starting to seem creepy with the intense eye contact, I glance down at her dripping clothes. "Are you all right? You look like you're having a rough morning."

For the briefest second, her face softens just the slightest, then, as quickly as it appeared, the stone wall returns. "Never better."

Pulling a towel out of the cooler, she drops it to the floor, steps on it with both feet, and uses it to wipe the floor of her tracks as she returns to the front door. "Enjoy your breakfast, sir."

With that, she's gone, leaving me alone again. I walk to the window and watch her slip and slide along the muddy path down the mountain, wondering why the hell she didn't drive up here in this storm.

NINE

Never Wear Mascara in a Storm

Emma

That's it. I'm done. I'm just going to pack up my things, get back on the speedboat, and tell Harrison I'm sorry but I can't do this. There is *no way* I am going to subject myself to another day and night from hell, complete with devious, evil houseboat neighbours. Okay, maybe they're not evil. It's not like they've tried to axe me in my sleep, but still. Trick knee, Alfred? Really? And I'd like to see those bunions, Phyllis.

On second thought, maybe not. I've never seen a bunion before.

I clomp through the rubber trees, the rain and my makeup stinging my eyes as I pass by the useless umbrella I tossed under a fern on my way up the mountain. The first gust of wind turned it inside-out and snapped one of those metal thingies that holds the fabric to the frame, which at the moment feels like some sort of metaphor for my life.

Gripping the nearest tree, I start down the steepest part of the path, my feet slipping out from under me. "Not again, muddy path. Not again," I say, trying to right myself.

Oops!

Shit. Again.

I fall, landing on my bum directly on a spot which I've certainly already bruised. The cooler slips out of my hands and slides down the rest of the way while I manage to dig my heels into the mud and stop myself. I struggle for a moment, trying to stand without putting my palms down in the thick mud, but it's no use.

Giving up, I let go and just allow myself to slide the rest of the way down to the beach, my pant legs filling with mud. By the time I reach the beach, I'm sobbing, which I haven't done since I was a small child.

I can't. I just can't stay here another minute. I sit, my shoulders shaking as I let it all go. After a few minutes, I feel like someone is watching me. I turn and look over my shoulder, seeing a large green iguana staring from inside a hollow log. He blinks slowly as though fascinated by the crazy, crying lady sitting near his house.

"Sorry," I say, feeling suddenly sheepish. "I'm not a crier normally. I'm actually very tough. It's just that I'm having a very bad week. I thought I was starting a glamourous new life as a head chef but really I've been sent out here to be a servant." I wipe the hair off my face, leaving a healthy dose of mud on my cheek. "I was going to invent Caribbean fusion food, write a cookbook, and possibly get my own show, but now I'm going to die alone on this stupid island, having never accomplished anything. Possibly sooner than later if my neighbours do turn out to be killers."

He stretches his head and sniffs the air, probably in search of food, then backs into the log a couple of steps. I don't blame him. I'd think I'm crazy, too.

Standing, I grab the cooler and start back for the houseboat from hell. I'm almost there when I'm struck by the greatest idea I've ever had: I'll offer to take over *two* of the restaurants and have two chefs work half-time out on Opposite of Eden Island.

That ought to work beautifully. Everyone will be happy. Me, because I won't have to deal with Mr. Snooty Pants or Mr. and Mrs. Lazy Jerks anymore, and the chefs that replace me because they'll only be working half-time. I can *easily* manage two restaurants at a time. As long as I don't have to sleep on a musty, cramped houseboat that sloshes and rocks all night, I can handle anything. Even if I worked sixteen hours a day back at the resort, I could still get a decent night's sleep in a proper cabin—somewhere with enough hot water to thoroughly wash *and* condition my hair like a civilized human being.

I pivot, and head directly to the speedboat, walking through the water instead of on the dock to clean my muddy pants a bit. I don't bother to pull the soft-top up to protect me from the rain. The boat is soaked and I'm soaked, so there really isn't any point. I forgo packing my things, telling myself I can always return later for them. I just have to get away from this godforsaken place before I completely lose it.

As I jam the key in the ignition, I glance at Phyllis and Alfred's houseboat and see them through the window. They're sitting at the table, looking completely cozy and dry. They're laughing at something, probably me.

Bunions, my arse!

Stellar hiring job there, Libby. You couldn't have maybe picked a couple of single hotties to be out here with me? Seriously?

The engine sputters just long enough for me to consider swimming home, then finally fires up. As I pull away from the dock, I hit full throttle, flipping the bird over my left shoulder.

Goodbye Mr. Snooty Pants. I hope your next book is a huge flop. See ya around, Mr. and Mrs. Downton Abbey Wannabes! I'll be sure to tell my replacements about your fake bunions and trick knees!

TEN

Canned Food and Spearguns

Emma

"**E**mma! What happened to you?" Rosy says, rushing from behind the reception desk in the lobby.

I blink back tears as she comes rushing toward me. "Oh Rosy, it's awful out there. Just awful."

She wraps me in a big warm hug in spite of the fact that I'm now soaking her bright orange blouse. Kissing me on the forehead, she says, "Did someone hurt you, Baby Bear? Because if so, somebody on that island is about to get an old lady ass-kicking. Is it that weird British couple? I *knew* there was something shifty about those two."

"No, it's nothing like that. They are a little creepy though." I nod my head, then sniff. "I just don't think this is going to work out."

"Come on with Rosy. I'll get you some dry clothes and a tea, then you tell me all about it."

"I'd like that," I say, nodding.

***

Ten minutes later, I'm sitting on the couch in the staff room, dressed in a clean, dry uniform of a white golf shirt and tan shorts with a towel wrapped around my shoulders.

Rosy places a hot mug of tea in my hands, then sits down on the armchair near me and pats my knee, reminding me of the many times we sat in this very spot when I was a child and needed some cheering up. I smile at her, feeling the full comfort of being around my resort mum once again. She'll understand me. She always does.

"Extra cream and sugar, just how you like it. Now, tell Rosy what happened."

I launch into the story about the axe murderers and the useless golf carts and rude, picky Pierce Davenport and trick knees and bunions, jumping from thing to thing so I won't accidentally leave something out. When I finish, I notice that Rosy's not sitting forward patting my knee anymore like she was when I started talking. Instead, she's sitting back staring at me with her eyes narrowed and her lips pursed. When I finish, she says, "So you had a bad week."

"Technically eight bad days with *horrible* nights in between," I mumble, holding the mug up to my lips.

"Seems to me you're overtired so you're panicking about all the responsibility that Harrison's given you."

"First of all, I'm not panicking," I say, scowling. "And second, *what responsibility?* I'm cooking for one guy." I hold up my index finger. "*One.* It's an insult that Harrison and Libby would stick me out there instead of trusting me *here* with a real kitchen and staff and a proper menu."

Rosy's head snaps back. "An insult? Have you lost your damn mind? That private island is the only thing that's going to keep the wolves from the door. If it's not occupied at least 80% of the year, this entire place is going to get handed over to the bank."

My stomach drops at the reminder of so much riding on my shoulders. "That may be, but even *Will* could handle this job and all he can do is open canned food. Seriously, my talents are being wasted out there."

"Oh, I get it. You're planning to run, aren't you?" Rosy shakes her head.

"Run? What is that supposed to mean?"

"You don't know you have a habit of running when the going gets tough?"

"I do not," I say, sitting up straight.

"Yes, Baby Bear, I'm afraid you do," Rosy answers, as she starts counting on her fingers and listing things I've quit. "Girl Scouts—"

"That scout leader had it in for me."

"—the soccer team—"

"The coach had a serious case of halitosis and all the other girls were so...girly."

"—culinary school..."

I gasp loudly. "I came home to help the family out when there was a crisis!"

Sighing, Rosy says, "You sure it wasn't because you were failing Sauces 201?"

Shit. "How did you know about that?"

"You left your email open when you borrowed my computer. I couldn't help but read it."

"There were special circumstances there... You know what? I don't have to explain myself. I've completed my training and now I want to make *proper* use of it. Running a *real* kitchen, not some tiny, duct-taped, three-burner, no broiler, laminate cupboards, dilapidated old houseboat." I set the tea down on the table and stand. "If you'll excuse me, I need to find my brother."

I start for the door but her voice stops me in my tracks. "Mmmhmm. You're running. I knew you would."

Spinning on my heel, I say, "I am *not* running. I'm just trying to make sure my talent and education are fully utilized for the benefit of *everyone* at Paradise Bay. It's called a win-win situation."

Rosy stands. "Call it what you want. You don't like the job so you're running, which means letting Harrison down."

Anger bubbles in my chest and I glare at Rosy. Damn her for being right. There is literally nothing I can say to defend myself, is there? "Thanks for the tea!" I bark as I swivel around again to leave.

"You won't find your brother. He's gone into San Filipe. To the *jewellery* store."

My shoulders drop and I turn back to her, the wind from my angry sails completely gone. "Is he proposing to Libby?"

Nodding, she says, "Tonight. He's got the entire thing planned. He's whisking her off to a beach house on the north side of the island for a few days. He wanted to do it the first chance he could and had planned to do it the day after Eden opened, but there was a crisis in housekeeping and he had to put it off," she says, taking a few steps toward me as she talks.

"Your brother and Libby have been working day and night to save this resort and they deserve to celebrate without any problems. But, if you want to ruin it because you're scared of the elderly couple living next door and you had to walk up a hill in the rain, he should be back in about an hour."

Narrowing my eyes at her, I say, "Have you always been this evil?"

"Yes."

"*Fine.* I'll go back." *But only until I find a way to get off that damn island.*

Rosy pats my cheek. "That's my girl. Be strong...and maybe bring a speargun to hide under your bed."

ELEVEN

Boat Show Models and Ill-Mannered Men

Pierce

I'm a one-hit-wonder. The guy whose moment of brilliance was fleeting and now...I'm a has-been at the tender age of thirty-one.

So, I might as well just lay here on the floor while the sun sets, tossing this stupid little ball in the air again as I listen to Bach's Orchestral Suite No. 2 in B Minor with the volume as close to maximum as possible without blowing the speakers, because let's face it, my life as I know it is over.

A face appears above me and I scream like a girl before I realize it's Ms. Banks with my dinner.

"I knocked but you didn't hear me over your music," she shouts.

Scrambling to my feet, I place the ball into the useless decorative plate that sits at the centre of the coffee table, then hit the pause button on my phone, silencing the Valcourt Symphony Orchestra.

"Hard at work, I see..." she says as she crosses the room.

That's it. I'm done feeling bad about being rude before. I don't need to be judged by some newbie cook who doesn't have the first clue how hard it is to write an entire epic novel. "Yes, actually, I was. If you knew anything about art, you'd know that it's imperative to let the mind flow in order to create."

Looking over her shoulder at me, she says, "Cooking is an art form. It's called the culinary arts for a reason."

"Yes, I know you chefs like to think that, but anyone can cook. You just have to be able to read and do basic maths, which most third-graders have mastered."

Narrowing her eyes, she says, "You know what else most third-graders have mastered? Manners."

"I don't think you've met many children." Ha! Score one for Pierce.

Silence falls as she turns her back on me and sets to work. I watch, our feisty exchange ringing in my brain. "Why isn't one of the other ones bringing me my food?"

"The other ones?" She asks, raising an eyebrow at me.

"Yes, I'd actually prefer to have one of them serve me." As soon as the words come out of my mouth, I regret them, feeling every bit the pompous arse. "I need to concentrate and I'm afraid you distract me."

Giving me a smug grin, she says, "Am I somehow *more* distracting than Phyllis or Alfred?"

Against my better judgement, I stare at her for a moment longer than I should, soaking in her beauty. "Yes, but not for the reason that your generous ego has concocted. It's because you're agitating." Liar.

"Well, until the path dries out, I'm afraid you'll have to be agitated. The golf cart won't make it up here and apparently, my coworkers are suffering from bunions and joint problems so they can't make the walk. So, for now, if you want to eat, you're stuck with a distraction," she says firmly. Her face lights up suddenly. "But if I'm too much of a problem, I could just leave the supplies here and you could cook for yourself in that amazing kitchen right there," she says, pointing in the general direction of the stove.

Something tells me she has an ulterior motive—probably so she can go back to the main island and shag the totally buff, adrenaline junkie boyfriend I imagine a girl like her would have. The thought of that is somehow more irritating to me than her presence. "I have neither the time nor the inclination to do that."

"Then, I'm afraid you're stuck with me." She sets to work arranging the food, her hands a blur of activity as she lights a candle to place under the food warmer on which she places a bowl of soup and a plate that is covered with a silver lid. A colourful salad is placed in front of my chair, which she has chosen for the view of the valley outside. A heavenly mixture of scents causes my stomach to make a most unrefined sound, and I find myself wishing I'd left the music on. Maybe she didn't hear it.

Oh, there it goes again. Shit.

And she definitely heard that one because she's very clearly trying not to smile, and has sucked both her lips in between her teeth, hiding them while she uncorks a bottle of white wine.

When she's finished pouring a glass, she turns to me, gesturing like a model at the boat show. "For your dinner this evening, I've prepared a feta-free Greek-style grilled asparagus salad with a homemade red wine vinaigrette, followed by Jerusalem artichoke and truffle soup. The main dish is handmade gnocchi with fresh pesto sauce and chicken sausage, and for dessert, a caramel mousse with a cashew cookie crumble. Bon appétit." She shuts the cooler and walks toward the door.

Somehow the thought of being here alone with this incredible view and what is certain to be a mouth-wateringly amazing meal makes me wish I was sharing it with someone. Not her, obviously, we hate each other. Some nice person, like Zach, maybe. She's a horrible distraction. A horrible, beautiful distraction.

"Good night, sir," she says opening the door.

"Wait!" I say, then go completely blank. I stare into her eyes while I try to think of a believable reason for stopping her. *Say something, you idiot!* "Please have my food left outside the door from now on."

She blinks, looking slightly hurt before answering. "I don't think that's a good—"

Holding up one hand, I say, "Please leave it outside. I can't afford to be interrupted again."

Glancing at the squash ball on the table, she smirks. "Fine. I'll let you get back to your masterpiece."

When the door shuts behind her, I let out a breath, somehow simultaneously relieved and disappointed that she's gone. Relieved because I won't risk making a fool of myself any longer, but disappointed...why? I have no idea.

TWELVE

Xena the Warrior Mermaid Chef

Pierce

When I started the series, I was certain that Lucaemor, the second son of King Draquen would emerge the victor, but as the story progressed, his younger brother, Matalyx, has outshone him in some ways that surprised even me. And in case you aren't familiar, both of them have done such heinous things in their quest for the crown that I'm honestly not sure I want *either* of them to end up wearing it.

But who does that leave? It must be someone strong not only in body and mind, but someone with all the integrity of the heavens and an ocean of courage. At least that's part of the prophecy as told by Mehesi, the immortal witch back in *The Blood Wars*. Why did I add that bit about the effing witch? I really screwed myself there...

Needing a break from staring at a flashing cursor on a blank screen, I walk out onto the veranda and stand, inhaling in the perfumed air. If I wasn't under the crushing weight of this deadline, I'd enjoy it here very much. It's stopped raining finally, and I squint while my eyes adjust to the sun.

The villa itself—and the jungle in which it is set—are idyllic. From up here on top of the small, lush mountain, I can see the wildest of spaces, leading down to the white sandy beaches and the turquoise sea beyond. If I can't find inspiration here, I'm certain I'll never find it again in my life. *Come on, Pierce. Everything is riding on this. Just decide who becomes king when the wars end and work your way back from there...*

A movement on the water catches my eye. Huh. A speedboat. And it looks like it's my chef driving it. What is she doing out there on her own?

I watch as she drives away from shore, then stops the boat and anchors it.

Going inside, I snag the binoculars off the console table and return to my previous position. Not because I'm some stalker or something, but we writers are a naturally curious bunch.

I adjust the lenses in time to see her strip down into her bikini—Holy Mother of God. Look at that body. She must be wanting to sunbathe. If she takes her top off, I'm definitely going to put down the binoculars and go inside, I promise. Otherwise, I'll keep an eye on her, you know, for her own safety. Honestly, I don't know what to hope for...

Instead of peeling off her top, she puts on a snorkelling mask, stands on the stern while she adjusts it, then executes a perfect dive into the water.

I stand, frozen in place, wondering if I should be trying to get to her somehow. Surely it's not safe to go off diving into the ocean alone.

Where is she? She still hasn't reappeared.

Shit. I should go. But, realistically, how would I get to her?

Just when I'm feeling fully panicked, she emerges, tossing something into the boat before diving back under again.

I adjust the binoculars to get a look at what she's thrown into the boat.

Dear God, is she...lobster fishing? In a bikini? Alone?

What kind of woman is this?

She's like Xena: Warrior Princess, the Little Mermaid, and Julia Child all rolled into one gorgeous package. I continue to watch until she pops back up again, this time with a lobster in each hand. She tosses them unceremoniously into the boat, pulls her mask off, then climbs the ladder.

Jesus, that was impressive. Too bad Mehesi didn't predict the throne would be taken by a ballsy gorgeous chef...

And just like that, everything suddenly makes sense. I *do* have the perfect hero to save Qadeathas. He's just not a he. The entire ending comes rushing to me in one giant Oprah Aha! moment. Rushing inside, I sit down and set to work.

THIRTEEN

Flowers Made of Fruit, Men Made of Steel, and Hallmark Cozy Mystery Murder Methods...

Emma

"Not an art form?" Priya says indignantly.

"I know, right? What an arse." I glance into my mobile screen which is propped up on the counter while I make hollandaise sauce. I'm making lobster benedict with my spoils from the ocean earlier this morning.

After years of cooking side-by-side with Priya, I've grown accustomed to talking to her while I work. I felt a nostalgic pang as soon as I started to prep breakfast and decided to call, knowing she'll be every bit as irritated by my first guest as I am.

Mimicking Pierce, I say, "Anyone can cook. You just have to be able to read and do basic maths, which most third-graders have mastered."

Priya shakes her head in disgust. "Unbelievable. What did you say?"

I wince into the camera. "More than I should have considering he's paying a disgusting amount of money to be here."

"Don't hold back on me, Banks."

"I may have said something about third-graders also managing to master the art of having manners."

Priya sucks some air in between her teeth. "Ouch. Say, when you get fired, I know a good chef who needs work."

"Still nothing?" I ask, feeling guilty for having ranted on and on for the past ten minutes without asking her how she's doing.

"Not a thing. Unless I want to flip patties at Mickey D's, which would definitely work against me as far as convincing my parents I have a viable future in the kitchen."

"I'm sorry, hon." Resting my hands on the counter, I look into the screen so I can give her my full attention. "Something's bound to come up though, right? You're a supremely talented chef. How can someone who was at the top of the class of the best culinary school in North America not find work?"

"If I didn't know any better, I'd say my parents are running around town after me trashing my reputation at every place I apply."

"They wouldn't do that, would they?"

"No." She shakes her head. "But only because they're too busy saving lives. Plus, they're completely confident that my 'little dream' is going to fall flat like that souffle you baked in first year."

I grin, thinking of how funny life can be—if it weren't for my sad little souffle, we never would have become friends. Priya stepped in to help me make a new one as soon as hers came out of the oven sitting a full three inches above the ramekin. "Have I thanked you for saving my butt that day?"

"Not lately," she answers with a wry grin.

"Thank you, Priya. Now, get your beautiful self down to the passport office because I'm sure something will open up here. I was serious about helping you get a job, you know."

"I know, and I appreciate it, but I'm honestly not meant to be in a tropical climate. I may be Indian, but us Bhatts are a sweaty bunch. My grandparents took the first chance to move to a temperate climate. Besides, even if we weren't sun-intolerant, the heat ruins your makeup, your hair, your clothes..."

"Your grandparents moved to the land of opportunity because of melting makeup?"

"Is there any other reason?" she asks. "Keep whisking that. You always stop whisking too soon."

I do as she says, reminding myself to slow down.

"Better," Priya says. "God, I miss cooking. I should get out of bed and make homemade noodles for supper."

"That sounds like a perfect idea. Maybe you can get your parents to come onside by appealing to their appetites."

"Not likely. They've already planned my day for me," she says, repositioning her phone to display a stack of papers that sits neatly on her night table. "These are applications to the top five med schools in the country. They mysteriously appeared here while I was sleeping."

"That's a little creepy."

"Right? I need to find a job so I can move out." She glances down at the glass bowl of sauce I'm whisking, then says, "Is that butter above 40°? It almost looks too hot to me."

I look at the sauce, realizing it isn't coming together properly. "I'll put it in the fridge for a minute."

Taking one step, I carefully place the bowl inside the tiny fridge, then pop back up into the view of the camera. "Would you like a tour of paradise while I wait?" I ask with a grin.

"Ooh, yes. I need to live vicariously through you right now until I can find a life worth getting out of bed for."

Picking up my mobile, I give her a quick tour, pointing out the duct tape, the 'ample' counter space, and the mysteriously missing burner before making my way to the bathroom to show her where I stand like a cowboy after thirty solid days on his horse to put on my makeup. The entire tour takes all of two minutes, and by the end we're both laughing at the ridiculousness of the situation.

"You should take the sauce out of the fridge now. I bet it's ready," Priya says.

"Good point. I should focus. I am, after all, trying to make the world's greatest hollandaise sauce and most beautifully arranged fruit plate to prove a certain snooty gentleman wrong."

"You sure you're not maybe just a teensy bit attracted to him?"

"No! Eww! Of course not. He's totally obnoxious."

"It's just that you talked about him non-stop for like ten minutes when you first called and usually that's a bit of a sign that you're into a guy."

"Can't I just bitch about some obnoxious jerk because he's an obnoxious jerk?"

"Hmmm...I'm not convinced that you can." Priya shakes her head and gives me a mock-serious look.

"Just help me think of the perfect fruit art display so I can prove him wrong."

"That's worth getting up for," she says, throwing off her covers and walking to her desk. After a moment, I can see her booting up her laptop.

"Mango rose flower?"

"I could," I say, tilting my head from side to side. "Or I could just poison his food and be done with it..."

Priya laughs for a minute and then her face suddenly grows serious when she realizes I'm not laughing with her. "You wouldn't really, would you?"

"No, of course not," I say. "Where would I even find some hemlock that can mimic a heart attack and leave no trace? It doesn't grow here."

"Did you look that up or something?" Priya asks, her eyes growing wide.

Shaking my head, I grin at her. "No, I saw it on a Hallmark cozy mystery."

We chat for another ten minutes while I carve a mango into what turns out to be a pretty impressive-looking rose. I slice a star fruit and carefully arrange it around the rose then add some fresh berries, positioning them just so. Covering the top with Saran to hold everything in place and keep it fresh, I place the fruit tray in the cooler, then get on with finishing preparations on the lobster Benedict.

"Here's a tutorial on how to make an avocado rose," Priya says, positioning her camera so I can see the picture of a swirl of avocado.

"Kind of looks like baby poop."

"Yeah, you're right," Priya says. "Hey, does he write sci-fi? Because if so, you should totally make these Darth Vader pancakes,"

"I doubt he writes sci-fi. He probably writes some supremely dull, highbrow fiction that nobody reads," I say, carefully positioning the lobster meat on the toasted English muffin.

"I'm looking him up. What's his name?"

"Pierce Davenport."

"What?!" she shrieks. "As in *People* magazine's hottest writer of all time, Pierce Davenport?"

Shrugging, I say, "Maybe. I haven't Googled him or anything."

She turns her laptop screen to face the camera. "Is *this* him?"

Squinting for a second, I nod. "Yeah, that's him."

"Oh my GOD!!! You're cooking for Pierce Freaking Davenport! He's a total genius! You've never heard of *Clash of Crowns*?"

"Wait. *He's* the *Clash of Crowns* guy? He is *not* what I was expecting," I answer, totally shocked.

"What did you think he'd look like?"

"Oh, I don't know, like maybe...an eccentric seventy-year-old man who wears jaunty hats and has a big white beard."

"You just described Santa Claus." After a second, she shakes her head in disbelief. "I cannot *believe* you're cooking for Pierce Davenport. Do you know how big he is? *Millions* of people per year are now travelling to the places where the show is filmed for vacations just so they can say they've been on the sets. It's gotten so bad that an entire village in Slovenia has had to set up gates into town and they can only let in five thousand people a day."

"Really? I knew it was popular but—"

"There is seriously no justice in this world. I'm a *total* Crownie—I've read all the books more than once and I haven't missed one second of the show, and there you are cooking for him and you don't even know who he is."

"Have you not heard a word I said? He's a total jerk! Cooking not an art form?! Hello?"

Priya sighs dreamily, completely ignoring me in favour of staring into her laptop screen. "He's got that Benedict Cumberbatch sophistication going on. And...oh my God, there's a shot of him at a beach without his shirt on. Looks like the paparazzi took it because he's not posing. Yum."

I stop working, my curiosity piqued. "Really? Show me."

"I knew it. You're into him."

"I am *not*. I just find it hard to believe that he could possibly have a good body under those rich guy clothes—oh snap! Is that really him?" I ask, staring at the screen.

Priya bursts out laughing, then says, "You totally want to do him. It's so obvious! There's no way you'd go to all this trouble for some snooty old dude."

"This is not about sex. It's about art, thank you very much. I'm trying to prove that what *we* do is every bit as artistic as what he does. I want to make him eat his words—literally."

"Lie all you want, but I know the truth," Priya says with a grin. "You're going to *way too much* trouble just to prove a point."

"That's just because I grew up with two highly competitive brothers so I have an unrelenting need to prove I'm right in every situation. I should probably go see a therapist."

"Or just sleep with Pierce Freaking Davenport, the god of all writers."

Rolling my eyes, I say, "I gotta go. I need to get this up the hill and slink away silently into the woods before he has the misfortune of having to see a mere mortal."

"Uh-huh. You better call me back after you bang him, Emma, because I bet it will be incredible and hearing about it from you is likely as close as I'll ever get to doing him myself."

"There will be no banging."

"Oh, there will be banging. And when it's over, there will be telling Priya everything."

***

Five minutes later, as I pull on my rubber boots, I smile to myself, satisfied to have created what really is a picture-worthy breakfast—even if it will be eaten by a total tea bagger.

Okay, I'd be lying if I said I'm not a little bit impressed now that I know *he's* the *Clash of Crowns* guy, but can you blame me? Very few people achieve what he has. And even fewer at a young age. And even less who also stride around with a super hot body. If he weren't such an arse, he'd be the whole package. But he is MOST DEFINITELY a total jerk which completely negates the body, the dreamy eyes, the money, *and* the fame.

Incredible sex. Pfft! I doubt that very much. He'd be adequate at best. If the way he acts is any indication, he's probably very selfish in the sack. No matter how hard his body is...

FOURTEEN

Sometimes a Man's Gotta Fight for His Fancy Breakfast

Pierce

Have you ever had one of those days where you could do no wrong? Where everything comes up your way and you want to stand on a stage in front of thousands of people shouting that you're king of the world *a la* James Cameron at the Oscars?

That's me today. Over the past four wonderful hours, I have written more words than I have in almost two years put together. But that's not all; they're *high-quality* words—the kind that sold this series to Sullivan and Stone in the first place. I finally found a way out of the corner in which I've been trapped, and not only that, it's brilliant.

No one is going to see it coming. Not even the biggest of the Crownies who spend more time spouting theories of how the series is going to end than I've spent writing the damn books.

Now that I think about it, I haven't had a writing session this good since I was twenty-four and I started the series.

And if I'm going to be completely honest, I've been just the tiniest bit worried that I really might be the lazy, no-talent hack that a certain former *Clash of Crowns* executive-producer called me in his interview in *Variety* last October. Not that I care about nasty criticisms, mind you. I just have an excellent memory for them.

My stomach growls, and suddenly I'm aware of the fact that I've neither eaten, nor had anything to drink, in quite some time.

It must be well past breakfast time. Now that I think about it, I'm pretty sure I heard a noise about ten pages ago, so perhaps that means there's a meal waiting for me. I stand and stretch, then stroll to the front door, grinning like a fool over having written so much after such a long drought.

Ha! I knew I was right to ask that my food be left outside. Without the burden of knowing I would be interrupted thrice daily, it's like the floodgates of creativity have been opened and one of the greatest works of my generation has begun flowing again. Yes, for once I'm making all the right moves.

Well done, Pierce, you beautiful genius.

Yanking open the door, I look down to see that my breakfast has indeed been delivered, but is now being enjoyed by a rather large bright green iguana. Damn. It looks good too, and a little bit fancy, even. He's chomping away on what looks to be a mango cut in the shape of a flower. My mouth waters at the thought of some fresh fruit while the iguana stares at me and stops chewing.

"Shoo!" I say, waving my hands at him. "Go on. Go find your own breakfast."

Instead of turning and fleeing like I expect him to, he maintains eye contact while bobbing his head up and down.

"What are you doing that for? Don't nod at me. I said shoo. Fuck off. That's *my* breakfast."

The scent of something amazing wafts its way to my nostrils. Even though it's still protected by the silver cover, the thought of eating it kind of gives me the heebie-jeebies in case it's somehow been infested by whatever disease disgusting lizards carry. But truth be told, I'm so hungry and it smells so incredible, I'm willing to risk it.

Why is he not yielding? I must be a threat to him, no? "Listen, you, I'm a *man*, and a hungry one at that. I would never normally hurt an animal, but in this case, I'm afraid I must insist that you leave."

The iguana continues bobbing his head and pops up that big thingy underneath his mouth at me, taking a step forward so he has now positioned himself over my fruit plate.

Okay, you can do this, Pierce. You can get rid of this iguana. He weighs, what? Twenty pounds? Maybe thirty?

I clap my hands loudly, then take a couple of steps forward to intimidate him.

Huh. That didn't work at all.

Leaning back slightly, I stick my flip-flop-clad foot out towards him, trying to nudge him away from the food. And that's when he makes his move, launching himself onto my ankle and clamping down with his sharp teeth while he scratches the living shit out of my leg.

"Ouch! Shit! Motherfucker!" I scream, swatting at him with my right hand which turns out to be the worst move ever because he has much faster reflexes than I thought.

I holler as pain sears through the hand that he is now attached to by his giant venomous teeth. I try to shake him off but he only grips harder, tearing the flesh on the back of my hand and my palm as he hangs from my appendage.

"Fucking hell!" I shout, aiming for the side of his face with my left hand so I can punch him with everything I've got.

He wriggles suddenly and I end up punching my own thumb which cracks loudly.

"Shithouse mouse!" I yell, for some unknown reason.

It worked! Thank the lord!

As soon as he drops to the ground, I use the opportunity to retreat into the villa. Slamming the door behind me, I lean on it, my heart pounding and my breath jagged as I hold it closed in case he tries to get in. When I finally process what I'm doing, I shake my head at myself. Lizards can't open doors. They don't have opposable thumbs.

The crisis now averted, my brain begins to process the pain that pulses through my right hand and my leg. "Shit, that hurts." I gingerly lift my shredded Theory chinos to examine my ankle, feeling slightly lightheaded as blood seeps from my wounds. "That's bad. That really hurts so much more than I thought it would."

My 'king of the world' moment was incredibly short-lived, wasn't it? I've been ousted from the throne by a fucking lizard.

Limping to the bathroom, I leave a trail of blood through the villa as I go in search of a towel. Suddenly, Emma and her attempt to dissuade me from having the food left outside pop into mind, and it becomes clear what she was going to say. She was likely about to explain that there are wild animals out here who will happily attack me for their share of my breakfast, but I was too pig-headed to listen. Instead, I shut her down as though she would know nothing of the subject.

Shit, I really am losing a considerable amount of blood. And thumbs are definitely not meant to hang limply from your hand. I need help. I start for the radio when I remember the damn golf carts can't make it until the path dries out. Shit. And it's not like any of the staff will be able to carry me down the mountain (not that I'd allow myself to be carried, no matter how badly I'm injured. I am a man, after all). I have to walk down myself.

Wrapping my hand in a towel, I limp to the front window to see if my scaly nemesis has left yet. Nope, he's still scarfing down my meal. "Bastard."

I'll go out the other way. Not that I'm scared of a lizard, mind you, but I'd likely kill him if he attacked me again, and I'd feel just awful about it.

I exit the villa through the patio doors that lead from the bedroom to the deck overlooking the jungle. Sneaking my way around the opposite side of the building, I keep a lookout for my opponent. When I'm safely several feet away from the house, I tiptoe through the grass to the path like Barney Rubble bowling. My ankle throbs with every step, and I suddenly realize I'm not entirely sure when I've had my last tetanus shot.

It's up to date, isn't it? Mrs. Bailey takes care of booking all my medical appointments. I'm sure she wouldn't have let it lapse. I should call her just in case, though.

I limp down the path that I've seen the staff use, hoping it's a short walk to wherever it is that the kitchen resides.

Oh, the irony of dying now, just as I've finally cracked the ending. After years of writer's block, I break free only hours before being savagely attacked and murdered by a rabid lizard, leaving millions of fans to wonder how it all ends...

Are iguanas lizards? Maybe they're reptiles. I really should have paid more attention in science class. Whatever they are, I know they carry some disease. I distinctly remember hearing that. Is it rabies or tetanus?

That would be an awful way to go—tetanus. The old lockjaw. I can just picture it—they'd find me at my computer several days from now, my entire body stiff, my shirt covered in foam from my mouth. Maybe I'm getting my illnesses mixed up. Is it hot out here? I feel terrible.

I can just picture the staff being interviewed on the six o'clock news, saying, "He said he wanted to be left alone, so we gave him his wish, only to have it be his doom."

People at home eating dinner in front of their tellies will say, "Why couldn't he have been nicer? It's really his own doing, even though it's sad since he was young and all. At least we'll find out how *Clash of Crowns* ends because the studio is going to finish the series for him."

A fluttering in the brush beside me has me jumping, then crouching into a ball in the middle of the path. "Fuck off. I will kill you if I have to."

I freeze in place, preparing for the attack. A pair of tiny yellow birds fly out from under the shrub, revealing the source of the sound. Straightening up, I chuckle at myself as I continue on.

Ten minutes later, I'm still in search of help, but am now feverishly hot, slightly delirious, and pathetically weak. I try to distract myself from the pain and dizziness by working out what I'll say to Ms. Banks. I clearly owe her an apology and a 'you were right.' Yuck. I'd rather eat iguana poop than admit I was wrong. Well, not really, because ewww, but still. Does everyone hate admitting they should have yielded to someone else's expertise? I'm sure I'm not alone in this.

Christ, I'm really sweating now. I *must* have been poisoned.

Okay, focus, Pierce. Better to apologize than die. Sort of. "Ms Banks, I have come to seek your forgiveness. I behaved rashly last night and should have listened to you..."

Or I could avoid her altogether and go straight to Mrs. Bailey's sister and her husband. Surely, they'll know what to do and there's no apology required. Phyllis could call Mrs. Bailey for me to find out about the tetanus shot.

By the time I reach the beach, beads of sweat are rolling down my forehead. My linen shirt is now sticking to the skin on my back. *Very posh, Pierce. Very posh indeed.* I unbutton it to let in a bit of the breeze, only to discover the air is as hot and sticky on my chest as it is on my face.

Is it really this hot, or have I developed a rabies-induced fever?

I stumble a bit over a stick, then trudge on in the direction of help. The blood from my hand has now soaked through the towel. Oh, that is not good at all. I'm going to die, aren't I?

Realizing my flip-flops are slowing me down, I kick them off, leaving them in the hot sand as I limp gingerly (and yet, in a very manly way) in what I hope is the direction of the staff quarters. When I come around the bend, I see two houseboats side-by-side. *Thank Christ.*

Which boat do I choose? Old, sickly couple? Or beautiful young woman I've horribly insulted? And how do I know which boat belongs to whom?

Oh, the heavens have answered my question in the form of the most magnificent, bikini-clad creature...

"Fuck me," I mutter. The vision of Ms. Banks sunning herself can't be real. That must be a mirage brought on by the poison. No one looks that good if they aren't on the page of a magazine.

My feet make my decision for me, heading directly toward the mirage. My breathing is laboured as I reach the boat, unsure of the etiquette required in this type of situation. I need her help, but clearly, I'm interrupting her coffee break. Although surely, because I'm dying, she won't mind being interrupted.

Hmm...How does one knock on a boat?

I stand for a moment, realizing she's on a phone call.

"Seriously?" Pause. "Oh fine, if it means that much to you, I can try to ask him, but honestly, I may not even see him again. He's demanded his meals be left outside." Pause. "He probably refuses to sign autographs for his fans. He's a total wanker."

Total wanker? That's rather crass, don't you think?

Feeling torn between guilt for eavesdropping and being highly insulted, I make a light coughing sound, deciding that it is the most appropriate way to address the situation.

She sits up suddenly, displaying the ample assets that are spilling out of her rather small, bright pink bikini in a way that would please any man.

Am I drooling?

Good God, I think I'm drooling. But I really can't blame myself—that's some serious *Sports Illustrated* Swimsuit Edition shit right there. Plus, I have rabies, so...

She ends the call quickly, then drops her phone on the deck before standing and wrapping a towel around herself. "What happened?"

"I've been attacked by a wild animal," I say, lifting up my pant leg to display my considerable wounds.

Her mouth drops and her eyes widen for a moment. "A wild...what?"

"Very large reptile with huge claws, enormous teeth, and sharp points on top of his head. He fought me for my breakfast."

"Do you mean an iguana?" she asks as she slides her flip-flops on and hurries to the ladder of the boat.

Nodding, I say, "A poisonous one. I'm certain of it based on his bright colouring. Quite possibly rabid based on his behaviour," I add, gravely.

Folding her lips between her teeth, she nods, obviously trying not to laugh. "In that case, I should take you to the hospital straight away."

"Thank you, yes. I'd say that's in order. I definitely need stitches and likely a large series of shots. Plus, my thumb might be broken." I hold my hand and show her my dangling thumb.

Emma gasps. "Yeah, pretty sure that's broken. Give me a second. I'll throw on some clothes and get the keys to the speedboat." I watch as she makes her way to the cabin door, her hips swaying under the towel in which they're wrapped. Lucky towel.

As I wait, I wipe the sweat off my forehead and try to pull myself together. I hear my father's voice in my mind: *Be a man, Pierce.*

I hobble over to the speedboat and get in, an immense sense of relief coming over me to get off my sore leg as I sit down. Emma reappears within seconds in a black t-shirt and some pink shorts that still offer a most lovely view in spite of her attempt at modesty. I *must* be delirious to be thinking about that right now.

"All right, let's get you to the hospital," she says, hopping down onto the dock and sprinting to the boat like one of those Ninja Warrior athlete people. She makes quick work of untying the boat and jumps in, firing up the ignition before she bothers to sit down. God, she's impressive. Every heroine in every fantasy should be exactly like Emma Banks.

"Thank you for this. I appreciate your haste." Closing my eyes, I sigh deeply, fear crawling through my veins as my hand and leg pulse. "I'm certain I've been poisoned. And if not, I may bleed out. The cuts on my hand are very deep. I may lose the use of it if we can't get to a surgeon straight away."

"I'll go as fast as I can. You just try to stay calm," she says, taking on the tone of a nursery school teacher, which I find oddly comforting. "You know, I doubt you've been poisoned actually. Salmonella, maybe, but that's about it."

"It's rabies, I know it. The sudden fever and the sweating. It's the only explanation," I say, shaking my head solemnly.

"Well," she says, tilting her head to the side thoughtfully. "Is it possible that it's because we're in the tropics, it's 40°C outside, and you've just been on a long walk?" There's just a hint of a smirk fighting to get out, but she holds it in.

I stare at her for a second, a sense of indignance brushing aside my pain. "Oh, I see. You're making fun of me."

"No, no. Not at all. Just trying to help you calm down a bit, and perhaps present a more logical solution to your symptoms. Although I am just a chef, not a doctor, so the fact that I grew up out here probably doesn't mean as much as it would if I had gone to medical school."

She's making fun of me. "How far is the hospital?"

"Another fifteen minutes."

"Please hurry."

"I'll have you there as fast as humanly possible," she says, pushing the throttle to full.

My head jerks back with the force of it and I close my eyes, praying this is not the end.

***

Thirty minutes later, we're sitting in the ER waiting room at San Filipe Hospital. Emma called ahead for a car to pick us up for the short drive here from the public dock.

I'm now drenched in sweat, nauseous, and terrified as I sit next to her in the brightly-lit room among the other patients. "I can't believe they're making me wait," I mutter. "I'm going to die waiting for help."

"You're not going to die. I promise," she says, patting me on the shoulder.

"Hey, aren't you Pierce Davenport?" a woman asks, pointing at me from across the room.

I nod slightly and attempt a smile.

"Oh my God! I'm like the world's biggest Crownie! Can I get a picture with you?" she asks, rushing over. *Seriously? Now?* I give her a pained look as I try to think of a graceful way to get out of this.

"Sorry, no photos. Hospital policy," Emma says, authoritatively. "He'd normally love to, though."

The woman's shoulders drop and she pouts a little. "My husband and I have watched every episode of *Clash of Crowns*. He won't believe I've met you."

"Thank you. I appreciate your support," I say.

"You're welcome. It's just such an amazing story," she says, her eyes lighting up. I know what's coming next. She's going to ask how it ends. "You can't give me a hint about how it all turns out, can you?"

"No, I'm afraid not. I'm under a strict NDA." I nod gravely as if to say it's such a shame because I'd love nothing more than to have a long chat while I bleed out.

Her face falls for a second, then she says, "My husband thinks Vilarr is going to come back from the grave and vanquish Zhordal."

Her husband is clearly an idiot. "He's not the first person to suggest that." I shift in my chair, trying in vain to move away from the pain in my leg.

The woman leans in closer and lowers her voice. "Can you at least tell me if he's wrong? He's wrong, isn't he?"

"I can't really tell you anything, except to say you are a very astute woman."

"I knew it!" She beams.

"I'm sorry, but Mr. Davenport really should rest," Emma says apologetically.

"Oh, right. Sorry," the woman answers, her shoulders dropping. She looks back at me and shakes her head. "Jeff will never believe I met you. Is there any way you could give me an autograph?"

"Sure," I say weakly. "Why not?"

She digs around in her purse for a second, then produces a pen and a crumpled-up napkin that I hope hasn't been used for nose-wiping (or any other type of wiping, for that matter). She holds them out to me, beaming as I lift my right hand to take it, only to realize I'm totally fucked. I can't sign my name. My hand is going to be useless for a very long time.

How the hell am I going to finish writing the series with one hand?

FIFTEEN

Confessions of Painkiller Pierce

Emma

Well, this is weird. Mr. Snooty Pants has asked me to come in with him while he gets stitches. At the moment, he's sitting on the exam bed while a nurse cleans his cuts. And even weirder, he seems...almost pleasant. He's actually smiling at me while she works on his leg—sort of an adorably sweet smile that makes his very kissable dimples pop.

He's also thanked me four times already for saving his life and for my quick thinking in the waiting area when that ridiculous woman was trying to get a photo with him. I mean, honestly? Who asks someone that when they're clearly very injured?

There's something so sincere about him right now. He's not the rich, well-put-together, cold man that I met a few days ago. This one is bleary-eyed and a bit vulnerable. From the looks of him, he hasn't slept in a long while, which I suppose makes sense since he's on some serious deadline.

His pants are rolled up, he's got bare feet, and he's left his shirt open, but likely because he's just too worn out to realize it and not because he's trying to show off his hard-earned abs. He reminds me of a castaway on a deserted island. A hot, highly intelligent castaway with a rock-hard body.

Okay, Emma, stop that or you'll forget he's a total jerk...

He winces just the slightest and I find myself feeling sorry for him. "You okay?"

"Never better," he says, even though that is clearly not true.

"I'll be back in a few minutes with the doctor to get you stitched up," the nurse says. "You're going to need an x-ray for that hand as well. I'm pretty sure your thumb is broken, although I can't imagine how an iguana would have managed that."

Pierce turns a bit red, then clears his throat. "He was unusually strong, I think. More like the size of a croc than an iguana."

She stares at him for a moment, opens her mouth, then closes it and leaves.

When we're alone, he gives me a guilty look that says there's more to the story than he's willing to tell. I narrow my eyes, then gesture to his hand. "So, the iguana did that? Really?"

"Umm hmm," he answers, avoiding eye contact.

"That just seems so hard for me to believe. I've lived here most of my life and I've never heard of such a thing. You weren't perhaps trying to challenge it for your breakfast?" I ask.

He lowers his voice until it's almost inaudible and says, "I may have done, yes."

"It would probably be better if we start bringing—"

"Yes, we should definitely have the food brought directly into the villa from now on, thank you. And my apologies for not allowing you to make that suggestion last night."

"Or just now," I say, raising one eyebrow.

A sheepish look crosses his face. "Right. I did it again, didn't I? Interrupted you. I apologize, Ms Banks. I'm afraid you've met me at what is one of the worst times in my adult life, which is no excuse, I know. Just...an explanation in hopes that you'll see it in your heart to forgive me. Is there any way we can start over under the provision that I attempt to let you see the non-wanker side of my personality?"

Oh crap. He heard me call him a wanker, didn't he? Even if it is true, that must not have felt very nice to hear. My face heats up with guilt. "I'd like that. I don't think I've exactly been at my best since we met either."

"No?" he asks, looking surprised.

"No. I'm normally not so..."

"Feisty?"

I chuckle a little at the description. "That's a kind way of putting it."

"It may come as a surprise—understandably so—but I am capable of kindness." He stares at me, his expression filled with regret and hope.

I'm about to make a very big mistake, aren't I? Yes, yes, I am. "In that case, I say we wipe the slate clean and start over."

"Good. Thank you, Ms. Banks."

We sit and smile at each other for a few seconds, and I find myself feeling a little awkward about having reached a truce with this man—this whip-smart, impossibly handsome man. I look down, needing to avoid the intense sincerity in his gaze, and focus on his hand, which incidentally, is positioned in front of his ripped torso. My cheeks warm even more and I scramble to think of a reason I'm staring in the general direction of his half-naked body. His thumb! I should say something about his thumb. "I just can't figure out how an iguana did *that*."

Pursing his lips together, he says, "All right, fine. I broke my own thumb."

"You...?" I start, then clamp my mouth shut before I start laughing.

"Yes. I was aiming for his head but I may have missed."

"With what?"

"My fist."

"So you...punched yourself?" I ask, holding my hand over my mouth to hide an involuntary grin.

He narrows his eyes but at the same time looks slightly amused. "I knew I should have kept that to myself."

I tuck my lips in between my teeth and clamp down hard to force myself not to burst out laughing. After a moment of making muffled squeaking sounds, I manage to gain my composure. "Sorry. Sorry. It's not funny. Not at all really. It's actually quite serious." I snicker again, then clear my throat. "I promise I won't tell anyone else how it happened."

Tilting his head, he gives me a dirty look which, for some reason, causes me to collapse into a fit of laughter, folding myself in half on the plastic chair.

"It pleases me to no end knowing I can amuse you."

Straightening up, I wipe the tears from my cheeks and shake my head. "Sorry. Last time, I swear."

"This may be funny to you but I'm in real trouble here. I don't know how I'm going to finish my book with one hand," he says, sighing. "I was on such a roll, too. After over two years of nothing, I was finally able to sort out how to end the saga. I had an epiphany this morning when..." He stops mid-sentence, his face turning slightly red, then says, "...I woke up. And if this hadn't happened, I'd still be typing away on my laptop."

There is very clearly something he's not telling me about how he managed to find his inspiration, but no matter how curious I am, I can't ask. It's absolutely none of my business. "I'm sorry this happened to you," I say. "Awful timing, really."

"Yes, it is rather unfortunate because now that inspiration has struck, I feel the need to get it all down at once before I forget any of it." He swallows hard, then says, "That probably sounds mad to you."

"Not at all. I've been working on this concept for a new sort of fusion menu and it's become a bit of an obsession. When I'm working on it, it's like this energy is flowing through me and the ideas are coming so fast, I can hardly keep track of them." I blush a little, expecting him to scoff at the comparison. "It's probably not the same thing, though. To you, thinking up a new type of cuisine probably seems trivial. Not like writing a wildly popular series."

His face becomes serious. "I deeply regret implying that you wouldn't understand what it's like to be an artist. I'm afraid I'm much better on paper than I am in person, especially when it comes to..." His voice trails off and he gives his head a tiny shake and scrunches his face, looking embarrassed.

Grinning, I ask, "Especially when it comes to what?"

"If you don't mind, I'd rather not finish that thought."

And before I can nudge him for a hint as to what he meant, the door swings open. The doctor and nurse come in, and the moment is lost, but I can't help but wonder if it's somehow related to what a 'distraction' I am to him...

***

Text from me to Priya: *You'll never guess who's sitting across from me. I'll give you a hint. He's famous and at this moment he has his very expensive shirt unbuttoned...*

Priya: *OMG! Tell me everything. How did this happen? Who opened his shirt? Why the hell are you texting me right now if you have a partially undressed hot man with you? And most importantly, can you get me a photo?*

Me: *An iguana ate his breakfast then attacked him, so he's currently being stitched up by a doctor (I took him to the hospital).*

Priya: *Nooo! Not the mango rose and the lobster Benedict?*

Me: *Unfortunately.*

Priya: *Seriously? Is he okay?*

Me: *Yes, he'll be okay, but it all looks rather painful. The doctor and nurse are betting on the number of stitches. She says fifty and he's guessing thirty-two.*

Priya: So NOT okay, then.

Me: Not so much. Here's the really weird part—he actually seems sort of sweet and he even asked me to come into the exam room with him.

Priya: *Because he's totally into you, you lucky bitch! You're going to end up marrying the freaking Clash of Crowns creator and live a gorgeous, incredibly rich life while I'll still be here with my damn parents.*

Me: *You can have him. A guy like that is way too much trouble.*

Priya: *Gotta go! Heading to the passport office now.*

Smiling to myself, I slide my phone back into my bag and glance at Pierce again. He's got his face scrunched up and his eyes closed and I can't help but feel really bad. I should have tried harder to convince him the food shouldn't be left outside. Although, he was being quite a wanker, so...

After a few minutes, he's taken to the x-ray department while I wait in the exam room for his return. For some stupid reason, I can't stop smiling. Okay, I know exactly what the reason is—my mind keeps wandering to his surprisingly muscular body. Even though I've only seen the chest and the lower half of one leg, I find myself wondering what the rest of him looks like under those clothes. In my imagination, he looks really freaking amazing...

Letting my curiosity get the better of me, I Google Pierce Davenport and spend the next twenty minutes reading all about him, starting with his Wikipedia page which gives a brief overview of his family's history as well as his writing career. He has two brothers. The eldest is Greyson, who is also insanely good-looking. Greyson is being groomed to take over the family business and is engaged to some beautiful socialite who rides for the Avonian Equestrian Team. Their younger brother, Leo—also on the ridiculously handsome side of the spectrum—seems like Pierce's polar opposite, a total playboy who hops from scandal to scandal. The latest rumour is that he's the reason Minka Kelly and Jesse Williams broke up.

Feeling strangely guilty at reading the gossip about his family, I search for images of him instead, finding dozens taken at various events over the years—some of them featuring a gorgeous woman who I'm pretty sure is a Victoria's Secret model. How cliché, Pierce.

His *Clash of Crowns* book covers are among the images, and before I know it, I'm one-clicking the first book in the series and settling in to see just what all the fuss is about...

***

I'm all the way to chapter ten when Pierce walks back into the room with his hand in a cast. Somehow, I've managed to get so lost in his words that I have no concept of how much time has passed. Feeling slightly disoriented to be back in the real world, I blink a couple of times, reminding myself of who and where I am.

"Well, it's official: it's broken," he says, raising his cast. "Six weeks minimum in this thing which means I'll have to have it removed when I get home."

"I'm sorry," I say, this time not finding it funny at all. "Should we get out of here?"

"Please."

I find myself wanting to hug him. Maybe it's that I was just reading a supremely tender scene he wrote where King Draqen was telling his son, Luc, how proud he was of him, but I suddenly have a feeling that there's a lot more to Pierce Davenport than the snooty rich guy he pretends to be.

***

Okay, so apparently Painkiller Pierce is funny as hell. I don't know what that doctor gave him, but I wouldn't mind some myself because he is very clearly feeling no pain. It kicked in about five minutes after we got on the speedboat and he's been hilariously and horribly honest since. Right now, he's sitting sideways in the passenger seat, facing me, while he talks about his family and I try not to listen because I'm sure Sober Pierce would be horrified at the secrets he's spilling.

"And another thing...I don't think they ever loved each other. Not even on their wedding day. It was an *arranged* marriage," he says, drawing out the word 'arranged' to make it last about ten seconds. "Yup. I bet you thought that only happened in places like India or in rural China, but it happens among the elite in the UK, too. It's a way to keep the wealth where it belongs—with the people who've always had it." Pointing his bad hand in the air, he says, "I'm being fastidious of course. I don't really agree with arranged marriages. Or any other type of marriage for that matter."

"I think you mean facetious."

"Oh yes, they are facetious. Both my parents. Sarcastic, too. And really rather neglectful. I don't think my mother has ever regarded her children outside the context of what we could do for her image. We were like little accessories, like Paris Hilton and her tiny Chihuahuas. That's a funny word, isn't it?" he asks, leaning so close to me, he tips over and has to right himself. "Chiiiiihuuuuaaaahhhhuuuuaaaa."

He then starts snickering to himself, repeating 'Chihuahua' a few more times before he closes his eyes and leans his head on the white leather seatback. "My brother is marrying someone he doesn't love, too. Does Whatever He's Told Greyson, that's my secret nickname for him. Sad really. She's got a face like the horses she rides. Oh, that was offside. Sorry, Porsche, I didn't mean to say that out loud. I only meant to think it."

I take a gentle right turn and soon the island comes into view, looking rather idyllic in the soft glow of the setting sun.

His eyes pop open again and Pierce says, "Just so you know, you don't have a face like a horse. You're lovely. I could stare at your beautiful face all day. Those eyes you've got are mesmmesing. Memorizing. Wait? What word am I trying to say?"

"Mesmerizing?"

"That's the one, love. Smart, too." He leans his chin on his hand and sighs deeply. "So smart. You're the kind of woman who could keep a fellow on his toes. Keep it interesting. I don't think I'd ever get bored of you, my sweet Emma. Have you got a fella? I bet you do."

"Uh, no, I'm not seeing anyone, Mr. Davenport," I say, trying to remind him this isn't an episode of *Blind Date.*

"Call me Pierce," he says, giving me an intense gaze. Closing his eyes, he starts singing at the top of his lungs, "Swwweeetttt Emmmmmmmaaa. Bah, bah, bah! Good times never seemed so good! I've been inclined. Bah, bah, bah! To believe they never would, would, would..."

Oh dear. Now he's gone full Neil Diamond on me. I hope he doesn't vomit in the boat. Although it is rather flattering that he's serenading me, isn't it? A rich, famous, hot guy serenading me. I'm going to let myself enjoy this moment because this is not something that happens to a girl every day. (Let's just ignore the fact that he's whacked out on codeine, mmkay?)

"...Hands! TOUCHING HANDS!!! REACHING OUT!!! Come on, Emma, sing with me!"

Oh, what the hell?

"Touching me! Touching youuuuuu!" we both sing, tilting our heads toward each other. I have to say, I haven't had this much fun since my last night in New York, which I really don't remember, but I'm pretty sure was a great time. We stare at each other while we sing and when I forget the words here and there, I laugh at both of us. Who knew snooty rich guys could be such a hoot? Not this lady...

By the time we reach the dock, the song is over and Pierce is out cold. I cut the engine, dock the boat, then stare at him for a minute. "Now what? I can't exactly carry you up to the villa."

His eyes pop open suddenly and he shouts, "I'm up! Is the elephant starting?"

"Umm...in a minute. We have to get you out of the boat first. We can take the golf cart, I think."

"Just exactly what is going on here?" Alfred's sharp voice cuts through the air.

I look up to see him standing on the dock with a very stern look on his face. "Mr. Davenport was attacked by an iguana earlier today and has been fixed up and given some excellent pain meds."

Alfred narrows his eyes at me. "Attacked?! You should have let us know."

Pierce sways a little and points his cast at Alfred. "Don't talk to my Sweet Emma that way or I'll be forced to thrash you."

Thrash him? Oh dear, he's definitely going to vomit, isn't he? I give Alfred (who looks scandalized) a satisfied grin. "I was in too much of a hurry to get Mr. Davenport to the hospital to pop by and ask you and Phyllis to have his room made up," I say, feeling emboldened by the fact that *I'm* our VIP's Sweet Emma. "Now, if you could be so kind as to help me get him up to the villa, it would be greatly appreciated."

"Yes, of course," Alfred says, looking slightly taken aback.

Pierce stumbles toward the side of the boat, trips and falls, gets back up while giggling hysterically, then grips Alfred's extended hand. "Thank you, Alfred. You really should lighten up, old boy. Life's too short to be so serious all the time."

"Yes, thank you," Alfred says, helping him onto the dock. "I shall try to...lighten up."

"Good show," Pierce says with a firm nod. He grins at me, then back at Alfred, then belts out, "Sweeeetttt Alllllfred! Bah, bah, bah!"

Huh. Now he's serenading the butler. Maybe not so special after all.

Alfred and I each take a side of Pierce and walk him to the golf cart while he continues to sing. We deposit Pierce into the backseat, then I climb into the driver's seat with Alfred next to me.

He finishes the song when we're about halfway up the mountain, then says, "Alfred, are you and Phyllis happy?"

"Quite, sir. We very much enjoy working with you."

"Stop sucking up, you wanker. Are you glad you got married or not? Because I've never been interested in marrying anyone my entire life. Except, now that I've met Ms. Banks here, I'm suddenly not so sure..."

Alfred gives me an alarmed look and I shake my head as I round the curve. "He's high as Snoop Dogg."

"What?" Alfred asks, clearly not understanding the reference.

"Patrick Stewart, then. He's a pothead, isn't he?"

"Patrick Stewart!" Pierce yells in a Scottish accent. "He's the best part of those X-Men movies. Emma, you should be in those movies. You'd look unreal in one of those superhero costumes. Rrwaaor!" He makes a cat clawing motion at me, then swings his head to face Alfred. "She would, wouldn't she, Alfie, old boy?"

"I wouldn't know, sir."

"I would," Pierce says, waggling his eyebrows. "You should see her in her bikini diving for lobsters..."

My eyes fly open and I suck in a breath at the thought of him watching me that day.

When I glance back at him, Pierce's eyes are wide. "I wasn't stalking you. At first, I was just curious about what you were doing out thereonthewater," he slurs. "Then I was worried 'bout your safety. A girl all alone on the ocean in nothing but a tiny bikini..."

Alfred scoffs in a very clear indication of his disapproval.

A second later, Pierce says, "I think I'll retire now. Good night, Sweet Emma..." Then he slinks down in his seat, closes his eyes and immediately begins snoring, just as we pull up to the villa.

SIXTEEN

So This is What It's Like to Be Famous...

Emma

Alfred and I manage to drag a passed-out Pierce inside and get him onto the bed, which is no easy feat with a trick-kneed old guy as your only help. Alfred pours him a glass of water and leaves it by his bedside while I remove Pierce's shoes and tuck him in.

I'm all business on the outside, but on the inside, I'm sort of all warm and mushy. He's just so adorable that I have an inexplicable desire to take care of him. And, to be honest, I'm more than a little flattered. I know he's crazy high, but there was a painful amount of honesty that came pouring out of him about his life, his family, and, as it turns out, his attraction to little old me. There's nothing wrong with enjoying the moment, is there? One of the world's most successful, most highly regarded, hottest writers fancies me. That's the kind of thing that could give a girl a major ego boost, if she let it.

I'm not saying I'll let it, but my back *is* a little straighter as Alfred and I make our way back to the golf cart.

Smiling to myself, I decide to crack open a bottle of wine and spend the evening reading more *Clash of Crowns* so I can figure out what makes a man like Pierce Davenport tick—other than me, of course. Wink, wink.

Once we've set off, Alfred says, "Emma, I have to say I'm disturbed by your terrible judgement with regard to Mr. Davenport's safety."

Wait. What now? "Excuse me?" I ask, hitting the gas pedal harder than necessary, causing Alfred to jerk back in his seat. "I got Pierce to the hospital as quickly as humanly possible. There's really nothing more I could have done."

"A good servant knows the guest sometimes makes requests that are not in his or her own best interest and therefore should be ignored, such as in the case of Mr. Davenport requesting his food be left outside. Your duty was to find a way to meet his best interests, of which safety is paramount above all else."

"Yeah, well, he demanded the food be left outside. I tried to talk him out of it but he wouldn't listen. What was I supposed to do?"

"Guard it until he was ready to eat."

"Guard—? Are you serious? You expect me to, what? Hide in the bushes so he won't see me while I make sure nothing gets into his food?"

"Yes, that is precisely what a dutiful servant would do."

"Okay, let's get something straight. I am *nobody's* servant. I'm a *chef,* and as soon as I can find a replacement, *I'll* be the one giving the orders instead of taking them."

I take a sharp curve much quicker than I should, taking out a large branch that's sticking out of the bushes. It snaps and I cringe inwardly, my heart pounding, but on the outside, I'm cold as ice and speed up even more as we wind our way down the mountain.

"This whole private cook thing is just a temporary mistake that is going to be rectified shortly, so there's really no need for you to lecture me on servitude because I am not now, nor ever will be, a servant."

Alfred grips the dashboard with both hands. "Oh, I've met people like you before. You think to serve others is *beneath* you," he quips. "And what, exactly, have you done with your life to rise above the station you currently occupy? May I point out, you finished culinary school less than two *weeks* ago, not two years. You probably didn't even pay for your education yourself. If I had to guess, I'd say you've been living off Mr. Banks your entire life, and when you decided you wanted to be a chef, you came to him to help make that happen."

Wow. Just...wow. "You know what, *Alfred*? Not that this is *any* of your business, but I worked my arse off in school, and it's perfectly fine for me to choose not to devote my life to servitude," I say, making a hard left when I hit the beach. "If that's your thing and it makes you happy, good for you. But just because I have no interest in obeying orders for the rest of my days, doesn't give you the right to judge me. You are not my employer, you are not my supervisor, and you are not my teacher, so spare me the lectures. I finished school already, thank you very much."

I slam on the brake, causing the golf cart to lurch to a halt, then hop out to plug it in, hoping that I've ended the conversation.

Alfred slowly gets out and I can feel him watching me while I work. When he speaks, his voice is eerily calm. "The only reason that Mr. Davenport is laying up there terribly injured is because you are a proud young woman who doesn't know her place. This entire thing could have easily been avoided and it is most definitely *your fault*. So, if that man wakes up tomorrow and decides to sue, or worse, to publicly *ruin* the reputation of this resort, he can bloody well do it. And if he does, the fancy restaurant you think your brother is going to hand you really won't be in operation very long, will it? Think about *that*."

"Whatever," I say, stalking away from him and waving one hand dismissively. I'm certainly not going to let some geezer like Alfred scare me. Even if he may have a point.

***

Okay, so it turns out, Alfred is not the only one worried about this. As soon as I poured a rather large glass of wine and sat down to spend the evening with the *Clash of Crowns* characters, Harrison and Libby called me and we've been on the phone for a really long time now discussing this entire matter

It turns out their engagement mini-break was interrupted by a panicked call from Rosy, who caught the breaking entertainment news as soon as she got home to make supper for her husband, Darnell. Some asshat got video of us together both at, and leaving, the hospital, and now the entire internet is buzzing with questions about what happened to

Pierce, why he's here in the Benavente Islands, and who his 'mystery woman' is.

Me. That's who.

Okay, I know I really shouldn't be enjoying this so much, especially if it turns out to be a very serious problem. But, *come on*, a mystery woman to the world's hottest living author? How could that *not* be a little thrilling?

But, back to the conference call. Libby's patched in the resort's lawyer, Twyla Brathwaite, for an emergency strategy session in case our VIP gets litigious. Twyla, by the way, is a friend of Harrison's from middle school who has been madly in love with him since eighth grade and is still holding on to the hope he's finally going to come to his senses and ask her to marry him. I wasn't in on the first part of this call, but based on her sour mood, I'm thinking Harrison told her what he and Libby are away celebrating.

Most awkward conference call ever.

Yet, it's also highly entertaining because Libby seems to have picked up on Twyla's hate for her/love for Harrison, and now the two of them are like a couple of ring-tailed lemurs in a stink fight. So now I'm sitting at the kitchen table, quietly sipping wine and nibbling on cheddar cheese while Libby and Twyla try to one-up each other in the 'who's smartest' department, which is making this conversation so much longer (and more fun) than it otherwise would have been.

I've already gone over in excruciating detail how 'the incident,' as we're now calling it, happened, we've brainstormed at least eight ways it could have been prevented, and moved on to damage control.

"So, here's what we've got so far," Twyla says. "Offer him a free weekday during off-season, a complimentary fruit basket—"

"The complimentary fruit basket is a nonstarter, Twyla," Libby says. "As a guest of Eden, he already has access to unlimited food, including fruit."

"Yes, you've already mentioned that, Libby," Twyla answers haughtily. "That's not the point. The point is to make *some type of gesture* which shows sympathy for his plight while not taking responsibility for the cause of it. There is a fine line you're walking here that I don't think you seem to fully appreciate."

"Okay," Harrison says in a much higher-pitched voice than normal. "I think we're making some really good progress here, but since Emma knows Mr. Davenport the best, why don't we hear from her? Emma? Any thoughts on damage control?"

Damn. This was just getting interesting. "Well, a few thoughts come to mind," I say, putting down my next slice of cheese. "He's already apologized to me for not listening to my advice about the food, which I think shows he isn't the type to sue. If he were, I think he would've started to blame the whole thing on me straight away, which he definitely is not doing. As far as our reputation goes, I'm not sure that we have to worry about it at the moment. The prospect of leaving isn't exactly simple for him. If you look at the backlash from the mere suggestion that he's on a vacation right now, you can see how complicated it would be for him to go home, or anywhere else for that matter. He needs a place to hide out until the media storm passes and there really isn't a better place than here. As long as nobody at Paradise Bay talks and gives away our location, we should be good."

"I'll get Rosy on that right away," Harrison says.

"Ooh, good thinking, hon," Libby adds. "No one will dare cross Rosy."

"Agreed. Rosy is the scariest," Twyla says. "Harrison, remember that time she caught you sneaking me into the pool after hours?"

"I think we're getting off topic," Libby says sharply. "Emma, what do you think the chances are that he'll seek some type of compensation for his injuries?"

"I really don't think he will," I say, realizing for the first time that Pierce Davenport has a lot more character than I'd first given him credit for. "He's already really rich, and to be honest, I think he'd rather not have the entire story of how this happened get out."

"Okay, let's say you're right," Harrison says. "What do we need to do to make sure he stays? If Eden sits empty for the next seven weeks, that's really going to hurt our bottom line."

Shit. I forgot about the bottom line. We *need* him to stay.

I close my eyes for a second. Time to take one for the team, not that I'd mind, really. "Umm, well, I'm not sure, but I think he might fancy me a little which may give him an extra incentive to stay."

"He fancies you?" Harrison asks, sounding none too pleased.

At the same time, Twyla says, "Excellent! Let's use that to our advantage."

"I'm not about to pimp out my little sister, Twyla."

Twyla laughs, then says, "Have you seen Pierce Davenport? I don't exactly think she'll mind."

"Wow. What a shockingly awful thing to suggest," Libby says.

"I'm not saying she should have sex with him or anything. Although, honestly, Emma, would it really be a hardship?" Twyla asks with a little chuckle, and if I'm not mistaken, I'd say she's trying to make Harrison jealous, which obviously isn't going to work.

"There will be no sex with anybody," Harrison says firmly.

"Agreed. I'll stop just short of prostituting myself. Maybe just some heavy petting or a blowie," I say, then laugh at my own joke. I wait until I'm pretty sure Harrison is on the verge of bursting all the blood vessels in his face, then say, "I'm kidding, obviously. Listen, at the moment, none of us knows anything other than the fact that he's injured, he's on some very good pain meds, and he is under what sounds like an insane deadline. Why don't we all take the evening to think about options, and I'll make him the world's greatest breakfast in the morning, go up and see how he's feeling, and try to get a sense of what he's going to do."

"I don't know," Libby says. "I think we should try to get out in front of this thing,"

"I agree with Emma," Twyla says. "This call is costing you a *lot* of money when really you may not have a problem at all. Although, it would be wildly unrealistic of you to think you *won't* have a problem, but if we discuss it during my regular business hours, it'll be much more affordable."

"Okay, thanks, Twyla," Harrison says, his tone anything but grateful. "Why don't you ring off? Emma, stay on the line for a minute. We have a few more things to talk about."

"Okay, good luck you guys," Twyla says, her tone sounding facetious.

There's a click, then Harrison says, "Listen, Emma, I think Libby and I should end our vacation early and be out there tomorrow morning to meet with Mr. Davenport. That would show we're concerned about what happened and how he's doing."

"Harrison, seriously, I've got this," I say firmly. "When I bring his breakfast, I'll tell him you intended to come but I told you that the last thing he needs right now is more interruptions. I'll do whatever I can to encourage him to stick it out for the entire two months—without resorting to prostitution, I promise."

There's a loud sigh that I recognize as Harrison's, then he says, "Will you call as soon as you've seen him tomorrow morning?"

"Absolutely. In the meantime, enjoy your holiday."

***

When I get off the phone, I polish off the rest of my wine and sit staring out the window into the black night sky. My stomach churns when I think about all the things that could go wrong here. How the hell did I end up with the future of the resort resting firmly on *my* shoulders?

The worst of it is that Alfred the Pius might be right. I may have let my irritation for Pierce lead us to ruin.

Pouring another glass of wine, my mind races through a number of horrifying scenarios, all of which end in me selling fish tacos from a truck by the side of the highway. No matter what, I have to prevent that from happening. Even if it means being stuck out here on this island for another seven excruciatingly awful weeks with Mr. and Mrs. McJudgy.

The fact is, this is my mess and I have to clean it up. I can totally do this. I will *not* let an iguana take my family down. Or some rich guy...who happens to think I have the prettiest eyes he's ever seen and thinks I'd keep a man on his toes and

I'd rock a superhero costume. So what if he's rich and sophisticated and talented? He's a man. And he's clearly into me. All I have to do is use that to my advantage.

Now, where can I find a Catwoman costume to serve breakfast in?

***

Text from Priya: *OMG! Call me now!*

Me: *Can't right now. Just on a conference call with Harrison, Libby, and the lawyer.*

Priya: *Have you seen the photos of you and Mr. Fantasy?*

Me: *I may have peeked, yes.*

Priya: *Call me ASAP. I have to know EVERYTHING.*

SEVENTEEN

A Leap of Faith

Pierce

"**W**elcome to the ABN Weekend Entertainment Update. I'm Veronica Platt, and joining me is Giles Bigly with the latest shocking news about *Clash of Crowns* creator Pierce Davenport, who apparently has been attacked by some sort of wild animal whilst vacationing in the Benavente Islands. Giles, what seems to be happening?"

Giles sighs deeply. "Well, Veronica, you've basically just given the story away again, haven't you?"

"Not at all, Giles. Just introducing it for our viewers at home."

Giles glares for a moment, tightening his jaw. "Yes, it would appear that there is some big, and not necessarily good, news today for all of the Crownies out there who've been impatiently waiting for the final installment of the *Clash of Crowns* series. As you probably know, Pierce Davenport, who at one point was dubbed 'Avonia's Greatest Literary Treasure,' is now well over a year late in publishing the final book on which the television show is based. This not only has been a source of huge financial losses for his publisher, Sullivan and Stone, but is also wreaking havoc over at the NBO studios where crew and cast members sit idly waiting to film the final season.

"While fans and studio executives alike reportedly believed he's been holed up in his upper east-side luxury apartment here in Valcourt, he actually has been on vacation in the Benavente Islands where he was attacked by some sort of wild animal. According to one witness who was in the waiting room at San Filipe Hospital where Mr. Davenport was spotted, he appeared to have broken his hand and also had several severe lacerations."

"Shocking, Giles. Any word on what type of animal could have done this damage?"

"Not yet, but the source did hear Mr. Davenport and his companion talking about an iguana or possibly a Komodo dragon."

"I see," Veronica says, shaking her head gravely. "Well, hopefully his injuries won't have lasting effects. Any word on who the companion was?"

"A Crownie managed to secretly video him in the emergency, then followed him and his mystery woman, with whom it appears he is vacationing, as they pulled away on a speedboat. At that point, the fan lost sight of Mr. Davenport, but some have suggested that he was likely returning to Oprah's mansion on the west side of the island."

The footage of Emma and Pierce in the waiting room plays with Emma clearly saying, "Sorry, no photos. Hospital policy. He'd normally love to, though."

The video pauses, the screen splits, and Giles nods. "You see there, her demeanour and how she speaks on his behalf, then she intimates that she knows exactly what he'd normally do…"

"Ah, yes, that suggests a very close relationship, doesn't it?"

"I'd say it does, yes. And apparently, later when he was brought into the examining room, she accompanied him."

"Interesting, Giles. There is a lot to unpack in this story. The first thing that comes to mind, though, is how disappointed his fans must be that he is not hard at work on the highly anticipated series finale."

"Indeed, Veronica. And they're not the only ones who are up in arms. Word has it that NBO studio head Kent Cromwell went on the warpath as soon as he found out about this breaking story. According to insiders at NBO, the legal team was brought in to discuss removing Mr. Davenport as one of the show's executive producers for the final season and they have already amassed a team of writers to pick up the saga where he left off and complete it without his input, which of course would be a huge disappointment to fans everywhere."

"Is there a possibility that he was there for work and not play? Like some sort of writer's retreat, for example?"

"It very unlikely," Giles says, pursing his lips. "Especially given the fact that he is clearly there with a young woman who looks like she could be some sort of swimsuit model or, perhaps, even a professional beach volleyball player."

"Absolutely shocking behaviour from a man who was once hailed to be one of the brightest stars of our generation." Veronica shakes her head gravely. "Okay, thank you very much for reporting. I'm sure you'll keep us up to date as more details emerge on this important entertainment story."

"Absolutely," Giles nods.

"After this break, we will be checking in with the royal family to see how the wedding plans are progressing in what's been dubbed Royal Wedding 2.0. We've got some surprising details about next month's upcoming nuptials between Prince Arthur and commoner Tessa Sharpe."

***

Voicemail from Bunny: "Pierce, it's your mother calling. I'm not sure if you heard, but the wedding is back on. Arthur and that woman of his have set a new date. It looks like they'll be getting married in three weeks' time, which is a great cause of concern for your father and I since you are out of the country. I'm just calling to see if perhaps you might wrap up your little book so that you can be back in time."

***

Email from the desk of Kent Cromwell
President in Chief, NBO studios

Pierce,

I understand you've been injured and I offer my deepest sympathies; however, we do need to discuss the future of the *Clash of Crowns* series. Call as soon as you get this email, even if it's the middle of the night. If I don't hear back from you within forty-eight hours, I will have to pass you off to our legal team.

Regards,
Kent

***

Text from Leo: *Hey, bro, saw the footage. How's your hand? If that's not the worst timing ever to be attacked by a wild animal, I don't know what is. Too bad you didn't join me in Bath instead of going off to the jungle. BTW, who's the hottie? Are you two an item or should I fire up the family jet and come 'meat' her?*

***

Well, if I thought I was fucked before, I had absolutely no idea what the phrase meant. Here's what's happened over the last eighteen hours: I've had my right hand stitched up and casted. Some arse at the hospital managed to take footage of Emma and me so now the entire world of Crownies is erupting on the Internet as they believe me to be on a relaxing vacation with a swimsuit model rather than completing the book. In this business, *perception is everything*, and unfortunately at the moment, the perception is that I'm a lazy ne'er-do-well who has no intention of finishing what I started.

To be honest, none of this bothered me too much for the first twelve hours because it turns out the medical staff at San Felipe Hospital are handing out some pretty good painkillers. But now that they've worn off, reality has set back in. I've got Kent Cromwell so far up my arse, I can smell his cologne, not to mention that the two biggest trending topics on Reddit are 'Who is Pierce Davenport's Mystery Woman' and, my favourite, 'Creative Ways to Kill off Pierce Davenport if He Doesn't Finish the *Clash of Crowns* Series.'

My hand hurts like a son of a bitch, too. I don't want to sound like a wimp or anything, but now that the drugs are out of my system, I'm left with a constant throbbing pain. But if I take more of the little blue pills they sent me home with, I'll be knocked out again, which means no writing, which means losing everything I've built over the past eight years.

Not to worry though. I just have to come up with a plan...

***

Text from Zach: *Pierce, just checking in to see if you're okay. A hand injury, that's bad luck, mate. Let me know if there's anything I can do to help you from this end.*

Text to Zach: *As a matter of fact, there IS something you can do. You pack, I'll arrange for a jet. I cracked the ending, but my right hand is completely useless, and at the moment I have no one else I can trust. Just sending this text has taken me twenty minutes of typing with my left hand.*

Text from Zach: *Unfortunately, there's no way I can leave town right now. Kennedy and I are in a couple's ballroom dance class for the next ten weeks. If I duck out now, I'll never hear the end of it. Sorry, old chap.*

***

Ballroom dancing? Does he not realize the entire fate of the people of Qadeathas is riding on this?

I stand and walk to the window to contemplate my fate, which may or may not include cliff-diving to my doom should I not sort out a suitable option. Honestly, it would be better to be dead than be a failure in my family. Well, not if you're Leo. If you're mummy's little cherub, you can fail all you want and still get showered with affection, but me, not so much. I've written one of the greatest selling series of all time (just behind Harry Potter, Lord of the Rings, and that awful Fifty Shades of Shite series), and yet, my parental figures remain unimpressed. *"Have you wrapped up your little book yet?"* Grrr.

Setting all that aside, I have to come up with a suitable response to Kent the you-know-what Cromwell, not to mention actually finish the damn book. I've got at least three hundred pages to go, no way to type efficiently, no one I can trust to keep the ending a secret, and no idea what to do.

Shit. Shit. Shit. How the fuck do I get out of this?

"Pierce? Are you all right?" Emma asks, standing at the door with the cooler that now has me reacting like a Pavlovian dog. "I knocked but you didn't answer so I got a bit worried."

"I was deep in thought. Come in, please." I smile, feeling somehow more relaxed at the sight of her lovely face.

"I thought maybe you'd taken more of those blue pills. They really knocked you on your arse." She smiles as she crosses the room. "How's your hand? And your leg?"

"Fine. No pain at all really." She must know that's a man lie, right? Yes, she does. I can tell by the smirk.

"I just can't believe you broke your own thumb. You must pack one hell of a punch." She opens the cooler and starts setting out my breakfast. "I thought I'd make you a one-handed meal. Nothing that requires a steak knife or seafood crackers."

"That's very thoughtful of you. Thank you, Emma," I say, trying not to limp as I walk over to the table. "What's on the menu today?"

"Sweet plantain hash and eggs, fresh banana cake, and Benavente cornmeal porridge."

"It looks delicious." I suddenly realize I'm staring at her, not the food, and my cheeks heat up. Clearing my throat, I glance down at the table, trying to regain my composure. When I look at Emma again, she's busying herself pouring a steaming cup of coffee for me, and if I'm not mistaken, she's blushing a little too.

"I thought you'd need a hearty breakfast after everything you've been through." Placing the carafe on the table, she looks up at me. "And everything you've got to deal with."

"Speaking of things I need to deal with, I owe you yet another apology. I'm not sure if you happened to read any of that garbage on the Internet last night or this morning, but apparently, some arse filmed us together and the brilliant folks in the media did what they do best—jump to conclusions without any proof." I jam my good hand into the front pocket of my chinos, feeling like an awkward fool. "Apparently, they think we're a couple and I haven't had time to set the record straight."

"Oh, I saw it, yes," she answers. "But don't worry, I don't mind as much as you might think about being mistaken for a swimsuit model."

"I'm glad. Some women would find that highly offensive."

"Would they?" she asks, looking skeptical. "Or would they just pretend?"

"Good question," I say, grinning at her quick wit. "So, um, those pain meds were a little on the strong side and I have found myself with some holes in my recollection of our trip back from the hospital."

Her eyes grow wide for just a millisecond, she blinks quickly, then replaces her smile with a poker face. "Pretty dull really. You mainly slept."

Shit. She's definitely lying. "Really? You're sure I didn't embarrass myself somehow? I seem to recall...singing."

"Oh, that was the radio," she says, waving one hand. "Seriously, you were fine. Nothing strange or otherwise embarrassing."

"Why do I feel like you're holding out on me?"

Giving me a half grin, she says, "Okay, you may have sung a little Neil Diamond, but you're very good, really. And don't worry. Your secret talent is safe with me. I won't mention last night's concert to a soul."

"Concert?" Oh, bugger. "That sounds like more than a little singing."

Emma finally lets herself laugh at whatever memory I've created for her, then says, "It was fine, really. Very fun actually. I may have even sung along. And think of it this way: at least you're a very nice sort when you're drugged out of your mind. Some people turn very nasty."

"Good point," I say, studying her long enough to decide she's not messing with me. I wonder if I could I trust her to help me.

"I spoke with my brother last night. He wanted to rush out to see how you're doing but I told him you're on a tight deadline and that it wouldn't be helpful," she says, maintaining direct eye contact. "They wanted me to pass on their deepest apologies for the incident and said to let me know if you're in need of anything at all to make the rest of your stay more pleasant."

"That's very kind of them."

"Is there anything you need?" she asks, tilting her head a little.

My heart leaps to my throat. I have to do this. I have no choice but to trust someone and it has to be her. "How quickly can you type?"

"How quickly can I type?" she asks, looking thoroughly confused.

Oh, this was a terrible idea. But I'm in it now, so... "I know that sounds rather unconventional, and it's absolutely within your right to refuse my request. I realize you're not a secretary and that helping me work on my book is insanely far outside of the scope of an executive chef," I say, running my hand through my hair, feeling like a complete idiot. "Not secretary. Executive assistant—I believe that's what they prefer to be called in the modern era. Did I just say modern era? Christ, now I sound like a man who's just time-travelled from the 1920's. I should just call you a dame and get it over with."

Emma starts to laugh, and the sight of it relaxes me the tiniest bit.

Clearing my throat, I continue. "It's just that I don't think that Phyllis or Alfred seem like the tech-savvy types, if you know what I mean. God, now I'm being ageist as well as sexist. I should just quit while I'm ahead."

"Please, go on," she laughs. "This is almost as fun as last night."

Shit. Pull it together, Pierce, you daft moron. "Allow me to start again. As you have quite likely deduced, I am not in the habit of asking for favours. But in this situation, as much as I hate to impose upon your time, I find myself without another viable alternative. I'm not sure if you're aware of the situation in which I find myself currently, but there's a bit of urgency to my work at the moment."

I nod. "I may have come across your rather bitter-sounding fanbase when I Googled you."

"That's putting it mildly. At this point, I'm getting more hate mail then Hitler...if he were alive and his address were made public, that is. Now I can't even string together a decent analogy. I should just stop talking." I shake my head at my idiocy, then take a deep breath. "Ms Banks, I know we got off to a bad start and it was completely my fault. And asking for this particular favour is so far out of my comfort zone, I can't even see the boundary from here. But I need someone who can be utterly discreet and would be immune to bribery because, should anyone figure out who is helping me type my book, they will undoubtedly stop at nothing to try to find out how this series ends."

"That sounds ominous," she says, her eyes growing wide.

"That didn't come out right. What I meant to say is that they'd likely hound you relentlessly and quite possibly offer you a great deal of money to spill the proverbial beans."

"Ah, that doesn't sound nearly so bad now," she says, looking slightly pleased.

"I can offer you just as much, if not more, money," I say, swallowing hard. "Name your price."

"I'm not interested in their money. Or *yours*, to be honest," she says, her face growing serious all of a sudden in a way that makes my stomach flip. "But there is one thing I need."

"Name it. As you can undoubtedly tell, I'm not only the world's worst negotiator, I'm also desperate."

Emma chuckles at me, then her smile drops again. "My family is worried that you might make some negative comments about the island after the incident yesterday, or possibly take legal action."

"Oh, no. That was my own stupidity," I say, shaking my head quickly. "You tried to warn me but I didn't listen."

"That's what I told them but they don't know you like I do. Not that I *know you* know you. I just...have a general sense of your character and you seem honest. Maybe a little too much so at times, but..." Her voice trails off and she turns a little red.

"Asking for what you want can be awkward as hell, can't it?" I say.

"Extremely."

"Is that all you need? Because I'm asking for a rather large favour here. I'll need you day and night for several weeks and I'd feel badly taking advantage."

"Well, if we're negotiating, what this resort needs is a champion of sorts—someone influential among people who can afford to stay here," she says pointedly.

"Done. I will happily tweet, Snapchat, and Instagram a plethora of soulful reviews and gorgeous pics as soon as I leave."

Her eyes narrow and I quickly add, "I can't reveal my exact location until I'm gone for what I'm sure are obvious reasons."

"Oh, right," she says with a nod.

'How about this? As soon as I leave, I'll not only sing the resort's praises on social media, I'll contact my inner circle and imply that none of them can afford to come here."

"Why would you do that?" she asks, looking slightly horrified.

"Because if there's anything that makes rich people want something, it's being told they can't have it. I'll have this place booked up for the next five years with three phone calls."

A huge smile appears on Emma's face and she nods enthusiastically. "Okay, I'll type for you and promise to keep everything that happens in the world of Qadeathas a *complete secret*. And, in exchange, you'll see to it that Paradise Bay Resort and Eden Island become the hottest celebrity destination in the world."

I extend my left hand to her to seal the deal, my heart pounding in my chest. "So we agree to trust each other, then?"

"Agreed."

We shake and I can't help feeling a warmth spread through me and a renewed sense of optimism for the future. Grinning, I say, "Nothing like equally desperate people to create the perfect deal."

"I wouldn't say were *equally* desperate," she says with a smirk. "I know how you broke your thumb."

EIGHTEEN

I'm Not Going to Sleep with Him, So Everyone, Please Relax

Emma

"I don't like it," Harrison says firmly.

We're on another conference call, this time without Twyla (one guess as to why). I've gone back to the houseboat to pack up food for the rest of the day and fill Libby and Harrison in on what I've worked out with Pierce. I expected Harrison to be thrilled, but he's pulling the 'protective big brother' nonsense instead.

"What's not to like?" Libby asks. "Not only is he *not* going to sue, he's going to stay on at Eden and promote it when he leaves. This is our best-case scenario and then some. Well done, Emma!"

"Thank you, Libby," I say in an overly gracious, I'm-glad-someone-appreciates-me tone of voice.

"Nope. Forget it," Harrison says. "I'll just hire someone from town to type for him. A stenographer or something."

I can tell by his tone he's shaking his head, and I bet he knows I'm rolling my eyes right now. "He wants *me*."

"Exactly," he quips.

"Not like *that*, you big jerk," I say. "It's strictly a smart business deal. Anyone else he would hire could be bought out for a lot of money to give away the ending before the book is published. I'm the perfect person to trust because I have skin in the game. If I spill the beans to anyone about how the series ends, he can ruin the resort's reputation. And if I'm not mistaken, our reputation was our big concern on the phone last night, no?"

"It was last night, but my focus has shifted to some guy trying to get his grubby hands on my little sister. No way am I agreeing to this. He's going to have you up in that villa all day and half the night for weeks. What if he tries something?"

"He's not a rapey guy. He's a desperate writer. Besides, do you actually not think I can defend myself against a guy with only one good arm?"

Libby interjects with, "Is this because of what Twyla said about Mr. Davenport being so hot? Because really, Harrison, I think Emma can resist him."

"Yes. Give me a little credit, please," I say, trying to sound highly offended by the very idea. "I'm not about to start snogging the guests like some cheap tart."

"Or like your brother," Libby adds with a little laugh.

She's referring to how they ended up together and I can't help but laugh along with her. It's nice to have an almost-sister-in-law.

"Oh, very funny, you two, but this is serious. There's a lot at stake here."

"Which is why I'm the perfect woman for the job," I say. "I know how much you've sacrificed for me and for the staff. I would *seriously* be *the last* person to let you down, Harrison. I owe everything I have to you. Not only that, but the future of this resort is my future, too, you know. This is my home and I'd never do anything to jeopardize it."

"I'm not questioning your loyalty, Emma. It's *him* I don't trust."

"Well, don't worry about him because I'm not interested in Pierce *that way* so there's really nothing to worry about. I'll type. He'll stay until he finishes his book, then give us a glowing review that will turn this place into the hottest vacation destination for the rich and famous. Nobody gets sued. Nobody has to turn their family business over to the bank. We all live happily ever after."

"See? All settled," Libby says. "So, Emma, you get straight to work with Mr. Davenport and let us know if you need anything brought out—paper, pens, another computer, whatever. In the meantime, I'll arrange for ready-made meals to be prepared for the two of you so you won't have to waste time cooking."

"Okay, perfect. We have enough food to get us through until lunchtime tomorrow," I say, hoping Harrison will consider himself overruled.

"I'll let Alfred and Phyllis know what's going on as well," Libby says. "They'll need to be ready in case you or Mr. Davenport need anything at all."

Oh, they are going to *love* that. "Thanks. I better get back up there so we can get started," I say.

"I still don't like it," Harrison says, but his voice is more on the 'defeated' side of the spectrum.

"You'll get over it," I say. "Now, please, let me be the hero for once."

***

Text to Priya: *Just wanted to let you know I may be incommunicado for a few weeks but I love you and I'm rooting for you to find your dream job.*

Priya: *That sounds ominous. Everything okay?*

Me: *Yes, but you may hate me once you find out what I'll be doing.*

Priya: *Which is...*

Me: *Working day and night with a certain writer typing the last Clash of Crowns book for him.*

Priya: *Are you freaking kidding me?! Because unless this is a prank, I pretty much have to hate you.*

Me: *I don't blame you. If I were a huge fan of his and the roles were reversed, I'd hate me too.*

Priya: *You could make it up to me by getting me an advanced copy of the book.*

Me: *I promise if I get an advanced copy, I'll mail it directly to you.*

Priya: *You're not going to get one, are you?*

Me: *Highly unlikely.*

Priya: *Maid of honour when you two get married?*

Me: *He won't be the groom but deal.*

Priya: *I don't know...a few weeks working closely together day and night...*

Me: *Nothing can happen. He's a paying guest. It would be very wrong of me (as Harrison pointed out repeatedly). Sleeping with him would be THE WORST thing I could ever do.*

Priya: *But you want to?!*

Me: *I never said that.*

Priya: *You just made a thorough argument for why you shouldn't sleep with him. If you didn't want to, you would have just sent a pukey face emoji. Plus, knowing you the way I do, the fact that your brother said you can't do it will make it all that more attractive to you.*

Me: *What?! My entire goal in life is to pay my brother back for everything he's done for me.*

Priya: *I'm not saying you WILL sleep with Pierce. I'm saying you hate being told what to do, which means that the fact that Harrison said you can't is going to make Pierce even more irresistible than he already is...*

Me: *I never said he was irresistible.*

Priya: *You don't have to. I saw that shirtless pic of him...*

NINETEEN

Girl Talk, the Masculine Way...

Pierce - Two Weeks Later

"Well, I don't hate it nearly as much as I thought I would, if that's what you mean." I'm on the phone with Zach while I stand on the veranda staring out at the jungle. It's the crack of dawn for him, but I knew he'd be up, and since Emma and I are taking a rare break, it seems like a good time to call. I sent him the first one hundred pages yesterday morning, and couldn't wait to find out what he thought, but he's refusing to talk about it until I tell him what it's like to work with another human being.

"You don't hate it. Is that Pierce code for she's wonderful, everything is amazing, and I've never been so happy in my entire life?" Zach asks, sounding all too amused.

"Obviously not. What we've got going here is a simple business arrangement. She helps me over the next few weeks, and I become the biggest influencer for her family's resort. It's a simple exchange of services and nothing more."

"You sure there aren't *other services* you'd like to exchange with her? I did see those photos in the *Weekly World News* and *wow*. Oh, but please don't say anything to Kennedy, because I told her I hadn't seen them."

"Would she really be angry at you for seeing a photo of a gorgeous woman in a tight tank top and short shorts?" We both know the answer, but I'm asking anyway on the off chance he'll come to the realization that marriage is a terrible mistake.

"You'll understand when you're married."

Nope. Didn't work.

"I highly doubt I'll ever understand this particular predicament. Now, more importantly, have you read the pages I sent?" I ask, feeling my stomach tighten as it always does when someone reads over my work.

"I have. In fact, I was up until after two a.m. because I couldn't tear myself away. You are one sadistic son of a bitch to put Ogden in the dungeon with Oona's tigers. And then you just leave that storyline for over fifty pages? Diabolical."

"Good, right?" I let out a sigh of relief, knowing that if Zach reacted this way, every Crownie out there will be in absolute agony.

"Honestly, Pierce, this is by far your best work. I don't know if it's the tropical air, the pain meds, or this chef-slash-typist of yours, but it's inspired, eloquent, and completely riveting. The way you handled finding Draqen's secret heir blew my mind. I woke Kennedy up because I yelled, 'Shut the fuck up!' as loud as I could."

"That must have gone over well," I say dryly.

"Oh yes, she was absolutely thrilled with me. If I get lucky again before I'm forty, it'll be a huge win."

"And you just turned..."

"Thirty-six, yes."

"Better stock up on hand cream."

"Already done," he says. "Now, back to the book. My only advice would be for you to hurry and get it wrapped up as quickly as humanly possible."

"Why, what have you heard?" I close my eyes for a moment, wincing in preparation for his answer.

"Kennedy had lunch with a showrunner at NBO. The word around the building is that the team is well into episode three already."

"Fuck."

"Sorry, mate. I thought you'd want to know."

"Yes, of course. Well, in that case, I should get back at it."

"Yes, you should. And don't let any beautiful brunettes distract you."

"Impossible. Although she is using my shower right now..."

"You dirty dog. You are doing her, aren't you?" Zach asks with a chuckle.

"Only in my overly active imagination. We've basically been working around the clock for the past fourteen days. A week ago, she started sleeping here—well, to be honest, it's more of a quick nap, then straight back to work—but it's all on the up-and-up. I'm on the couch, she's in my room. It's all fine, except..."

"Except that you wish it weren't strictly professional?"

"I am a man, and she's...well, as close to perfect as I suppose a woman can get."

"Holy shitballs. I never thought I'd hear you say that about a woman. You sound almost...affected."

"I'm not affected. I'm just...it's just probably being in a tropical paradise. I think it puts ideas in a man's head."

"Well, you have to take a break from writing at some point. Why not *enjoy* those breaks?"

"Because my editor was just lecturing me on how urgently I need to finish this book."

"Righto. Get to it, sir," Zach says.

"Yes, yes, I will," I answer, suddenly dreading the next scene. "There's just one problem. The next chapter is *the one* everyone's been waiting for since the series started."

Zach gasps. "You mean Oona and Luc are finally going to do it?"

"Yes, and it's not like it's a scene I can exactly skim over. Not after making people wait for over seventeen hundred pages for them to consummate their relationship."

Zach lets out a puff of air, then says, "Well, shit. That's going to be a little awkward, no?"

"More than a little. Maybe I'll just type one-handed and give Emma the evening off."

"I'd say tackling that one alone would likely be one of the smarter decisions you've made since you left Valcourt," Zach says.

"As opposed to picking a fight with a Komodo dragon over breakfast?"

"I thought it was an iguana."

"Iguana, unusually large Komodo dragon...who's to say?" I ask.

"You are, if you're telling the truth."

"Look at the time. I really should be running to get this book finished."

***

When I walk back inside, Emma is coming out of the bathroom in a lovely white sleeveless sundress, her hair leaving drops of water on her tanned shoulders. She no longer wears her chef's uniform now that she's no longer cooking for me. She doesn't take the time to put on makeup either (not that she needs it) so she won't delay my work in any way. Alfred and Phyllis have been making trips back to the resort to bring back ready-made meals that Emma can heat up in the oven or stovetop in the villa.

God, but she's pretty. I find myself staring at her longer than I should—an embarrassing habit I seem to have developed over the past couple of weeks of working with her. Her cheeks develop a pinkish glow and she looks down for a moment, then clears her throat. "I was thinking I should put that lasagna in the oven, then we can get started on the next scene while it cooks."

I watch as she turns to the kitchen and sets to work, opening a bottle of red wine Alfred chose to go with our dinner.

Our dinner.

How strange a thought. Since I left boarding school, I have never lived in such close proximity to anyone. I've had a couple of somewhat serious relationships in the past, but never with anyone to whom I suggested they leave so much as even a toothbrush at my flat.

And I know this isn't a relationship. I'm not delusional or wishful, so you can get that out of your mind right now.

It's just oddly intimate to not only share every meal with someone, but to share my work before it's ready to be seen by another person. She's seen it all over these past days—the frustrations and highs, the frantic pace, the dreadfully slow moments when ideas simply won't come. She's heard me stumble over a sentence repeatedly until I get it right. She's erased entire paragraphs when I go down the wrong path.

Emma waits patiently, never making suggestions or asking questions, for which I'm grateful.

And even though I wish it didn't matter, I can't help but watch for signs that she's enjoying the story. Will she smile or laugh at the right moment? Does she look horrified when I want her to or disgusted when I write something disgusting? Do her eyes fill with tears when we reach a particularly emotional passage? Somehow her reaction has replaced my own instincts in knowing if I'm on the right track or not, which sounds pathetic, I know. But in a way, maybe having the immediate sort of feedback that I'm getting from her would be useful for every writer.

Forcing myself not to watch as she bends to put the tray of lasagna in the oven, I busy myself looking over the outline I've painstakingly scratched out with my left hand for this next scene. My heart thumps loudly as I stare down at the page.

"Okay, now, where were we?" Emma asks, seating herself next to me at the table and powering up the laptop. God, she smells good. What *is* that shampoo she uses? It's like every heavenly scent blended together. Or is that just her?

Okay, dumbass, forget about how amazing she smells. "We're just about to start chapter twenty-eight, I believe."

Placing her hands on the keyboard, Emma smiles over at me. "I'm ready when you are."

Rubbing the back of my neck, I give her a sheepish look. "The thing is, this next bit might be a little awkward."

She immediately starts to type what I'm saying, and then gives me a questioning look because that indeed would be a strange way to start a chapter.

"Oh, no need to dictate this part," I say, smiling at her for a second before avoiding her gaze so I can get this next sentence out. "I'm afraid this chapter is a rather steamy, intimate scene, so if you'd prefer not to assist me with it, I completely understand. I wouldn't want you to have to do anything that would make you in any way uncomfortable."

"If I made it through that decapitation scene and the bit where the elves drown Surryn in that swamp, I'm sure I can make it through this."

I give her a hard look. "You sure?"

Emma bites her bottom lip, then smiles up at me, making me wonder if her answer isn't solely about the book. "This isn't my first time, Pierce."

"You mean you've transcribed sex scenes for other men before?" I ask, giving her a half-grin.

Laughing, Emma says, "Yes, many times. Now, fire away. I want to see what you've got hidden in that deviant brain of yours."

TWENTY

Is it Getting Hot in Here?

Emma

Oh my. This man has imagination to spare when it comes to the bedroom stuff. I can hardly type. I want to smoke an entire pack of cigarettes, and yet Luc and Oona are both still almost fully dressed. Is my face bright red? I bet it is because I'm like a cat on a hot tin roof. Is the cat they're referring to in that play super horny? I've always thought it was a sexual reference but I could be way off base. If it isn't about sex, it should be.

"Luc runs his hand up her spine, then gives the string a sharp tug, allowing the bow to disappear. He listens as Oona makes the slightest little moan, and forces himself to make this moment last. On the battlefield, he may be aggressive to the point of insanity, but here, he must restrain himself."

Oh no, don't restrain yourself, Luc. Go for it. She wants you to really go for it.

"He must show her that when he removes his armour, there is a gentleman underneath who knows how to please a woman. Her pleasure is his. Reaching up, he lifts her long, auburn curls and sweeps them over her right shoulder so he can begin the torturous task of unlacing her dress. Her neck calls to him and he lowers his mouth over her collarbone, running his lips along it and tasting her flesh for the first time. His entire body reacts with lust and...is this okay, Emma?"

"Oh God, yes," I say, my voice breathy, and I finally realize I've just been staring at him.

"It's just that you've stopped typing," Pierce says.

"Sorry. I got...a little distracted," I answer, flushing as I turn back to the laptop. "We were at the bit about him tasting her flesh for the first time."

"Righto, thanks. Okay...*His entire body reacts with lust as he grips her hips and pulls her back toward him. Oona arches her long body and rests her head on his shoulder, raising one hand above her head to reach for him as he plants hungry kisses along her neck. 'We cannot undo this, Oona. Once I have you, you will be mine forever,' Luc whispers. She spins her body to him and stares up at him. 'Then take me, Luc. Take me now. I can't wait any longer to be with you.' Her breasts heave as Luc claims her mouth with his own...*"

Oh my God. Are my breasts heaving too? I think they are. *Stop that, girls! That is completely inappropriate.* Did he notice? Dear Lord, I hope not....

"*The fabric silently falls to the floor and he lifts her off her feet and carries her to the bed.* Or maybe he should carry her to the bearskin rug in front of the fire. I did say earlier the room was chilly and the bed is quite far from the fireplace. What do you think Oona would enjoy more?"

"The rug, definitely the rug. There's more friction on the floor."

Grinning at me, Pierce says, "I thought you were going to say it would be more romantic."

"Right. That too," I answer, quickly. "Now what's he going to do to her?"

"Good so far?"

"Very. I mean, your readers will probably like it," I say with a shrug.

"I hope so," he says, giving me a knowing grin. "Let's continue then."

"Yes, let's," I say, swallowing hard.

"*Luc lowers to his knees with her in his arms, gently lays her down on the thick white rug, then runs his hands up and down her naked body, relishing the feel of her silky skin. He traces her breasts with his thumbs, then—*"

BEEP. BEEP. BEEP.

"Oh, dinner's ready."

Now, lasagna? Really? "Brilliant. Are you hungry?" I ask.

"Starving," he answers, staring at me, and if I'm not mistaken, he's not talking about the food.

I stand quickly before I do something stupid like climb into his lap and kiss him full on the mouth, which is exactly what every cell in my body is telling me to do right freaking now. "Why don't I whip up a salad while the lasagna sets?"

"That would be lovely," he says, staring at the laptop screen. Lifting his left hand, he taps out a few words and I can't help but wonder what they are. But maybe it's better I don't know because as it is, I'm ready to give my left ovary for a vibrator and about five minutes alone.

Swinging open the oven door, I grab at the pan without remembering to put on oven mitts. "Shit!" I say, my hands snapping back before I register what an idiot I've been. I glance at the tips of my fingers and see that they're okay.

"Are you all right?" Pierce asks, his voice much closer than I thought it would be.

I turn, feeling silly and holding up my hands. "Totally fine. I pulled my hands back in time."

He takes my hands in his and inspects them while I stare at him, helplessly filled with a longing he created without really meaning to. Or did he? The feeling of his hands on mine have my bosoms heaving again. *Dammit, bosoms.* Is he staring at them? No, he's looking at my hands. God, he's handsome up close like this. Those eyelashes are seriously thicker than Justin Theroux's. I can see why Jennifer Aniston wouldn't have been able to resist.

And what is that cologne he's wearing? I bet it's called Sexy Sex Man Who Can Deliver the World's Greatest Orgasms. Or something like that. I really need to unpack the rest of my things and find my personal massager.

His eyes meet mine and we both just stare at each other, speaking volumes without saying a word. I lift myself up onto my tiptoes, my brain screaming at me not to kiss him. He is a guest. A VIP guest. *Do not kiss him, Emma! You don't even know if he wants to kiss you.*

He lowers his face toward me and I suddenly am pretty damn sure he wants to kiss me. Oh yes, let's forget the food and *do this.* I close my eyes, afraid to see him pull away. One of us should come to our senses but it isn't going to be me because

I'm desperate to feel his lips on my lips, his tongue against mine, to taste and touch and nuzzle together in our shared euphoria.

But he doesn't get the chance because his mobile phone suddenly starts buzzing, saying "Zach Calling." And the moment is officially over. Murdered by his best friend-slash-editor calling with an urgent update from his publisher.

And Zach has just officially become my least favourite person on the planet.

***

"This is delicious," Pierce says, taking another bite of the pasta.

While he was on the phone, I set our dinner up on the table for two out on the screened-in veranda. The lighting is low out here, having been designed for just such a meal. The sounds of the waterfall in the distance and the frogs croaking fill the air while I pull apart a soft white roll and pop a piece into my mouth.

Luckily, we both seem to have come to our senses and the sexy haze we were under has lifted. Pierce tells me about his call with Zach and fills me in on what's going on back in Valcourt. Things are erupting in the worst way possible for his career and the tension on his face is visible. While I listen, it suddenly becomes clear to me why he was so surly when he first arrived.

"Anyway, enough whining, right?" he says, pouring more wine in each of our glasses.

"Whining? You've had the weight of an entire cable TV network on your shoulders for years now. I can't even imagine the pressure—all the crew members and cast relying solely on your imagination for their livelihoods, and the network having all that money tied up, not to mention your publishers hounding you at every turn."

"And let's not forget the outraged Crownies all over the globe."

"Them, too," I say, shaking my head. "The fact that you're still upright is a wonder to me."

"Thank you," he says, with a small smile. "It's not all bad though. I know it's every writer's dream to be in this exact scenario. Well, maybe not exactly, but the bit about the hit series."

"I suppose, but I doubt they'd consider the cost of it," I say. I look out at the inky jungle, then back at Pierce. "Can I ask you a question?"

"Certainly."

"Why does this matter so much to you? You could just quit and let NBO finish the whole thing if you wanted. It's not like you need the money, so why kill yourself and take all the abuse?"

He chuckles a little, then nods thoughtfully. "This will sound stupid, but I feel like I owe it to the characters. I know they're not real, okay, so no need to have me committed or anything," Pierce says with a wry smile. "It's just that I created this world, and all these lives within it that are hanging in the balance. It may sound conceited, but I don't think another writer would do them justice."

"That doesn't sound conceited at all. It sounds loyal."

"Yes, I'm very loyal to my imaginary friends," he says. "Maybe I *am* insane."

I smile and shake my head. "No, you're not. It's the right thing to do—finishing it. And the fact that you could just drop it and spend the rest of your life on vacation makes it all the more commendable."

"I don't know about that, Emma. It's not like I'm searching for the cure for cancer or something."

"Maybe not, but you've created something incredible—something that *millions* of people have fallen in love with and are gripped by." I watch him for a moment, hoping for some sign that he's pleased with himself, but only seeing that look of concern firmly in place. "Your parents must be very proud."

"One would think," he says, looking out into the night sky.

"But, how could they not be impressed by having one of the world's most successful writers as a son?" I ask, wrinkling my nose in confusion.

Sighing, he looks back at me. "They would have preferred to have two versions of my older brother Greyson.

Easy to lead. Does what's expected. Says the right thing in every occasion."

"Ah, I see," I say, even though I don't see how any parent could be disappointed to have him for a child.

"Oh, don't give me that look. It's fine, really. We were never close to begin with so it isn't like I lost anything I once had." He looks suddenly shocked. "Well, I didn't expect that to pop out of my mouth. What is in this wine?" he asks, picking up the bottle and pretending to exam it.

"Don't try to change the subject."

"Shall I lay down on the couch, doctor?"

I give him a thoughtful look. "Won't work. You were talking about the fact that you never had your parents' approval. Tell me more about that."

"It's really not worth talking about. Not every family is close-knit. It's not a tragedy."

"I'm not sure I'd agree with that." I reach across the table and cover his hand with mine. "I'm sorry, Pierce."

"Why are you sorry? You didn't make them the way they are."

"Still," I say, giving his hand a little squeeze. "I don't think it would have been very nice to grow up in your home."

"Guessed it in one," he answers with a wry smile. "What about your family? You seem like the well-adjusted type who probably has supportive, wonderful parents who doted on you day and night, hung on every word, and celebrated every tiny success."

"Yes, I did, but my parents died when I was seven," I say, doing my best to look okay with it.

"So not such an ideal upbringing then," he says, his eyebrows knitting together in concern. He flips his hand so he's holding mine now. "I'm sorry to have assumed."

"That's okay. You said I seem well-adjusted so I'll take that as a compliment." We share a moment of pure connection, then without thinking about it, I launch into an overview of my childhood—the perfect life, the car accident, the quick move to Santa Valentina Island with an uncle we'd never met, and my odd-but-kind-of-cool upbringing at the resort.

When I'm done, he looks at me for a long time before saying, "What was the hardest part of losing them?"

Oh, so we're doing a deep dive, I guess. "So many things. Being pitied isn't fun, I suppose. Making everyone you meet feel sad when they ask about your parents," I say with a little nod. "But I suppose the worst bit is the wondering. Would they be proud of me? Would they have liked me as an adult? Like, *really liked* hanging out with me, you know? What advice would they give me when I mess up or when I couldn't figure out what to do with my life? Just never knowing and having to sort it out for myself," I say, taking a sip of wine. "That, and my mom's spaghetti sauce. I can still taste it but I haven't managed to recreate it, no matter how hard I try."

"Is that why you wanted to become a chef?"

"Maybe," I answer with a sad chuckle.

"But you figured the rest out for yourself in the end. I suppose a person has to, *and can,* when they come to the biggest truth of life—that you can't actually rely on other people."

Wrinkling up my nose, I say, "I don't think that's the truth at all. You *have to* rely on others—that's one of our basic human instincts. We're pack animals."

"Not me. I'm more of a lone wolf," he says, looking down at our intertwined hands for a second, then pulling his hand away in favour of holding his wine glass.

"I thought wolves were pack animals."

"Not this one," he answers, taking a sip. "This one doesn't rely on anyone and never will."

"Well, in case you haven't noticed, you've been relying on me and I don't think I've let you down. You and I have been relying on Alfred and Phyllis and the staff back at the resort to keep us fed and they haven't let us down. And from the sounds of things, you rely on your friend, Zach, quite a bit too."

"Yes, well, this is what I would call an extraordinary circumstance," he says, holding up his casted arm. "Besides, you're all being paid."

Ouch. I take a deep breath but say nothing as I try to let the sting of his words fade.

"I didn't mean it that way. You've been lovely and I really appreciate everything you've been doing to help me. I only mean that in my experience, money breeds reliability better than any other form of motivation or attachment."

My heart breaks a little at this glimpse into his fractured soul. "How very sad."

"Please don't tell me you're feeling sorry for *me*. Believe me, Emma, I want for nothing." He takes a long swig of the wine, but when he lowers the glass, something in his face says that it tasted sour.

"Nothing?"

"Nothing. I am perfectly happy on my own, and that's the way I intend to stay."

The memory of Painkiller Pierce comes to mind and I think about how he told Alfred he'd never considered marriage (until he met me, that is). I raise one eyebrow and give him a long, hard look. "So, you don't ever think you'd want to get married and have a family? Even if you met the perfect woman?"

"Never. That's literally the stupidest thing a person can do. Marriage equals misery." He looks me straight in the eye while he talks but there's something hollow about his words— like he's repeated this mantra many times to convince himself it's true. "You can't spend fifty years with someone and not let each other down at some point. Or just generally grow to hate one another."

"Wow," I say quietly. "I guess you've got it all figured out then."

"Yes, I have." He gives me a firm nod. "I'd think you'd agree with me after suffering the loss of your parents."

"Because I've been hurt before?"

"Precisely."

"But the thing is, once you've been loved so fully and unconditionally, you know it's real and that it'll happen again."

Pierce stares at me, considering my words. "That surprises me. Were I in your shoes, I would have come to the opposite conclusion—that people leave you so it's best not to get too attached."

Shaking my head, I say, "I love having people I can rely on and trust. And even though I didn't have my parents to help me figure it out, I always had Harrison and my Uncle Oscar until I was eighteen. And a lot of the staff at the resort have helped guide us and teach us what we need to know. One woman in particular, Rosy, who works in the office at the resort, has been a lot like a mum to us since we got here." I sigh, thinking of how angry I've been with Rosy for the past couple of weeks. "She gives us shit when we need it."

"Sounds lovely," he says sarcastically.

"It is, actually. Rosy and her husband never had children, so in a way, we've become the family we each needed."

"I'm glad you had that, Emma. Unfortunately, I didn't grow up in a world where any of that would have been possible." Pierce stares down at his empty plate for a moment, and when he looks back at me, he smiles too brightly. "But I suppose we should get back to work, shouldn't we?"

"I suppose we should. It must be getting late by now."

We stand and bring the dishes into the kitchen, Pierce managing to tuck the empty wine bottle under his bad arm and carry a considerable amount with his other hand. "Don't feel sorry for me, Emma. Please. I'm happy the way I am. And I'm smart enough to know to be grateful for what I've got."

I stare at him for a moment before putting the dishes in the sink and turning on the water to rinse them. Somehow, this little act reminds me of what I am to him. No matter what I was feeling earlier, no matter how intimately we were just speaking—I am just a means to an end because in his mind, money breeds reliability in a way nothing else will.

TWENTY-ONE

Meaningless Things You Don't Ever Want to Forget

Pierce

Thoughtful silence fills the space while Emma does the dishes. I help somewhat uselessly with one hand, not knowing what to say and wishing we could go back to where we were before dinner, before we were honest. I find myself worried that I've disappointed her somehow with my views on family and the general lack of reliability of the average human. I tell myself it shouldn't matter what she thinks.

I've never really cared what anyone thinks, come to think of it. My entire life, I've just drawn my own conclusions and gone on my blissful way, so I don't see why today should be any different. Just because I've spent every waking moment with her for days, and I find her ridiculously attractive, doesn't mean I should upend everything I believe just to please her. The reality is that we're nothing to each other, no matter how many pheromones flood the room when we're together.

Glancing over at the table, I see my laptop sitting open, waiting for us to finish the scene that would come off sounding false were I to go back to it now.

I give Emma an easy smile. "I say we make some cocktails and lighten the mood in here."

"Certainly. What would you like me to make?" Emma asks in a very formal tone that says she, too, feels the need to remind herself of what we are to each other.

"Have you ever had an old-fashioned?"

"I thought those went out with Model T."

"They're delicious. I say we bring them back." I open the top cupboard and take down two tumblers. Emma moves over to the liquor cabinet and before she can ask what ingredients to get out, I say, "I can handle this one-handed. You relax for a few minutes." She gives me a skeptical look until I say, "Grab my phone over there and put on some music for us."

"What would you like to hear?" Emma asks, walking over to the table.

"Ladies' choice." I place a teaspoon of sugar into each glass, and then sprinkle a few dashes of bitters, then a bit of water. Taking a spoon out of the drawer, I muddle the mixture until it's dissolved, then fill the glasses with ice and add whiskey almost to the rim. Opening the mini-bar, I'm pleased to find some cocktail cherries. The unmistakable sound of Mumford and Sons starts up, and I force myself not to tell her that they're a nice group of guys. I despise name droppers, even though at this moment, I wouldn't mind impressing her.

Emma walks over and opens the jar of cherries for me. "When did you learn to make those?"

"My parents used to host a lot of parties when I was young. They refused to invite me until I mastered the art of mixing cocktails."

"Oh," she says, sounding horrified. "How old were you?"

"Seven or eight, I guess."

"Really?" she asks, her face falling.

"No. Not really," I say with a hint of a grin. "The movie *Cocktail* was on the telly once when I was going through my 'I want to be the best at everything, just like Tom Cruise' phase when I was a teenager. Since I wasn't old enough to be a fighter pilot or a lawyer, and our nanny had a love for libations, she was only too happy to be my taste tester."

"I don't know which story is sadder—the sob story you made up or the real one," Emma says.

"Neither is cause for pity. I promise, I'm fine." I pick up one of the glasses and hand it to her, delighted when her fingers brush mine. "Let's see if I've still got it." Raising my glass in the air, I say, "To Luc and Oona."

"May they have a dozen little warrior babies who can tame dragons and wield a hammer like Thor." Emma grins over the rim of her glass as she takes a sip.

***

Three hours and four cocktails later, we haven't exactly gotten back to work, but we have spent one of the most enjoyable evenings I can remember in a very long time. Somehow, we got on the subject of exes and I found myself sharing way too much about my first girlfriend—a certain airheaded teen pop music sensation that, if you think back to the year 2005, you'll most definitely remember.

We've just been laughing ourselves silly, swinging on the side-by-side hammocks under the stars as I regale her with tales of my efforts in memorizing pickup lines à la *Night at the Roxbury.*

"Okay, worst part about being a writer..." Emma says swinging wildly on her hammock.

"Editing, hands down. Well, to be honest, two years of writer's block wasn't exactly a cakewalk, either. Oh, and I suppose the signings aren't exactly my cup of tea."

"Yes, it sounds dreadful—all that smiling and talking to people who adore you," Emma says, giving me a sideways look.

"Not to mention how sore my hand gets from signing my name by the hour."

"Awful. Have you considered work as a coal miner?"

"Obviously, but none of them would be tough enough to take my place as a writer, so..."

She laughs, and I lie back and revel in the delicious sound of making her happy.

"Your turn. Worst part of being a chef."

"Scrubbing pots."

"Is that why you want to get out of here and run a proper restaurant kitchen? So someone else can do that bit for you?"

"Would there be any other reason?" Emma asks, grinning over at me. She reaches up both hands over her head and smiles up at the night sky, looking very dreamy, I might add. "I missed the stars," she says, her words slurring together ever so slightly.

"When? As far as I recall, they never went anywhere."

"Hardy har har. When I was living in New York, even though I *knew* they were there, I hated not being able to see them. Here you can see them *all*."

I stare up at the millions of tiny lights framed by the treetops and slow my hammock to a stop with one foot. "They really are rather brilliant," I say after a moment of reverence. "I can see how you'd miss them. Once you know they're all up there."

"I don't think I could ever give them up again."

"That's too bad." Shit, did I just say that out loud?

"Why is it too bad?" she asks, narrowing her eyes at me in confusion.

Son of a bitch. I really did say that out loud. "I have no idea. I must be drunk. Whose idea was it to drink anyway?"

"Pretty sure it was yours."

"Must have been. I'm not as bright as people give me credit for. I really should be working."

"Yes, as much as I didn't want to tell you, you're under a terrible deadline."

Chuckling, I find myself reaching out for her hand when we swing toward each other. I take hold of it and we both stop and just look at each other. Her skin is warmth and satin and is absolutely irresistible to me. Rubbing my thumb over her knuckles, I glance at her beautiful mouth and let myself wish for a moment. For what, I don't know, but for something other than the existence I've known. Maybe I'd like to see the world through her eyes, missing the stars, unabashedly trusting people, and believing love could be real.

We're both fully clothed and yet I feel stripped bare in front of her. Even though I'm a little buzzed, I can't help but still feel like this is all too much. More than it should be, more than it can be, and yet...

Maybe she's feeling the same way, because she suddenly closes her eyes. Grinning, she says, "Let's sleep out here tonight."

"All right, Emma. Anything you want."

A moment later, her breathing becomes heavy and her grip loosens. Her arm drops down beside her hammock and I feel a strange pang as I watch her sleep.

I stare at her just long enough to burn her image into my brain so I'll be able to recall her lying next to me even when I'm ninety-five. After a few moments, I decide enough is enough. I steady myself as I stand, and carefully lift her out of the hammock and carry her inside. I know my hand will hurt like a bugger tomorrow, but at the moment, I couldn't care less. I have her in my arms now and that's all that matters, really.

I walk her to the bedroom and lay her down on the giant bed, then, unable to stop myself, I brush the back of my forefinger against her cheek.

She smiles without opening her eyes and turns toward my hand.

Covering her with the duvet, I whisper, "Good night, beautiful girl."

Then I take a deep breath, turn, and walk out to get back to work.

TWENTY-TWO

Chocolate Cake and Other Dangerous Cravings

Emma

I wake feeling disoriented and pat my hands on the bed, trying to figure out where I am. The last thing I remember is the stars and Pierce's smiling face. Were we holding hands? Yes, I think we were.

I open my eyes and blink for a moment, seeing that the sky is starting to light up ever so slightly, causing a muted orange glow to the room. I listen carefully but don't hear anything coming from outside the bedroom. I'm not sure what I was dreaming about, but I know it had something to do with Pierce because of the warm gooey feeling in my chest like melted chocolate in fresh-out-of-the-oven chocolate chip cookies.

I want him.

That is an undeniable fact that I haven't told anyone else. I've never met a man like him before—someone so sure about everything, including how hopeless humans are as a species. I wholeheartedly disagree, but at the same time, I can't help but respect the hell out of his conviction. There's nothing wishy-washy about Pierce Davenport. Nothing soft (especially not that body, but I digress).

Our evening's conversation comes rushing to mind and I feel sad for him in a way that I haven't felt for anyone before. I may have lost my parents when I was a little girl, but as far as I can tell he never had any to begin with. When you know you're loved and that you matter to people in this world, even if they disappear suddenly, you take that love with you wherever you go and you know without a doubt that it exists. I don't think he has ever felt like he mattered to anyone, and the thought of that is absolutely unimaginable.

Tears fill my eyes and I sit up, trying to convince myself not to feel sad for him and to remind myself that this is not what my heart thinks it is. It's just a business deal, and we're just using each other to get what we each need. I help him and he'll let me be a hero to my friends and family. He'll also put me years ahead in my plan for world cuisine domination.

But still, it's probably okay to let myself dream a little about what it would be like if this was the start of something wonderful...

His smile pops into my mind and his deep, full, sexy-as-hell laugh. The smell of his aftershave comes to mind next. He carries the light scent of a man who has it all, including the answers. Now, the words I typed earlier fill my brain and warm my insides. They call to me to go find him and experience his touch for myself, even though I know it would be both wrong and a complete disaster.

Well, wrong, yes, but calling it a disaster might be a bit dramatic. How much of a disaster would it really be to have multiple orgasms provided by a ridiculously hot man who happens to be asleep on the other side of that door?

And how *wrong* really? It's not like either of us would be betraying anyone. We're both decidedly unattached. We're both consenting adults. Well, if we consented that is. And we'd both receive a great deal of satisfaction from the experience, wouldn't we?

Yes. Yes, we would.

And even better, we'd both know exactly what it is and what it isn't. It's not long-term. It's not a 'relationship.' It would just be lots of amazing sex between two consenting, lust-filled adults who happen to be on a private island paradise together for a few weeks...

Okay, Emma. That's all just crazy talk. You can't have him now and you never will, so just try to think of something else to satisfy you.

Chocolate. There are two slices of Belgian chocolate cake in the fridge that we left uneaten. If Pierce didn't get to them after I went to sleep—okay, passed out, I can admit it—they both have my name on them.

I stand and sneak to the door, telling myself I'm not going out there for sex. Only for chocolate. I won't even peek at his mostly nude body. He sleeps in just his boxer briefs, a little fact I figured out two nights ago when I needed a drink of water.

I open the door and tiptoe across the moonlit living room, catching sight of him laying on the couch. Even in the dark, you can see he's hot AF. How did he come by those muscles? Okay, maybe I can peek for just a few seconds, then stuff all my lust deep down inside while I gorge myself on cake. Yes, that's a solid plan. Just like that solid man laying right there.

What a gentleman really, to give me the bed when he's paying an exorbitant amount to sleep in it. What a very hot, only-in-his-boxer-briefs, super-buff, incredibly talented gentleman. Oh yes, mummy likey.

Licking my lips, I watch him sleep for long enough to be considered very creepy. At least I hope he's asleep. I finally tear my eyes from his abs long enough to look at his face.

Oh shit. His eyes are open.

"Can I help you?" he asks.

Jumping back a little, I whisper, "I thought you were sleeping."

"So, you thought you'd watch me?"

"Of course not. I just came out to get some of that chocolate cake and...I wasn't sure if maybe you'd want some, so..."

"So you thought you'd stare at me?" he asks, sitting up and rubbing his scruffy chin with his hand.

Is he grinning at me? Yes, the hot bastard is most definitely grinning.

"I wasn't *staring*, I was just trying to ascertain your level of awakeness." Yeah, I'm making up words now, so what of it?

He bursts out laughing and then stands, letting his eyes roam over my body. I'm still in the dress I put on after my shower but the look on his face makes me feel completely nude (and happy about it).

"Did you put me to bed?" I ask.

"I thought I would return the favour from the other night when you brought me home from the hospital."

"Thank you. In that case, I'll share the cake with you," I say over my shoulder as I walk toward the kitchen.

"You mean you were going to eat both pieces yourself?"

"I thought you were a gentleman. A gentleman would never ask a lady how much cake she plans to eat." I switch on the stove light which, in my opinion, sets just the right ambiance for sunrise cake eating.

"A lady wouldn't eat all the cake in the house without offering the gentleman some." He takes a couple of forks out of the drawer while I retrieve our snack. Each piece is in its own take-out container, so I take the lids off and pass him one while he deposits a fork in my container.

Opening the fridge again, I get out a jug of milk, and when I turn back, he's already gotten two glasses down for us. "Milk's a must with chocolate cake," I say.

"Agreed." With one hand, he manages to hop up on the counter so he's sitting with his back against the cupboards. In only his underwear, but I should probably stop focusing on that.

"Impressive," I say as I put my cake down and use both hands to lift myself onto the counter next to him. I sit in the corner, my knee barely touching his.

He's right there. I could reach out and touch *all* of him from here. *Nope, Emma. Cake. Just eat the cake.*

"You couldn't sleep either, or was it my creepy stalking that woke you?" I ask, taking an overly big bite.

"I was already up. I finished that sex scene after I put you to bed and it left me feeling a bit...wired."

Laughing a little, I say, "Wired? Is that author speak for randy?"

"Maybe," he answers sheepishly before lifting his fork to his mouth. When he swallows, he has a long gulp of milk, then says, "Having a beautiful woman asleep in the next room doesn't help much in that regard, I'm afraid."

The look he is giving me is a definite 'let's do this' expression. He glances at my lips, then his eyes flick back up to mine.

"Do you want me to start sleeping on the houseboat again?" I ask, feeling my heart thump away in my chest.

Reaching up, he wipes a tiny bit of chocolate off my lip with his thumb and sucks it into his mouth. "Not at all. Do you want to go back?"

"Not a bit," I say breathlessly.

Leaning toward me, he lowers his mouth over mine, keeping it poised so close to mine, I can almost taste him. *Please don't let anything interrupt this moment. I will literally explode if he doesn't kiss me right now.*

I close my eyes and move toward him, suddenly terrified that he's going to come to his senses and pull away. My heart pounds in my chest as I wait for him to make the next move.

Will he leave me wanting or will he lean in and make this happen? He doesn't pull away. He doesn't disappoint me with an abrupt distance. Instead, I feel his palm on my neck, warm and steady as he draws me so near. I can feel the warmth of his mouth even though we aren't quite touching yet. And suddenly, I fall into a dream, the most perfect one I've ever had in which the perfect man is giving me a soft and perfect kiss. There's an unexpected tenderness to his touch, a quiet desperation that hints at a wild need to be held.

His kiss is careful at first, as though he's checking once more to see if I want this. And I do. I want this in the worst way, even though it's the last thing I should want. This is just business. He'll be gone in a few weeks. And yet, I'm still parting my lips to make room for him to take what he wants from me.

Oh my, now he's kissing me full on the mouth, and wow, this is one toe-curlingly amazing kiss. I melt like butter in a hot pan, moaning a little as I drop the cake and my fork on the floor. Reaching up, I cup his jaw with one hand and run my fingers along his abs with the other.

His mouth feels so right, the way it moves, thrilling me to my core. It's all so new and yet it somehow feels as though we've kissed a thousand times before. There's something about the way we move together that promises it will always be a thrill with him, no matter how many times we do this.

Pressing my hand to his chest, I feel his heart beating and it seems to speak to me, telling me yes with every pulse.

We stay like this, caressing and kissing each other for what could be minutes or hours. I lose all track of time and place, and of who I am. There is only overwhelming desire and the perfection of this moment. We kiss until I'm so breathless and frenzied that I have to pull back and rest my forehead on his to recover.

We sit side-by-side, panting, before starting again. The only thought that I can hold onto is that I want this. I want more. I don't ever want to stop. We stay like this, sitting beside each other, making out for way longer than my lady bits can handle, then finally, he slides down off the counter and positions himself in front of me, spreading my knees so he can get closer. Pulling me to the edge of the counter, he gives me a preview of what's waiting for me inside those briefs. And I could not be more thrilled. Because, wow.

He drizzles kisses down my neck that have me wrapping my legs around his lean back. "Emma, I don't want to lead you on."

"I was thinking the same thing," I say, biting his earlobe. "We can't really do this. You're a guest and if we do this, I could get in a lot of trouble. Plus, I wouldn't want you to think I'm using you for a good recommendation, when really..." Kiss. Kiss. Kiss. "I'm using you for your body."

"Perfect," he says, crushing my mouth with his. We let our tongues do the talking for a minute, then he pulls back. "Wait. We're really doing this though, aren't we?"

"Fuck, yes," I say, looking him dead in the eye. "We're definitely doing this but only unofficially."

"I promise. I'll take this to my grave," he says, sliding his hand up under my dress.

"Where's a bearskin rug when you need one?" I ask as he starts to lift my dress over my head. I help him out, then he tosses it behind him, leaving me in only my lacy white just-in-case knickers.

"It's my writing that did it for you, isn't it?"

"Will you be disappointed if I say yes?" I ask, reaching down and groping his considerable package.

"Nope," he says. "Not a bit."

I slide down off the counter and wrap my arms around his neck so we can keep going. We keep our mouths locked while he guides me in the general direction of the bedroom, although to be honest, I don't really care where he takes me as long as it's only a few more seconds until I can get back to all that delicious grinding sans knickers...

TWENTY-THREE

Not-So-Best-Kept Secrets...

Pierce

"That was...magnificent," I say, smiling up at the ceiling like a happy fool. My heart is pounding and I am trying to get my breathing under control so she won't think me out of shape. Although we did just do it—and rather well for only having use of the one hand—three times, so really, is there any chance she'll think me a slacker in bed? Probably not.

"Magnificent?" Emma laughs, her delightfully naked body strewn across me. "I've never heard it described quite that way before."

"Would you prefer stunningly wonderful? Breathtakingly satisfying? Remarkably grand?"

"Only if you mean it."

"Oh, I mean it. You are quite the apt cowgirl. Giddy up," I say, slapping her on the bottom lightly and making her squeal with laughter.

"Was it good for you?" I ask as I run my fingers lazily along her spine, feeling deliriously happy for once in my life.

"Yes. You're much better than I expected," Emma says.

"What?" My hand freezes in place.

Emma lifts her head to face me. "Well when I first met you, that is. I figured you were too pompous and self-centred to be good at the sexy stuff."

"No offence, though..." I say, raising one eyebrow.

"Come *on*, you can't tell me you wanted me when we first met. It's not like I was exactly looking my best."

"Oh, I wanted you all right. In that tiny, left-nothing-to-the-imagination uniform? Big turn-on for any man. The way your breasts were stuffed in there. I spent the entire conversation secretly wishing those buttons would pop." I smile at the memory.

"Seriously?"

"Yes. I'm a man. We're a little pathetic that way. But, now that I've been given the coveted 'better than expected' review, I can die happy," I say sarcastically.

"Wow, as an author, I would have thought a mediocre critique would bounce right off you by now," she says, shaking her head and trying not to laugh.

"On the contrary," I say, flipping us both over so I'm now on top. "Poor reviews spur me on to levels of greatness previously unknown to humankind."

Emma wrinkles her nose, pretending to be skeptical. "I kind of doubt it, but I'm willing to let you try again."

"How kind of you," I answer, working my way down toward her lovely breasts.

The sound of the front door closing has us both freezing in place. "Was that...?" I whisper.

"Hello, it's Alfred!"

"Shit. Shit. Shit!" Emma says, squirming out from under me.

We both scurry around the bedroom to find clothing.

"My dress is in the kitchen!" Emma hisses, grabbing a tank top and some shorts out of her overnight bag.

I yank on a pair of khaki pants and a T-shirt—no easy feat with this stupid cast.

"Sir? Mr. Davenport? Your breakfast is ready," Alfred calls.

I exit the bedroom trying to wipe the sheepish 'I've been caught diddling the help' expression off my face. A breakfast of scones, pastries, and fresh fruit has already been laid out for us on the table.

"Ah, yes. Brilliant. Thank you, Alfred."

"You haven't seen Ms. Banks, have you? Her brother has been trying to reach her for a few days now." Alfred's gaze lands on her dress, which is strewn across the fruit bowl on the island at the moment.

And, of course, that's when Emma walks out of the bedroom with an unmistakably guilty look on her face.

Alfred makes a *tsk*ing sound and raises his eyebrows at her. "Mr. Banks needs you to call him immediately."

"Yes, of course. Thank you," she says, biting her lip.

Turning to me, Alfred says, "If there's nothing else, I shall leave you to your morning."

"Thank you," I answer with a nod. "Listen, Alfred..."

Holding up one hand, Alfred says, "I assure you I'm nothing if not discreet, sir."

"I appreciate that, Alfred," Emma says, letting her shoulders drop a tiny bit. "It's nice to know you understand."

"Please don't mistake my consideration for Mr. Davenport's privacy for approval of your actions," he says coldly.

"That's hardly fair, Alfred. Emma and I are both at fault here."

"Yes, but as the guest, you're under no obligation to conduct yourself according to a code of servitude," he answers, narrowing his eyes at her in a way that makes me want to punch him. "Ms. Banks, however, *is*."

"That will be all, Alfred," I say, matching his tone.

We both stand perfectly still waiting for him to leave. When the door closes behind him, Emma lets out a long sigh and covers her face with one hand. "This is bad. Very bad."

I stride over and take her hand away from her face, then gently lift her chin so she's looking up at me. Giving her my best rogue smile, I say, "Is it really so awful for someone to know you slept with me?"

"This is serious, you big dope," she says swatting my arm. "I'm supposed to be showing how responsible I am, not...doing very naughty things with our most important guest. If my brother finds out, he's going to be furious with me."

Wrapping my arms around her waist, I pull her near. "So what? My brothers and I spend most of our lives being angry with each other. Is it really worth giving up the greatest sex of your life for?"

Emma grins in spite of herself. "I said better than expected."

"But you meant it was the greatest sex of your life. It was in the subtext," I say, happy to see her smile again.

All too quickly, the line of worry reappears between her eyebrows. "We should stop," she says, breaking away from me and pacing the room. "First of all, you really can't afford to waste even a moment right now. It's coming down to the wire here. You're in a race to the finish, and if you lose...well, I don't even want to think about that possibility. Those NBO hacks will ruin this perfectly amazing series," she says with an indignation I can't help but adore.

"See, when you say things like that, it makes it damn near impossible for me not to want to get you back into bed."

"I'm trying to be serious here, Pierce. I didn't spend the last two weeks typing until my wrists are killing me just so the world will get some third-rate version of *Clash of Crowns*. No, thank you. There's *no way* I'm going to let that happen, even if it means cutting you off from the most magnificently grand sex on the planet."

"Do we really have to stop completely? There's only so long each day I can write," I say, but I can see my words aren't registering, not with the look of panic on her face.

"Oh God, if anyone else finds out about this, I'll never hear the end of it. I don't know if I can trust Alfred and Phyllis farther than I could throw them. They might be a pair of old gossips for all I know. Shit. How am I supposed to convince my brother to hand over an entire restaurant to me if he thinks I'm going to be some loosey goosey rule breaker? I had this whole plan to get myself off this hellhole island and now..." She trails off, biting her thumbnail for a moment, completely lost in thought. "He did not put me through culinary school so I could end up in bed with every guest that happens to fancy me."

Every guest? "Emma, do you think you might be panicking a little bit unnecessarily here? I highly doubt you're going to end up in bed with *every* guest."

Emma stops pacing and looks up at me. "Oh yeah? So far, I've slept with 100% of the guests I've served since I finished culinary school! *100%, Pierce.* Those are not good odds!"

I walk over and put my hand on her shoulder. "Emma, stop. It was one night. I promise you, you haven't ruined your life. If they talk, you can always deny it. Big deal. We both walked out of the bedroom. So what? It's not like he has video proof of us doing it on the counter or something."

Emma points to her crumpled dress. "He saw that! He knows."

"Maybe you're messy. It's his word against yours. And he may not say anything at all," I say. "He doesn't strike me as the type to gossip. He gets off on being a pious perfect servant. There's no way he's spilling anyone's secrets. He's more likely to hold his disapproval over you until the end of time."

"Oh, much better," she says sarcastically.

"It'll be fine. You're not planning to stay out here anyway."

"True," she says, nodding quickly.

There's a shift in her mood and a budding hope rises in me that we can pick up where we left off before Alfred arrived. I lower my face to hers. "Everything will be okay, I promise." I take her hand in mine and rub her wrist with my fingertips. "Did you say your hands are sore?"

She nods, looking up at me and shrugging. "A little, yes."

"Here, let me help," I say in a low tone, massaging her hand.

"Pierce. I'm serious, we can't do this anymore."

"I know. I heard every word you said, Emma, and I promise I'm not trying to get you back into bed," I say, glancing at her pouty lips. "This is a professional courtesy hand massage."

"It better stop at my elbows. I'm serious," she says, her voice thick with lust.

"I promise not to give you a happy ending," I answer, licking my lips.

"Good. I hate happy endings anyway," Emma says, gazing into my eyes in a way that says she absolutely adores happy endings. "We'll chalk last night up to cocktails and...the residual effect of working on a sex scene together."

"Absolutely. We'll take a giant step back to strictly business territory."

"Yes, we'll be strictly professional from here on."

***

171

Okay, so we may have not stuck with the whole 'keeping it professional' thing yesterday. But we did manage to last until well after ten in the evening before giving in to our lust, so I'd say that's a win. Then it was off to bed to work off our collective sexual energy before getting a solid night's sleep.

This morning, we're off to an early start, having woken with the birds at the sunrise. After a few minutes of cuddling, Emma hopped up out of bed and said, "Come on! I need to know if Ogden is going to live."

So now she's whipping up a fast breakfast while I shower (with a plastic bag over my hand—very sexy, I know) and try not to think about her naked body. Shutting off the water, I take a towel off the rack with a loud snap. Whistling, I dry off quickly, hoping to be all dressed and suave before Emma finishes preparing brunch. I fill the sink with hot water and spread some shaving cream on my face. Glancing at the man in the mirror, I see a guy who cannot stop smiling.

It's the series, I promise you. Nothing feels as satisfying as writing after such a long dry spell. Unless it's you-know-what with the perfect woman after a self-imposed sex exile (or sexile, as I call it) while I was trying to crack the ending of the series.

My mind wanders to having Emma on my lap after dinner last night. She really is the perfect woman—well, as perfect as they get, anyway. She's so fun, and sexy, and smart. Gorgeous, too. That long, auburn hair of hers just does it for me. The lean curves and those long legs, too. Wow.

But it's not just her looks. There's so much more to her. She's so committed to my book, and she has this general sense of optimism that keeps me going when I'm tired of writing and feel like giving up for the day. She's a real ball-buster too, which I don't mind in a woman, quite frankly. Not literally, of course. Were someone to literally bust your actual balls, that would be no bueno. I was referring to the 'no excuses' thing she's got going on. Just do it. She's like a gorgeous Nike ad come to life.

I'm torn between spending the next few weeks madly writing and telling NBO to do whatever the hell they want to my world so I can spend the entire time in bed doing very naughty things to Emma. But it's not just the naughty things I want to do. I want to tell her everything I've ever thought, show her every word I've ever written, find out what she thinks about every topic under the stars. And between you and me, I've never wanted to do *any* of those things before. I've always been 100% certain those types of sentiments only existed in greeting cards men buy their wives to make up for decades of neglect. But now, I'm not so sure...

Strolling from the *en suite* into the bedroom in the buff, I stand in front of the closet trying to figure out the perfect thing to wear. I don't want to make it look like I'm trying too hard, but after her seeing me all rumpled and down-trodden, it would be nice if I could make a good impression.

I'm going with my favourite white T-shirt that displays the fact that I *do* work out regularly and a pair of low-slung cargo pants for a bit of a tough guy look. Show her I'm not just some rich guy who can string a few words together. I'm a man.

Socks or no socks?

Good God, Pierce, pull it together. You sound like a fourteen-year-old boy. You might as well douse yourself in Lynx body spray and floss for her.

When I exit the bedroom, I see her standing in front of the stove. "Mmm...smells yummy." Walking up behind her, I wrap my arm around her and nuzzle her neck for a moment while she stirs the eggs in a pan.

"You smell kind of nice yourself. And your face is so smooth," she says.

"I may have decided to get rid of the scruff in case you were getting sick of whisker burn."

"That's rather presumptuous of you," she answers, giving me a sassy look. "What if I don't want to sleep with you again?"

"That would surprise me greatly."

"And why's that?"

"Because of all the moaning and grinding you did before you left to make breakfast."

"I did not grind," she says, her eyes wide with shock.

"Tell that to my balls," I say. "They'd argue that you most certainly were grinding."

Clapping her hand over her mouth, Emma bursts out laughing, her cheeks turning a delightful pink. "You're terrible."

"Never said I wasn't." I lean down a little and nuzzle her nose with mine. "Now, where were we?"

"Talking about your delicate balls," she says, grinning.

"Hey, they're not delicate. They're very sturdy. Just because you were trying to grind them into a fine powder, doesn't mean they aren't very manly balls."

"As opposed to womanly balls?"

"Exactly. Now, stop trying to change the subject because we were talking about how badly you want to kiss me again."

Lifting herself onto her tiptoes, Emma gives me a lingering kiss. "Mmm. Smooth like jazz."

I chuckle, wrapping my hand around her waist and pulling her close. "Shall we free-style it?"

"You're such a nerd," she murmurs, brushing her lips against mine. "And a very naughty boy who needs to work."

A few minutes later, we're sitting knee-to-knee digging into a most delectable breakfast. She's made so much food, I honestly don't know where to start: the raspberry compote-filled crepes, the fresh fruit, the scrambled eggs, the bacon, or her. I watch as she takes a bite of a strawberry and decide I need to let her eat. If she's anywhere near as hungry as I am, it would be the kind thing to do.

After our first few bites, she wipes her mouth with her napkin. "Now, I think we should set down some ground rules."

Uh oh. Ground rules sounds so...ruley. Pausing my hand halfway between my plate and my mouth, I say, "Like what?"

"Well, it's clear that you can't get enough of me, and I understand, I really do. But you have a serious deadline, and there's no way I'm going to get in the way of that, no matter how badly you want to shag me."

"Damn. You're right. So what do you propose?"

"I think we should agree not to do anything physical again until you finish the entire thing and it's been sent off."

"No deal. That'll take weeks." I shake my head and have a sip of my coffee. "I have a counter-proposal. After every scene I complete, we take a break for a specified amount of time to drive each other wild."

"No way. You don't have time for that. End of each day but only if your brain is too exhausted to write, and no pretending just so you can get into my knickers."

"You drive a hard bargain, but I'll accept."
"Smart man."

***

Three Weeks Later
So, the whole 'my brain is too tired to write' thing is a bit of a moving target. To be honest, these last few days, we've moved more to a schedule that resembles writing as a break when we're too tired to have sex. It's honestly not been that good for my productivity, but damn, if I'm not having the best time ever.

The good news is that the pages I've been sending to Zach have been received every bit as well as I'd hoped, and I only have three more chapters to finally be free of this series forever. We should easily get through those today, which is why I suggested we take an early morning dip in the infinity pool to wake us up.

Breakfast has been served so we know we have this entire island to ourselves until we call for lunch. There's a tremendous feeling knowing you have this kind of uninterrupted privacy—it's like the world's greatest aphrodisiac. Unless you're one of those people who likes the idea of getting caught. Then you'd hate it here.

Emma stands in front of me in the water, then leans back to dip her hair in, her lovely, perky breasts rising up so I can see them. Mmm yes, I think I'll start right there. I can only use one hand and my other one needs to stay on the pool deck so as not to wet my cast, but it's totally going to be worth it. Pulling her to me with my good hand, I lift her up and hold her in place while she rubs up against me and we kiss like it's the first and last time rolled into one.

"Emma, what the hell?" a male voice calls out before a loud laughing sound comes from the same general direction.

We freeze in place, then we both turn our faces to see who exactly is watching us. It's her brother, Harrison, who I met when I checked in, and a younger-looking version of her brother, who I can only assume is also...her brother. Well, if that won't ruin a perfectly good erection, nothing will.

"Ha ha ha! Emma! You lady dog!" the younger one says.

Unwrapping her legs from my waist, Emma crouches in the water and closes her eyes for a moment, then says, "Will, when did you get back?"

"Late last night," he says, looking much more amused than the older one.

"Emma, I'd like to talk to you," Harrison says, looking like a vein is about to pop in his neck. "*Now.*"

He grabs one of the bathrobes off the chaise longue next to the pool and holds it out to her, then turns his back to us while Emma hurries out of the water and puts it on. The two disappear around the corner toward the front of the villa, leaving me completely nude with their little brother.

"I'm Will. Emma's my big sister."

"Pierce."

"I know. I'm a huge fan of the show," he says with a wide grin. "How's the ending coming along? Are you going with happy or horrifying?"

"At the moment, it's looking like it'll be horrifying."

TWENTY-FOUR

Once the Cat is Out of the Bag, There's Really No Getting It Back in...

Emma

And, just like that, our perfect little fantasy bubble has burst.

I hurry behind Harrison as he stalks across the deck and around the corner, my wet feet slapping on the smooth wooden planks. My heart pounds and my stomach churns as I scramble to think of how to spin what is an impossibly bad situation. When he reaches the far side of the villa, he turns, crosses his arms, and gives me a stern look from under his eyebrows like he used to do when I was twelve and he was sixteen and I was in major trouble.

"You probably should have called ahead," I say, going for a pre-emptive strike.

"Oh, is *that* what went wrong here?" he asks, his head snapping back. "I didn't call ahead to make sure I wouldn't interrupt the naked chef serving up a little breakfast spread?"

"Calm down, Harrison. It's not a big deal."

"Not a big—?!" he starts, then shuts his mouth and glares, zeroing in on my neck that might as well just have a sign attached to it that says 'Pierce was here.' "Jesus. Is that a hickey? You know what? Do *not* answer that."

I close my robe a little tighter, feeling thoroughly exposed. I can't see my own face, but I'm pretty sure I look guilty as sin.

"How long has this—" He gestures repeatedly to me and in the direction of the pool. "—been going on?"

177

"About three weeks," I answer in a voice so quiet I can barely hear it.

Apparently, he heard it, because he says, "Three—!" He stops and shakes his head, then takes a deep breath. "All right, I'm going to try to stay calm until I have all the facts. Have you two talked about a future together over the past twenty-one days or has it just been...*that* in the pool back there?"

"The second one," I mumble. "But technically that was the first time in the pool, so..."

Holding up one hand, he says, "I don't need that level of detail. I'm just trying to determine whether I need to go kick his ass or not."

Rolling my eyes, I say, "For God's sake, Harrison, I'm a grown woman and it's not 1802. If I want to have a bit of a fling, it's hardly going to scandalize the entire island."

"So, this is okay to you? Some meaningless fling with a guy who's just going to up and leave in a couple of days?"

"Well, it's better than nothing!" I snap. "It's not like I'm going to find Prince Charming while my brother has me sequestered like a nun out here in the middle of nowhere."

Leaning down, Harrison lowers his voice. "Are you actually trying to blame *me* for this?"

"No, of course not. It's just not exactly easy to be out here alone all the time."

"Well, you haven't exactly been lonely since your first week here, have you?" Harrison waves the thought away with both hands, then says, "You know what? It doesn't matter. You're done here. Pack up your stuff because you're coming back with me to the resort where I can keep an eye on you."

"No, I'm not," I say, folding my arms across my chest. "Pierce needs me."

"Excuse me? Did you just say no?" Harrison asks, his nostrils flaring. "I don't think you understand. *I'm* the boss, not you. And I'm also your big brother. Mr. Can't Keep It in His Pants is lucky I'm not giving him the ass-kicking of a lifetime right now."

"I'd like to see you try. *I* could kick your ass." Okay, that bit is not at all true. Harrison is ridiculously tough, but I couldn't think of anything else to say. "Now, in case you hadn't noticed, I'm an adult, which means my love life is my own business! Besides, he's *desperate* and I'm the only one who can help him," I say firmly. "There's no way I'm going to abandon him in his hour of need."

"Are you really this naïve? You fell for the lonely, desperate writer routine?" Harrison shakes his head at me.

I jut my chin out defiantly. "That's *not* a thing." It's not, right?

"Sure it is. The old, 'I need you, you're the only one who can save me' bit. Trust me, it's a thing. He's just using you."

"You don't know him. He's not like that."

"And you think you do? What the hell do you think is going to happen here, Emma?" Harrison says, lifting his arms out to his sides, then letting them drop. "He's going to fall in love with you and move to Santa Valentina where he'll write books and you can cook for him for the rest of your life?"

Yes, yes, I do think that. "No, of course I don't think that," I spit out. "I know exactly what's going on here and I'm fine with it."

"You're fine with being used and thrown away."

"Maybe *I'm* using *him*. Did you ever consider that?" I ask, raising my voice.

"I sure as hell hope not because if that's what kind of person you've turned into, I did a shit job of raising you."

Ouch. That would really sting if let it. I make fists and jab them into my hips. "You know what? You should be *thanking* me. He's not suing us over his injuries, *and* he's already told me he's going to have this place booked solid for years to come."

"Is that how he got you into bed? By promising to pimp out our resort to his rich friends in exchange for a little action?" Harrison's face twists in disgust. "And what exactly are *they* going to expect when they get here, huh?"

"Okay, first of all, he has no intention of pimping me out to anyone. In fact, I'm certain he'd be highly insulted by the idea, *as am I*. Second, are you really accusing me of prostituting myself? *Seriously*?!" I whisper-yell. "I would *never* do that, so for you to stand there and..." I stop mid-sentence, unable to string together the rest of that thought as rage courses through my body. "You know what? Fuck you, Harrison."

"You're actually mad at *me*? *You're* the one in the wrong here. You know that, right?"

"What's going on between Pierce and me is *none* of your business. All you need to know is that he offered to be an influencer for us *before* I started sleeping with him. The rest is private."

"But it's *not* private, Emma, because he's a paying guest and I'm your boss." Harrison sighs deeply and closes his eyes for a long second. When he opens them, his expression is grave. "Do you know why I sent you out here? Because *you're* the person I trust the most in this world—other than Libby, of course. You are *the most important* chef cooking for *the most important* guest we will ever have. *You're* the difference between us being able to provide a home for ourselves and good jobs for the entire staff, and having to hand it all over to the bank and walk away with nothing. And you've risked everything for...for what? If things go bad between you two, we have no way of forcing him to keep his word. He can do whatever the hell he wants, including *ruin* us."

His words feel like they could very well crush me and I look down to avoid the grief in Harrison's eyes. I chew on my lip for a second, then say, "He wouldn't do that."

"You are *so* naïve."

"I am not," I say, my anger flaring again. "I know exactly what I'm doing. And no matter what you think of Pierce, he's a man of his word."

"Oh yeah? Did he promise to break your heart? Because that's exactly what he's going to do."

"My heart isn't involved in this, so don't worry about it."

Running his hands through his hair, Harrison shakes his head. "That doesn't make it better, you know. I can't believe you would put a bit of fun ahead of the needs of everyone who works for us, ahead of your family...after everything I've..." He stops himself, but I know he was about to say 'after everything I've done for you.' "I've never been as disappointed in you as I am right now."

And there it is. I've done the very last thing I wanted to do—I've disappointed my big brother. I feel my eyes fill with tears. "I'm sorry, Harrison. I didn't expect this to happen. I was trying to do the right thing for you, and for the resort, but then...I just got caught up...but I can fix it, okay? I'll make sure when he leaves, it's on a good note. It'll be all right, I promise."

"You can't promise that."

"I'll do whatever I can to make it right," I say, wiping the tears from my cheeks.

Harrison gives me a long, hard look, then sighs, but says nothing so I take the opportunity to try to smooth things over. "He's leaving in like...thirty-six hours. I'll help him finish his book, then we'll part ways like two mature adults, and everything will be just fine. You don't have to worry about anything. Seriously. I know I've been reckless, but I'll make sure everything turns out okay."

Rubbing the back of his neck, Harrison says. "I don't have any choice but to say yes, do I?"

"Not really."

"Fine then, but we are *not* done with this."

We walk back around the house, neither of us saying anything. When we turn the corner, I see Pierce, who is now standing on the deck with a towel around his waist looking very uncomfortable. Will, however, is stretched out on a lounge chair sipping a beer and wearing an expression of delighted amusement that makes me want to slap the smile off his face.

Harrison ignores Pierce and looks at Will. "We should go."

Will stands and says, "Great to meet you, Pierce. See you tonight!"

Tonight? WTF? "Umm...what now?"

"You guys are coming to Rosy's for my welcome home dinner," Will says with a broad grin.

No effing way is that happening. Shaking my head quickly, I say, "I don't think so. Pierce is under a seriously tight deadline and—"

"Oh, well, he said he'll definitely finish in time and he didn't want to make you miss a big family get-together," Will says, pointing back at Pierce with his thumb. "Good guy, this one. You picked a good one, Em."

My mouth hangs open as I watch Will stroll closer. He gives me a light punch on the arm. "Six o'clock. Don't be late."

TWENTY-FIVE

So, This is What a Normal Family Dinner is Like...Maybe

Pierce

"We don't have to do this, you know," Emma says as she pulls the parking brake on the jeep we picked up at the resort.

We're currently in front of Rosy and Darnell Brown's house, whom I understand to be sort of surrogate parents to the Banks children. Why they need that, I have no idea. They're all adults, as far as I can tell. Maybe not Will though. He seems like a thirteen-year-old boy with a pituitary gland issue.

"I want to do this, Emma." That's a lie. I most definitely do not want to spend the next three to four hours at Rosy and Darnell's tiny house in San Felipe having an awkward meal with Emma's relatives who likely all think I'm some type of nefarious bastard. But *not* doing it would make Emma look like a poor judge of character, so I insisted we attend for her sake.

"Yeah, it's just that you *really* don't understand what you're about to walk into," she says, closing her eyes and rubbing the bridge of her nose in a way that has me slightly concerned.

"Please. I can handle myself. I assure you I have been in situations with much greater stakes than this," I say, taking her hand in mine and giving it a squeeze.

"But you don't have time for this. We should be working," she says, chewing on the inside of her lip.

"There's only one chapter left and it's already the middle of the night in Avonia, so whether I get it to my publisher now or a few hours from now, it really won't matter. We'll go in, have a nice dinner, then go back and finish the book."

"But they're going to—"

Holding up my hand, I say, "I have to do this. If I don't, your entire family will think you mean nothing to me, and I can't have that."

"Why not?"

"What do you mean, *why not?*"

"Seriously. According to you, you don't even care what *your own* family thinks of you. You're leaving here tomorrow night and you'll never see any of these people again. Why put yourself through this?"

I sigh heavily, not wanting to think about life a day from now. "First of all, are we so certain that I won't see them again? Second, even if that does turn out to be true, I don't want them to think differently of *you.* I don't want them to question *your* judgement, so if you'll allow me to please go in there and make an excellent impression that will reflect well on you, I'd greatly appreciate it."

"Fine," she says, yanking the keys out of the ignition. "But I'm telling you, you do not know what you're getting yourself into..."

Tilting my head, I give her what I'm sure is a condescending look. "Listen, if you experienced the viper pit in which I grew up, you'd know that this evening will be a total breeze for me."

A slightly evil grin crosses her face that has me feeling a tad less cheeky than I did a few seconds ago. "Let's go in then, Mr. Cocky Pants."

"Let's save the cock talk for later," I say, raising my eyebrows up and down. "Time to go wow the fam."

***

"Baby Bear!" an extremely loud voice booms across the lawn as we walk up the sidewalk. "There's my girl!"

A short woman with pulled back black hair and the most colourful dress I've ever seen comes hurrying out of the house, accompanied by two yappy little Jack Russell Terriers. She pulls Emma in for a vigorous hug while the little dogs jump up and bark, trying to get in on the action.

When she lets go, she says, "And this must be your new man!" Looking me up and down, she says, "Mmm mmm mmm. He'll do. Bring it in and give Rosy some sugar."

Emma gives me a 'how are you handling it now?' look, grinning broadly as I'm sucked into a bosomy perfume cloud while one of the dogs nips at my ankle and the other one jumps up, trying to get a hold of my cast. I can't move, however, because Rosy just might squeeze the life out of me in her effort to get every grain of sugar she can. Just when I feel like I'm going to lose consciousness, she lets me go.

"Starsky, Hutch! Get down!" An older man, who I assume is Darnell, comes out the front door. "That goes for you, too, Rosy." He's got a thick Caribbean accent and even thicker black hair. He's wearing a broad grin, a loud shirt printed with enormous green palm leaves, baby blue shorts, brown leather sandals, and black socks pulled up over his considerable calves.

The dogs and Rosy all ignore him and he gives up, moving on to greet Emma while either Starsky or Hutch tries to hump my leg. Not to be outdone, his partner in crime tries to hump *him*.

I try to pry off my furry attacker but Rosy impedes my progress, holding my cast in one hand and groping my bicep with her other one. "Poor dear. How's your hand?"

Seriously, is no one going to stop them?

"Emma! Our little chef returns," Darnell says, the pride written all over his face. "Why haven't we seen you sooner? You've been home for nearly two months." He pulls her in for a big hug, then turns to me. "Is it because of dis guy?" he asks, narrowing his eyes at me.

"Yes, it's all his fault, Darnell. He's kept me busy day and night actually," Emma says, gesturing for me to come over. "Starsky! Stop that!"

I manage to slip away from Rosy's grasp and try to shake off Starsky while I walk over, but it turns out, he's got quite the grip for such a small dog, so I end up dragging him for a few feet until I reach Darnell.

He bends at the waist and swats the dog away, shaking his head. "He's a humper, dat one. No matter what we do, he just won't stop." When he straightens up, Darnell gives me a little nod. "So, you've been keeping Emma busy, eh?"

"Uh, yes. She's been helping me with my book."

Shaking his head, he says, "Your book? Kids these days. I can't keep up wit all the new slang."

"Come on. Let's get out of this damn heat," Rosy says, gesturing for us to make our way up the front steps.

When we walk inside the house, a blast of air conditioning hits me, immediately drying out my eyeballs. Good God, it's cold in here. But on the plus side, the dogs seem to hate it too and they scurry through the living room, through the small kitchen, and out the doggy door into the backyard.

Rosy stands in front of the noisy air conditioning unit for a moment and closes her eyes. "Ahh, that's better."

"She's been gettin' them hot flashes so she keeps the place like an icebox," Darnell mutters.

"You don't be telling my secrets, you old fool, or I'll start telling everybody how many times a night you get up to go pee," she says, narrowing her eyes at her husband.

I can't help but laugh inwardly at their exchange, trying to imagine what my mother would do if my father mentioned anything to do with menopause, even to her. *She* doesn't even want to know how old she is, let alone have it broadcast to strangers.

"You two are a little late so everybody's out in the backyard," Rosy says. "Emma, you stay inside and help me with dinner. Pierce, you go relax and have a beer so we can talk about you without you hearing."

I look at Emma to see if she's okay with this plan. She smiles widely, then leans in and murmurs, "Remember, you're the one who wanted to come here."

A moment later I follow Darnell out into the small but lush garden. Tall palm trees line the space, filled in with flowering, leafy shrubs that surround the cement patio. A wooden picnic table sits under a makeshift awning that looks like it's made from a sail that has been repurposed. In the far corner, a turquoise wooden boat is flipped upside-down, resting on a couple of sawhorses. Based on the bucket of sandpaper and rags, I'm guessing it's being refurbished. Smoke rises from a barbeque and the smell of charcoal briquettes blends with the floral scent of the air.

Darnell takes a beer from an ice-filled cooler and hands it to me. "Now, have you met everybody yet?"

"I've met Harrison and Will, yes," I say, raising my beer to the two brothers who are sitting in metal folding lawn chairs. (One of them is grinning and the other is not. You can probably guess which one is which.)

"Yes, we've seen a lot of Pierce, actually," Will says, standing and shaking my hand.

"Really?" Darnell asks, looking confused. "I thought you just got in last night?"

"I did," Will answers, then turning to the woman next to Harrison, he says, "Libby, have you met Pierce?"

"Not yet," she says, blushing a little when she gets up to greet me. I can tell by the look on her face she knows exactly what happened this morning but she's trying not to think about it.

I extend my hand to her. "Libby, it's a pleasure to meet you. Emma has nothing but the best things to say about you."

"Aww. Thank you. She's like the little sister I never had."

"She's like the little sister *he* should never have had either," Harrison mutters.

"What's that?" Darnell asks Harrison. "You got to speak up, man. My hearing isn't what it used to be."

Libby gives Harrison a sharp look, then settles back into her seat next to his. Will flops down onto his chair as well, while Starsky gives Hutch a look that somehow sets off a full-on dog fight, complete with rather vicious-sounding growling. I watch for a moment, wide-eyed, but since it doesn't seem to concern anyone else, I decide to leave it be. Besides, better they're having a wrestle than trying to hump me.

"So, Will, Emma tells me you're filming a television series," I say, smiling as I take a seat on the end of the picnic table bench.

"Oh, yeah. Just on a quick hiatus between locations. We were in the Brazilian rainforest for a month and next we move on to Nepal to wrap up."

"Excellent. She said it's an adventure show?"

Will nods. "I'm a bit of an adrenalin junkie so I guess you could say I've gotten lucky to be able to make a career out of it."

"You have to go back home soon, don't you, Pierce?" Harrison asks, his expression saying that can't happen a moment too soon for his liking.

"Tomorrow, yes."

"Right," he says, running his tongue across his front teeth. "So, when will you be coming back, then?"

"Excuse me?" Okay, now I'm onto him. He's going to put me on the hot seat for shaboinking his sister.

He has a sip of his beer. "I'm assuming you're coming back since you and Emma are together now."

The door swings open and Rosy and Emma emerge with their hands loaded down with bowls and dishes. I jump up, happy for the diversion, and help carry what I can with one hand.

"Old man, how's the chicken coming?" Rosy asks.

"Almost spicy enough, my queen," Darnell answers, brushing more sauce onto lumps of meat that are so saucy already, they are literally unidentifiable. "Just needs a little more heat or it won't singe off Pierce's taste buds." He gives me a wink that is not in any way a comfort to me.

"Will and Harrison, would you boys carry my air con machine out here for me?" Rosy asks. "If we have to be out in nature, I'd rather not know about it."

A few minutes later, we're squeezed in around the picnic table with the plastic table cloth flapping wildly in the frigid wind of the air conditioner. Unfortunately, Rosy wanted me seated next to her so instead of enjoying a light, warm Caribbean breeze, I'm being blasted by 12000 BTUs that the Bryant Breez-o-matic is pumping out. Without thinking, I lift the pepper shaker off the stack of napkins and they go flying all over the yard. Luckily, Starsky and Hutch are on the case, both of which get a hold of a few and start tearing them apart while Emma, Will, Libby, and I chase the rest down.

Dinner consists of a three-bean salad, coconut rice and red beans, a pineapple pepper slaw (heavy on the green peppers—blech!), enormous prawns with something called a Green Scotch Bonnet Pesto, and the world's spiciest, messiest chicken. Good thing the dogs have most of the napkins. After a quick grace, everyone digs in, and I decide it's time to turn on the charm.

"So, Libby, I hear congratulations are in order," I say with a smile. "Have you two set a date yet?"

She blushes and nods, chewing her mouthful of food. After she swallows and wipes her lips, she says, "Thank you. We're thinking of October which *is* hurricane season but it's also slower that time of year so we should be able to take some time off."

"I'm sure it'll be lovely." Unless there's a hurricane, that is.

"Who knows?" Rosy says, nudging me with her elbow. "Maybe there will be a double wedding."

Oh. *Now* I understand why Will invited me—for his amusement. What a fucker. I can't help but kind of like him though...

"Rosy, could you please pass the pepper slaw?" Emma asks urgently.

Rosy gives her a strange look. "It's right in front of you, Baby Bear."

"Baby Bear? I noticed you called Emma that earlier," I say with a warm smile.

"Yes, she's my Baby Bear. Harrison's Honey Bear, and Will is my little Cuddle Bear because he was always the cuddliest of my three bears," Rosy says with pride. Then her face falls a little. "But he's off zipping around the world so much that Big Mama almost never gets any cuddles."

"At least you've got Darnell," Will answers, taking a bite of chicken.

Rosy shrugs. "Meh."

"What about Starsky and Hutch? They seemed very affectionate when we got here," I say, trying hard not to sound facetious.

"Yes, they're real love bugs, but they can't replace my Cuddle Bear."

"Well, I'm here now, Rosy," Will says, wiping about a gallon of sauce off his chin. Seriously, it's impossible to eat this chicken without looking like a cheetah feasting on a gazelle.

"Yup. You certainly are here, so I'm just going to have to stock up." Rosy lifts herself up off the bench and reaches across the table to pinch his cheek. When she's done, she sits down and turns to me. "Now, back to you, Mr. Author. What are your intentions with my Baby Bear?"

"Oh, did we forget the buns? I think we left them in the kitchen," Emma says, standing quickly and disappearing into the house.

"I don't know what's wrong with that girl this evening," Rosy says, looking over her shoulder at the door. "First, she doesn't see the enormous bowl of salad right in front of her, and now she's imagining she saw buns. Now, Pierce, what exactly are you and Emma thinking about your future?"

Did that air conditioner start blowing really hot air just now? Because I'm suddenly feeling uncomfortably warm. "I...um...you know, it's early days, Rosy," I say, feeling like a complete cad.

Rosy's smile wipes off her face and I get the awful feeling it's not going to return any time soon. "What is that supposed to mean?"

"Nothing. Just that we've only met a few weeks ago and haven't really had time to explore where this is going."

"Really? Because it looked like you were doing quite a bit of exploring this morning in the pool," Harrison says, glaring at me.

"Ha! That's for sure," Will says, chuckling.

Here we go.

"Where is Emma with those buns?" I ask in a desperate attempt at changing the subject.

It fails, of course. Rosy crosses her arms and gives me a look that would intimidate Vlad the Impaler. As hard as it is to hear with the Breez-o-matic going, I'm relatively certain I just heard Libby mutter, "Oh, God help you," from across the table.

"I hope you're not thinking of *exploring* things and then taking off forever," Rosy says.

"It's just very complicated. You know, because of our careers," I say.

Emma walks out at that very moment, presumably thinking she's missed the worst of it, but something tells me she hasn't. As soon as the screen door slams shut behind her,

Hutch wakes up from his nap and loses his mind, taking Starsky with him. I've never been so glad to hear yapping dogs in my life. I glance around, looking for an escape route, but the fence is an eight-foot cement block structure with no gate.

Darnell tosses each of the dogs a mostly eaten chicken bone and they silence immediately for a second before they both decide they want the same one and the fight's on again.

"Baby Bear, don't tell me this is one of those Tundra hook-ons I've been reading so much about on Facebook," Rosy says.

"Tinder, Rosy," Will offers helpfully. "It's Tinder, and it's a *hookup,* not a hook-on."

"And they didn't meet that way. He's our inaugural guest at Eden, remember?" Harrison says. "She's his chef-slash-secretary-slash-hookup partner."

Darnell stops with a chicken leg halfway to his mouth. "Wait a minute. Wait just a damn minute. Is this guy not your boyfriend, Emma?"

Emma shoots Harrison an icy glare, then says, "We haven't really *defined* things, but I assure you what we have is built on mutual respect."

The chicken leg drops to his plate. Darnell swipes the last napkin off the table, then starts wiping his hands menacingly. "I don't like the sound of that at all."

"Really, it's just...can we just...not talk about this?" Emma asks. "We're supposed to be celebrating Will's return."

"Hear, hear," I say, picking up a chicken leg and taking a bite. *Fuck me, that's spicy.* I start to choke, stifling a cough as I desperately grasp for the napkin on my lap. A low growl comes from the general vicinity of my crotch and I look down to see Hutch bearing his teeth at me. He snatches the napkin off my lap and takes off, leaving me with saucy hands, and lips, according to the burning sensation. I start to cough again and pick up my beer to try to wash down the spices that are now burning a hole clean through my esophagus.

How am I the only one having trouble with this?

Turning to Emma, Darnell says, "Why'd you bring him for a family dinner if you two aren't serious."

"I didn't invite him. Will did. Do you think I want him here?"

"That's not very nice, Emma," Rosy says, "You're going to hurt his feelings."

At the same time, Darnell, who is clearly offended, asks, "What is that supposed to mean? Are you embarrassed by us?"

"No, of course not. I didn't mean I don't want him *here*, I meant I don't want *him* here."

"Ouch," I say, before realizing that she's not wrong about that. I don't exactly fit in at the moment, what with my saucy hands and lips.

"Not like that, Pierce." Emma looks up at the dark sky and groans. "Dammit. Will just asked him here to torture him."

"I did not," Will says, pretending to be highly offended. "I thought it would be a nice gesture since Harrison was so pissed at you two this morning."

"Why would Harrison be mad at you? Is it because this is just a hook-on?" Rosy asks.

"I wasn't angry. I was...ummm...surprised and concerned," Harrison says. "But Emma assured me she's happy so that's all that matters in the end."

"Yeah, she did look pretty happy this morning," Will puts in, tilting his beer at me.

"Shut up, Will," Emma says, fixing him with a dirty look. "Look, not that it is *any* of your business, but Pierce and I aren't in a long-term relationship, okay? We're just enjoying our time together before he has to go back to his life and I go back to mine. There is no future here. None. So you can just forget the double wedding and the cute little pale babies, Rosy. When he leaves here, he's going to help get us some high-end clients, and that will be that. Done. *Finito*. And if it doesn't bother me, it shouldn't bother you."

Huh. Something about the way she's so sure this is over already doesn't sit well with me. She's right, but...I don't like it.

Rosy puts her hand on mine and makes far-too-intense eye contact. "Is this what you want, Pierce? Some meaningless hook-on?"

"No, Rosy. Emma is not some meaningless hook-on to me. She's one of the finest women I've known and I want her to have every happiness." I look up at Emma.

Our eyes meet and, for a second, there's a deeper connection than I've felt with anyone in my life. Deeper even than my fondness for my favourite nanny, Tatiana, who had long blonde hair and enormous boobs. I swallow hard, staring into Emma's hazel eyes and feeling a strange sense of longing, even though she's just across the table from me. But there's an honesty in our exchange as well that says we both know where this is heading. Nowhere, and far too fast for my liking. I might as well help her out a bit while I'm here.

"Emma is just getting her life started here and has some very big plans. Unfortunately, my life is in Avonia and I'm in the middle of something I cannot abandon."

"So, you're going to abandon her instead?" Darnell says gruffly.

I sigh, not knowing how to answer that. "We both have obligations and people who are relying on us. Does that mean we shouldn't enjoy the time we have together?"

A resounding 'yes' comes from around the table.

"See, Emma? I'm not the only one who's concerned," Harrison says.

"Oh for..." Emma says, rolling her eyes. "Can you all just leave this alone, please? You know, Harrison, it's not like you and Libby were thinking of eternity when you first started 'seeing each other,'" I say, doing air quotes. "So why is it okay for you but not me?"

Libby nods and points a chicken leg at her fiancé. "She's got you there, Harrison. I tried to warn you to stay out of it."

"It's not the same thing."

"Why, because I'm a woman?" Emma asks.

"Because you're my little sister and I'm supposed to protect you from sharks like this guy."

"He's not a shark," Emma says, glaring at Harrison. "And you know, I'd think you'd be a bit nicer to the man who is going to save our arses."

"I don't want his help. Not like this," Harrison says, folding his arms and turning to me. "Thank you for the offer, but no thank you. Please *do not* use your fame to help us book up our resort."

"That seems rather short-sighted," I say without thinking. "I can make your lives very comfortable."

"Do *not* do that," Harrison says. "Because if you do, you'll basically be turning my sister into a prostitute, and I won't allow that."

"A prostitute?! Are you crazy?" Emma asks. "I'm not sleeping with him for the recommendation on TripAdvisor! I'm sleeping with him because I want to."

"That's it. You've insulted Emma enough." I stand and wedge myself out of my spot at the table. "The only business transaction Emma and I have is that she's typing for me and in exchange, I'm going to help promote your resort. And believe me, *I'm* getting the better end of that deal because Emma has spent *weeks* helping me, day and night, until her hands are sore, and what I'm going to do for you will take three phone calls and a couple of posts on Instagram. The other...*aspect* of our relationship has grown out of very real feelings for each other." I look up at Emma and say, "Right?"

"Yes," she says firmly. "That's right. Very real."

Our eyes meet again and we stare at each other, shell-shocked. What the hell just happened here? Emma swallows hard and gives me a small grin. And I go from being shocked to being foolishly happy in a millisecond.

And that's when Starsky decides it's time to hump my leg again.

"Starsky! Stop that!" Rosy says, tossing some chicken at the ground beside him.

"Thought so," Will says smugly.

"You thought what?" Emma asks, scowling at him.

"That you want a real relationship with Pierce, but you were too stubborn to admit it."

"So, that's why you invited him here?" Emma asks, raising her voice. "To back us both into a corner so we'll admit we like each other *more than friends*?!"

"Pretty much," Will says. "You're welcome, by the way."

"For what?" Emma stands. "Saying we have feelings for each other doesn't change the reality of the situation. He's still leaving tomorrow and I'm still staying here," she says, throwing her arms up in the air.

"But at least you both know the truth, which means you can *do* something about it," Harrison says, cutting into the conversation. "Do you think it was easy for Libby and me to admit we were in love?"

"It wasn't," Libby says, shaking her head. "I had just been jilted at the altar when we met and I was in *no* condition to start a new relationship."

"But we did," Harrison says, smiling down at her.

"And it worked out," Libby answers, grinning back up at him.

Harrison looks at Emma. "Listen, I'm sorry I got so mad this morning. Clearly, you two have something worth pursuing here. The way Pierce stood up for you says a lot about his character."

Emma sighs. "As much as I appreciate your intentions on this one, you don't know the first thing about Pierce," she says. "He doesn't believe in love or marriage or really any type of happiness that has anything to do with other human beings. He likes being a reclusive, miserable, lonely writer, and you know what? I'm fine with that. I don't need anything more from him than what he's got to offer while he's here. You may not understand that, but it works for me, okay?"

"Oh, Baby Bear, you're going to run again," Rosy says, shaking her head. She stands and walks over to Emma, taking both hands in hers. "Don't be scared. You don't have to run."

"Oh my God! Is no one here listening? I'm not running. I'm not scared. I'm just...*a realist*," Emma says. "Now, if you don't mind, we're going to leave. We have another 24 hours of meaningless fucking ahead of us and I'd like to make sure we get to it."

She storms into the house, leaving me standing with her family. Well, this is awkward in a way few things in my life have been. "Umm, thank you for your hospitality," I say, looking from Rosy to Darnell. "Delightful evening, really. Delicious food, lovely company."

"Pierce!" Emma calls from inside the kitchen.

"I should go."

TWENTY-SIX

Emotional Rollercoasters, Awe-Inspiring Endings, and a Feast for a King

Emma

"What the hell was that?" Pierce asks as soon as we pull onto the tree-lined freeway.

"My family. I tried to warn you," I say, shifting gears roughly as I change lanes.

"Not them. *You.* What was that crap about me being a lonely recluse and the meaningless fucking?" he asks. "Was that really necessary?"

I feel a twinge of guilt, but push it away. "Sorry. I didn't mean the thing about you being lonely."

"But you meant the bit about the meaningless fucking?" he asks in a hard tone.

Instead of answering, I take the next corner too fast, throwing us both off balance for a second.

"Slow down," he says. "I don't need to get killed because you're in a pissy mood."

"I'm not in a pissy mood," I answer, accelerating to beat the red light. "This is just how I drive."

We ride along in silence all the way back to the resort. It isn't until I pull into the stall that I remember we're staying here for the night rather than risking the trip back to Eden in the dark. We've got a suite booked and had planned to wrap up the last chapter, then spend the rest of the night doing all sorts of fun, sexy celebrating. But obviously that's off the table now, isn't it?

I cut the engine, then we sit for a moment, not looking at each other. Finally, I say, "We should get to work."

Pierce turns to me and tilts his head. "So, that's it then? We just pretend none of that happened and go back to the way things were?"

"Look, I don't have all the answers here, okay, but I do know we have a job to do. The rest can wait."

"Fine."

***

Three hours later

It's close to midnight which means that back in Avonia, people will just be getting into the office. Pierce has already avoided two phone calls from NBO, one from Sullivan and Stone, and a text from Zach that said: *Call NOW. URGENT.*

He's closing in on the end of the story, and I had no idea what an emotional journey this would be. As I type, I'm pulled along with the two remaining sons of King Draqen—Lucaemor and Matalyx—who finally unite to battle Zhordal mo Rhandar's army. After years of betrayal, lies, and pain, they have formed an alliance foretold by Mehesi the witch way back in book two. But I'm kind of crapping here because she foretold that only one heir would survive the great war, and honestly, I can't decide who to root for, since they've both had to do such evil things to survive the unending night, but they're also so incredibly brave and amazing at the same time.

I've all but forgotten what happened at Rosy and Darnell's, and I couldn't care less that we're spending the night in the uber-romantic Palatial Suite because I'm so swept up in what's happening in the realms of Qadeathas. I *have* to know how it will end. My heart pounds and I feel like I might literally die if Luc doesn't make it out of the battle alive and find his way back to Oona, who has been wandering hopelessly in a terrifying labyrinth for four days. She's pregnant, starving, exhausted, and she can't sleep because there's a damn manananggal stalking her who is definitely going to kill her, then suck the heart out of their unborn baby.

I wait breathlessly as he pauses and thinks.

"Damn," Pierce says, running his hand through his hair. "I can't do it," he says, looking up at me.

"Do you want me to type that or are you saying that to me?"

"Don't type that." He stands and crosses the room to the bar.

God, he's handsome. You should just see him right now. He got too hot while he was pacing and dictating so he's now barefoot with his linen pants rolled up a bit and his shirt is unbuttoned. Yum. Too bad I'm never going to see him again after tomorrow. A pang hits my chest and I blink quickly, forcing myself to look out the window at the moonlit ocean view instead of at his perfection. That moon will still be here. So will the sea. I may not care that they're there, but at least it's something to cling to...

"Ah, shit," he says, sucking back a quick shot of whiskey. "I know what I have to do but I can't."

"Don't tell me..."

Pierce lets out a frustrated chuckle. "I just realized why I have stalled for two years on finishing this. I'm nothing more than a sentimental idiot."

He stares at me with a grave expression. "He must die. It's the only way for the House of Dalgaeron to survive."

"Not true. You're the author of his fate. You get to decide, don't you?" I stand, suddenly wanting some booze myself. "Can't Luc live, then go rescue Oona, and they rule the kingdom with their cute little heir...maybe pop out a few spares while they're at it?"

Pierce shakes his head as he pours me a glass. "If he survives, his son can't. There can only be one heir the morning after the endless night. That's the prophecy."

"That's the prophecy." I sigh, then take a swig of the whiskey and feel it slide over my tongue and burn the back of my throat. Swatting him on the arm, I say, "Why'd you have to write that stupid prophecy, anyway?"

"Apparently, I'm a sadist," he says. "Okay, let's do this."

***

It's after two a.m. when Pierce hits the send button. We're sitting side-by-side on the couch with the French doors open to let in the air. The breeze causes the white sheers to billow as he sits back and lets out a long sigh. We're both wrung out. I've used a box of tissues and am still doing that hiccupping breathing thing you do after an enormous cry. Other than when I lost my parents, I can't remember a time when I've felt so raw.

"Are you all right, Emma?" he asks, resting his hand on my knee. His eyes are red too, and even though he hasn't bawled like a baby (or like me, for that matter), he's exhausted in a way that I've rarely known myself.

I nod, sniffling. "It's just...so bittersweet." My face crinkles up again and my eyes fill with tears.

Pierce puts his arm around me and pulls me onto his lap, where I curl up and bury my face into his neck. Kissing me on the temple, he says, "It's over. I'm in shock."

I sit up and nod a little. "I bet. You've spent years of your life on this."

"Eight years of thinking, writing, rewriting, dreaming, and fighting with myself over it," he says, staring out the window. "And with two little words, it's over. The End."

"Maybe that's why you got stuck for so long," I say, cupping his face with my hand. "Maybe you didn't want to say goodbye to them."

"Apparently getting attached to fictional characters is as ill-advised as attaching oneself to real humans," he says, chuckling softly.

"Worse, even," I say, laying my head on his shoulder.

I'm pretty sure we're both thinking about the next hard moment we'd both like to avoid. Closing my eyes, I nuzzle his neck with my nose, then feel both of us moving so that our mouths find each other. His mouth is warm and comforting. He tastes like whiskey and feels like exactly what I need right now to make everything okay again.

I turn so I'm straddling his lap and soon our clothes are off and we're comforting the hell out of each other on the tile floor. And there's something different this time. It's honest. We're in this together and there's no hiding from each other. This feels like the real thing. Our eyes stay locked on each other as he moves over me and there's a story we're writing together with just this look. It's the story of us. It's deep and filled with everything we need to be happy and whole.

When it's over, we lay together on the floor, panting and kissing, not wanting this moment to end.

"You must be exhausted," I say finally.

"I am, but I don't want to sleep. I don't want to miss a second of being able to look at you."

We kiss again, our tongues saying what we can't with words. After a few minutes, I pull back. "Let's stay up then. Until you get on the plane."

He grins and shakes his head a little. "You're magnificent, you know that?"

"Yes," I shrug, making him chuckle. "Come on. I want to show you something amazing. At least, I hope it'll be amazing."

***

Forty-five minutes later, we're in the kitchen of the Japanese restaurant, having snuck into the buffet to get some of the ingredients we need so I can test out the culinary concepts I've been working on for the past several months. The sounds of Andrea Bocelli play quietly in the background as Pierce watches me work from a stool on the other side of the stainless-steel island. Having him here makes me chop faster, dice with more precision, and sprinkle herbs with more flare than I ever have before. I want to impress him like he has impressed me. I want to make a meal he will never forget, even when he's ninety-eight and can no longer remember the names of his characters or how Lucaemor came to his end (a hatchet to the head, in case you were wondering).

Anyway, back to the food. I want him to be able to smell this meal and taste it in his mind. I want him to know he was here with me.

Turning the flame up to high, I drizzle olive oil into the centre of a carbon-steel skillet, then slide the minced garlic off of the cutting board and into the oil with the side of my knife. The garlic sizzles, filling the air with the first of many aromas to come before we eat. I quickly stir as I glance back at Pierce. "Bored yet?" I ask.

"Riveted actually," he says, with a smile. "I could happily sit here and watch you cook all day."

"Full disclosure? I'm really nervous to cook like this for you."

"But you've already made so many meals for me. Is it because I'm watching you?"

"No, it's because I'm making something totally new. Something I've only dreamed about but never tried."

"Really?"

I nod. "I call it Carib-Asian food—it's Caribbean with an Asian twist. It could be god-awful," I say, tossing the prawns in the pan. "Or, it could be the next best thing."

"I'm guessing the latter of the two."

Taking a deep breath, I grin at him for a second. "Either way, I'm terrified to let you try it."

"Now you know how I've felt these past few weeks with you bearing witness to the most vulnerable creative moments of my life."

An hour later, as the sun comes up, I clear the island, wipe it off, then set the feast in front of Pierce.

Taking two white plates down from the cupboard, I set two places, then add a dollop of sauce to each. "These are jerk pork spring rolls. The concept is to take plain spring rolls and use jerk spices, as well as a pineapple and coconut chutney to give them an island feel." I add the next appetizer to our plates. "This is a Thai chicken satay served on a bed of alfalfa and coconut, with a mango peanut sauce."

"Smells amazing."

"I agree," I say, excitement fluttering in my tummy. "Our first main will be ginger shrimp with coconut milk, calabaza squash, and a lemongrass stock served over rice noodles, and garnished with sliced avocado and chopped cilantro. Next will be chicken with rice and peas blended with annatto seeds for a slightly sweet and peppery flavour that adds an unmistakably Caribbean flowery scent to the dish."

I stare at my creation, feeling elated in a way I haven't in the past. This is it. I know it. This is my future. Right here on this island.

"Finally, we have lobster tail on coconut and pineapple rice with a lemongrass sauce to make it really different. Dig in," I say, picking up a fork.

"Wait," Pierce says, standing. "We need to document this." He takes his mobile out of his pocket and walks over to the opposite side of the island.

I sit, hold my arms out to the side, and smile, bursting with pride and possibilities.

"Perfect," he says. When he sits back down, he holds up his glass of white wine and says, "To your bright, shiny future."

Laughing, I say, "God, I hope so."

I watch him intently as he takes his first few bites, trying to gauge his reaction. He closes his eyes and moans, which is either a testament to my creation or to his own acting ability.

"Incredible, Emma," he says. "Truly."

Truly incredible? My entire body hums with pleasure.

"You should eat too," he says. "You're making me a little uncomfortable with all this watching."

"Right, sorry. Most of the fun is in seeing you enjoy it though," I say, picking up one of the pork rolls.

"You know what's funny? As a writer, you almost never get to see anyone enjoy your work. You just hear about it after the fact, if that, even. But having you work with me was a completely new experience."

"Was it both terrifying and exhilarating?"

"That's exactly the right description."

We take a moment to smile at each other before we eat, and without saying it, I know he understands exactly how I feel at this moment.

When we've stuffed ourselves, I sit back, feeling a sense of complete satisfaction at having created that which has been brewing in my mind for so many months. It's like the greatest non-sex orgasm ever.

"Was it good for you?" I ask with a little laugh.

"Magnificently moving and wonderful. You're very talented, Emma. Should you want to, you could really go places."

"Oh, I want to," I say, fully meaning it.

His face grows serious for a moment and he gives me a thoughtful look. "Would it be strange if I tell you I'm proud of you?"

His words threaten to bring tears to my eyes and I have to look away for a second to dull my emotions. Finally, I manage to say, "No, it would be nice. Would it be strange if I tell you that I'm proud of you?"

"I'd very much welcome that sentiment."

TWENTY-SEVEN

The Pathetic Hero's Return...

Pierce

"Pierce, you didn't tell me you were rich," Emma says, tongue-in-cheek, as she pulls the keys out of the jeep's ignition.

I glance at the Learjet waiting for me. "It's really just a way to get from point A to point B."

Emma stares reverently at the plane, which at the moment has a particularly sleek glow from the pink and orange sunset, then she shakes her head. "No, it's not. *That's* a whole different life, right there."

I see the plane through her eyes and feel suddenly ashamed by the level of luxury to which I've grown accustomed. Trying to slough off the shame, I quip, "It's the perfect way for a reclusive writer to travel."

She gives me a small, hollow smile that reminds me of what's happening.

I'm leaving.

I swallow hard, thinking about her words, and knowing that what she really means is that it's a world into which she wouldn't fit. She may not be wrong about that, either. *I* don't even fit in there.

For a moment, I consider an alternate ending that doesn't have the word goodbye as the closing line. After all, the sun is setting on what has been a perfect day, and if this were one of those cheesy romance movies, she'd be getting on the plane with me to start our happily ever after.

But this is real life, and she's *not* getting on the plane with me and we both know that in a very short time, the word goodbye will come into play.

"Would you like to come aboard and have a look?" I ask, wanting to extend our time together by even just a few minutes.

"Maybe another time," she says casually.

"Listen, Emma," I say. "I just want you to know that today was quite possibly the best day I've ever had." I reach for her hand and rub her knuckles with my thumb. "You are an extraordinary woman, and I truly mean that. The next few months are going to be insanely busy, but maybe once I get through all of the editing and—"

Shaking her head, Emma says, "What if we don't do the bit where we make promises we may not keep? In fact, I think we should agree to leave it here and not say we'll 'keep in touch' because that's inevitably going to lead to one of us being the last one to contact the other one, then that person will be waiting to hear back and..." She takes a deep breath, then says, "A clean break is best."

"Right. Brilliant," I say with a little nod. "Well, in that case, please allow me to say I've never met anyone like you, and I couldn't have done any of this without you."

"Okay, I'll let you say that," she answers with a wry grin. "Before you go, there's one thing I have to know. Have I perhaps restored your faith in humanity, even just the tiniest bit?"

"I'm afraid only in you. Everyone else can just sod off."

Emma laughs a little and then a quiet grows between us as I try to force myself to either come up with something incredibly clever and/or charming to say.

Total blank. Bugger.

Emma sighs. "This would never have worked anyway. I don't think I could go my entire life without cooking with sun-dried tomatoes."

I laugh, wanting very much to kiss her hard on the mouth and forget this whole 'going back to my real life' thing. "How is it that you really exist?" I ask, drinking in the sight of her beautiful eyes one last time. "You spent the last several weeks helping me day and night, not to mention all the very meaningful fucking, and now you're trying to make this easier for me."

"Why would I make this hard for you? We knew what we were doing the whole time, and we knew where it would take us."

"I suppose we did," I say, searching her eyes for some sign that she wants me to stay, because at this moment, I'm pretty sure if she wanted me to, I would.

Emma glances at the plane, then says, "You should go. They're waiting for you."

When I look up at the jet, I see Yvonne, the flight crew leader, standing at the top of the stairs, waiting to greet me.

"I'm going to be horribly cliché and ask you to promise me one thing..."

"Don't worry, I won't speak a word of any of it to anyone, I promise," Emma says firmly. "Well, that's not entirely true because my best friend, Priya, knows you were here. I mentioned your name before I knew you were famous, and she sort of guessed what was going on, but I would *never* give her any details other than general girl talk like 'it was a-MAZ-ing.'"

God, she's cute. How the fuck am I going to force myself to get on that plane? "Actually, I wanted you to promise you won't give up on your dreams, no matter what. You have a rare and quasi-magical talent and it would kill me if you wasted it making boring meals for middle-aged idiots and their infantile third wives."

She reaches up and touches my cheek with her hand. "I promise. Nothing is going to get in the way of my world cuisine domination."

"That's my girl."

The look on her face says she won't let anyone get in her way, not even me.

And for that, I'm glad.

***

Email from Gwen Sullivan, President, Sullivan and Stone Publishing, Inc.

Dear Pierce,

I understand you're on your way home victorious. Zach has shared some of the pages with me, and I could not be more thrilled. See you as soon as you get in. I cannot wait to sip some wine and read the finished product.

Warmest regards,

Gwen

***

Text from Zach: *Just finished. Brilliant way to close the series! Seriously. It's so much better than I could've expected. Madly working on edits. Call me as soon as you land.*

***

Text from Leo: *Not sure when you'll be home, but I just wanted to let you know I'm using your flat. A bit of a problem at the house in Bath has left me without a place to stay and I knew you wouldn't mind putting your little brother up for a while. I'm afraid Mum and Father are rather pissed at me at the moment so I'm persona non grata over at their place. See you when you get back.*

***

Voicemail from Kent Cromwell: *Pierce, Kent here. I knew you'd get the job done if I applied some pressure. The talk over at S & S is that it's one of the most brilliant works they'll ever put out so well done, both of us. I need you to authorize pages to be sent over here immediately for adaptation. Call me as soon as you get this.*

***

I should be on top of the world right now. I finally broke the *Clash of Crowns* curse. Every ounce of pressure has been lifted off my shoulders after two years of suffocating under the weight of it. I won. I beat Kent Cromwell and the rest of the clones at NBO.

So, why don't I feel elated? Thrilled? Utterly satisfied? Instead, I feel shell-shocked. Empty. Numb.

It's because I'm exhausted. That's the reason.

I should be sleeping. The fact that I don't even know how long I've been awake is a testament to the fact that I have no business *being* awake at the moment. I've written like a madman for nearly two solid months, not to mention all of the stunningly wonderful sex and the delicious verbal sparring— that combination would wear out any man. Yes, I'm just tired. The smart thing to do would be to sleep eight hours straight so I can hit the ground running when I get home tomorrow.

I pull back the covers on the bed, glad that I sprung for the plane with the master suite. Turning off the light, I lay down and try to get comfortable.

Okay, that's it, Pierce. Go to sleep...now.

Shit.

Hmm, maybe I'm forgetting something? I definitely feel like something is missing.

Oh, now I remember. I promised Emma I'd help them book up Eden Island. I sit up, flick on the light, grab my phone off the nightstand, and open my photo gallery. When it opens, I'm met with Emma's smiling face as she displays the incredible meal she made us this morning. Not sharing *that* one with the world. She's just for me. Look at that face. She truly is a stunning woman, and not just that, she's brave and strong and so very talented.

I scroll through and find a few scenery shots I took over the month, then post them on IG with the caption 'My writing retreat for the past two months. Very inspiring. For all you #ClashofCrowns fans out there, you may be happy to know that as of this morning at 3 a.m. the series has been completed. #writinglife #EdenIsland #ParadiseBay'

Putting my phone on airplane mode, I shut the light off, lay back down, and wait for sleep to come.

Huh. Normally I sleep really well on the jet. It's pitch-black in here, there's a climate-control setting set to an optimal temperature of 17°C, the engines create ambient noise, and I'm in a queen bed with 1000 thread count sheets. What more could I ask for?

Emma beside me.

Oh, wow, Pierce, that was just pathetic.

But I suppose I did get rather accustomed to listening to the rhythmic sound of her breathing at night, and the way she'd tuck herself against me with her arm slung across my abs, and the scent of her skin. Oh, and how her head fit perfectly in the crook of my neck when she was snuggled up beside me.

It'll take me a night or two to get used to sleeping alone, but, honestly, what's not to like? I can stretch out across the entire bed if I want. I can snore freely, or binge watch *Black Mirror* without worrying about keeping her up. Yes, this is definitely better.

Closing my eyes, I tell myself to just go to sleep already. Go to sleep, and when you wake up, you'll have begun to forget all about Ms. Emma Banks, chef extraordinaire. Adventurous, independent, beautiful Emma.

Okay, so it may take a few days, but definitely by the end of the week, this whole thing will be just a delightful memory.

I hope.

TWENTY-EIGHT

Awful Smug Rich People and the Bitter Women Who Serve Them...

Emma

Is there anything worse than being in limbo? Well, I suppose there are much worse things, really—like being sentenced to life in a Turkish prison, for example. But as far as life *outside* of a crowded, dank jail cell goes, being in limbo is absolute crap.

It's been over two months since Pierce left and this entire time, I feel like I'm just waiting for my real life to start. And, I don't know about you, but I absolutely *hate* waiting. At any given moment, my stupid heart is expecting Pierce to come bursting through the door to the houseboat to pledge his undying love for me, and I'll start crying (a dainty, pretty cry, not the ugly version) and say, "Shut up. Just shut up. You had me at hello."

But, that's just ridiculous and my brain knows it. He's *not* coming back with a capital NOT, but somehow my heart isn't taking messages from my brain at the moment. So my poor brain is also stuck waiting for my heart to finally accept reality.

The truth is, it's not just Pierce or my stupid heart that I'm waiting for, it's also my chance at getting off of Eden permanently. And the way things are going, I honestly don't know when I'll get my chance, because things have changed drastically since the beginning of June. Thanks to a certain famous author, the Island of Eden, and in fact, the entire Paradise Bay resort, has become the hottest sun destination on

209

the planet. Obviously not weather-wise. I don't actually know the literal hottest place on the planet. I'd guess in a desert somewhere, maybe in Africa. I meant hot as in everybody and their aunt's cat wants to book a holiday with us.

When Pierce left for the other side of the planet, he posted the most incredible shots he'd taken of the island on his Instagram account. Who knew he's basically a professional photographer on top of the whole writer/sex god thing? Not that it matters because he's gone. Gone. Gone. *Gone.*

But his parting gift to me was a hell of a lot of rich people booking the island. Other than two days in October, we're booked solid until next August. Next August! Can you imagine?

Not only that, the people who can't afford to stay on Eden—which includes 99.8% of the world's population—are booking at the main resort. This has meant Harrison and Libby have been swamped trying to find new hires in all departments and keeping up with the incredibly steady turnover of guests.

Things have been a little bit prickly between Harrison and me since the dinner at Rosy and Darnell's. I think he feels upset about how our success came about, like it's all tainted or something. He hasn't brought it up, but he's definitely different around me now. He's kind of quiet and isn't so quick to smile as he used to be, which honestly leaves me feeling kind of awful about being so irresponsible but also simultaneously pissed at Harrison for making me feel like a crap bag.

Well, maybe I'm the one doing that to myself. Even though things have turned out so much better than we could have hoped as far as business goes, I still can't escape the fact that I played pretty fast and loose with the future of the resort and everyone who works here, all for a guy. I feel so bad, I haven't even brought up my brilliant idea of switching with two of the chefs at the main resort so I can get off of Eden. I've just been out here hating my life and waiting for something to change.

Not exactly my normal take-charge, kickass self, am I? Instead, I'm a crabby serving wench, who pretty much hates everything and everyone. But can you blame a girl who's just ended an amazing non-relationship that felt like *the most incredible* relationship two people have ever had, who then finds herself surrounded by happy couples 24/7?

It's natural to feel a little bitter, no?

And by a little, I mean I pretty much want to poison all the newlyweds I've served in the past ten weeks. Every disgustingly blissful, self-satisfied pair of them.

Yes, happy couples are the worst—especially rich, entitled ones. If I thought Pierce was snooty when I first met him, he had nothing on the people he's sent our way. Take, for example, the couple we've got here at the moment. I've dubbed them the Duke and Duchess of Spray Tans. The Duke has got to be in his late 60s if he's a day, and his very new Duchess looks like she could still be young enough to think starring in *Lindsay Lohan's Beach Club* is a wise choice. The Duke himself must think he's fooling everybody with his hair and eyebrows that have been *Just for Menned* into an unnatural black colour that looks like he rubbed his hair with shoe polish. The missus isn't exactly what I'd call a natural beauty either. She left her ombre blonde hair extensions on the kitchen counter yesterday (eww) and when I happened to catch the pleasant sight of him chasing her around the villa naked (terrifying), her double Ds didn't even bounce the slightest bit and it was very clearly a case of the carpet not matching the drapes.

At the moment, I'm cursing the pouring rain beating against the houseboat. It's the third 'no golf cart' day in a row which means in a few minutes, I'll be slopping my way up the mountain to serve them breakfast where I'll likely bear witness to something that will leave me with PTSD. (Post Traumatic Servant's Disorder—look it up. It's a thing.)

I get my mobile off the table and video call Priya because misery loves company, and we're two of the most miserable people on Earth these days.

When her face appears on the screen, she looks about as bad as I feel. She has dark circles under her eyes and her hair looks like it hasn't seen a comb (or quite possibly shampoo) for a few days now. "Have you heard anything from him?" she asks.

"Nothing. Any word on the job search?"

She holds up a form to the screen and I squint to read the text at the top. "So, you're actually filling them out now?"

"Yes, I might as well just give up and be a doctor." She

slumps in her chair. "What are you making?"

"An uninspired vegan, gluten-free breakfast. Mango almond smoothies and a scrambled veggie fry-up."

"Sounds disgusting."

"Oh, it is. But Duke Spray Tan is needing to stay in shape for the new missus."

Priya stares down at the plates while I unceremoniously dump the tasteless mixture onto them. "God, how could any woman be worth eating that for the rest of your life?"

"Based on the sounds coming from the bedroom, I'd say she helps him forget the shitty menu."

"Eww."

"Yeah, eww. And it's supposed to rain for another two days which means subjecting myself to trauma six times a day with meals that fit his Body for Wife diet."

"Okay, time to cheer ourselves up," Priya says, opening her laptop. "Let's see what Mr. Davenport is up to this week."

"Let's not. It's not as fun as it used to be." As in, 'it's not as fun as it used to be when I thought he might come back.'

"You have to be patient, Emma. He'll come to his senses soon. In the meantime, let's keep tabs on him."

I can see she's already off cyberstalking him by the look on her face and the fact that she's typing.

"Who is *that* be-otch?"

"What be-otch?" I ask, freezing in place.

"Looks like he was out last night celebrating with...oh! That's what she looks like in real life." Priya says scrunching her face up.

"Who?"

"Destiny Poulsen. Boy, does she ever look different without that wig and all the dirt on her face." Priya screen shares a photo of Pierce, looking stupidly handsome in a tuxedo standing next to Destiny Poulsen who plays Oona in *Clash of Crowns*. In the photo, she's wearing a dress that's so low-cut, I swear I can see the top of her navel. My heart sinks to my feet and I feel suddenly pukey.

"Urgh. You probably don't want to hear this," Priya says, coming back on the screen.

"I don't, but tell me anyway."

"Well, according to *Weekly World News E- Gossip*,

Pierce and Destiny have been suspected of having an intimate relationship, but no one's been able to confirm it. According to a source on set who asked not to be named, the pair have always gotten on very well and she wouldn't be at all surprised to see them couple up at some point in the near future."

"On second thought, don't tell me."

"Sorry, hon."

"Not your fault that I'm utterly forgettable."

"You're not forgettable! It's probably just malarkey. The Weekly World News isn't known for their dedication to accuracy in reporting."

"They were right about that man that had a baby," I say, sighing loudly.

"True, but I'm sure they have this wrong. Plus, you're the one who came up with the whole 'let's not keep in touch' thing, effectively slamming the door on any future possibilities."

Oh right. I keep forgetting how I shot myself in the ovary with that one. "Hey, I had a good reason at the time. I thought if I pretended to be an ultra-cool, breezy girl, it would make him come rushing back."

"You should call him and tell him you made a mistake."

"I can't. From the start, we both agreed it was casual and temporary. I can't go back on that now and say, 'whoops, turns out I want forever.'"

"Why the hell not?"

"Because it would be setting myself up for guaranteed rejection—he's made it really clear he loves the single life. I pretended I was super on board with who he really is. I can't very well go back on that now and tell him I lied and I'm actually just like every other woman out there who wants the ring and the monogrammed towels. As soon as I do that, he'll know I'm a big, fat liar, and he'll lose all respect for me."

"So, you really pretended your way into a corner."

"Yes, and now I'm waiting for the paint of shame to dry." I let the truth of my words sink in a little even though they feel like third-degree burns on my insides. "I should go so I can get my boots on, hike up the mountain, and serve this disgusting slop to an even more disgusting couple, then maybe I'll just walk directly into the ocean and end it all... Oh, wait, I can't. I need to plan the menu for my brother's wedding supper, and go get fitted for a bridesmaid dress because, in a couple of weeks, I'll be celebrating something I'll never have—true love. But don't worry, because when that's over, I'll be back to serving an endless stream of copulating couples."

So, at least there's that to look forward to...

TWENTY-NINE

Men Being Childish and Churlish

Pierce – Valcourt, Avonia

"**J**esus Christ," I say, staring at the mess of little white bits all over my 3D Lego Qadeathas model. I pick up one of the bits and press it between my fingers. "Leo, you wouldn't happen to know why the realms of Qadeathas, as well as my $12,000 dining room table, has been sprayed with some sort of waxy substance, would you?"

Leo, who is lounging on my couch watching *Shark Tank*, glances up to take a peek at what I'm talking about. "Oh, *that*. I was making wax fingers earlier."

"Wax fingers?"

"You dip your fingertip into melted wax from a candle."

For fuck's sake. "And why exactly would you do that?"

"Because it's fun. It feels nice and warm and just the slightest bit dangerous in case you get your fingers too close to the flame. I made little *Clash of Clash* action figures for you. See?" He stands and walks over to the table, pointing to the tiny wax ghost-like things that have been drawn on with a Sharpie. "Oona, Luc, Matalyx..." He holds up the biggest one. "I used my thumb to make Zhordal."

"How many street drugs have you taken? Seriously, Leo, if you had to estimate your lifetime use..."

Leo rolls his eyes at me. "None, obviously, if you don't count Mary Jane or a little Molly."

"I actually do count those. But setting your brain functioning aside, you didn't think that perhaps you should clean up after playtime?"

"Isn't Mrs. Bailey going to be here tomorrow morning?"

"I don't employ her so she can clean up after my toddler brother." I walk over to the living room, pick up the remote control, and shut off the telly, feeling very much like I would were I the father of a twelve-year-old boy. Good practice I suppose, should I ever accidentally have a child of my own. "Clean it up. Now."

Leo rolls his eyes at me, then walks over to the kitchen to get a roll of paper towels. "What flew up your arse?"

"Oh, I don't know, perhaps that my idiot brother moved in while I was out of town and won't leave?"

"If by 'idiot' you mean young at heart, fun-loving, and charming, then I'll take that as a compliment."

"It's not, and please don't. Now, cocktails start at eight. Are you going to be ready in time? Because I'm not waiting for you." *There you go, Pierce. Set firm limits and stick with them. It's the only way he'll learn.*

"Oh, I'm not coming," Leo says, shaking his head. "I'm afraid I'm not invited."

"I'm sorry? You're not invited to our father's birthday dinner?"

"Oh, yeah, well, technically I *was* invited and have now been uninvited," Leo says, "I went over there yesterday to smooth things over and see if perhaps Father'd be ready to welcome me back into the fold, but then there was this lovely new maid they've hired and one thing led to another and—"

Holding up one hand, I say, "Got it. I really don't have time to hear the rest, anyway. I need to finish getting ready."

I stand in front of the mirror in the living room and make quick work of my bowtie while Leo does a rather ineffective job cleaning up his wax fingers leavings.

When he's done, he says, "I signed my name to your card. I hope you don't mind, but I'm a little short on funds at the moment, and I figured you probably got him something pretty good."

"A new set of custom-made golf clubs."

"Well, that was very generous of us," Leo says with a wide grin.

Swiping the card off the counter, I sign my name to the bottom and stuff it in the envelope. "Perhaps while I'm gone, you could think of ways to earn some money so you can get the fuck out of my flat permanently."

"Not very generous of you," Leo says, feigning shock. "But don't worry about it, that's why I'm bingeing on *Shark Tank*. I'm learning about business."

Sighing deeply, I rub the bridge of my nose. "Brilliant. Maybe when you're done, you could make a list of things for which you have a decent aptitude. There must be *something*. Figure out what it is, get a job, and get the hell out."

"I have an aptitude for being irresistibly charming, but I'm afraid I haven't got much else to offer."

"The only person who finds you irresistibly charming is our mother."

"And as of yesterday, her maid."

"Oh, yes, we mustn't forget her," I quip. "But, for realsies, Leo. I have a very busy life and I really cannot have you here any longer. So *do* use this evening to figure out what your next move should be—or more accurately, *where*. And in the meantime, keep your grubby hands off my Lego. It's not a toy!"

***

"Cheers! There you are, Pierce," my mother says, sweeping across the room in her sequined gown. She gives me the ever-comforting air kisses on both sides of my face, careful not to ruin her hair or meticulously-applied face. "Where's Leo?"

"He thought it best that he not attend."

"Well, how is that going to look to everyone?" my mother hisses at me.

"Honest."

Having had enough of this conversation, I make a beeline for the bar to get myself a drink. Unfortunately, Greyson has had the same idea, so I shall now be forced to converse with my older brother.

"Pierce," he says, glancing at me as he tosses a couple of ice cubes into a tumbler.

"Greyson. How's almost-married life?"

"Perfect. How's your hand? I understand you got into a bit of a dust-up with a gecko."

"Giant Komodo dragon, actually. And I'm just fine, thank you."

He has a sip of his drink and smacks his lips. "So, you've finished your revenge series. Did you kill off the whole family now or am I still the only one you secretly want to off?"

"You know, Greyson, if you'd been alive when Carly Simon wrote *You're So Vain*, you'd be certain that song was about you." I take a quick swig of bourbon, then pour more in the tumbler.

"Oh, I get it. You actually have the nerve to be offended that I'm offended you killed me off in your book."

I sigh audibly, wishing I'd stayed home. "You'll be happy to know I've killed Leo," I say, pausing for effect. "Myself as well." I know I shouldn't tell anyone this, but Greyson is one of few people I can trust with this information. He's a total wanker, but he's not a big mouth.

Raising one eyebrow, he says, "Really? But I suppose you get some sort of heroic ending rather than getting poisoned and shitting yourself to death in an outhouse like me."

"You'll have to read the book to find out."

"There you are, darling," Porsche, Greyson's fiancée, says, sidling up behind us.

You have to be careful around Porsche—I swear she went to finishing school at an academy for spies.

"Pierce, the man of the hour," she says as we give each other a customary, if not cold, air kiss. "I hear the buzz over at Sullivan and Stone is that you've really pulled one out of your arse this time."

"What a delightful way to put it," I say.

Ignoring my insult, she says, "We've all had a bet going on how everything would turn out. Greyson and I were both firmly on the 'he'll never finish it' side of things, whereas your father believed you would finish it, but only several years after the television series wrapped up. You'll be happy to know Leo had every faith that you would manage to squeak it out under the wire. But he's prone to childhood fantasy, isn't he?"

"And yet, he won," I say, tipping back my drink. "I hope you didn't bet all the money you've been saving for your rhinoplasty. It would be a shame if you had to continue walking around with those uneven nostrils much longer."

Porsche gasps and lifts her fingers to her nose. "Oh, piss off," she hisses before storming off.

"Why'd you have to wind her up like that?" Greyson says, shaking his head at me. "Now she'll be booking in with mum's plastic surgeon before the night is up."

"She started it."

"You're such a child," he says, tipping back his drink before going in search of his fiancée.

I watch as he crosses the room, leaving me in the happiest scenario possible at this type of event—alone with the booze. I should not have come. I could've easily told them I was far too busy, but for some idiotic reason, I found myself feeling sentimental about my old man turning sixty-five and decided I might as well show up. But now that I'm here, I'm filled with regret. I'd kill for a pair of humpy little Jack Russells to liven things up a bit.

I curse Leo for not coming. As much as I'm glad to be away from his asinine behaviour for a few hours, at least I would have been mildly amused. When *is* the last time I had fun? *Oh, brain, don't answer that. You do not want to know. What happened on the Benaventes wasn't real life and you know it.*

Other than my time at Eden, my life is a series of phony obligations broken up by intense periods of loneliness. I believe that shall be the theme of my next book, The Chronicles of the Mysteriously Depressed Author Who Has It All and Should be Enjoying Every Minute of His So-Called Perfect Life. The title's a work in progress, but you get the idea...

I pour myself another drink then turn when my father's oldest friend and his new wife are announced by the butler. My mother scurries over to greet Lord and Lady Winthrop. I watch them for a moment, wondering what Emma would think of any of these people.

Actually, I know she would see right through their phony smiles and even phonier bridge work. If she were here right now, we'd be sharing a laugh about the very obviously dyed hair and eyebrows of Lord Winthrop, who apparently hasn't ever heard the term 'age gracefully.' My father went to Eton with him and they've been best of frenemies ever since, one-upping at every turn. The only area in which my father hasn't chosen to take him on is in the new wife department, having decided to stick it out with my mother rather than split the family cash in halfsies. Lord Winthrop, however, is on his second wife upgrade and Lady Winthrop 3.0 looks to be in her mid-twenties, so I'm sure their love is completely authentic and has nothing to do with his millions.

Oh Christ, here they come with their hideous matching spray tans lighting their way across the room.

I have another sip, deciding to drink just enough so that I can bear being here, but not so much that I start saying things I really mean.

"There's the pride of Avonia," Lord Winthrop says, slapping me on the back. "Have you met my new wife, Brittany?"

"No, I'm afraid I haven't had the pleasure," I say, plastering a polite smile on my face.

Brittany blinks quickly and grins up at me, her cheeks turning slightly red.

"She's a huge fan of your work, Pierce."

"Well, not the books," she admits sheepishly. "I'm not much of a reader but I *love* the show. No chance you'll give us a hint at the ending?"

"Wish I could but I'm under an iron-clad NDA."

Her face falls a little, then her eyes light up again. "Do you know James Prescott personally?" He's the actor who plays Matalyx—he's got a real dark, smouldering thing going that the ladies love.

"Yes, nice fellow. Very talented."

Lord Winthrop looks slightly panicked and quickly changes the subject from the man I'm certain she's thinking about whilst playing with her husband's wrinkly old balls. "We just got back from the Island of Eden, actually. Tad and Tatiana showed us pictures of their trip and Brittany just had to go. Quite the perfect spot for our honeymoon." He drapes an arm around his wife's waist and pulls her close.

My ears perk up at the mention of the island, and suddenly I'm very much interested in what they have to report. "Yes, it's quite lovely there. Excellent food, too," I say, hoping to lead the conversation over to Emma. Not because I am missing her horribly or anything. More like I'm just curious about how she's doing.

"It was an amazing holiday," Brittany says. "Although the chef left a little something to be desired."

Her husband nods quickly. "True. There's not much a chef could do with our restricted diet—no gluten, no salt, no animal products, and no processed sugar."

"But for what we were paying, it could have been served with more flair."

I bite my tongue, forcing myself not to home in on the word 'we' in that sentence. I can let that one go, but I'm afraid I can't say the same about the flair thing. "More flair?" I ask, feeling my spine straighten.

"Maybe flair's the wrong word," Brittany says, seeming to pick up on my irritation. "Perhaps enthusiasm. She was just sort of...depressing to be around."

Lord Winthrop laughs and looks at his wife. "Now that you mention it, she was, wasn't she?"

Narrowing my eyes, I say, "Oh, so it's amusing to come across someone who's down in the dumps, is it?"

Lord Winthrop looks taken aback. "No, I didn't mean it like—"

"Did you ask her what was wrong?" I say, cutting him off.

They wear matching confused expressions, and I have the urge to knock their stupid heads together.

"Excuse me?" Lord Winthrop asks.

"Did you *bother* to ask her if she was all right? Or did you just go on your merry way, pretending she didn't exist?"

"No, of course I didn't ask her. It's none of my business," Lord Winthrop says.

"And why would you? It's just another human being who's obviously in pain. What would that possibly have to do with you?" I say, leaning in toward him in a rather menacing way. "I suppose she doesn't matter at all. She's just one of the help, right?"

I hear the sound of a throat clearing and look to my left to see my father standing next to me. He gives them an overly gracious smile, then says, "Brittany, love, have you tried any of the pâté? Bunny had it flown in from Norway this morning."

Glancing at me warily, Brittany, says, "I haven't yet, thank you." Looking up at her husband, she says, "Let's go."

As soon as they are out of earshot my father gives me a cold look. "It appears as though I've banished the wrong son from the party. I thought perhaps you'd be in a decent mood now that you're a big success again, but I can see your disposition is very much the disappointment it was before."

"On that note, I believe I'll take my leave. Happy birthday, Father."

***

By the time I'm home, I feel slightly less numb than I did when I left, which is strange considering how much I've had to drink. Suddenly, the reason pops into my mind and I wince internally, realizing that I really am a sick bastard. This little spark of life is brought to you by knowing Emma isn't happy and the depraved part of me thinks it's because she might be harbouring feelings for me.

I think of her there on that island, serving the likes of Lord and Not-a-Lady Winthrop, and an indignant rage builds inside me. Yes, I do know I wasn't exactly a real treat when I first got there, but at least I had the self-awareness to realize it. Not like those two idiots who probably think they were doing *her* a favour by being there.

I stand under the rain shower head, scrubbing my hair far too vigorously as I think about Emma having to cook gluten-free, vegan, salt-free, sugar-free slop. The rage is now a full-blown inferno, and it strikes me that it's a great injustice in this world if someone with her talent is being forced to waste even a precious day cooking for ungrateful ingrates.

I push the button that turns off the steam and water and turns on the warm, dry air. As I stand being air dried by the vents embedded in the tiled walls, I think about how pointless it all is for me to be here with every advantage when she is so far away with absolutely none.

Seriously, what's the point of all this money, if I can't improve the life of someone so deserving?

THIRTY

Hurricane Penny Comes to Town...

Emma

"**O**kay, people," Libby says, walking around the lobby handing out lists to everyone present. "Now, we knew this might happen, but it's all right, because I've got a plan."

Of course she's got a plan. She's Libby—the most thoroughly organized bride I've ever seen. She's calm in an almost eerie sort of way, considering the fact that we've had to shut down the resort and most of the island has been evacuated because of the potential for tropical storm Ernie to become a class four hurricane within the next few days.

I find myself watching Libby's mum, Penny, who happens to be the complete opposite of her daughter. Penny Dewitt is one of the flightiest people I think I've ever met. She arrived two days ago with her super young boyfriend/puppy dog, Jorge, and according to Rosy, she's done nothing but drink by the pool and pretend she's not vaping weed (which she most certainly is).

Jorge looks like he spends far too much time in front of the mirror working on his top knot and keeping his beard looking just so. Apparently, Penny picked him up in Argentina, and it's clear to everyone in the room, including him, that she's ready to take him back there and drop him off. She's been making some obvious advances in Will's direction which couldn't be more inappropriate since Will is about to be her daughter's brother-in-law. Also, she seems to have no regard for poor Jorge, who looks like he might just burst into tears at any moment.

She is the least motherly mother of the bride I can imagine. She either calls Libby 'Mini-Me,' which makes no sense since they're total opposites, or she calls her Breeze—Libby's original name apparently, which is rather ironic since there's really nothing breezy about her.

"We'll most likely lose power at some point," Libby's saying when I finally get back to paying attention. "This means we need to have torches and emergency candles at the ready. We'll all be staying in the main building for the duration of the storm, and since we're all together, we're going to go ahead with the wedding. Fidel has gotten his minister's certificate online, so he'll handle the formalities this evening. Emma, how's the dinner coming along? Do you need any help with that?"

"I'm all set," I say with a smile. "The only hiccup would be if the power goes out in the next couple of hours but I rounded up a couple of headlamps for Junior and me to use, and we can use a lighter to start up the stove burners and the oven so long as we don't lose gas, we'll be fine."

"And if we lose gas?" Libby asks.

"Then we'll be eating very fancy peanut butter and jelly sandwiches."

Libby nods and smiles. "Sounds perfect."

Harrison, who's been boarding up windows with the crew, comes walking in looking much happier than one would expect given the circumstances.

Libby grins up at him. "All set?"

"All set," Harrison says, putting his arm around her.

I can't help but feel sorry for Libby. She's given up everything for Harrison and here she is on her wedding day without her grandparents who raised her or her best friend, none of whom could fly in because of the storm. But maybe I shouldn't pity her. After all, she really looks incredibly happy. "Okay," she says. "I guess we should get ready. We'll meet everyone here in the restaurant at 5 p.m. for the ceremony. Dinner will be at six."

***

Junior and I spend the afternoon in a mad rush, trying to prepare everything while the power is still on. It's a little weird since this is *his* kitchen but *I'm* the one in charge of tonight's menu, so it's hard to know exactly who's in charge. He's been a head chef here since I was in middle school, and from the way he acts, he hasn't quite accepted the fact that I've grown up.

We're doing a Carib-Asian meal that he's not familiar with and he clearly doesn't trust that I know what I'm doing because he's asked me at least twelve times now if I'm sure about this. His lack of faith is doing a number on my confidence because I'm really *not* sure this meal will work out, having only made these dishes once before for Pierce. Not that I'm letting Junior know that. Outwardly, I'm like the ice woman—cool, collected, and confident. But inside, I'm pretty much a nervous wreck.

Honestly, the pressure at this moment is clinical-strength-antiperspirant stressful. I should have stuck with a tried and true lobster dinner, instead of going for a showy, unforgettable menu. If I mess this up, the only thing unforgettable will be what a crap chef I am.

Too late to change it now. The ceremony starts in less than an hour and we have a lot left to get done. There's a total of twenty-four guests, including Darnell and Rosy, who brought Starsky and Hutch so that they can hunker down here at the resort until the storm passes. The dogs are running around the front of the restaurant at the moment, but will be shut up in a suite during the actual ceremony. I hope.

They arrived a few hours ago and Rosy's been in and out of the kitchen all afternoon, sampling food and sneaking treats out for her dogs. The rest of the time she spends barking orders at Harrison, Darnell, Will, Fidel, Nelson (Harrison's best friend), and a few of the staff members who are all doing their best to turn the Brazilian steakhouse into a romantic chapel.

Libby and Harrison decided to have the wedding and reception here since it's the only restaurant attached to the main building, and it's a really cool space. It has a high wood-planked ceiling, white smooth stucco walls, tall potted plants sprinkled throughout, and rust-coloured tile flooring for a bit of a South American flair. Even if they didn't do much other than move the chairs and tables around, it's a lovely place for a wedding.

Fidel's wife, Winnie, who is currently very pregnant with their second child, is up in the Palatial Suite with Libby, helping with her hair and makeup. Their son, Harrison Junior, is having a nap in his stroller in the restaurant while Darnell waits impatiently for him to wake up so he can play with him.

"Emma, you should go get yourself ready. I can handle the rest of it," Junior says, as he chops an onion.

Glancing at the clock, I see I've got about forty-five minutes to shower and get wedding ready. "Okay, thanks." I quickly put the bowl of pineapple mango chutney I've made into the refrigerator and say a silent prayer that the power holds until after dinner.

I rush to the stairwell and take the four flights up to the Palatial Suite. When I walk through the door, I can't help but have a slight pang, remembering the last time I was in here. (Okay, not slight as much as a ginormous, knock-you-on-your-arse pang.) I can picture Pierce pacing the room while he dictated. I close my eyes to blink away the image and remind myself that today is about Libby and Harrison's happy ending, not mine. (Not *that* type of happy ending, eww.)

It's been four months since I've seen Pierce, and every day that I'm busy is a day I'm grateful for because it allows me to stay distracted. On the plus side, I've gone from thinking about him a thousand times an hour to about a hundred times a day, which I would say is definite progress. Excruciatingly slow, horribly painful progress. But I knew what I was signing up for when I started the whole thing, so I might as well shut up about it.

Thirty minutes later, I'm sitting on a stool with a very pregnant belly in my face while Winnie applies my makeup. Libby, who's all set to go, is sitting at the desk on the other side of the suite, probably writing thank you notes already, and looking elegant in her airy chiffon sleeveless gown. Her normally wild red hair is swept up in a twist and her tastefully applied makeup gives her a timeless look.

Her mum, Penny, is here as well, and for some reason, Jorge has joined the ladies for the pre-wedding prep. He's standing in front of the mirror rubbing stinky beard oil into his long, brown beard to get it nice and...what? Oily?

Every time he looks at Libby, he gets all misty-eyed and says how proud he is of her, which seems a little weird for several reasons including, but not limited to, the fact that Libby's only met him once before—on her first wedding day (and they only spent about five minutes together before the entire thing was called off), he's six years younger than her, he's sporting a plethora of tattoos including some lovely neck artwork, and Penny, who is his only connection to Libby, keeps insisting they're 'keeping it casual.'

Penny, meanwhile, is wearing the shortest mother-of-the-bride dress a person could get—it's more of a long, floral, off-the-shoulder shirt than a dress, really. She's got the legs to pull it off, but it's still not quite the right look for her daughter's wedding.

Winnie does some very fast contouring with one hand while she eats a pastry with the other. "This baby must be a girl," she says. "I never had a sweet tooth like this with little Harrison."

"I don't know," Penny says. "Look at how low you're carrying her. Just a minute. Let me do the ring trick and we'll know for sure." She removes a gold chain from around her neck and slides a ring from her pinky toe onto it. When she straightens up, she stops for a moment and gives Winnie a thoughtful look. "Oh, unless you don't *want* to know, that is. There's a certain excitement in the unpredictable."

Winnie grins. "Let's do it."

With Winnie and Penny busy scientifically determining the sex of her child, I get up and walk over to Libby to check on her. "How are you doing?" I asked quietly.

"Good," Libby says, smiling up at me. "I think we've got everything under control. As long as we have the rings and a minister, that's all we need to get this done, isn't it?"

I stare at her for a moment, trying to determine whether or not she is really happy or if she's just pretending, but it's impossible to tell. "Are you really okay, Libby? I know this isn't the beach wedding surrounded by your closest friends and family that you had planned."

"None of that matters," Libby says, reaching out and taking my hand into hers and giving it a squeeze. "Not when you're with the right man. This is honestly the happiest day of my life."

I feel myself tearing up and blink quickly, trying not to ruin Winnie's handiwork. "I'm glad you're happy," I say, giving her hand a squeeze back. "Truly."

"Thank you, Emma. And I know you're going to be this happy one day in the not-too-distant future," she says with a confident smile.

If only that were true...

***

"Will you, Harrison Theodore Banks, take Liberty Dawn Dewitt to be your lawfully wedded wife? Will you love her, honour her, remain faithful to her, and support her in her dreams for as long as you both shall live?" Fidel asks.

"I will," Harrison says, holding both of Libby's hands in his and staring into her eyes.

Okay, now I'm just pathetic because tears are uncontrollably running down my cheeks as I watch the two of them together exchanging their vows and wish more than anything that our parents could be here in this moment for him.

Rosy, who's standing next to me, sniffs loudly and says, "Oh, this is just so beautiful."

I take a moment to look around the restaurant and smile at everything that Harrison and the rest of the crew have managed to do. They've covered all the boarded windows with billowy white cloth and there are candles lit everywhere, giving the room a warm, romantic feel. A makeshift altar has been set up using a wooden archway from one of the gardens. It's been covered with golden trumpet vines for the two of them to stand under. Eight-foot-tall potted palms have been moved into position with three on each side of the archway to create a focal point for the ceremony. Light linens cover all of the chairs that have been set up for the guests on this side of the room. The other side of the restaurant holds a horseshoe-shaped table for the twenty-four of us to share in our feast as soon as the ceremony is over, provided I don't cock it all up.

Fidel grins at Libby and says, "You may now kiss the groom!"

I stand back while the rest of the party congratulates the happy newlyweds, and for some reason, I can't seem to stop crying.

"You all right?" Will says, bumping me on the arm.

I look up at him, surprised that he's standing beside me and embarrassed for him to see me all emotional and girly. I give him a quick nod and clear my throat.

"I know. I'm missing Mum and Dad too, today," he says, his face screwing up a little bit with sadness.

I sniffle, dabbing my wet cheeks with the backs of my hands. "It sucks so hard that they're gone."

"Agreed," he says, shifting his gaze to the happy couple. "I think they would have loved Libby."

"Me too."

I loop my arm through Will's and rest my head on his shoulder for a moment while we watch Harrison pop open a bottle of champagne. It hurts so much to wish for something you can never have. Every cell in my body aches to see my parents again, to hug them tightly and talk to them—Mum especially, because she would know what to do about all these feelings that I can't seem to ignore. She would know just what to say to help me forget about a certain famous author.

Every day I think about ringing him up under some lame pretense, or just hanging up once he answers just so I can hear his voice. But I don't let myself. I can't. I spent so much time pretending I was 'Miss I Love Casual Sex' that trying to reach out now would be an utter humiliation. It would mean he knows I'm actually 'Miss I Want Forever,' which was never part of the deal.

Taking a deep breath, I decide I have to just get on with it. Time to cook.

And that's when it happens—the room becomes suddenly quiet. The air conditioning shuts off at that same moment the emergency lighting turns on.

Oh perfect. Now I need to prepare a wedding feast in the dark.

***

Forty minutes later, I stand surveying the results of my work, wiping the sweat off my brow with a dish towel. I no longer look like a wedding guest, but a chef in Hell's Kitchen. I'm in my uniform with a headlamp on that has totally ruined my hair. I'm so sweaty that I'm sure my makeup is down around my neck by now, but I couldn't care less. I'm on the verge of pulling off an unforgettable meal—in the good sense of the word.

Junior and I bring out the appetizers, and before I go back to make the mains, I stand and watch as the guests take their first bites. I fight not to think about the expression on Pierce's face when he ate this exact meal on our last day together, but there's no use. The smells, the textures, even the satisfied faces remind me of him. *Forget him and enjoy this moment, Emma.*

I glance over at Will, who has somehow ended up next to Penny (and I think we all know how). He gives me a desperate look while she tries to feed him some of the chicken satay off her fork. Poor Jorge is sitting on the other side of her, tapping on her arm to get her attention. When she ignores him, he starts kissing her bare shoulder loudly. Penny brushes him off with one hand and turns back to her new prospective conquest.

Darnell, who is digging into his fourth jerk pork spring roll, says, "Harrison, the girl *can cook.* Why have you been hidin' her out on some deserted island all this time?"

I grin to myself as I hurry back into the dimly-lit kitchen to plate up the main course. Junior is already getting started. He smiles at me when I return, blinding me for a second when his headlamp points directly into my eyes. "Emma, I tried the sauce for the lobster tails—complete perfection," he says, putting his fingers to his lips and making a kissing motion.

"Thank you, Junior. That means a lot coming from you." And it does.

"The student has become the master," he says with a little wink.

The two of us work together quickly to get the meals plated while the rain pelts the boarded-up windows and the wind howls. Once we've served everything, the two of us sit down to eat.

Harrison, who is seated next to Libby in the centre of the horseshoe, raises his glass of white and mouths, "Well done!" to me.

I shrug and mouth back, "De nada."

After a few minutes, Harrison and Libby both stand, and Harrison clinks the side of his glass with his fork to get everyone's attention.

"Hey, we're supposed to do that," Rosy says haughtily.

"Kiss her!" Darnell shouts.

"Wait till you're in your room!" Will calls, earning him a laugh.

"Libby and I would like to thank everyone for being here to make this happen. We know it was a lot to ask for you all to come here and to have to stay here to ride out the storm with us."

"At a five-star resort with a stocked fridge?" Nelson says. "I don't think anyone minds as much as you think."

Harrison grins at his best friend, then looks around the table. "It's on a day like today that you really realize how lucky you are to have family and friends to share your life with," Harrison says, his eyes looking a little misty, if I'm not mistaken. "On an occasion like this, you can't help but think about the people who couldn't be here. In particular, Libby's grandparents who are back in Avonia, and her best friend, Alice, but also my mum and dad, who I know would have loved knowing my beautiful bride. We lost them at such a young age, and it made me aware of how important it is to make the most of the time you've got, and how you need to keep the people you love close." Harrison looks right at me when he says it and gives me a meaningful look. I tear up and blow him a kiss.

Looking at me, he says, "So, thank you for sharing this day, and our lives, with us."

Libby puts her arm around her new husband's back and says, "Yes, thank you *all* for turning this space into the perfect place for us to get married. And I'd like to extend our eternal gratitude to Emma and Junior for this incredible meal. Emma planned the menu herself and it was a delightful surprise for us. We didn't know what she had in store, but we knew it would be wonderful, and it was. Truly spectacular, Emma, especially given the lack of power."

"No problem," I say, revelling in the moment.

"Seriously, Emma, this was amazing," Harrison says. "I think this may be the best meal I've ever eaten. I had no idea my kid sister was so talented." He holds up his glass and says, "Please raise your glasses to Emma."

"To Emma." Murmurs of agreement come from around the room and I sit feeling awkward. Okay, maybe awkward isn't the right word. Maybe thrilled or proud or ecstatic would be more accurate.

Harrison holds up his glass to me. "Today has been perfect, and that's because of you."

Libby gives me a little wink, then takes a deep breath and says, "Harrison and I also have an announcement to make. If all goes according to plan, in six months, we'll be welcoming a new addition to the family."

"We're having a baby!" Harrison says, beaming.

Rosy bursts into tears, sobbing audibly as she gets up and walks over to squeeze the life out of both of them. Tears fill my eyes and my mouth hangs open.

From across the room, I hear Penny say, "Wait. I'm going to be a grandma?"

***

It's late in the evening and I'm alone in the kitchen wearing a headlamp while I scrub the pots and pans. I decided to get the job over with when Libby and Harrison went up to their suite. I told Junior to stay at the party, which is still going as strong as the rain outside.

My mobile buzzes and I glance at it, my heart skipping a beat like it has for the sixteen weeks since Pierce left. It's not him of course, but an alert from the Benavente Weather Service stating that the storm has been downgraded and won't be turning into a full-blown hurricane. I let out a sigh of relief knowing that we've escaped massive damage and the months of cleanup that comes with it.

The power hasn't come back on, but I don't even care. I don't care if I'm standing at this sink for another week because

I'm still riding the high of making the perfect Carib-Asian wedding feast.

The door swings open and Harrison walks in, his bowtie hanging loosely around his opened shirt collar.

"I thought you went upstairs already," I say.

"I did, but Libby was out like a light about thirty seconds after we got in the room." He smiles, looking completely content as he opens the fridge and takes out two beers.

"She must be exhausted."

"Yup. It's been a long couple of days for her, especially considering she's pregnant." He twists the tops off both beers and sets one down next to the sink for me, then has a swig of his before picking up a dish towel.

"I can't believe you guys are going to be parents," I say, picking up the bottle of beer and clinking it to his. "Cheers, bro. Congratulations."

"Thanks. I honestly don't know if I'm more excited about being married or the baby," he says with a huge grin.

"Baby for me. I'm going to be Auntie Emma."

He has a sip of beer, then says, "I hope I'm ready for this."

"You've been ready since you were eleven. You've already got the dad jokes down."

"Ha ha."

"Seriously, you'll be amazing and so will Libby. That's one lucky little baby."

He smiles for a moment before setting his sights on me again. "You doing okay, Emma?" he asks, giving me a concerned look. "Are you happy?"

"Of course I'm happy. It's been such a terrific day—in spite of the storm. I'm going to be an auntie, and the dinner turned out pretty damn well, if I do say so myself."

"It was an amazing meal, Em. You've got talent to spare, kid," he says. "But what I mean is, are you happy being back home again?"

"Absolutely," I say, turning back to the pot I'm working on to avoid eye contact. "There's no place in the world I'd rather be."

"Liar. You're miserable. Everyone can see it, even the guests."

"No, they can't," I say scoffing.

"One of them left a comment on TripAdvisor about the super depressing chef."

"So?" I roll my eyes. "That doesn't prove anything. Some people are just really picky."

"I know you, Emma. You haven't been yourself since Pierce left."

"Whatever," I say, scrubbing the pot extra hard. "I've just been in a funk but it's got nothing to do with him. I didn't want anything long-term with him anyway. It would never have worked out."

"Oh, that's too bad because he called here to find out when you'd be getting some time off."

My knees feel weak and I freeze in place. "Wh...when? What did he say? What did you say? Why would he call *you* and not *me*?"

"This morning. He started out trying to sound casual, like he was checking to see if things were going well and if we needed any more help promoting the resort now that he's got some time," Harrison says. "Apparently, he's been working day and night so the book can go to a rush print or something but he wanted to reach out the first chance he got."

"Really?" I ask my heart relocating to my throat and pounding like Junior tenderizing a T-bone.

"That's what he said." Harrison lifts his eyebrows like he's not sure if he believes it or not. "I got the sense he wanted to find out if you'd moved on without upsetting you."

"Exactly what did he say that gave you that impression?" I ask, tapping my foot impatiently.

"I don't know. Nothing specific. It was just his tone."

Gah! Men are awful at girl talk, no? "Describe it."

"What? I don't know. Kind of muted, I guess, if I had to pick a word."

"Don't pick one word. Pick *all* the words. Be specific and precise. What did he say and how did he say it?"

Harrison shakes his head, looking confused. "He asked how you were and I said you were fine. I asked how he was doing and he said fine...or okay. He might have said okay..."

"Which is it? Fine or okay?"

Shrugging, Harrison says, "I really can't remember."

"Oh my God! You are *terrible* at this. Why couldn't Libby have answered the phone?"

"Jesus, Emma. Forget the details. The point is, after a few minutes, he finally came out and asked if I could give you some time off so you can come see him."

"And?!"

"And I told him you had some time right now because of the storm, but that it was also the reason you won't be able to go anywhere for a few days..."

Not bothering to dry off my hands, I pick up my beer and take three long gulps.

"Thought so," Harrison says with a reluctant smile. "He's sending a plane for you as soon as the airport opens up. He wants you to go see him in Valcourt."

A plane? Valcourt? My brain feels like it's going to shut down and I don't know what to focus on first. I turn on the water and rinse the pot, my mind racing through what Harrison has just told me. *Nope. Do not get your hopes up, Emma. Not after spending four miserable months trying to forget him.* "The smart thing for me to do would be to just try to forget him. I have a life here and he has a life there, and that's that."

"True, but if the two of you are meant to build a life together, you'll find a way to make it work," Harrison says, turning the water off and taking the world's most thoroughly rinsed pot out of my hands. He dries it, letting his words float in the air.

Build a life together? I don't think that's going to happen. He probably wants more meaningful casual sex. I let the water out of the sink and watch as it swirls down the drain. After a moment, I say, "He doesn't believe in building a life with someone. He's a lone wolf."

"That's stupid. There's no such thing. Wolves are pack animals."

"Right? That's what I told him." Shaking my head, I say, "I'm not going to go. It would be a really bad idea. I know I said I was cool with the whole temporary thing, but to be honest, I have been struggling to get over him. I shouldn't put myself through that again."

"Yeah, you're probably right," Harrison says, nodding his head. "Although, to be honest, I'm not sure you'd have to get over him again."

"Why? Did he say that?" I ask, swallowing hard.

"Not exactly. It wasn't so much what he said but how he sounded," Harrison says, having a sip of his beer.

No beer sipping! Only girl talking!! "What did he sound like?"

"Like a guy whose heart was broken."

THIRTY-ONE

Long Haul Booty Call

Emma – Somewhere Over the Atlantic Ocean

"What are you up to?" I ask, smiling into my mobile screen.

Priya holds up perfectly shaped tortellini. "Making dinner while I wait for the mailman."

"Yum. What's the filling?" I say, wondering how long it'll take her to realize I'm on a freaking private jet at the moment.

"Chicken and truffle."

"Nice. Cream and chive sauce?" I ask, holding up a glass of champagne and taking a long sip. *Come on, look at the screen.*

"Yup," she says, brushing egg wash on a circle of dough.

For the past several weeks, Priya's been putting her culinary skills to use at home while she waits for an acceptance letter for a med school she doesn't want to attend. She's started cooking again, but says each meal she makes feels like a goodbye to the real Priya, so it's more like a torturous 'looking for closure' thing than anything else. So far, she's had two rejections and no answer from the other schools, and somehow the 'noes' have depressed her even more. But I get it. Rejection feels awful, even if it *is* for something you never wanted in the first place.

"Wait? Are you wearing a scarf?" she asks, squinting. "What are you dressed up for?"

"I thought I'd try to bring back the days when a woman would get all dolled up to go on a plane." I hold the mobile at arm's length so Priya can see I'm dressed in long black dress pants, a long-sleeved black sweater, and a Burberry knock-off scarf that I picked up yesterday. I turn the phone so she can get a look at the luxury with which I'm surrounded.

"Did you say you're on a plane, because that looks like a living room in some rich person's...oh my God, is that Pierce Davenport's plane?" she asks, her voice rising two octaves.

"Umm-hmm. He sent his jet to pick me up for the weekend. No biggie," I say nonchalantly.

Priya screams so loud that I glance around, hoping that none of the flight crew heard that. I'd hate for them to know I'm not exactly used to living the lifestyle of the rich and famous.

"You've been sent for?" Priya asks, her eyes wide.

"I have," I say, stretching my entire face into a grin so big it almost hurts. "He would have come himself but he's had to make some last-minute changes to *The Fire of Knights*. He'll be done by the time the plane lands."

"Oh my God, that's so romantic." Priya clutches her heart with both hands.

"To be honest, I'm not sure if it's romantic or not yet. I'll find out when I get there."

"What? He sent a plane for you. That is firmly on the romantic side of the spectrum."

"Or is it just a rich guy booty call?" I ask. The awful, yet familiar, tightness in my stomach comes back. It's come and gone every few minutes since Pierce texted with the flight details.

"No way. A guy doesn't fly a woman halfway around the world just to have sex. There are probably thousands of women within a two-mile radius of his house that would gladly hop into bed with him."

While the thought of thousands of women clambering to have sex with Pierce isn't exactly comforting, she makes a good point. If this was just a fling, would he really go to all this trouble?

I've been doing my best not to hope for more than the right here and now—well, more like *there* and *in a few hours*, I suppose, but you get the idea. I've been miserable without him but I'd be a fool to think that he's going to ask me to spend the rest of my life with him. He's not that type of man and according to Oprah, when someone shows you who they are, you should believe them. "Honestly, Priya, when someone's got the kind of money he has, they can afford to be picky. He knows we have a great time together, and that he can trust me to be discreet. It really might just be a few days of shagging."

Her face falls. "Don't you think you should have found that out before you left? It's been hard enough for us to get over him the first time."

Rolling my eyes, I say, "For you maybe. I've been doing really well."

"Seriously? You actually believe that?"

"Okay, *fine*. It would be nice to know if this is something in the long-term territory, but I'm trying *really hard* not to go in with unrealistic expectations. Could be that he wants some sort of long-distance arrangement where we meet up whenever one of us has time off."

"*Or*, he's flying you all the way there so he can ask you to marry him," Priya says, looking hopeful.

"Not him. Trust me," I say, shaking my head. "But that's okay. Maybe this will be the start of a sophisticated, mature relationship—one that allows each of us to be independent and have our own lives, but still get together every couple of months to have some fun as a fabulously unconventional globe-trotting power couple."

Priya screws up her face, looking very skeptical. "Is that really the kind of relationship you want?"

"Maybe. I won't know until we have *the talk*. But I think I'd be fine with that." I nod firmly, trying to convince myself. "Besides, is *any* relationship perfect? I think not."

"Yeah, I guess so..." she says, sounding completely unconvinced. "But, most of the time you just hear how hard the long-distance thing is. One person usually gets more attached and wants to live in the same place but the other one refuses so they break up. *Or* one of them moves so they can be together, then winds up resenting the other one for ruining their otherwise great life, and they end up miserable, which means they either break up or just live together with a simmering hate between them."

"Wow. Thanks, Debbie Downer," I quip.

"I'm just trying to help. I don't want to see you get hurt."

"Well, as much as I appreciate it, I think Pierce and I need to define things for ourselves. We're not like other people. We don't need all the traditional stuff everyone else thinks is so important. This could work for us quite nicely."

"Okay, two things come to mind. Number one: you just said 'for us,' which clearly means you're expecting this to be more than just a long-haul booty call. Number two: what you're describing doesn't sound like sharing your life with someone. It sounds more like just chronically missing him with a few days of relief and shagging here and there."

"Okay, well, *thanks* for the advice. I should let you go so I can get back to enjoying my flight," I say in a hard tone.

"Sorry for wanting you to be happy," Priya says sarcastically.

"I *was* happy until I talked to you."

"Being in denial and being happy are not the same. I want you to be happy for more than just a few days, but if you don't think you're worth more than that, I guess that's up to you."

"What's this obsession with 'being together forever' that people have?" I ask, feeling completely irritated. "So, this may not fit into your definition of the perfect relationship. So what? The only thing that matters is what Pierce and I think."

"Hey, I'm not trying to ruin your fun or anything. I'm just worried about you. But if you think this is really what you want, then I'll get behind it."

"This is really what I want."

"Great," she says without a trace of enthusiasm. "Then I'm happy for you."

"Thanks. I should let you get back to your pasta."

"Right. Yeah," she says. "Have fun."

"I will."

When I get off the phone, I sit staring around the plush white carpet and the large windows that are so clean you could eat off of them—well, if they weren't upright, that is.

The ball of tension in my gut has now tripled in size. As much as I can't admit it to anyone else, there's a tiny part of me that's worried I may be within range of serious heartbreak. Honestly, I'm a little freaked out that I *may*, in fact, want the full meal deal—the marriage and the kids and the falling asleep next to each other every night, and sipping coffee together in the morning, and getting irritated with him for leaving the toilet seat up, and the knowing he's mine every damn day for good. But knowing him the way I do, I don't think he's going to want any of that. And it's not like I can admit to him that *I* want it. Not after pretending I'm totally supportive of his 'lone wolfiness.' I can't be that girl that suddenly says, 'I love you just the way you are, now change everything.' I can't even be the girl who says 'I love you' because he doesn't believe in love. Dammit. Why did I get on this plane?

THIRTY-TWO

Operation Ruin Your Chance at Happiness

Pierce

I am currently sitting in the back of a limo parked just off the tarmac at the private flight hangar of the Valcourt International Airport. It's an unseasonably cold, grey November morning, and I find myself wishing it were warm and sunny for Emma's arrival. I glance at my watch for the third time in under a minute, bouncing my knee with nervous energy. After months of no contact, I've made a leap of faith that for some reason feels absolutely right.

If all goes well, by this time tomorrow, Emma and I will be celebrating our new future together with her as the head chef at Intermission, the top restaurant in all of Avonia, which I acquired last week. It's a prime piece of waterfront real estate that borders downtown Valcourt. The view of the North Sea is one of the best in the kingdom, and, better still, the kitchen was designed by the three-time CEDA Grand Prix Award winner, Johann Petersburg, who apparently in the culinary world is a pretty big deal. The front of house, as they call it in the business, is trendy and elegant, with a modern sleek design, and it has a rooftop terrace that allows patrons to enjoy the view along with their dinner on a warm day. It's fully staffed, wildly popular, and is waiting for Emma to slide in and make it her own.

Once word gets out that I own it, it should be nearly impossible to get a reservation for years to come, especially because *The Fire of Knights* comes out next month, just in time for Christmas. Sullivan and Stone have pulled off a publishing miracle, pushing back all other publications by two weeks so they could do a rush print on the hardcover.

Speaking of Sullivan and Stone, that's where we're heading right after I show Emma Intermission. We're meeting up with Gwen Sullivan to score Emma a book deal so Carib-Asian cuisine can become the best thing since sliced garlic bread fresh from the oven. Then, finally, I'll whisk her over to my fortress of solitude so she and I can have incredible 'we're starting the most amazing life together and living our dreams' sex non-stop for the next several weeks.

Yes! The plane is pulling up. I do a quick breath check and decide another Listerine melt-away is in order, even though I've used nearly an entire pack in the last ten minutes. I am pathetically nervous and excited. My heart feels like it's going to pound right out of my ribcage and onto the car floor.

But, seriously, why should I be nervous? I'm about to give Emma everything she's ever wanted. How could she possibly say no?

***

As soon as the door to the plane opens, I get out of the limo and hurry to the bottom of the staircase. I get there in time to see her as she comes through the open doorway. Unable to wait any longer, I take the steps two at a time while she rushes down them. We meet in the middle, and I wrap my arms around her waist while she crushes my mouth with hers. We kiss like that soldier and nurse in the famous photo from after World War II. (Except not quite because I read somewhere that the nurse didn't know him, didn't expect him to kiss her, and totally wasn't having it, whereas Emma is most certainly having this.) If it weren't so bloody cold, we'd strip down right here and go for it on the stairs.

When we pull back, I say, "My God, you're beautiful. I almost forgot how stunning you are." I kiss her again, thoroughly enjoying the feeling of her warmth against me and breathing in the scent of her skin.

"Thank you. I have to say, that greeting was worth flying halfway around the world for," she says in a slightly breathy voice.

A particularly big gust of wind reminds me that she must be freezing, being in no way used to this kind of weather. I pull off my wool coat and wrap it around her shoulders. "Come on. Let's get you into the limo."

"I won't argue with you on that one," Emma says. "How about next time you come to me?" she asks, following me down the steps.

"I may have an even better idea," I say as we hurry across the tarmac.

"What?" Emma asks.

"I'm afraid it's more of a show than a tell sort of thing..."

We make out in the back of the limo the entire way to the restaurant. By the time we arrive, I've all but forgotten our destination and am now wishing I was taking her straight home so we could do all sorts of catching up without any further delay. But then I remind myself that the whole point of this is to show her this is more than just a fling. I'm going to give her everything she's ever desired, and *then* get on with the sexy sex.

The limo stops in front of the darkened one-story brick building bearing a long black awning that reads "INTERMISSION" in muted gold letters. Through the large front windows, you can see the perfectly set empty tables waiting for patrons. Excitement overtakes me and I feel like this is the moment before the moment that will change my life forever. I look down at her with a wide smile, happiness bursting inside me.

"It doesn't look like they're open yet," she says, turning to face me.

"You're correct. They're not." I dig around in the pocket of the coat Emma is wearing and pull out the set of keys.

She stares at me, looking adorably confused and small in my wool jacket. "Did you rent it out so we can have a private meal?"

"Not exactly," I say as I unlock the front door. Silence and warm air greet us when we walk inside. I lock the door behind us and flick on the lights. "This is considered the trendiest, best restaurant in all of Avonia. Everyone who's anyone is seen here on Saturday night. It seats eighty inside and the rooftop patio seats another forty during the warmer months. The kitchen has been designed by Johann Petersburg. Have you heard of him?"

"Umm yes. He's like the JK Rowling of kitchen design," she answers with a little grin. "Just kidding, he's bigger. He's like the Pierce Davenport of kitchen design."

"Ha! Nice save," I say, feigning irritation. "Come on, let's go see the best part," I say, grabbing her by the hand and rushing her to the back.

We walk into the large, bright, stainless steel kitchen and I start the tour.

"First, you'll notice three separate preparation areas have been installed to allow for temperature control and prevent cross-contamination because apparently certain raw foods don't play well with each other. If you look up, you'll see state of the art fire-suppressant systems in all the cooker hoods—well, I suppose you can't see them really because they're on the inside of those vents but I'm assured they're there. Emergency shutoffs on each wall," I say pointing to the red buttons scattered throughout the space. "All the services, including the ventilation, temperature, humidity, and even the four walk-in fridges, are controlled by a computer in the office back there, and the head chef can even access it from a mobile phone which I thought was pretty cool."

"That *is* cool," she says as I continue to pull her around the kitchen.

Turning to her, I stop and smile. "It's fully staffed, runs like clockwork, and, best of all, is ready for you to put your stamp on it."

Emma stares at me for a moment, her mouth open, but doesn't say a word.

Shit. What is that look? Shock? Yes, she's in shock. "I know, this is a lot to take in. You've been flying all night and I imagine the last thing you thought I'd do is say, 'Here darling, I bought you a restaurant.'"

"You could say that," she answers, turning a slow circle and staring at the large space.

"Do you like it? When I saw it, I immediately imagined you standing here," I say, grinning as I quickly move to the grill area. "Or here," I say, sliding to the food preparation area.

"Plating meals, calling out orders, stirring sauces, making Carib-Asian food the most popular trend in all of the UK."

"It's amazing," she says with a smile that fades all too quickly. "But I don't understand. You *bought* this for me?" she asks, her eyebrows knitting together.

"Yes. It's all yours," I answer, rushing over to her and wrapping my arms around her waist. "Every fork, every napkin, every bloody square inch of it."

She stares at me. "So it was up for sale and you walked in and just said, 'I'll take it,'" she says, doing a pretty reasonable impression of me.

"Not quite. I did a little research to determine which restaurant was the best in the city, then I made them an offer they wouldn't refuse." God, that sounded impressive, no? I really am quite the romantic.

So, why isn't she jumping into my arms, kissing me senseless whilst we peel off our clothes so we can break some health code violations?

This is probably one of those life surprises that is so overwhelmingly wonderful that you can't react because it's almost too much. Yes, that's it. "I've shocked you. Sorry. I was just so excited for you to see it all that I thought we'd come straight here. I probably should have given you some type of hint or something." Kissing her on the lips, I then say, "But *this* is where you belong, Emma." Letting go of her, I place my hands on the counter-top. "Here, in this state-of-the-art kitchen so you can create whatever you like without having to answer to anyone, or serve irritating honeymooners or grumpy arrogant authors who don't give a damn what they eat...or wait for your chance at greatness or...or ever have to wash another pot again."

"But, I didn't...this isn't mine. I can't just *take* a restaurant from someone and pretend it belongs to me." She shakes her head in a way that is more than a little concerning.

"Of course you can." I lift my hands to her face and cup her cheeks. "You deserve this, Emma. I can't let you waste your talents at Eden when you should be here getting the recognition that is rightfully yours."

"It's lovely, Pierce, really, truly lovely of you to do this," she says lifting onto her tiptoes to give me a soft kiss. "You believe in me which is honestly the greatest feeling in the whole world, and as far as kitchens go, I couldn't have dreamed up a better one."

"But?" I ask because I can see in her eyes that a big ass 'but' is coming my way.

"I don't deserve this, Pierce. I've done nothing to earn it." She takes my hands from her face and backs up a couple of steps. "I don't want to be given something because I'm good in bed. I want it because I'm a great chef."

"I'm not giving you this because I like sleeping with you—which I do, by the way. I'm giving this to you because you're a talented chef and I want to see you fulfil your potential."

"But I didn't earn this," she says with a shaky sigh.

"I beg to differ. Without you, I'd have never finished the series. You *saved* me, Emma. You saved the entire *Clash of Crowns* franchise. My publisher, the entire cast and crew at NBO, all of us. Without you, my legacy would have been ruined," I say taking both of her hands in mine. "Let me save you back."

"Save me from what?"

"From a lonely, dreary existence on a deserted island. Save you from obscurity when you have so much to offer the world."

"It's not *that* bad," she answers. "It's not great, but it's where I'm supposed to be right now—paying my dues."

"Skip the dues." I give her a quick kiss. "Skip them. You don't have to pay them anymore. You can start your *real life* now. *Here*," I say.

"But I already have a life. I have a family that needs me and responsibilities and obligations," she says, pacing a bit. "I can't just up and leave. Not after everything my brother's done for me."

"I've already thought of that," I say smoothly. "I'll cut Harrison a cheque for your education and we'll find someone who can slide into your place at the resort so he won't have to do that himself. What about that friend of yours—the one you went to school with? I bet she'd take your old job in a heartbeat."

"That sounds almost like you're going to buy me from him," she says with a laugh that sounds more horrified than amused.

"No, I didn't mean it that way. I just meant you won't have to feel obligated to him anymore," he says.

"I'm not working there because I'm paying off some financial debt. I'm there because that's my family's business—*it's our life*. Will and Harrison and I have always been there for each other, our entire lives. It's our *home*. They're my family. I can't just abandon them."

"It's not abandoning them. It's starting a new life. Harrison loves you and he wants you to be happy. He said as much on the phone," I say. Okay, change of tactic. I'll be cute about it. Nothing else seems to be working... "If this will make *you* happy, it will make *him* happy. So, really you'd be doing him a *favour* if you move here."

"It's not that simple, Pierce," she says, shaking her head.

"It is if you want it to be. Your brother will understand and I think you know it." Crikey. This is not going at all the way I thought it would. "It's easy enough to find a chef, there are loads of them out of work."

Her head snaps back. "So, we're a dime a dozen? Is that what you mean?"

"No, of course not. None with your passion or talent," I say, starting to feel rather annoyed at the fact that she's not being more gracious about my gift. "Christ, this really isn't the reaction I was expecting."

"Well, I'm afraid your expectations weren't very realistic if you thought you could just decide my entire life for me without bothering to consult me," she says, staring at me in a way that makes me not so sure I want her here at all. "What did you think? That after five months of nothing, I'd fall into your arms and say yes to all of this?"

Yes. Yes, I did. "I certainly expected you to be more grateful," I answer in an icy tone.

"Oh for—" She pauses and takes a deep breath. "I don't even know what we *are* to each other. I'm certainly not moving halfway around the world without knowing what this is," she says, pointing back and forth between us.

"It's a relationship. It's me saying that I've missed you and I want you here." I run my hands through my hair in frustration. "I don't know what will happen, but for the first time in my life, I want to give it a go with someone. With you."

"But *this* isn't the way to do it," Emma says, gesturing wildly in the air. "I've heard basically nothing from you for *months*, then suddenly you send for me, and expect me to turn my back on my family and move here at the drop of a hat?"

"First of all, the no contact thing was your idea, not mine, so please don't throw that back in my face. Second, you, *of all people*, know what kind of pressure I've been under with the publisher and the network up my arse. I have done literally nothing but work and attend the odd promotional obligation since I left. And as soon as I could, I came up with a plan for us to be together," I say, my voice rising. "This is the king of all grand romantic gestures that you women seem to need. I thought you'd be thrilled, yet it sounds like you'd rather make me pay for not ringing you up enough to chat."

"That is *not* what I meant and you know it!" she answers, her voice rising to meet mine. "For all I knew, we were over. And then you suddenly decide we should give it a try, so you jump in and make all the decisions for both of us with absolutely no thought of consulting *me* on where I'd be spending the rest of my life."

"To be honest, I didn't think it would be a tough decision for you." I tap my chin, pretending to be deep in thought. "Hmm...Let's see, I could live in a luxurious flat and run the best restaurant in the entire kingdom, or I could spend the rest of my days on a crap houseboat with a three-burner stove and a bar fridge. Tough call. How will you decide?" I say, oozing sarcasm.

She glares at me, her entire face red with fury. "There's really no need to be a sarcastic arsehole about this."

"No? I'm offering you everything you've ever wanted and you're not only turning it down, but you're also implying I'm some controlling bastard for doing it!" Every muscle in my body tenses with anger. I take a deep breath and lower my voice. "I've clearly made a mistake. This won't work."

"You're right. This won't. But not because I'm making a bad choice. It's because you have no idea what it means to love someone."

"This coming from the person who's saying no to a future together?" I scoff.

"If you knew what love was, you'd know it means finding a way to fit into *each other's* lives instead of expecting me to give up mine."

"And just how are we supposed to do that when we live on opposite sides of the planet?" I ask, throwing my hands up. "One of us has to give up their life and since *mine* is far superior, it's only logical that *you'd* fit into *mine*." Oh, now that was just rude, wasn't it? I should not have said that, no matter how true it may be.

Emma's shoulders drop and she stares at me for an uncomfortably long moment. When she finally speaks, her voice is quiet. "If you really believe that between the two of us, *you're* the rich one, I feel sorry for you. All you've got is money."

I roll my eyes and shake my head. "Oh please. Spare me the 'all you need is love' routine. If that were true, why is the entire world obsessed with the rich and famous? Could it *be* because they desperately want the lifestyle that goes with it?" I ask. I give her a hard look, then nod firmly. "Yes, I'm pretty sure that's it."

"Not everyone is like that."

"Even Mother Teresa was in it for the fame," I say. "And in case you've forgotten, *you're* the one who wants to have your own cooking show, a chain of restaurants, and all the juicy star power that comes with it. Is that because you just want to 'share your vision with the world?'" I'm doing air quotes now to really drive my point home. "No. It's because you want to be rich and be admired by the world."

"Wow. You really are jaded beyond repair, aren't you?"

"Thanks for the psychoanalysis, Dr. Kubler-Ross. Perhaps you should turn your skills on yourself so you can begin to understand why you're saying no to the best thing that's ever happened to you, because I assure you, I'm *fine*."

"No, you're not, Pierce." She shakes her head slowly. "You're turning on me because I can't just drop everything at the snap of your fingers. I'm not the type of person to abandon her family just because someone sends a private jet for me."

"But you *did* get on the jet," I say. Oh, now I'm just being nasty, but I can't seem to stop. It's like my tongue is a runaway train with no brakes. I can see I'm about to crash but I cannot stop it from happening.

Tears fill her eyes. "I came because I wanted to see if there could be some sort of future with you, not because I'm a gold digger."

"In case you haven't picked up on it, *a future* is precisely what I'm offering you—and one that's a damn sight better than what you've got sorted out for yourself—but if this isn't enough for you, say no and I won't bother you again." I stuff my hands in the front pockets of my jeans and give her a hard look.

"So, that's it then?" she asks, wiping the tears from her cheeks. "I either give up my entire life and take your offer, or I can just fuck off?"

"It's a hell of a good offer. Most women would jump at it."

Lifting her chin, she says, "Well, I'm not most women, am I?" She gives me one last look before storming out of the kitchen.

I watch the doors swing wildly while my brain tries to catch up with what just happened. I'm not going to chase her. I offered her everything any woman could ever want. If she's too thick-headed to take it, that's her problem. Better to find out now, I suppose, than a few years down the line. Besides, if she doesn't understand what all of this means, this never would have worked anyway.

Then why is every cell in my body telling me to run after her and fix this?

Because the body is prone to forcing you to do stupid things. Something to do with being biologically programmed to procreate. The brain, however, is smarter, and my brain is telling me to just let her go.

THIRTY-THREE

The Consolation Life

Emma

Text to Priya: *Hey. On my way home—economy class on Cheapo Airline. They're de-icing the sketchy-looking wings so I have a few more minutes with Wi-Fi, and maybe to live, if the engine is as dodgy as the rest of this aircraft.*

Priya: *Shit. So, it didn't work out then?*

Me: *Not exactly. He bought me a restaurant in Valcourt.*

Priya: *Ummm...and that's bad, why?*

Me: *Would you respect a head chef who only got the job because her boyfriend bought out the owner?*

Priya: *WHAT DOES THAT MATTER? HE BOUGHT YOU YOUR OWN FREAKING RESTAURANT!! I'd kill for a rich boyfriend who would buy me a restaurant. Or just a restaurant. Or just a boyfriend, broke or otherwise.*

Me: *I know it sounds insane but there are three very good reasons: 1) I didn't earn it. 2) I'll never respect myself if I take it. 3) He'll likely lose all respect for me if I take it, so really it'll be the beginning of the end and I'll be stuck in a foreign country alone. 4) He thinks I shouldn't have any say in where I live my life. 5) He just assumed I'd give up my entire life at the snap of his fingers. 6) Harrison and Libby are having a baby. They need me. I can't just abandon my brother after everything he's done for me.*

Priya: *That's six reasons.*

Me: *I'm too depressed to do math.*

Priya: *In that case, maybe you should get off the plane and try to sort it out with him.*

Me: *It's over. Trust me...*

Priya: *Damn. What happened to the whole mature, sophisticated globe-trotting thing?*

Me: *It didn't come up. It was either take his offer or leave, so I left. I'm not the kind of girl who can let a man make all my decisions for me.*

Priya: *I'm sorry, hon. I wish it had worked out.*

Me: *It's okay. The way he acted today is actually going to make it much easier to get over him.*

I hope.

***

"What are you doing back here already?" Rosy asks as I climb out of the backseat of the jeep.

I had planned to sneak back to the resort, then take a boat and go back to Eden, tell Phyllis and Alfred to fuck off and leave me alone, then hide on the houseboat a few days. But it turns out two of the resort's guests were on the same flight as me, and Justin was there to pick them up when I walked out of the terminal. He offered me a ride and I couldn't think of a good excuse not to take it.

The entire drive was excruciating, both physically and emotionally. Physically, because the couple I was with are huge over-packers, so I had to share my half of the backseat with two enormous suitcases, one of which was resting on my legs that are already sore from not being able to stretch them out for the past ten hours on the plane. And I'm still in my damn 'classy plane outfit' that I've been wearing for two days. So now I'm yet again returning a sweaty mess, being way too hot in my black pants and sweater combo. I left my carry-on in Pierce's limo when I stormed out of the restaurant, so I haven't been able to change clothes, brush my teeth, or put on some emergency deodorant. Not that I care what I smell like, really. Smelling good is irrelevant for people who are doomed to live their lives alone. Well, not really, but I feel like being dramatic at the moment, so please let that one go.

As if that weren't bad enough, emotionally, the ride sucked hairy balls because it turns out they're not only huge over-packers, they're also huge Crownies, and are only coming to the resort so they can stay in the room where Pierce wrote the final scene of the series. They kept yapping excitedly about the series and what a genius Pierce is and have either of us met him... So at least I've had a cup of unrefined sea salt vigorously rubbed into my fresh wounds, which is always nice.

But, back to Rosy who is standing directly in the sun on the steps of the lobby with both hands on her hips. She looks pissed. I'm not sure who at, but I know I'll find out in a few seconds.

"Things didn't work out, so I decided to come home," I say with a shrug. Attempting to put an end to the conversation, I start walking in the general direction of the pier.

"You mean you flew all that way just to get on a plane and come home?" she asks, walking down the steps and following me.

Stopping, I turn to her. "Listen, Rosy. I'm in a crap mood, and the last thing I need is a lecture on how I shouldn't run from trouble or how I should try to make it work with a fine piece of man candy like Pierce or whatever else you're planning to say. He wanted me to move there. I turned him down, but not because I'm running. It's the right thing for my family and for me. It's over. We're never, ever, ever, ever, ever getting back together. And that's all I'm going to say about that."

Rosy's shoulders drop and she takes a few steps toward me and gives me a huge hug. "Oh, Baby Bear, I'm sorry."

"I'm fine," I say, my voice cracking as I feel my strength dissolve in her warm, cozy hug. "Really, I'm okay," I sob.

Before I know it, I'm standing in the middle of the path bawling my eyes out on Rosy's shoulder while she pats my back and shushes me. I can feel the eyes of all the staff and tourists zipping past us on golf carts or strolling by, but I don't even care.

"Shh...shh...it's okay, Baby Bear," Rosy says, patting me. "You'll feel better after a nice shower and some soap," she says, trying to pull away from me.

I clutch her tighter and keep bawling, needing this so badly right now.

When I'm finally done crying, Rosy lets me go and says, "You did the right thing, Emma, and you'll meet some nice island boy to spend your life with. In fact, my nephew, Tyson, and his wife seem to be on the rocks. If they end up divorced, he'd be a real catch."

"The cop with four kids?" I ask.

"Ready-made family," she says, waggling her eyebrows.

I bark out one of those delirious 'I can't believe this is happening' laughs.

Taking me by the hand, she tugs me along the path. "Now, come with me. I have some news that will cheer you right up."

***

"Retiring? Really?" I ask Junior for the third time.

Junior, Harrison, and I are standing in the reception area of the Brazilian restaurant so we'll be out of the way of the staff who are in full dinner service prep mode.

"Yes," he says, smiling at me. "You don't have to keep begging around the resort for someone to swap with you anymore."

I stare at Harrison for a moment. "Really?" I whisper.

"Really, Emma. You've earned it. You stuck it out on Eden for six months and you pulled off a miracle for our wedding dinner," he says, putting his hands on my shoulders. "I'm really proud of you, kiddo."

"Thanks," I say, looking around at my new life. Maybe it's true what they say about God opening a window when a door slams in your face.

Junior beams at me. "You're going to be great. And I've been telling Harrison I think you should test out your Carib-Asian idea one night a week to start. See how it goes over."

"I'd love that," I say, smiling, even though I'm not as happy as I wish I were at this moment. I'm basically trying to fake that I'm delighted because, to be honest, even though I'm taking another giant step forward in my career, and even though I don't have to live on that crap houseboat anymore, I'm still terrified that I just made the worst mistake of my life yesterday. Oh, shit. I think I did. Tears fill my eyes and I try to blink them back inside.

Harrison tilts his head. "You okay, Em?"

Nodding quickly, I say, "I'm just so happy."

One of the servers pokes her head out the kitchen door and tells Junior he's needed. He gives me a wink and says, "As of Monday, she'll be calling *you* to put out the fires."

"Hopefully only figurative fires, not real ones," Harrison adds.

I smile, still stunned that this is happening on the heels of the worst day of my life. I follow Harrison out the door and down the path toward the beach. I can feel him staring at me so I keep a big smile plastered on my face. I know I should be saying something—lots of things about how excited and grateful I am--but somehow, I can't find the words right now.

We take the few steps down onto the sand before Harrison says, "So, tell me what happened."

"I'm fine. Honestly. We're just too different. It wouldn't have worked," I say, concentrating very hard on keeping my voice strong and steady.

"You sure?"

"Yeah, of course. I feel a little stupid flying all that way when we probably could have figured it out with a quick phone call, but otherwise, I'm great," I say, nodding confidently at him. "How could I not be?"

"At least you know now, right?" he asks, bumping my shoulder with his. "You won't have to wonder anymore."

"Exactly. Knowing is *so much better* than not knowing."

That, by the way, is the biggest lie people tell themselves right behind 'I'll start working out on Monday.' Hoping Pierce and I would end up together was *so much better* than knowing it's over for good. Knowing is the dog's bollocks because now I have to move on with absolutely no hope whatsoever. And I have to pretend everything's hunky-dory when it's really not hunky-dory at all. There's no hunky or even a little bit of dory. It's just crap.

Not to mention the fact that I can't actually talk about the reason I came home with anyone here. There's no way Harrison and Libby can find out that one of the biggest reasons it didn't work out is so that I can be here for them. If that happens, they'll be putting me back on the next flight to Avonia themselves, and to be honest, I'd rather eat spiced kidney than get back on another plane right now.

And even if I *did* fly back, rush to Pierce, and tell him I changed my mind, it's not like we left things in a very nice place. I don't even *want* to get back with someone who thinks Mother Teresa was in it for the fame. Seriously, what kind of man says things like that? I mean, it's sort of witty—I'll give him that. But it's also exceptionally rude and I'm not going to spend my life with someone rude.

No matter how badly I want to.

THIRTY-FOUR

The Part Where the Guy Goes Out Drinking So He Can Forget...

Pierce

"**A**nother round for everyone!" I shout, my voice barely making it above the sound of the thumping beat. A roar from the crowd of clubbers drowns out the music. I turn to Leo, screaming in his face, "And that's how it's done!"

"Yes, I get it. You know how to party," he yells back. "You've more than demonstrated this fact over the past four nights. You're a total rock star. Now, can we please get out of here?"

Leaning into his ear, I say, "Why on earth would we do that? Have you seen all the women in this place? It's like a lady buffet and I'm feeling rather peckish at the moment."

"No, you're not," he says, rolling his eyes. "You've been using that same creepy line every night now, but when it comes down to it, you don't want to sample the menu. You're just going to stand here being utterly picky because none of these women is you-know-who. Then we're going to go home where you'll sit at the kitchen table sipping tequila until the sun comes up and force me to listen to you go on about how you're *so glad* you didn't let yourself get tied down."

"Thrilled, actually!" I say, tipping back the bottle of champagne I'm holding and guzzling down as much of the bubbly liquid as I can in one go (which is quite a bit, in case you're wondering). Wiping my mouth with the back of my hand, I shout, "I'm no chunder bunny!"

The people around us cheer as though I've just won the World Cup, and I hold up the bottle and yell, "Now, which of you lovely ladies wants to come home with me?"

***

"There you are," I say, stumbling through the door to my flat and finding Leo on the couch watching Peaky Blinders. "What happened to you, you wanker?"

"I got sick of watching you self-destruct. It's not as fun when *you* do it," he says without looking up at me.

I flop down onto the couch next to him and kick off my shoes.

"So, where's the woman you were going to bring home?" he asks.

"Meh, no one there I fancied enough to let into the fortress of solitude," I say, rubbing my chest. Apparently, if I drink to excess several days in a row, I end up with a wicked case of heartburn.

Tom Hardy comes on the screen, and we're both transfixed by his skill to transform into an insanely entertaining rum runner.

"I wish I'd written this show," I mutter.

"Instead of *Clash of Crowns*?" he asks.

"No, along with it. This is the one show I can never predict. Everything else I see, I can tell you what the characters are going to say next, but not this one." I burp a little, then tell my stomach to keep it all in. *Keep it in or you'll turn me into a liar* and *a chunder bunny.*

"Yes, you've always been drawn to the unpredictable, haven't you?" he asks, staring at me.

"Who isn't?" I ask, turning back to the show.

"I suppose you could call that chef of yours unpredictable," he says after a minute.

"Just a sec," I say, feigning excitement. "Let me go get the nail polish and some sheet masks." Folding my arms and leaning back, I drop the enthusiasm from my voice. "I don't need some heart-to-heart pep talk, Leo, so let it go already."

"You're a miserable git, you know that?" he asks, punching me on the arm.

"If you don't like it, leave," I say. "In fact, even if you *do* like it, please leave anyway. You're like Marvin K. Mooney—unable to take a bloody hint."

Shaking his head, Leo says, "Everyone thinks you're the smart one, but when it comes to love, you're a complete imbecile."

"Have you been talking to Emma or something?" I ask, narrowing my eyes. "She said exactly the same thing. Well, not exactly, but basically...and you know what?" I say, pointing an unsteady finger at him. "You're both full of shit. I offered her *the world* and she said 'no thanks.' I handed her the best restaurant in all of Avonia on a silver platter. Not the second best. Not third. Not some shit start-up nobody's heard of. The best fucking one. And she said 'no.'"

I stand, needing to move while I rant. "*No* to all of it. Instead of being grateful and living happily ever after with me, she called me a controlling arsehole...except she didn't use the word arsehole. But she did say controlling which I *am not*. I just thought maybe she'd appreciate having someone give her everything she's ever dreamed of. I thought maybe she'd want to be with me...but she doesn't. So *screw her*. If she wants to live on some shit boat and be a servant for the rest of her life, she can do that. I don't care."

Spinning back toward the telly, I see Cillian Murphy on the screen looking rather put out about something as usual.

"Thomas Shelby doesn't need a woman to make him happy. Smart man right there."

"Pierce, can I ask you something and get an honest answer?"

"Probably not," I say, wavering a little on my feet.

"Why did you become a writer?"

"Because I ran out of good things to read," I say, shrugging.

"That's not true. When you finished your first book, I asked you that question and you said, 'Because fictional characters don't disappoint you like the people you meet in real life.'"

"Yes, well, so fucking what? We had a fucked-up childhood, in case you didn't notice. It's not like our parents were people we could ever really count on. Turns out the rest of the world is just like them, Emma included." I sigh heavily, then drop onto the oversized ottoman, spilling a stack of books onto the floor. "Maybe she's right. Maybe I'm too damaged to be able to love someone properly."

"Maybe," Leo says thoughtfully.

"Thanks for that," I say sarcastically. The lead ball in my stomach seems much heavier now and I desperately want to get rid of it. "There's no such thing as love, by the way. You must know that."

"No, I don't know it," he answers, sounding utterly sure of himself. "I don't think we've had a good example of how to do it properly, but I do know couples who seem to have it right."

"Name one." This should be good.

His face lights up. "Zach and Kennedy."

"Don't even. Of all the harpies in the world, Kennedy's their leader," I scoff.

"Maybe to you, but to Zach, she's everything. They both want to make the other person happy, even if it means giving up something they really want," Leo says. "He takes those stupid dance classes because it makes her happy. He'd much rather be at home watching the telly than doing a foxtrot with a bunch of seniors every Tuesday night, but he goes anyway. And do you really think she wants to go to the Ashes every couple of years and spend an entire week watching cricket with him? She doesn't even like cricket. She'd much rather be off shopping and eating at the best restaurants in Paris or New York, but they don't have the money for it, so she ends up drinking beer and eating meat pies with him all day in the stands. And she doesn't even complain. She just makes the best of it because he loves it so much."

"Ah, so love is an unending series of doing shit you don't want to so the other person will have sex with you again," I say. "Good thing I got out of it then."

"That's not what I said. Love is doing shit you don't want to do just to see the look in her eyes," he says. "Or so it seems. I haven't found the girl I'd give up my life for yet. But when I do, I'm not going to let her get away. I can tell you that."

"Well, take it from your big brother, don't bother. I tried to give her what she wanted, but believe me, Emma did not have that look."

Leo screws up his face looking skeptical. "Did you really? I know you're have a blast being a martyr and all, but the truth is, you did something you thought would guarantee you'd get what *you* want."

"You think I want to own a bloody restaurant?" I ask, feeling a sense of righteous indignation nudge out my heartburn.

"I think you wanted to find a way to fit her neatly into your life without you having to give up anything you care about. The money was nothing for you to spend—a drop in your enormous bucket of cash. Totally worth it if it meant you didn't have to change anything about your life other than making room for her toothbrush in your cabinet."

I start to protest, but he cuts me off.

"You wrote the ending you thought you should have. You treated her like one of your characters and assumed she'd go along with it. But you were forgetting something—she's not some puppet on a string. She's a real person with ideas and hopes and fears, and things that matter to her."

"Christ, I obviously know that she's a real person. I'm not mental." I look down at the scars on my hand, feeling that ridiculous tug in my chest that comes when I envision her taking care of me. "Whatever. It's over now, so I'll just get on with my remarkably wonderful life. She made it clear she doesn't need me and I definitely don't need her."

"Okay, fine. Be that way, but I know the truth and deep down so do you. You didn't try to make her happy. You tried to make yourself happy and now you've put a pout on because she didn't go along with it." Leo shuts off the telly and stands up. "You're right about one thing though. It's best you broke up now. You don't deserve her. She needs a real man who'll be willing to sacrifice, even just a little, to show her what she means to him."

He turns and walks away while I sit and stew. After a few seconds, I shout, "What do you know about relationships, anyway? You've never had one last longer than a one-night!"

I expect him to come back and argue, but he doesn't give me the satisfaction. I call out, "I'm not going after her! I can tell you that much."

Muttering to myself, I say, "I'm not. I am not going to chase her. No thank you."

THIRTY-FIVE

Sisters Before Misters...And Other Lies

Emma

Today is quite possibly going to be the greatest day of my life.

Now, I know a person really shouldn't think thoughts like that because it's considered a jinx. It's like calling a perfect game before the ninth inning is over. But, in this case, I *really believe* it's true. Not that I'm naïve enough to think there won't be the odd hiccup. Something *always* goes wrong when you're in the restaurant biz—a tiny grease fire (been there, have the baking soda on hand to stop it), or a leaky sink (I have a small toolkit packed and ready to go)—but I'm as ready as I'll ever be.

After a week of working side-by-side with Junior, getting the lay of the land and taking notes on all of his old guy chef tricks, I've learned all the little quirks of the Brazilian steakhouse. The second oven is always 10° higher than it shows on the display. David the dishwasher is prone to bouts of irritable bowel syndrome when there's a particularly large pile of dishes, meaning it gets handed off to his twin brother, Daniel, the kitchen porter. This will spark a fight that ends in fisticuffs unless I intervene early. Lastly, but most importantly, never *under any circumstances* ask Martha the floor manager about her divorce (or that suspicious-looking mole on her neck).

To be honest with you, I'm kind of nervous. Well, *very* nervous really. A week isn't exactly a long time to soak in the knowledge that took a lifetime for Junior to gather, but on the other hand, some of the ways he does things are a little bit old-school and I know I can improve upon his methods. Not right away, of course. I need to let the staff get used to a new sheriff in town, and I fully intend to respect their knowledge about the workings of this particular kitchen. After all, *I'm* the new guy here.

Look at me, embracing my new challenge with some humility. Pretty good, if I do say so myself.

I do a quick check of my light dusting of makeup in the bathroom mirror. I don't need to straddle a toilet like I did on the houseboat now that I'm settled into a small-but-functional staff cabin at the main resort. It has a mirror above the sink, right where it belongs, so things are definitely looking up.

Yup, I look decently head-chefish. My hair is pulled back in a sensible-yet-stylish low bun, and my uniform fits just so.

Taking a deep breath, I stare at my reflection. "This is it. This is the moment you've been waiting for."

So why don't I feel happy? I'm going to be serving meat on swords, which has always been one of my dreams.

It's just nerves. By the end of today, I'll be right as rain because I promise you this melancholy has *nothing* to do with a certain rich guy who is most likely about to run Avonia's best restaurant directly into the ground with his complete lack of knowledge about the business. There really is no justice in the world, is there?

Oops. I seem to have taken a trip down Bitter Girl Lane. I keep winding up there for some dumb reason. But never mind. Once I get started on my new life, I'll spend all my time at the intersection of Moving On Avenue and I Can't Even Remember What He Looks Like Street.

Yes, twelve hours from now, when I return back to my comfortable, not-sloshy-with-the-tide cabin, I'll be too knackered to think about Pierce and his stupid perfect restaurant and his dumb rock-hard abs. I don't even like hard abs. They're very uncomfortable if you're trying to nap on them. Maybe I'll find myself a nice squishy fellow who will celebrate my brilliance as an artist while I rest on his comfy body.

But first, it's time to get over to the Brazilian steakhouse so I can begin my journey to culinary greatness...

***

Four Hours Later

"He did what?" I say into my mobile screen, walking out of the kitchen and straight outside.

"He offered me a job at his restaurant," Priya says, looking completely dumbfounded.

"But...why would he...how did he...*Pierce*? As in the guy I never want to see or hear from again?!" My pulse speeds up as I find a spot in the shade of a palm tree so I can see Priya.

"Yes, same guy—and I'm very sorry to bring him up to you, but I thought you'd want to know. He said you'd mentioned my name but he had to look me up."

Okay, this is SO not what I needed on my first day as head chef. Things aren't exactly working out as planned—one of the servers called in sick, the meat guy shorted me by twenty pounds of picanha, and one of the dishwashers died. Oh, not a person, an appliance. We could all smell burnt rubber, and by the time we located the source of it, smoke was already pouring out.

I literally just told the team that we'd had our three mishaps for the day and that the evening was going to be smooth-sailing when my phone rang. Aaaannnd, now there's this...

"So, what did you tell him?"

"I'm not going to take a job with your ex," she says, snorting like it's the most absurd idea she's ever heard. "No way. You're my bestie. Sisters before misters, right?"

"Damn straight," I say firmly. "Why *you*, anyway? No offence. It's just that he could hire any number of great chefs to work at his stupid restaurant." My anger simmers like the coconut rice I just left on the stovetop. "Is he doing this just to piss me off or something? So you'll tell me all about what an amazing job it is and I'll rue the day I turned him down?"

"Or so I'll tell you when he comes in with some new woman on his arm. Pfft!" Priya says, making a 'he's crazy' face.

"As if you would ever do that. Apparently, he doesn't know who he's dealing with, am I right?"

"Oh girl, you are so right," Priya says. Yes, we're two sassy best friends out to conquer the world.

"So what did he say when you turned him down?" I ask, starting to feel a little giddy about him being rejected by both of us.

"He said he understood why I might feel uncomfortable and that he wanted to make sure I knew the only reason he was offering me the job was because you told him I was supremely talented and he trusts your opinion about these things above anyone else's," Priya says, with just a hint of sheepishness in her voice. "He also told me the offer stands if I change my mind."

"Urgh. That is *so him* to be all gentlemanly about it," I say, rolling my eyes. "I mean, come on! You can't just swoop in and take my best friend."

"No doubt," Priya answers, nodding quickly. "So, that's that then...I guess."

Ignoring that last bit which seemed a lot like trepidation, I say, "Any word on your med school applications?"

"Nada. But I did apply for a bit of a quirky chef's position actually."

"*Cool.* Where at?"

"Starbutts."

The connection must be crap here. I could have sworn she said Starbutts but she definitely said Starbucks. "I didn't know they needed chefs there."

"Oh, yeah, definitely. Everybody gets hungry—customers, dancers..."

Well those are random examples, no? "I don't get it. Will you be in their head office in Seattle? Are you going to be designing ready-made meals for them or something?"

"Uh, no, just regular cooking," Priya answers vaguely. "I actually don't think they have a head office. Well, Tony, the guy who owns the place, has an office in the back next to the change room."

"Wait a second. We're talking about Starbucks, the giant coffeehouse chain, right?"

"No," she says, shaking her head. "Star*butts*. It's a strip club just outside of town. Tony wants to try to attract a higher-end clientele so he's looking to change up the menu. That's where I'd come in. *If* they offer me the job, that is. They had two other chefs they were interviewing that day and apparently one of them said she'd be willing to dance when the kitchen is slow. He asked me if I would, but I said no."

Sweet Jesus.

Okay, Emma. You cannot let your best friend be reduced to flipping burgers at a strip club. Especially not when she's been offered the world's most perfect opportunity. Stop being a selfish be-otch. "You should take the offer from Pierce," I say, the words tasting like recycled tobacco juice.

"No way," she says. "That is *off* the table. Like, swept off into the trash and the garbage truck already came and took it away so there's no chance of retrieving it. Sisters before—"

"Take the job, Priya. It's the perfect opportunity. The restaurant is absolutely gorgeous and the kitchen is to die for."

"It is, isn't it?" she says, bursting with an uncontainable excitement. "And the *location* is just...wow. I looked it up online after I got off the phone with him. I even think I'd like the weather there."

Oh, she totally wants this so badly she can taste it. I force a bright smile. "Valcourt really is a lovely city. I lived there until I was seven, you know. There's so much to love about the entire kingdom, really. Plus, you'd be getting away from your family, which may not be the worst thing in the world."

"It is kind of perfect for me. He said he can fast track my work visa because he knows someone, so I could be there by the end of the month. But honestly, only if you're one thousand percent sure," she says firmly. "Because if this would *in any way* upset you, even just the tiniest littlest bit, I won't take it."

"It won't upset me, I swear," I say, keeping the grin plastered to my face. "As your best friend, I want you to be happy. And it's not like Pierce and I were married for five years and just went through some messy divorce because he was cheating with his floosy of a secretary. We had a few fun weeks together and then we realized it wasn't going to work. That's it. You go. Take the job and don't worry about me."

"You're sure?" she asks, wincing a little.

"I'm sure. Just maybe don't mention if he comes in and happens to look devastatingly handsome or says something particularly witty."

"I'll pretend I never saw him."

"Perfect." I give her a big grin, then say, "I better run. I left some rice on the stove and I don't want it to boil over."

"Thanks, Emma. You're the best friend ever."

"I know," I say, winking at her. "Now, you go call what's-his-name back before he finds someone else."

I hang up and start back toward the restaurant just as the kitchen door bursts open. David and Daniel spill out onto the ground, punching the hell out of each other while an elderly couple, who happened to be walking by, gape at the display.

Taking a deep breath, I say, "You wanted this, Emma."

THIRTY-SIX

The Mother Teresa of Breakups

Pierce

As much as I hate to admit it, it appears as though I may be nothing more than what the great Ms. Tina Turner called a typical male. I'm not sure, having never been in this situation before, but I suspect I may be suffering from a serious case of man grief, characterized by the incessant need to distract oneself from any reminder of a certain woman from whom you've recently parted ways.

In my case, I have pathetically been doing all of the archetypal things men do—the partying like it's nineteen ninety-nine, the seeing her face everywhere I go, the throwing myself into my work with wild abandon (which is utterly ineffective when you have no work-in-progress to distract you, and every time you try to think of a new storyline, you end up with characters who resemble the very woman you're trying to forget). I've now moved on to the bulking-up phase, which entails spending several hours per day in my home gym. This is where I am at the current moment. It's cardio day, so I'm running on my treadmill at a punishing level ten incline. Impressive, no?

The bulking-up phase is an attempt to become insanely shredded (should I meet someone who will distract me from the cavernous hole that resides just to the left of my right lung lobe), but also should serve as an effective means of exhausting myself in an effort to try to get a full night's sleep. It's not working, by the way. I'm still staring at the empty pillow next to mine for half the night while I torture myself by going over every second of our last moments together in excruciating detail. What could I have said or done that would have led to a different outcome? What if I had taken her home first and we spent a couple of days together 'bonding?' What if I had asked her if she'd ever consider moving *before* I bought the damn restaurant?

No matter what I do, I can't escape the truth, which is that Emma was right, as was Leo, surprising as that may be. My grand romantic gesture was, in fact, a very selfish act designed to get exactly what I wanted with the least amount of effort possible, allowing me to dress up my demands as a gift and hold it against her should she say no. The crazy part is that I think deep down Emma knew that, had she accepted, I would have quickly lost interest in her because she's not wrong—I was essentially trying to buy her, no matter how nicely I packaged it. And here's the irony: it seems as though I can only love a woman who won't allow me to use my money to manipulate her, but in attempting to reassure myself that she couldn't be bought, I've lost her.

Because she couldn't be bought.

And, like a total boob, I tried to buy her.

Sadly, this brings me to the inescapable conclusion that I, Pierce Davenport, am simply not capable of love or of sustaining a long-term relationship. You'd think coming to this sort of major revelation would help me move on, but it's an utterly useless bit of knowledge. If all I can do is think about Emma day and night, knowing that I can't have her, I pretty much am screwed as far as enjoying the rest of my life goes. I'm not even enjoying my fortress of solitude anymore, and it used to bring me unbridled joy.

Leo has taken off with some friends to the south of France for a few days, and instead of revelling in my delicious seclusion, my mind is focused solely on the fact that I am very much alone, a state which used to thrill me to no end but now feels pathetic.

I've creeped on her Instagram page where she showcases the meals she's been working on. She's changed her profile to read "Head chef, Paradise Bay Resort Brazilian Steakhouse/Part-time creator of Carib-Asian Cuisine." Based on her posts, it would appear that Thursday nights are Carib-

Asian night at the steakhouse, and I can't help but feel a strange sense of pride and excitement for her that she's finding a way to make her own dreams come true.

I slow to a fast walk and open my Instagram app. There she is. Well, not her exactly, but a photo of some braised beef ribs she made today. I run my fingertip over the screen like an imbecile. Somehow, the sight of those brown hunks of meat that I can neither smell, nor taste, brings me a strange sort of sustenance inside.

Oh, Christ, I really am the *most* pathetic of the bunch, aren't I? The mighty Pierce Davenport, lone wolf, intellectual, creative genius—brought to my knees by a feisty chef.

I know I shall never get her back, and I can live with that (sort of), but only if I can find a way to make it up to her. Because if she's feeling even a tenth of the anguish that I am at our parting ways, I don't think I could stand it. So far, the only thing I've thought to do is to hire her friend Priya (who really is a great chef, by the way) because I hoped it would make Emma happy. But I'll think of other ways, I promise.

Until I kick off (likely very prematurely from the loneliness of having to live without her), I shall find ways to quietly improve her circumstances because if I could at least know that *she* is happy (and that I had a hand in it), it would bring me some sense of peace. So really this all just reinforces the fact that I'm a selfish bastard because, at the end of the day, I'm only trying to make myself feel better.

Yes, I'll be the Mother Teresa of breakups. Next stop, sainthood.

THIRTY-SEVEN

How to Make a Total Arse of Yourself in Three Easy Steps...

Emma

Two Months Later

It's late afternoon for me as I do the mental math calculation to figure out what time it is for Priya. I have a few minutes before the dinner rush starts and I *really* need to talk to her.

Let's see, four p.m. here so it's got to be...eleven o'clock for her. Perfect. She'll be available. The two of us have had to adjust to our new time zone difference/incredibly hectic head chef schedules, which has left us with a very narrow window of time when we can speak. Unfortunately, it's always when we're both at work—before my big rush and after hers. Otherwise, one of us is always sleeping or she's hanging out with her new boyfriend, Ivan, a handsome and deliciously nerdy Avonian who's doing his masters in Zoology.

I'm happy for Priya. I really am. It turns out Intermission is the cat's pyjamas as far as jobs go and Ivan sounds like a great guy. They're super cute together and it warms my heart to see her go from down in the dumps to on top of the world.

So overall, things are looking great for both of us. I'm honestly too busy to be wasting my time thinking of what's-his-face, which is for the best because when his face *does* intrude on my day, it's like a kick to the lady junk.

Priya picks up on the second ring.

Oh goody! Time to forget Mr. Famous.

273

I take a deep breath and pretend to be thrilled with life. "You'll never guess what's happened!" I tighten my shoulder grip on my mobile (why didn't I get a damn headset already?) and awkwardly slice a clove of garlic. "I got a call from a producer at ABN's Weekend Edition. They want to come down to Paradise Bay to do a piece on Carib-Asian food!"

"Are you serious, Emma? That's *huge!*" Priya answers, and I can hear the sounds of pots clanging in the background.

"Right? Now for the big question. Did you, by any chance, have anything to do with this? Because I can't for the life of me figure out how they would have heard of me." I crack open another clove of garlic with the side of my knife.

"Pinky swear I had nothing to do with it," she answers before she takes the phone away from her mouth and I hear her say, "That's not clean. Look at the bottom."

"So hard to find good help these days," I say under my breath.

"Preach, sister," she answers quietly. "But back to your big television appearance. Could Will have tipped them off? His show is on that network, isn't it?"

"I already asked. He said he had nothing to do with it."

"I suppose it's possible they just heard about you by chance. Most of your guests *do* come from this part of the world."

"Yeah, maybe. I just have this feeling someone gave things a push..."

"Are you thinking that a tall, dark, and well-read someone had a hand in this?" she asks.

"No," I scoff. "We've had no contact for months. I'm sure he doesn't even remember my name. Besides, he's in full-on publicity mode at the moment for the book. He's even letting the cameras into his luxury flat for some sort of 'Lifestyles of the Rich and Fabulous' thing. Not that I'm stalking him. I just happened to catch a promo for it on the telly the other day."

"Right," she says, sounding utterly unconvinced. "He hasn't been in to the restaurant, by the way."

"You don't need to tell me that, you know. I couldn't care less where he goes, or with whom, for that matter."

"Sure you don't," Priya answers. "And you're also not cyberstalking him every chance you get."

"It was an ad during the news, thank you very much."

"Since when do you watch the news?" Priya says.

"I was over at Rosy and Darnell's for breakfast on Sunday. They had it on. I just happened to see it."

"And I suppose you haven't memorized the time and found a way to make sure you don't miss the special."

"Coy isn't a good look on you, Priya. Why don't you just say what you really mean?"

"Fine," she says, firmly. "You desperately want to get back together with Pierce. You cannot stop thinking about him and you know ending things the way you did was a ginormous mistake, and you'll likely never be truly happy again until you figure out a way to make it work with him because, as much as you wish it weren't true, he's your beaver."

"What?" I ask sounding disgusted.

"Ivan and I were watching the nature channel this morning. Did you know beavers mate for life?"

"No, I wasn't aware of that, and as cute as that analogy is, you've got it wrong. Pierce and I are finished. We're not going to build a dam together and have little beaver babies—"

"They're called kits, actually."

Well, that's helpful. "We're not having any kits or kids or getting a rescue dog and matching Argyll sweaters. It's over and that's a *good thing*. Just look at all the wonderfulness coming my way since we broke up. Instead of focusing on a *man*, I'm doing exciting and challenging things, I'm making a name for myself, none of which I would have done if I was spending all my time rolling around in bed with some *writer*." I suddenly realize I'm talking loud enough that Daniel and David, both of whom are working on the other side of the prep station, have just heard every word. Shit. "Anyway, I should go," I say, shifting to a very professional tone. "I have a lot to do before we start seating people."

"Somebody heard all that?"

"Yup."

***

"Welcome to ABN Weekend Edition, coming to you live from the Benavente Islands! I'm Veronica Platt, and joining me this morning is chef Emma Banks, co-owner of the Paradise Bay Resort and creator of the Carib-Asian food craze that's got everyone talking."

Oh, shit. This is really happening! Keep smiling right into the camera. Wait. Didn't they say *not* to look into the camera? Yes, maybe that was it. I can't remember.

Shit. Am I sweating? I think I'm sweating. Can they see how badly I'm sweating? We probably shouldn't have filmed this outside. It's got to be at least 50° C and I'm pretty sure my uniform is drenched with sweat. *Don't look down, Emma. Just keep smiling at the camera. No, at Veronica.*

"So, Emma, your Carib-Asian creations are creating quite a buzz. How did you come up with the concept?"

"I... If something... When you..." Shit. Deep breath! Okay. "Back in culinary school in New York, we were given an assignment to pair up two different, unusual food combinations, and I wanted to bring in a Caribbean flavour to my project since I grew up here. On Santa Valentina Island. Well, from the time I was seven. My parents died in a car accident and our uncle took us in. I used to live in Valcourt before that, actually, not Asia. But I still wanted to incorporate an Asian flair into my project because Avonia isn't known for its cuisine. Not that it's not good, because it is. It's just not *Asian* good." Asian *good?! Oh Christ! Stop talking!*

Veronica's smile is still in place even though her eyes are looking slightly panicked. "So you could say this concept has been in the works since you were a little girl?"

"Yes. I mean no, I didn't actually start thinking about cooking this way until, well, probably last year I suppose." Dear God, that didn't make any sense at all. How much longer will this be?

Veronica's smile falters for a second, then she fixes it back on her face and asks, "What are you making for us today?"

"Today I'll be making jerk pork spring rolls, spicy ginger shrimp with calabaza squash served over rice noodles, and coconut lemongrass mochi ice cream for a little *dolce*." *Now I'm speaking Italian? Good God.* "These are a few of the featured dishes that we've been testing out for the past few months with great success."

"Well, it looks wonderful," Veronica says. "Can we zoom in on this food as it sizzles away here?" Veronica says. "For those of you back home, let me tell you, this smells ah-MAZ-ing."

I turn the heat up on the prawns and stir them with shaky hands. So much for my dream of having my own cooking show. When will this nightmare be over?

***

"Well, that was wonderful," Veronica says, shaking my hand. "Really delicious, and you did so well on camera. You're a natural," she lies.

"Really? Because I felt very nervous."

"Oh, you'd never know," she says. Turning to the co-producer, she says, "Right, Kennedy? You couldn't tell Emma was nervous, could you?"

"Not a bit," Kennedy answers smoothly. "Well done."

She gives me one last look and then says to Veronica, "We should really take a look at the itinerary for tomorrow's parasailing segment. The network wants you to sign off on some extra waivers apparently."

"Okay, well, thanks so much," I say, as I pack up the dirty dishes. I quickly make my way into the restaurant with my arms loaded up, then go back out for another load, feeling like a complete muttonhead. I know I did a crap job. If I hadn't, the entire resort staff wouldn't have scattered the moment the cameras turned off.

Veronica and Kennedy are standing with their backs to me talking in low voices as I reach the outdoor kitchen area.

"I don't know. He thought she'd be brilliant on camera," Kennedy says. "Well, let's just leave it, okay. I don't want to rock the boat with him until his special airs."

"Christ, he's definitely making us pay for getting access to his stupid fortress of solitude," Veronica says, causing my ears to perk up.

"You know Pierce and his diabolical love for making peoples' lives difficult," Kennedy answers. "If I didn't love Zach so much, I'd definitely tell Pierce where to stick his novels."

"As soon as we get what we need, you mean."

"Yes, of course," Kennedy says, sounding annoyed. "*After* the interview."

I crouch behind the grill and hold my breath, desperate to hear the rest of their conversation.

"No matter, we just need to get this shit over with, then he'll give us full access to his entire life," Kennedy says. "It'll totally be worth it."

"Yes, well, let's just hope the person in charge of my parasailing experience is a little more professional than the mumbling amateur cook," Veronica answers. "I'm liable to end up paralyzed."

Mumbling amateur? That wasn't very nice.

"She was an absolute disaster, wasn't she? I can't believe *that's* the woman Pierce has been carrying a torch for all these months."

He's carrying a torch for me? I hold in the scream that wants to erupt from my chest.

"Are you sure *she's* the right one?" Veronica asks.

"As shocking as it might sound, I'm positive it's her," Kennedy answers.

"He could do *so* much better," Veronica says, stressing the so for far too long, if you ask me.

"Meh. He looks great on paper—rich, handsome, brilliant—but once you get to know him, he's a total wanker," Kennedy says. "Let's just say there's a reason he's a writer. He doesn't exactly play nicely in the sandbox with the other kids."

Total wanker? My fists curl up in tight balls and I feel the sudden need to hop out from behind this grill and start throwing punches. Why the hell I want to defend *him* is beyond me though. Is it because he's carrying a torch for me? Could that be right? *Of course not. Don't think about that, Emma. You'll only backslide.*

"I need a drink. Which way is the beach bar?" Veronica asks.

"I'm pretty sure it's over here," Kennedy says, her voice sounding nearer.

Shit! I close my eyes, following the two-year-old logic that if I can't see them, they won't be able to see me. Curling up in a ball, I hold my breath.

"Emma, what are you doing?" Fidel's voice rings out.

Busted.

I open one eye at a time and see not only Fidel, but Veronica Platt and Kennedy Carter-Shulman staring down at me.

"Praying," I say rocking on my heels and straightening up to stand. I bow and gesture over my head, heart, and stomach with both hands. "It's part of the Carib-Asian philosophy of life. One must pray after the successful execution of a meal...to thank the food gods." I nod knowingly, then continue to ramble on, even though none of them are buying it. "It's sort of a cross between a Buddhist Zen thing and a voodoo prayer of thanks. Anyway, enjoy the rest of your stay, ladies. The beach bar is that way," I say, gesturing with my hand to the far right before I realize that I have just now confirmed that I was indeed eavesdropping.

Both women stare at me for a moment looking horrified before Fidel says, "I was heading that way myself. Why don't I show you?"

And that's how it's done, folks. That's how you make a complete arse of yourself in three easy steps.

***

It's early the next morning and I'm hurrying along the path to the restaurant under a large hat and a pair of oversized sunglasses that I hope will help me remain incognito. There's a lot of activity over near the pier, and I know that the crew is getting set for their day on the water. Perfect. This means none of them will notice me.

Lowering the brim of my hat, I step up my pace. Once I'm in the safety of the kitchen, I can stay there until these people leave this evening.

"Emma!" Kennedy's voice calls out from behind me.

Damn. Foiled again.

I pause slightly and then continue on, hoping she won't know that I heard her.

"Emma Banks! I know you heard me."

Son of a...

I stop and spin slowly on my heel, wincing as I turn to face her. Standing perfectly still, I watch as she strides toward me, looking every bit the high-powered television producer that she is. I kind of (read: definitely) want to karate chop her in her smug throat and yet, for the sake of the resort, I know I have to resist the urge.

When she reaches me, she lowers her voice. "I don't quite know how to say this, but yesterday... Well, Veronica and I may have said a few things that, if someone happened to overhear and take them out of context, it could be disastrous."

"Oh, you mean when I was praying? I may have heard bits and pieces, but I promise not enough to put any of it into any type of context."

"You heard what I said about Pierce, didn't you?" she asks, taking her sunglasses off so she can get a good look at me.

"May have, yes. But I promise, it was unintentional."

"Yes, I'm sure it was. To be honest, I can't afford to have anything we said get back to him. I didn't mean any of it, you understand. We were just blowing off steam, but it could have a major impact on my career if he found out."

"Mum's the word, I promise."

"Thanks, Emma," she says, letting her shoulders drop a bit. "And I'm sorry if we said anything that hurt your feelings. I was just in a bad mood yesterday with the jetlag and the stress of running this entire production."

"No harm done." I give her a bright smile, then try to turn away but her voice stops me.

"The thing is, you seem like a nice enough girl, and I just thought I should warn you that if you *are* thinking of getting involved with him, it's probably not such a good idea."

My heart drops to my feet and I consider running away with my hands over my ears. Instead, I sigh deeply and turn to face her. "Trust me, I've already figured that out for myself, but I appreciate the heads up."

"Good, because he really does believe his own lone wolf bullshit." Kennedy nods quickly. "And I just don't think that he's the type of man who would make life easy for his partner. He's really very selfish for the most part, although I have to say, *you* must be really something for him to agree to let the public catch a peek into his sad life," she says. "I've been begging him for years to let the cameras in, and until now, he's never wavered even the slightest on his decision. It's always been a hard no, regardless of what carrot I dangled in front of him—and believe me, I've dangled some pretty impressive carrots. So when he called me, I jumped at the chance."

I stand perfectly still, not daring to move a muscle or even take a breath for fear of missing anything that she's saying. My mind is spinning so fast, I can't think of any type of response.

"Anyway, I have to run. Do what you will with this information. The only thing I ask is that if you do decide to act on it—and I strongly advise you don't, knowing Pierce the way I do—please don't tell him that you know he was behind all of this. It was one of the key elements to our deal. Complete secrecy."

"But why wouldn't he want me to know?"

"He didn't say, but if I had to guess, it was because he wanted you to think you'd done this on your own."

***

So this is one of those awful moments in life when you have a big, nasty secret that you have to keep until you go to your grave.

I'm currently at an impromptu staff celebration at the beach bar at which almost everyone I care about in the world is feeling gloriously elated about Paradise Bay's newfound fame. Bob Marley is playing, people are singing, and Lolita, the head bartender, has cracked the seal on the new Bellini machine. She's got it working overtime to keep the glasses filled, and even *she's* smiling for a change.

I'm on one of the swings that line the side of the bar closest to the beach. My sandals are off and my feet are dragging through the sand as I move back and forth slowly, feeling completely detached from the festivities.

It's awful to have a secret like this—to watch people around you be excited about something that is essentially a sham. ABN didn't show up here because of our stellar reputation for world-class service, or for our incredible menu, or because of the extra TLC we give our guests. They weren't here because of the snorkelling or the parasailing or the day on a private island beach. They weren't even here for the Carib-

Asian cuisine, as much as I wish they had been. They were here for one reason only—because, for some unknown reason, Pierce Davenport cut them a deal.

I slowly sip my cool drink through the straw as I watch Harrison and Libby give each other a big hug, making room for her expanding belly. He kisses her on her forehead. I'm not much of a lip reader, but I'm pretty sure he just told her he's really proud of her and she has returned the sentiment.

Yes, Emma Banks will never tell a soul about how this really transpired. I shall take the crushing truth to my grave, alone in my misery.

***

Mmm...I know there was a time a million years ago when I thought Bellinis were a terrible idea, but I was so wrong. They are most definitely a very good idea.

I'm delightfully tipsy and have now moved to the pool deck so I can dangle my feet in the refreshingly cool water while I sip my third drink. This is much better over here because I'm alone and the sun's gone down, meaning I can cut all the fake smiling that was starting to hurt my face.

"Hey, you," Libby says, managing to get herself down beside me. Sliding her feet slowly into the pool, she sighs happily. "That's better, I've never been pregnant before, but I have a feeling the Caribbean isn't exactly the easiest climate for it."

I glance at her swollen feet, wishing I could do something to fix them for her. "Maybe you'll have to spend the next few months in the pool."

"I won't be able to. We're going to be far too busy from now on, thanks to you," she says, poking me on my shoulder.

"Oh God," I say, shaking my head. "All I did is botch a live internationally-televised interview."

Giving me a stern look, she says, "I'm not talking about the interview. I'm talking about how that camera crew ended up here in the first place. That was all you."

"What?" I ask, giving her my innocent look.

"Spare me the act, Emma. I figured it out days ago."

"Does Harrison know?"

Shaking her head, Libby says, "No, and let's not tell him, okay? He's so proud of the team—which he should be. We provide a kickass place to vacation so it's about time someone recognized it."

"Thanks, Libs. I didn't want to spoil the moment for anyone—especially Harrison."

"Look, I don't know exactly what went wrong between you two, but I do know you're miserable without him. So unless he did something unforgivable like cheating or treating you poorly, I'd say it's time for you to figure out how you and Pierce are going to make a go of things." Libby says pointedly.

"We can't. I rejected him. Hard. And I don't think there's any coming back from that."

"Huh," she says, rubbing her round belly. "I never took you for a coward, Emma."

"I'm not a *coward*. I'm just not stupid enough to think that something insanely complicated between two people who basically have nothing in common and live on opposite sides of the earth could possibly work. So, if that's what you mean by coward, I guess I'll have to wear that label, although I'd prefer the term smart."

"Emma, do you think it was easy for Harrison and me to make the leap? I mean, talk about *nothing in common* on paper—he's this adventurous, athletic guy, and I'm... well...more risk averse. And when I decided to go find him and tell him how I felt, I had *no idea* how this was going to work out. Or if it would. I didn't know I was going to end up living here, and that the two of us would get married and start a family together. All I knew is that I wasn't going to be happy again without him."

"I'm happy. At least I will be. It's just gonna take me a few more weeks—"

"You're utterly miserable. It's as plain as the nose on your face." Libby pats my knee with her hand. "And I'm afraid that feeling isn't going to go away. Sometimes, picking the sensible thing isn't the *right* thing. If I did the sensible thing, I'd be back in Avonia married to the wrong man."

"I'm pretty sure Pierce is the wrong man."

"Well, I'm pretty sure he's the right man."

"What makes you think that?"

"Because he very clearly wants you to be happy, whether he can be with you or not."

THIRTY-EIGHT

The Making of Emma Scissorhands

Emma

Three Days Later

So, after a night of non-stop thinking, I decided Libby was right. I'm not going to forget about Pierce. Ever. And I shouldn't. Here's a man who sacrificed his privacy—which is a HUGE deal for him—and he did it for me. Not only that, he did it *after* I rejected him and told him he was too damaged to love (the thought of which makes me feel slightly nauseous).

He bought me a frigging restaurant, which, although utterly misguided, was a lot more thoughtful than, say, handing me a heart-shaped box of chocolates or some edible undies when I stepped off the plane. And he could have easily done nothing other than send a private jet for me, shag me senseless for a few days, and send me home. I was up for that. But he didn't. He tried to give me a future. And I ran. Not that I didn't have a reason to run, because I did. I *do* have a family that needs me, and responsibilities, and career aspirations. And if I left them, I'd be running from all that, which would still make Rosy right about me.

But I'm not a runner. I did run from Pierce, but only because I was forced to choose between two things to run from. So it shouldn't count because I ran from the thing I *wanted* in order to stay where I'm *needed*.

My big mistake was that I didn't even *try* to work it out. I didn't say, 'How about you move to the Caribbean? You can write there.' I just said no full stop and left.

He then hired my best friend, sight unseen, because he trusted my professional opinion (or so he said, but for my ego's sake, I choose to believe it). He could have stopped there, too, but he didn't. He's now traded his privacy for my success, which actually makes it *more* difficult for me to pick up my life and move to Avonia, which, surely, he must know. He's trying to make me happy even though he knows this means we won't be together, which is really rather sweet, and it means that he actually *does* know what love is all about. Plus, he's really good at all the sex stuff. Like really friggin' can't-stop-thinking-about-it good.

So, now I'm in a cab in New York City on my way to 2XFanCon (Fantasy Fan Conference, in case you're not a complete nerd). Pierce will be there for another three hours signing books, along with some of the cast of *Clash of Crowns*. And since New York is a whole lot closer to the Benavente Islands, and I know exactly where to find him, I decided this was my best shot at getting my beaver back. The mate-for-life beaver, not the vaginal one.

You know what? I'm just going to forget that analogy altogether.

Let's just move on because, although I look very presentable and sophisticated in my dark grey wool mini-dress and tall boots, I have no idea what I'm going to say when I get there. I've had days to think about it too—while I packed, at the airport, on the flight over—and nothing.

So, I'm going to have to wing it. Secretly, I'm hoping the very sight of me will cause him to rush to me, wrap his arms around me, and say, "Emma. You are the love of my life. You don't have to say anything because I told myself if you showed up, I'd never let you go again. Marry me now." Or some such thing that will get me out of having to come up with some super romantic, emotionally-charged way to win him back.

Oh! We're here. Now all I have to do is talk my way into this sold-out event, find Pierce in this massive building filled with thousands of weirdos, and hope he really does still have feelings for me.

I pay the driver and get out, feeling a blast of chilly air as I hurry to the entrance of the Javits Convention Center. My heart is pounding now and I take a few deep breaths as I push the revolving door and get out of the wind. Taking a second, I pat down my hair as I try to get the lay of the land. This is an enormous building, and it's chaotic, too, with scores of costume-clad people milling about the glass lobby. I see a folding table with some official-looking people sitting at it. A sign hangs from the table that reads:

2XFan Con Registration Desk.
All patrons MUST have a valid badge and,
for the comfort of our other guests, be in costume.
NO EXCEPTIONS.

Okay, so I don't have a costume or a badge. That's okay. I can make this work.

I walk over, smiling brightly as I choose a woman about my age to help me out. The entrance badges sold out months ago but she'll understand. In fact, I'm pretty sure we're kindred spirits. I can tell by the way she's scrolling on her phone. Although, she does sort of have a no-nonsense vibe going with her very serious tortoiseshell glasses, short, perfectly straight fringe, and a crisp white button-up shirt with *all* the buttons done up. Even her nametag reads Sloane, which is kind of a serious name. Hmm. Here goes nothing...

"Hi there," I say in a quiet 'I have something really important to do here but I don't want anyone else to hear' voice. "Sloane... Pretty name, by the way. I'm wondering if you could help me out."

She looks at me over the rim of her glasses wearing an expression that says 'I'm not here to help you out.' "Sold out. Next year, buy tickets earlier."

"Oh, no...you don't understand," I say with a chuckle. "I'm not a fantasy fan. There's someone inside who I must speak with *urgently*. I've come a long way, actually all the way from the Benaventes, and I just need to get inside for a few minutes so I can talk to him. Then I'll leave straight away, *I promise*," I say, giving her a confident nod.

"If I had a dollar for every time I heard that, I wouldn't be sitting here all day. Nobody gets in without a badge."

Walking around the table, I crouch a little and wrap my arm around her shoulder, "Yeah, here's the thing, I need to get in there to see Pierce Davenport. And trust me, he'll *want* to see me. In fact, he'll probably be *so* happy to see me, I could easily score you an autograph or a picture with him if you like."

Why did I think this would work? I am *way* too close to this strange woman. Like 'I can smell her coffee breath' close. This is awkward even for me.

Shifting away from me, Sloane says, "Okay, you're going to need to step back onto the other side of the desk before I call security."

"Righto." I straighten up and do as I'm told. "Now, about getting me..." My voice trails off and I gesture in the general direction of the exhibition halls with my head, "Inside."

"Yeah, not happening."

"I really do know Pierce Davenport."

"And Jo Rowling's my bestie. In fact, as soon as my shift ends, she's picking me up on the roof in her helicopter so we can go for drinks," Sloane says dryly.

Nodding quickly, I say, "I can totally see why this sounds insane, but I assure you *in my case*, it's true." I lean down a bit and say, "Woman to woman here, Pierce and I were an item and I sort of messed things up but I *know* he wants to get back together. And if you'd just let me inside, you'd become part of an epic love story."

"Aww, in that case," Sloane says, clutching one hand to her chest, "no."

Picking up a walkie-talkie on the table, she stares at me while she says, "I'm going to need security at the reception desk. We've got another Davenport stalker."

"I am *not* a *stalker*," I say indignantly.

"Tell it to him," she says, pointing with her thumb to a very large man who is suddenly standing to my left.

He's dressed in a wannabe cop uniform, but the look on his muscles say he's not messing around. "Let's go, lady."

My shoulders droop as I follow him to the door. I sulk as I make a half-circle in the revolving door out into the late afternoon air.

Now what?

I stand on the sidewalk, staring back at the building while I try to think of a plan. I watch as Wonder Woman and Batman hop out of a cab and rush inside, grinning at each other. Hmm...I wonder if Batman has one of those grapple hook things on his belt and he'd be willing to help me scale the wall, get onto the roof, and in through an air duct.

He trips on his own foot and nearly falls but Wonder Woman rights him just in time.

Nope.

"You get in the Green Lantern line, and I'll go straight for Lucamor Dalgaeron," he says.

"Other way around," Wonder Woman answers.

Nerds.

Happy, happy, nerds.

A lone thin man walks out dressed in jeans, a ball cap, and a wool coat. He's carrying a large plastic bag and has weird white makeup all over his face, except the areas around his eyes have big black circles of makeup. He looks as dejected as I feel. And then it hits me. The answer to my conundrum is about to walk away.

***

Ever wear a wig that a strange man just removed from his own head?

Up until today, the answer to that question would have been a hard no for me, along with a 'I just threw up in my mouth a little' joke. But, now, as I stand in the skeevy bathroom of the 7-11 in full costume, I stare in the mirror. "He better fucking love you."

After a stop at a bank machine, I'm now dressed as Edward Scissorhands, scissors and all. Well, one scissorhand so far. I need help with the second one. The costume cost me a painful $200 USD, plus $100 USD for the badge, and I had to buy five dollars worth of stuff to get the keys to the bathroom, but I'm now unrecognizable to the security team.

I hope.

I didn't have white makeup on me (weird, right?), so I bought some cake donuts covered in icing sugar to pat all over my face and I wet the eyeliner and mascara I'm wearing and smudged it around to make circles. My coat, sophisticated dress, and purse are all stuffed in a bag.

A bang at the toilet door tells me it's go time.

Oh, by the way, that banging is Calvin, the guy who sold me the costume. He's sticking around to help me finish dressing and give me pointers so I can go 'Full Scissorhands' as he calls it. "Are you all right? You've been in there a long time."

"Great, thanks!" I answer. Taking a deep breath, I unlock the door and shuffle out.

Oh, did I mention this costume restricts movement in the legs? Yeah, Calvin said, "It's an exact replica of the one Johnny Depp wore in the classic 1990 film featuring one of the most underrated actresses of our time: Winona Ryder." Except Calvin went one step further with it and had the legs sewn together just under the buttocks so that he wouldn't break character by taking too big a stride. So at least I can't run away if I get made...so that's another thing I've got going for me.

No matter. It'll all be worth it when Pierce and I are living happily ever after...

Calvin looks me up and down, then nods his approval. "Noice. You've gone Full Scissorhands. Those cake donuts worked out much better than I thought they would."

"Thanks," I say, with a little shrug. "The trick is to dampen your skin first."

"Really? Good to know if I'm ever in a pinch."

After affixing the second scissorhand to me, Calvin walks me back to Javits Center, all the while regaling me with little known facts about the film. Apparently, Tim Burton originally wanted Tom Cruise for the role, and according to Calvin, it's a damn good thing he didn't get it because there's no way Tom has the sort of vulnerability Johnny does. Also, Johnny Depp only says 169 words in the entire film. Calvin counted to verify that little fact after he read it online a few years back.

So, this all seems totally normal and not in the least bit scary, right?

"Okay, well, we're here. I better give this a try," I say turning to Calvin and holding my hand up to shake his.

He jumps back a little. "Jesus! You can't shake hands with those things on. In fact, keep your hands down and whatever you do, don't trip because you could really hurt yourself...or someone else. And if it's someone else, you will *definitely* get sued."

"Or run out of town and into a castle in the hills where I'll have to live out my days making ice sculptures," I say with a little chuckle.

He narrows his eyes. "That's not...it's a very serious film about isolation and the frailty of the human condition."

"Sorry, Calvin. You're absolutely right. I'll make sure I don't lift my hands or...trip." In these ridiculously restrictive leather pants.

Okay, Emma Scissorhands, time to go get your man...

THIRTY-NINE

A Day in the Life of the King Nerd

Pierce

These are my people. These sad, pathetically lonely 2XFanCon attendees. And I am their equally lonely, pathetic leader. Even though I'm not a virgin. Even though I don't live in my parents' basement. Even though I don't have reptile-filled terrariums lining the walls of my flat, I understand my people and the pain of rejection that we all share.

I wonder if getting a tarantula would ease the pain?

Closing the copy of *Blood Wars* I've just signed, I hand it to the painfully thin teenager dressed as Matalyx and give him a long, thoughtful look. "I'm thinking of getting a pet. You wouldn't happen to know anything about tarantulas, would you?"

"Do *not* get a tarantula. It's literally impossible to get a girl to come home with you if you tell them you own a giant spider."

"I could just not mention it..."

Shaking his head, he says, "She'll see it when she gets there, and believe me, she won't stay."

"Oh, fair point, yeah," I say, nodding.

"Go with an iguana," he says, authoritatively. "Most girls don't hate them."

I wince at the memory of the last iguana I met, then say, "I don't know. I had a bad experience with an iguana once. What about a gecko?"

"Even better. Chicks think they're adorable."

Hope, the assistant Sullivan and Stone sent to help with crowd management, clears her throat. "I don't mean to rush you, Mr. Davenport, but the line is not getting any shorter."

I glance down the length of the hall, seeing she's right. Unlike her, I'm in no rush to get this over with because I really have no desire to go back to my empty hotel room. Giving my new friend an apologetic look, I hold out my hand for a fist bump. "Thanks for the advice."

"Any time."

A middle-aged woman in a slutty Oona costume is next in line. She giggles and thrusts her copy of *The Fire of Knights* at me. "Can you make it out to Tammy-Lynn, the real Oona?"

"Sure," I say, trying not to glance at the considerable cleavage spilling out as she leans over the table.

"I just want you to know, I never doubted you for a second. I knew you'd finish the series and that it would be better than anything that has ever been written."

She's the one-hundredth person to say that today, by the way, which is weird since the last one of these I did, it was literally a five-to-one odds that the next fan in line had turned on me and had shown up with the sole purpose of blasting me for being in there at all.

"Thanks. I appreciate your faith in me." I hand her back the book and give her a smile that says 'I'm nice but also busy, so move it along, Slutty Old Oona.'

"Do you have a girlfriend?"

Hope takes this as her cue to cut in. "Sorry, Mr. Davenport has a lot of fans waiting, so he needs to continue on to the next person."

Tammy-Lynn looks highly offended, but moves along, making way for an enormous guy dressed as Zhordal mo Rhandar, the evil overlord of the underworld in *Clash of Crowns*. He's so tall, he could actually pass for the real guy if he wasn't holding a mobile phone in one hand and a book in the other. I'm temporarily blinded by the flash as he catches a great shot of me with my mouth open, about to ask him to whom I should make out the inscription. He thrusts his copy of *The Chamber of Dragons* at me without a word.

Yes, this socially awkward man suffering from gigantism is my people. Like me, he is destined to never have sex again. "Hello, that's quite the Zhordal costume. Well done, you."

Sensing another lengthy conversation, Hope leans toward him and says, "Whom should he make it out to?"

A loud yell from the other side of the hall distracts Zhordal, who turns, lifting himself on his toes for a better look at what's going on. He mutters, "What the hell?"

Standing, I wait until I see the cause of the murmurs going through the crowd—a man dressed as Edward Scissorhands is scurrying along with his arms at his sides whilst glancing over his shoulder. Behind him, a team of security guards and a woman in a white blouse are attempting to chase him through the throngs of people and calling for him to "Stop right there!" But Edward keeps going. Slippery little fellow.

"Is this some sort of art performance piece?" Hope asks. "Are they re-enacting the scene where he gets chased out of town?"

"Somehow I think this is real," I answer, unable to peel my eyes off the terrified-looking Edward as his wild black hair bobs with every step. Huh, there's something familiar about him. I find myself cheering for him for some unknown reason. He just looks so...vulnerable.

"Why doesn't he just start running?" Zhordal asks.

"Because you shouldn't run with scissorhands," I say, chuckling at my own joke.

Oh goody. He's headed this way.

I put my Sharpie down while Zhordal breaks character long enough to video the ensuing chase.

"Stop! We know who you are, lady!" the woman calls out.

Lady?

"I only need one minute!" Edward calls back in a high-pitched voice. "One minute and then I'll leave! I promise!"

Uh oh, now she's locked eyes with me and she's literally making a beeline for me. "Pierce! It's me!"

Fuck me. I stand, my body feeling suddenly numb. "Emma?"

"Yes! It's me!" she shouts just as she's tackled by the woman, who has outstripped her security counterparts.

Emma falls, her hands flying out in front of her, stabbing Captain Kirk in the arse as she goes down. Captain Kirk shrieks in pain as he's thrust onto the ground with Emma on top of his legs. The security guards pile on top of the woman who's on top of Emma.

My heart pounds in my chest as my brain scrambles to catch up with what's going on. Emma is *here?!*

Emma is here!

And she's dressed as Edward Scissorhands. And she's obviously in some sort of trouble with the authorities. Well, the 2XFan Con authorities anyway. And I'm standing here like an idiot. "I have to get to her," I say to no one in particular as I start fighting my way through the crowd that's formed.

"My ass! My ass!"

"I'VE GOT HER!"

"I'm so sorry! I didn't mean to—"

"You fucking dickhead! You stabbed my ass!"

"She's right here!"

"Holy shit! Edward Scissorhands just shanked Captain Kirk!"

"This is awesome!"

"Greatest 2XFanCon EVER!"

"Somebody call an ambulance!"

"Is there a doctor in the house?!"

"I did not intentionally stab your arse! I'm so sorry! Please do not sue me!"

By the time I squeeze through the wall of people, Emma is facedown on the floor with a knee in her back. The woman in the white blouse is tugging at her scissorhands while a security guard holds her down. The woman glances up at me. "Stay back, Mr. Davenport! We've caught your stalker!"

"Get off her now!" I bark, crouching beside Emma. "You're going to hurt her."

"I can't move until we remove her weapons," the guard says.

"My ass!" Captain Kirk whines, writhing on the floor. "I am going to sue you! For every penny!"

"Oh, for fuck's sake," I mutter, gently lifting Emma's left arm and unsnapping the contraption from her leather costume.

Brushing the woman's hands away, I take off the other set of scissors. "There. Let her up."

A seductive-looking Storm Trooper kneels beside Captain Kirk. "I'm a doctor. Take your hands away from your bottom so I can see the extent of the damage."

"It's bad, doc," he whines. "I don't think I'll be able to sit again."

Emma, who has been freed, crawls over to the man. "I'm so sorry. I was trying to keep my hands down but I got pushed and..."

"She totally did, man," Han Solo says. "I've got it all on film. She got tackled and skewered your ass by mistake."

"Looks like you'll need about four stitches. Maybe five," Dr. Storm Trooper says.

"Mr. Davenport, this woman claims she knows you. Is that true?" the guard asks.

"Yes, I know her quite well."

"So is she a stalker or not?" the woman in white says.

"Not."

"We're still going to have to take her into custody," the woman says. "She did sneak in with a used badge and stabbed a man."

Glancing at the woman's name tag, I then give her my best celebrity grin. "Sloane, is it? Pretty name." Holding my hand out, I say, "Pierce. Thank you for your vigilance. I truly appreciate it, but is there some way we could work something out so Emma here doesn't have to get arrested?" I look at Emma and smile. "I really do need to talk to her."

FORTY

If This Is How It Has to Happen...

Emma

Five Minutes Later...

Pierce and I are alone in the small green room for celebrity guest use. Two police officers wait outside the door to keep people out and keep me from running off while they review the videos and decide if they're going to press charges.

Pierce gives me the once over, looking shocked and amused and happy and confused all at once. Obviously deciding to act casual, he asks, "So, how've you been?"

Doing my best to pretend everything is totally normal, I shrug. "Good, yeah. Really good," I say, then start to laugh, covering my face with one hand. "Oh Christ. I must look insane with this stupid costume on."

I tug the wig off, wishing I could wash the icing sugar off my face.

Pierce chuckles, shaking his head in disbelief. "I can't believe you're here. And that you've really changed your style so much...and that you've turned into a stabby criminal since I last saw you."

"These past few months have been a time of exploration and personal growth for me," I answer wryly. We stare at each other, then I shake my head, my heart still pounding wildly. "Yeah, this is not exactly how this moment was supposed to go."

"Really? Why ever not?" he asks, feigning confusion.

"I was going to change into my sophisticated 'getting my man back' outfit before you saw me," I say, fear coursing through my veins as I process the fact that I just called him 'my man.' "Also, I didn't think I'd be facing possible assault charges."

"'Getting your man back' outfit? Tell me it's the tiny chef uniform," he says, grinning.

I laugh and nod my head. "Of course. I know how much you liked it." I stare up at him, longing to wrap my arms around his neck and plant the biggest, wettest kiss on that mouth of his. "Pierce, I was wrong. Not about everything...but about what I said about you being damaged. I didn't mean it and it's been haunting me ever since I took off and I'm just really so sorry because I think you're my beaver."

Looking genuinely bewildered this time, he says, "Come again?"

"Oh God. Forget I said that, okay? I just...I've been having trouble coming up with what to say when I found you. I'm not a writer," I say, feeling overheated in this leather suit. "I know you were behind ABN featuring the resort. And I know what you did for me and for my family."

"I don't know what you're talking—"

"Kennedy told me."

"I've always hated that woman."

"I'm not a huge fan of hers either, to be honest, but without her, I wouldn't be standing here in this used leather costume asking if maybe you could consider giving us another chance. And I don't know if that's a good thing for you or not, but..."

Oh, *thank God*, he's kissing me and I don't have to talk anymore. And wow. I so badly want to do this with him forever.

The way he's kissing me is saying a lot of wonderful things about our future together. And I'm kissing him back with everything in me, hoping beyond hope that he can feel that I, Emma Scissorhands, love the hell out of him and always will.

He pulls back a bit, then gives me a quizzical look. "Is that...icing sugar?"

"A good chef knows how to improvise."

Grinning down at me, he says, "Brilliant and beautiful," before crushing my mouth with his again.

***

Three Hours Later...

We're currently in the penthouse suite at the Hyatt. Captain Kirk agreed to drop all charges in exchange for a private meet and greet breakfast with Pierce tomorrow. Pierce also managed to get the event manager to let me slide on the whole 'used badge and running from security' thing in exchange for his promise to come back to 2XFanCon next year.

We've had the world's greatest makeup sex in the shower, then on the bed, then on the ottoman, then in the bathtub, had a break to eat uninspired fifty-dollar room service hamburgers and fries, followed by more orgasmicly sexy sex.

It's late in the evening now and while we're both deliriously happy, we've been avoiding 'the talk.' I think we're both just so happy to be able to do this again that we wanted to enjoy the moment before things possibly go off the rails when we discuss THE FUTURE.

Pierce lies on his side facing me. He's running his fingertip over my face in a way that is completely hypnotic. I stare at his incredible dark eyelashes trying to memorize everything in case somehow this doesn't work out. I don't want to forget a thing.

Propping his chin on his hand, he sighs. "I have a confession to make."

My heart drops at his words. "What kind of confession? Something dark and awful, like you've got a red room back at your pad in Valcourt? Or you shagged a hundred women while we were apart and now play host to a slew of STIs?"

"Christ, no. Why would your mind go there?" he asks, looking horrified. "I was going to say I'm wildly, helplessly, hopelessly in love with you."

"Oh, so not bad at all, really," I say with a sideways grin.

"I hope not." He glances at my lips.

I kiss him quickly before he can take it back, my heart bursting with fear and joy, then say, "I also have a confession to make. I don't want this to be some casual thing. I never really did because I'm also pretty much horribly and completely in love with you. Like so much so that I was willing to wear the very recently used wig of a strange man."

"Oh, so that sounds serious," he says.

Swallowing hard, I say, "I'm afraid so."

"Well, in that case, we're going to have to figure out what to do about this." His smile fades. "But first, I have to admit you were right about me. Back in Valcourt, when you said I didn't understand love, you were bang on. I didn't. I think I'm starting to get it, but before...I really had no clue.

"From what I gather, love means putting the other person first, not trying to force them to fit into your life for your own convenience...even if I did try to dress it up as giving you everything you ever dreamed of." He gives me a small smile and shakes his head. "You, Emma Banks, are the only person to see through my bullshit. You're also the only person who has ever made me believe that love might not be a total fucking sham. And that's why I have to find a way to spend my life with you. So that you can hold my feet to the fire when needed and make me believe that there's good in the world. I hate myself for the cliché that's about to come out of my mouth, but I'm afraid I can't help it. You make me a better man."

Tears fill my eyes and...uh oh, I have that ugly cry face happening. I try to straighten it out but I think I'm only making it worse. Although, the look on his face doesn't say he's exactly put off by it.

Lifting one hand to my cheek, he continues. "I want to spend the rest of my life giving you absolutely everything you've ever wanted, just so I can see you smile. I want to make you laugh and drive you nuts and taste every dish you create—even the ones with sundried tomatoes, should they come back in fashion. I want to rub your feet when they're sore after a long shift and serve you a glass of wine or a whole bloody bottle when you've had a bad day. I want to go to all your family dinners with Rosy hitting on me and Starsky and Hutch humping me and Harrison glaring at me in a way that says I'll never be quite good enough for his little sister—he's right, by the way. But I promise you I'll spend every day of the rest of my life trying to be the man you deserve."

"You already are," I say, smiling through my happy tears. "And even better, you're the one I need. And I know together, we can figure out how to make this work."

"Agreed. We definitely can sort it out," he says pressing his forehead to mine. "What if—and I'm just spit-balling here so if you have a better idea, just say so—what if I move to Santa Valentina? We could get some fabulously private place on the beach—close enough to the resort for you to bicycle there every day but far enough away for us to have our own little retreat. I could write books while you're off being an incredible chef. Then when you come home, we can shag until the early morning hours."

I laugh through my tears, nodding quickly. "That's perfect for me, but not if you don't want to live there. I don't feel right asking you to give up everything you've got in Avonia."

"What exactly have I got? A very expensive, very lonely flat? A family I can't count on? I'm relatively certain I can give that up without much heartache, especially if I know you're coming home to me every day. As someone pointed out to me once, of the two of us, you're the one with the rich life. I've just got money." He gives me a lingering kiss. "What do you say? Do we have a deal, Ms. Banks?"

Giving him a skeptical look, I say, "I don't know. Will you sing Neil Diamond to me every once in a while?"

"Only after a few drinks."

"I can live with that."

Pierce grins widely. "Thank God because I've always dreamed of having a happily ever after."

"Liar."

"Okay, maybe not always, but since I first laid eyes on you."

"Oh, you're good," I say, snuggling closer to him. "If this whole fantasy writing gig doesn't turn out, you could write romance."

"I just might," he says, letting his lips hover over mine. "Or I might give it all up and live off a certain amazingly talented chef I know."

EPILOGUE

There's Always Room for One More...

Pierce

One Year Later

"Two minutes 'til showtime!" Emma's voice cuts through the considerable noise in our normally quiet beach house. Her entire family, and I'm pretty sure everyone they know, have amassed here this evening to watch the season opener of the final season of *Clash of Crowns*. Excitement buzzes around me as I finish filling a tray of champagne flutes to serve our guests—well, the adult ones, anyway.

Harrison is in the kitchen heating up a bottle for their adorable little ginger baby, Clara (named for Libby's grandmum), who I must say, seems to favour her Uncle Pierce above most people. Clara is currently being bounced on Darnell's lap whilst Rosy plays peek-a-boo from behind the sectional.

Emma pulls an enormous tray of appetizers out of the oven warmer and sets it on the island, along with the trays of fruit, veggies, and bowls of crisps. "Appies are ready!" she calls, eliciting an enthusiastic murmur along with a mass exodus from the living room furniture in the general direction of the island.

Oh, in case you're wondering, we bought a massive open-concept bungalow that sits on the southeast side of Paradise Bay. It's beachfront (obviously) and is set on a private estate nestled in the jungle (but not so close to the jungle that, say, any hungry iguanas will challenge me for breakfast). From here, Emma really can cycle to the resort every day. Most days I go with her and drop her off at the restaurant, then go back to pick her up in the late evening after she's done working for the night.

I pass out drinks while the opening credits start, feeling the thrill of anticipation flow through my veins. Our light grey sectional is packed with an eclectic group of people who I've come to know and trust over the past year since I moved to Paradise Bay.

As soon as the first notes of the theme song start playing, a cheer erupts from around the room, scaring Winnie and Fidel's baby, Oliver, who starts crying. This initiates a shift of bodies on the couch, as Will, who's been holding the little one for the past half hour, hands him off to his dad for comfort.

Emma wraps her arms around me and gives me a kiss on the cheek. "Can you believe it? Our book is on TV," she says with a little grin.

She's been calling it *our book* to bug me, but since she's the one who saved my sorry arse, then gave me a life worth living, I don't mind a bit. When you love someone the way I love her, you want to share everything, even if it's credit for the greatest masterpiece of modern-day fantasy literature. I'm actually starting to understand how John Lennon allowed Yoko Ono to ruin the Beatles. He must've loved her the way I love Emma.

She shushes everyone in the room as soon as the credits finish, even though we both know the chances of us being able to actually hear the show among this crowd are about as likely as her getting into her Emma Scissorhands outfit again.

Two years ago, if you'd have asked me if there was *any* possibility I'd enjoy sharing an experience like this with my family, I would've laughed in your face. But that's because I was with the wrong family. In fact, it was my idea to invite them all tonight. Emma wanted to watch the show alone with me, but there's no way I wanted to deprive everyone else of having this moment. I glance around the room at their happy faces, knowing I made the right choice. Not just today, but back in New York when I decided to move here for the rest of my life. I used to believe so strongly that to avoid disappointment a man could—and should be an island—but that was a load of bollocks. Because a life surrounded by people who you can take care of, and who will take care of you right back, is truly the richest form of existence.

"Come on," Emma says, tugging on my hand and pulling me onto the ridiculously big, faux fur beanbag chair that she insisted we buy. And, like most things, she was right about it, because it's so damn comfortable, it's actually where I do most of my writing now.

I'm working on a new series, by the way. I won't tell you what it's about because it's not fair to everyone else out there who is waiting patiently. I do, however, find myself running all my ideas past Emma every morning when we eat breakfast together. I get up early, just so we can have some time together before she's gone for the bulk of each day at the restaurant. I know, I know—I used to make fun of Zach for the very same thing. But once you get it, you really get it.

Speaking of Zach and Kennedy, they're doing well, and she doesn't hate me anymore since I let her use me to boost her career (while I was using her to boost Emma's). We actually stayed with them a few weeks ago when Emma and I were in Avonia, and the four of us had a rather lovely visit.

We also spent a lot of time with Priya and Ivan which was actually quite educational. We got to talking about wolves, and it turns out they're not loners at all. They're pack animals. And so am I. Who knew?

Harrison blocks my view of the telly for a split second as he passes baby Clara to me, gently setting her on my lap before handing me the bottle. "There you go, little peanut. You can sit with your famous Uncle Pierce."

I stare down at the beautiful little girl and say, "Would you like your bottle?"

She reaches out with both hands and grabs it, sticking it greedily into her mouth and making me chuckle.

"Uncle Pierce is going to close your ears and Auntie Emma will shield your eyes on the bad parts, okay? This isn't exactly a child-friendly show."

Emma smiles up at me for a moment, giving me that look she gets sometimes—it's a mixture of wistfulness and pure bliss, and I've noticed it happening more often when little Clara is around. She turns back to the show, resting her head on my shoulder.

"You know, we should have one of these," I murmur to her.

"One of what?" Emma asks distractedly.

"A mini us."

Without looking at me, she says, "Oh, I wouldn't want to do that unless we were married."

I stare at her for a moment, then whisper, "In that case, we should do that, too."

Turning to me slowly, she gives me a look. "Are you proposing to me right now?"

"No. I'm just floating the idea to see if perhaps it interests you. I wouldn't want to be presumptuous and go out and get a ring without checking with you first."

Giving me a half grin, she says, "I think this is one situation where you should just feel free to be presumptuous."

"Thank God, because I've been wanting to ask you for months now, but didn't want to rush you."

Reaching up with one hand, Emma cups my cheek and draws me in for a lingering kiss. When we finally remember where we are and pull back, I smile down at her, my heart feeling like it's going to erupt with happiness. "I take it you're happy about me proposing to propose."

"Uh, yeah," she whispers in my ear. "Let's just say you are going to get so lucky later."

"How soon do you think we can get these people out of here?"

"At best, two hours."

"Damn. I don't know why you insisted on inviting them," I mutter, tongue in cheek.

A voice calls from the front door, interrupting the moment. "Hello? Is anybody here?"

Emma gives me a confused look which I return. "That sounds exactly like Leo."

I turn my head, only to see my baby brother standing next to the island. "Oh good, I haven't missed it then."

He helps himself to a glass of champagne, then heaps some spring rolls and prawns onto a plate while Emma and I stare at each other, dumbfounded.

Walking over toward us, he sits on the ottoman next to Emma and me as though he's just come from the corner store instead of the other side of the planet. Giving Emma a quick peck on the cheek, he says, "Hi Em. You look lovely."

"Thanks, Leo..." she says, her eyebrows still knit together.

"Do you know how hard it is to find your house?" Leo asks. "It's like everybody on this island is determined not to give away your whereabouts. I finally had to show the cabdriver my passport and some photos of us together from a newspaper article before he was willing to bring me out here."

He takes a bite of spring roll and chews. Glancing down at Clara, he says, "That's not your baby, is it?"

Oh, for God's sake. "No, Leo. She's our niece. Don't you think I would mention if I had a daughter?"

"I suppose you would. Cute little thing." He places one finger under her hand and shakes it, then says, "Hello sweetie. What are you drinking?"

Baby Clara takes the bottle out of her mouth with a pop and giggles at my brother. Of course, she's immediately enamoured with him. Women of every age love the little bastard.

"It's great to see you, Leo," Emma says, laughing a little in shock that he's here. "Have you come all this way just to watch the show's premiere?"

His gaze is now fixed on the screen where Oona is just about to walk into the labyrinth. Without looking at us, he says, "Oh, no. I've been ordered to leave Avonia for a minimum of six months or I'll be disinherited. I was hoping I could camp out here for a while."

"Oh, Christ, Leo," I say, covering the baby's ears. "What the hell did you do this time?"

"I'll tell you later. I'm trying to watch the show. I can't wait to find out how the series ends."

"Have you not read the book?" Emma asks, sounding slightly offended on my behalf.

"Oh, no, I haven't read any of the books. They're a little slow-moving for me. That's why I prefer the NBO version." He takes a bite of a prawn, then says, "Delicious appies, by the way, Emma. You've outdone yourself."

Emma and I exchange a long look, speaking volumes in a single moment. I'm apologizing for my brother showing up out of the blue and wanting to invade our lives, and she's telling me that it's all right, and I should try to be patient with him. Giving me a quick kiss on the cheek, she whispers, "It's going to be wonderful."

"What is?"

"All of it."

She smiles confidently at me before tucking her head back onto my shoulder.

And she's right. It will all be wonderful because no matter what comes our way, we are in it together...

NOVELIST MONTHLY

BEST OF THE DECADE ISSUE

THE WAIT IS OVER!

CLASH OF CROWNS
Book 4 has arrived!

Get a sneak peek inside Pierce's
Very Own Fortress of Solitude.

THIS MONTH WE'RE CELEBRATING
ALL THINGS FANTASY
OR SHOULD WE SAY ALL THINGS
PIERCE DAVENPORT?

MUSINGS FROM A FANTASY MAN

THE WORLD'S BIGGEST AUTHORITY ON ALL THINGS FANTASY FICTION

I HAVE NEVER BEEN SO SORRY IN MY LIFE

WRITTEN BY JOE 'FANTASY' WILCOX

I have just finished the final book of *The Clash of Crowns* series and I have to extend my deepest apologies to Mr. Davenport for my inexusable lack of faith in his abilities, his talent, and his work ethic.

I am sorry I amassed a group of angry Crownies outside your flat. I'm sorry I accused you of not caring about your fans. I'm sorry I didn't trust your genius.

The Fire of Knights is by far the greatest ending to the greatest fantasy series of all time. There will never be another story that will grip me the way this one has, unless, of course, Pierce Davenport starts a new series.

It's not the ending I expected, but it was utter perfection.

Thank you, Mr. Davenport, for giving us the world of Qadeathas. We will forever be in your debt.

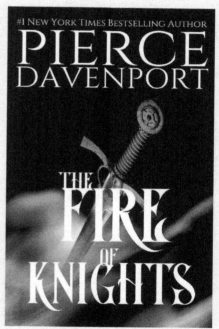

RATING: 5 SWORDS

Join me on Twitter at #sorrypierce to discuss all things *Clash of Crowns*!

Carib-Asian Night

• CARIBBEAN ASIAN FUSION MENU •

APPETIZER

Jerk Pork Spring Rolls with Tamarind & Honey Sauce

Jamaican Chicken and Cabbage Dumplings with Coconut Dipping Sauce

Roti Stuffed with Stir-Fried Sweet Potato & Pineapple Chutney

ENTRÉE

Thai Chicken Satay Served on a Bed of Alfalfa and Coconut, with a Mango Peanut Sauce

Spicy Citrus Tuna Tiradito Topped with Sliced Red Onion, Pickled Jalapeños, Truffled Shishito Glaze and Crunchy Ramen Noodles

Spicy Ginger Shrimp with Calabaza Squash Served over Rice Noodles

DESSERT

Coconut Lemongrass Mochi Ice Cream

Mango Rice Pudding

Red Bean Empanada Trio

Fried Banana Cakes with Coconut Sauce

AVAILABLE NOW

The Suite Life
~ *A Paradise Bay Romantic Comedy, Book 3* ~

From best-selling author Melanie Summers comes a seriously romantic, laugh-out-loud tale of a single mum and the man who restores her faith in love...

Handsome, rich, and charming, Leopold Davenport has always been the life of the party, but when he takes things too far, his father banishes the twenty-seven-year-old from his homeland of Avonia for six months. Threatened with disinheritance, Leo must find a job, get a home, and grow up. With nowhere to turn, Leo moves to Santa Valentina Island, where is sister-in-law helps him find work as a bellboy at the Paradise Bay Resort owned by her family. Little does he know that dealing with people's baggage will make him examine his own. Will he check out or find that a long-term reservation is on his itinerary?

Twenty-six-year-old single mum Brianna Chance (a.k.a. Bree) never believed in fairy tales—and after being abandoned by the father of daughter, Isabelle, Bree has lost her faith in love. A law student by day and concierge at the Paradise Bay Resort at night, Bree's focus is on giving her daughter the life she never had. With Isabelle starting kindergarten soon, Bree needs to come up with the money for private school. She'll do anything, including renting out the tiny garden shed in her yard to Leopold Davenport, a man who's determined to make her work-life a living hell.

Can Leopold make the leap from ultimate playboy to become the man Bree needs in her life?

Will Bree allow herself to believe in happily-ever-afters or will she play it safe and hang a do-not-disturb sign on her heart?

A NOTE FROM MELANIE

I hope you enjoyed going on this adventure with Pierce and Emma. I hope you laughed out loud, and the story left you feeling good. I hope that you fell as much in love with them as I did. If so, please leave a review.

Reviews are a true gift to writers. They are the best way for other readers to find our work and for writers to figure out if we're on the right track, so thank you if you are one of those kind folks out there to take time out of your day to leave a review!

If you'd like to find out about my upcoming releases, sign up for my newsletter on www.mjsummersbooks.com.

All the very best to you and yours,
Melanie

Special thanks

I am forever working at a ridiculously fast pace, which means I need a LOT of help to keep things flowing. Time to acknowledge the many people who have made this book possible, including:

- You, my lovely reader friends, without whom, all of this playing around with imaginary friends would mean people would look upon me with a mixture of pity and fear. Instead, I get to call myself an *author*, which has a markedly better reaction,
- Kristi Yanta, editor extraordinaire who made Pierce and Emma's story the best it could be,
- Melissa Martin, an amazing proof-reader/copy editor, and wonderful friend,
- Janice Owens, a terrific and patient proof-reader who taught me a lot of neato stuff,
- Kelly Collins, who is as close to a writing partner as a person could get without actually working on the same book. She kicks my butt when needed, is always there to listen and help me figure things out. She's truly one of my closest friends, even though she lives really friggin' far away,
- My dear friend and talented writer Jenn Falls for always helping me when I get stuck and listening when I'm panicking about a book. Pierce would not be Pierce without her genius ideas,
- My Chick Lit Think Tank Pals: Whitney Dineen, Tracie Banister, Kate O'Keeffe, Virginia Gray, and Annabelle Costa, for sharing their knowledge and cheering each other on as we write, edit, release, repeat,

- Tim Flanagan, my marketing, maps, formatting, print covers, and other graphics genius who took my crazy fun idea and made it happen,
- Christine Miller, my author assistant, who keeps my social media stuff going while I'm lost in Paradise Bay,
- My oldest and dearest friends, Nikki Chiem and Karlee Chance, who are always there for me no matter what. Thank you, ladies, for getting me through this rough time,
- My mom, who helps out SO much around here (including with proofreading) so I can work, especially when I'm under a deadline,
- My dad, whose unwavering faith in my abilities will go with me wherever life takes me,
- My kids for bringing humour and hugs to my days,
- And, last by certainly not least, my husband and best friend, Jeremy, for always supporting me and being such an inspiration when it comes to both romance and comedy.

Thank you to all of you from the bottom, the top, and the middle of my heart!
You mean the world to me,
Melanie

ABOUT THE AUTHOR

Melanie Summers currently resides in Edmonton, Canada, with her husband, three young children, and their goofy dog. When she's not writing romance novels, she loves reading (obviously), snuggling up on the couch with her family for movie night (which would not be complete without lots of popcorn and milkshakes), and long walks in the woods near her house. MJ also spends a lot more time thinking about doing yoga than actually doing yoga, which is why most of her photos are taken 'from above'. She also loves shutting down restaurants with her girlfriends. Well, not literally shutting them down, like calling the health inspector or something. More like just staying until they turn the lights off.

Melanie is a member of the Romance Writers of America, as well as the International Women's Writing Guild.

Melanie would love to hear from you! She does her best to respond to all inquiries and emails personally. If you would like her to attend a book club meeting via Skype please contact her to book a date.

Website: www.mjsummersbooks.com
Email: mjsummersbooks@gmail.com
Facebook: https://www.facebook.com/MJSummersAuthorPage
Twitter: https://twitter.com/MJSummersBooks
Newsletter Sign-up:
https://mjsummersbooks.wordpress.com/secret-scenes/

Made in the USA
Coppell, TX
26 March 2020